cpm

Dear Romance Reader:

This year Avon Books is celebrating the sixth anniversary of "The Avon Romance"—six years of historical romances of the highest quality by both new and established writers. Thanks to our terrific authors, our "ribbon books" are stronger and more exciting than ever before. And thanks to you, our loyal readers, our books continue to be a spectacular success!

"The Avon Romances" are just some of the fabulous novels in Avon Books' dazzling *Year of Romance*, bringing you month after month of top-notch romantic entertainment. How wonderful it is to escape for a few hours with romances by your favorite "leading ladies"—Shirlee Busbee, Karen Robards, and Johanna Lindsey. And how satisfying it is to discover in a new writer the talent that will make her a rising star.

Every month in 1988, Avon Books' *Year of Romance*, will be special because Avon Books believes that romance—the readers, the writers, and the books—deserves it!

Sweet Reading,

Susanne Jaffe
Editor-in-Chief

Ellen Edwards
Senior Editor

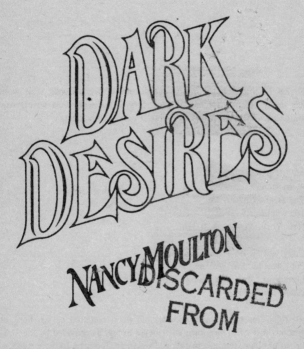

DARK DESIRES

NANCY MOULTON

AVON BOOKS ◆ NEW YORK

AVON BOOKS
A division of
The Hearst Corporation
105 Madison Avenue
New York, New York 10016

First Avon Books Printing: May 1988

To Heather Lynne and Ryan Patrick,
the greatest kids a mother could ever have—
I love you so very much.

And to Barbara Brooks—kindred spirit.

True friendship knows no bounds.
Thanks with all my heart to
Barb, Jane Luman, my Mom and Dad,
and all my many other cherished friends
and family
for walking a dark path with me
into the bright sunlight.
God bless you.

Chapter 1

Loneliness seemed to fill all of Christa Haviland's being as she gazed out the dormer window of the music room on the third floor of Haviland Court. Dark, storm-laden clouds brought deep shadows to the ebbing afternoon, and the rising wind played havoc with the colorful autumn leaves blanketing the extensive formal garden fronting the red-brick mansion. The lengthening shadows gave eerie shapes to the neatly trimmed privet hedges, deepening Christa's melancholy. She shuddered as a chill swept over her. After living here for two years, the estate still didn't feel like home to her. Would it ever?

A knock on the hall door drew her attention there. "I beg your pardon, madam," the elderly majordomo apologized when she opened the door. Ambrose's usual dignified control was absent as he stood before her holding a glass-globed oil lamp. Christa noticed how pale and nervous he looked. The lamp visibly shook in his hand.

"What is it, Ambrose? What's wrong?"

"Dear me, I cannot explain it here, madam. Please come to the kitchen. It's most urgent."

"Yes, of course. Let me get my shawl." She went

1

quickly to the silk-covered divan and caught up the wool wrap. "Go ahead with the lamp, Ambrose. I'll follow you."

Because of noise, odors, and the danger from fires, the cooking facilities at Haviland Court were located in a separate building behind the main house. A sharp crack of thunder pealed overhead and giant raindrops started to pelt down on Ambrose and Christa as they stepped out into the night and hastened to the kitchen house.

Christa was stunned by what awaited her in the brightly lighted room. A man sat slumped in a straight-backed chair with Hester Baldwin, the fifty-year-old head cook of the estate, bent over him.

"Thank the heavens yer here, Mrs. Haviland!" she declared. "I sent the scullery maids to bed when Ambrose told me somebody was hurt outside, so's there wouldn't be many of us knowin' about him. He's babblin' somethin' about rebels bein' after him."

Christa rushed to the figure and stooped down to get a better look at him.

"Christa . . ." the injured man's hoarse voice ground out.

"Marcus? My God, Marcus, what's happened?"

"He's bin shot, near's I kin tell," Hester answered for him. "Soaked up two of my best dish-dryin' towels, bleedin' bad. But I think the flow's slowin' some now."

Marcus Desmond was ash pale, his handsome face drawn into a tight grimace of pain. "My leg—ball went straight through," he managed to say through gritted teeth. "No time to explain, Christa. I need a fresh horse. Had to let mine loose so they wouldn't find it. Patrol of Continentals after me. Have to get away . . ."

As if his words were an announcement, the clamor of horses' hooves sounded outside.

"At least six riders," Ambrose called out anxiously from a back window.

The estate guard dogs contributed a frenzy of loud barking to the pandemonium of the patrol's arrival.

"We must hide Marcus!" Christa exclaimed, fighting down sudden panic as she tried to think. "In the pantry. No, the canning storage cellar! Yes, there. Ambrose, take a lamp and go outside. Stall them as long as you can."

The majordomo looked stricken at being given such an assignment, but in a moment he recovered and left the kitchen.

"Come, Marcus, we must hide you. Hester, help me with him. And use care," Christa directed.

With surprising agility, the portly cook swung Marcus Desmond's arm around her shoulder and took most of his weight upon herself so that Christa could hurry to open a trapdoor in the wood-plank floor.

"This way, quickly!" she exclaimed, assisting Hester in guiding him down the narrow stairway. He was breathing hard and was clearly weak from loss of blood. "Lie still down here, Marcus," Christa beseeched as she helped Hester ease him to the dirt floor. She was breathless from the effort of getting him down the stairs. "We'll return as quickly as possible."

Marcus said nothing. Christa could only pray that he'd be all right as she and Hester hurriedly returned to the kitchen and banged the trapdoor into place behind them. She snatched up an oval rag rug and threw it over the cellar door.

Just then Christa spied one of the bloodied towels in full view on top of the baking table. She grabbed it and jammed it into a copper kettle hanging from a low ceiling beam.

In the next instant, three men wearing worn American army uniforms burst into the room through the back door. Ambrose tried to follow, but he was hampered by the effort required to hold onto the collar of a huge, viciously snarling mongrel. Christa's heart jumped into her throat when she saw one of the soldiers whirl around and point a pistol at the barely controlled dog.

"No, please, don't shoot!" she cried. Without thinking, she dashed to put herself between the man and the guard dog, speaking fiercely to the animal. "Be still, Wolfgang! To heel!" She pointed her arm down sharply at her side and the dog immediately ceased to struggle against Ambrose's hold. But a low, threatening growl still sounded in the animal's throat as the butler released him and he came to stand at Christa's side.

"That's a nasty animal there," the soldier snapped angrily, glaring at the ferocious mixed-breed beast, but he lowered his pistol anyway.

Though Christa was trembling with relief, she tried to regain her composure sufficiently to present a bold front.

"You have no right to invade this house! What is the meaning of this?" she demanded, her chin high, inwardly only too aware that the man's weapon could easily be pointing at herself next. The two men with the soldier held muskets at the ready.

The same man who'd spoken earlier now eyed Christa with a different kind of interest. His face was half hidden by an unkempt, bushy red beard, but Christa easily read his lewd expression as his gaze swept brazenly over her. Instinctively, she pulled her wool shawl closer to cover the low-scooped neckline of her dress. When he finally answered her question, his manner was gruff.

"I am Lieutenant Luther Cosgrove of the United States Continental Army. My men and I are looking for a Tory spy. He may be wounded. We intend to search these premises."

"Lieutenant, you must know this city is held by forces loyal to our sovereign, King George. Dragoons vigilantly patrol this area. I demand you leave at once!" Christa tried to preserve her brave front as she spoke, but she feared the loud pounding of her heart would give away how frightened she was.

"So you are *loyalists* here." The officer spoke the word contemptuously. "What household is this?"

Before Christa could answer, a fourth soldier stepped forward from the shadows. "I'm from this area, Lieutenant, and know this to be Haviland Court, the estate of Orin Haviland and his family. Mr. Haviland is a wealthy and influential man with a strong voice in the Continental Congress. It's said he has King George's ear as well. I believe he's abroad in England at this time. This is Mrs. Nevin Haviland, his daughter-in-law. Her husband is now serving with the king's forces against us."

Christa's eyes widened in shock when she saw who was speaking. "Elias? You've joined the rebels?"

Elias Gilroy's home bordered Montclaire, Christa's own family estate. The men of that family were staunch king's men—or at least they had been. Elias's words just now had been boldly spoken, though he hadn't met Christa's gaze.

"Private Gilroy has chosen the side of independence and righteous freedom in our revolution against tyranny!" the lieutenant declared angrily. "There's been enough delay. Begin the search at once! Take the spy alive, if you find him, for the information he carries. The three of you investigate the main house, and use haste."

His men saluted and immediately departed. The lieutenant began to move cautiously around the large kitchen and side workrooms, making his own search. When he stepped on the oval rug to look out the back window, a plank of the trapdoor under his feet creaked from his weight. Christa stopped breathing as she watched to see what he'd do next. But he didn't seem to notice anything amiss as he continued across the kitchen to the scullery.

While he looked into that room, Christa's gaze slid involuntarily to the woven rug on the floor. Quickly realizing the danger in that, she forced herself to look away from the telltale spot. Fear made it hard for her to think. She touched Wolfgang's head absently, trying to decide what action to take. The tension she felt in the big animal's body matched her own.

Lieutenant Cosgrove returned and openly stared at her. "A husband would be a fool to go off to war and leave a pretty wife like you pining away at home. It must get lonely around here, not having your man around. For one inviting look from those smoky blue eyes of yours, I'd be glad to ease that loneliness or anything else ailing you."

Christa slapped him hard across the face. Angrily, Cosgrove grabbed her wrist and gripped it tightly, causing her to wince in pain. Wolfgang rose to his feet, baring his sharp teeth and snarling a warning. The lieutenant frowned menacingly and raised his pistol toward the dog. At that moment, Elias Gilroy returned to the kitchen.

"Private Gilroy reporting, sir!" he declared with a smart salute. "I found no fugitive on the main floor of the house."

The other two soldiers returned, too, and repeated Gilroy's actions. "Perhaps we should continue the search elsewhere, sir,'' Gilroy suggested. ''It's dangerous to remain in one place for too long.''

''I'm aware of that, Private,'' Cosgrove growled in disgust as he roughly pushed Christa away. She grabbed Wolfgang's collar while the lieutenant motioned his men toward the back door.

''Another time, lovely lady,'' he told her, flashing her a lecherous look as he led his men out to join the rest of the patrol.

Gilroy was the last to follow. Christa touched his arm to make him pause.

''Thank you, Elias,'' she whispered.

He said nothing, but his serious expression seemed to soften as he gave a slight nod and then left.

Ambrose had no more than closed the door behind him when several maids and two grooms entered the kitchen from the main house.

''Please, calm down,'' Christa directed when they all began to talk at once. ''They're gone now. We have nothing to fear.'' She hoped the servants wouldn't notice her own trembling as she tried to make her words sound convincing. ''Now, all of you go back to the house.''

Ambrose locked the door behind them as soon as they departed. Moving quickly, Christa snatched up an oil lamp and ran across the room to the trapdoor.

Chapter 2

Christa carefully descended the ten steps into the cellar, followed by Hester and Ambrose. When the lamp's circle of yellow light fell on the hard-packed dirt floor, Marcus Desmond's still form appeared just where they'd left him. Christa tried to steel her already strained nerves for what she might find as she knelt beside her friend and gently took his head in her lap.

"Marcus," she called as she brushed her hand across his cold, clammy forehead. Was he alive?

How she longed to see the shy, boyish smile that came easily to his lips when they chatted together. His brown eyes always warmed with pleasure when he goaded Christa into a heated debate. At age thirty-five, Marcus Desmond was a wealthy and highly respected barrister, well known for his fiery dissertations in court.

Slowly his eyes opened and he blinked to focus. "Christa?"

"Marcus, thank heaven you're awake," she exclaimed. "Don't try to move. You've been badly hurt."

"I—I can't stay here, Christa," he argued haltingly. "Rebel patrol . . . too close. Danger to all of you." He tried to rise, but Christa held him back.

"The patrol's come and gone. You're safe here for the time being. Please lie still." She turned toward the old butler. "Ambrose, send Herman to General Howe's headquarters to tell him about the rebels. Then have him fetch Doctor Hinton. He's the closest physician."

Marcus shook his head. "No, the danger increases the longer I stay. Now that I've had a chance to rest, I can go on. I must get the information I have to the proper sources as soon as possible. Lives depend on it. Ambrose, lend me a hand."

Gritting his teeth, Marcus clutched the butler's extended arm, but as soon as he attempted to stand upright, his injured leg buckled under him and he lurched forward. Only Christa's and Ambrose's quick actions to catch him prevented him from falling.

"Now, will you please listen to me, Marcus?" Christa begged as they eased him down to the dirt floor. "You can't stand on that leg, let alone ride." She looked at the servants. "See to sending the message to the general and bringing the doctor, Ambrose. Hester, get the chest of medicines in the pantry. We'll do what we can to tend this wound until the doctor arrives."

The two loyal servants nodded and hurried up the stairs. Christa loosened Marcus's collar to make him more comfortable as she held him against her lap.

"I had no idea you were involved with such clandestine activities, Marcus, but no information can be important enough to jeopardize your life."

"It is, Christa—vitally important to General Zachary's offensive strategy. General Howe's victories have forced George Washington and his rebel army into full retreat. But indecisive action now could reverse that gain. I *must* deliver the dispatch I carry." He pressed a hand over the breast pocket of his coat and grimaced as he gasped in pain.

"Well, you can't do it, Marcus. Someone else must take the dispatch."

"Impossible." Marcus shook his head. "I'd never trust a servant with this communiqué."

"Not a servant. *I* could deliver it for you," Christa suggested impulsively.

"What? *You?* That's unthinkable. You're a woman. It's much too dangerous."

Christa bristled at how quickly he dismissed the idea. He sounded so much like her husband and father-in-law in his condescending attitude. She tried to control her temper.

"Don't you trust me, Marcus?"

"Of course, I trust you. That's not the issue, Christa."

She could see by his expression that he was in pain. "Please don't waste your strength arguing with me, Marcus." Keeping her voice calm, she attempted to find the right words to convince him. "From what you've told me, the crucial issue is the dispatch you carry and its importance to our military objectives. It must be delivered as quickly as possible. You can't travel. A servant can't be trusted, and there's no one else here to do it. I'm the only logical alternative. I want to help His Majesty's cause. I'll take Wolfgang with me."

In the flickering lamplight, Marcus stared up at Christa, then he sighed as if in resignation. "If anything were to happen to you . . ."

"Nothing's going to happen to me, except that I'll aid you and my king. Now come, tell me what must be done."

Marcus knew he was defeated. Time was of the essence, not only in getting the communiqué delivered, but also because he could feel himself slipping toward unconsciousness.

"Very well. There's no other choice. Listen carefully."

He reached inside his coat, drew a folded leather packet from his breast pocket, and handed it to Christa. "I was to deliver this information tonight to Captain Trace Cavanaugh at the Wild Boar Alehouse on Sterling Street. He's my contact in the intelligence network and General Zachary's right-hand man. Tell Trace this: 'The rook is the king's pawn,' and he'll know I've sent you. He'll answer with the code word, *checkmate.*"

Christa nodded, remembering everything.

Marcus had to wait a few more moments before he had the strength to go on. As he gazed up at Christa, he couldn't keep her features in focus.

"T—take the greatest of care, Christa," he pleaded haltingly. "Disguise yourself somehow. If you're caught . . ." The thought caused him more pain than his injury. "T—try to destroy the packet. If you're found with it . . . you could be shot for spying."

Marcus's words stunned Christa. In her impulsive haste to help him, she hadn't considered what the consequences of her actions might be. Still, she couldn't go back on her word. If she could help the loyalists by delivering the dispatch, then she must. She'd just contact this Captain Cavanaugh and come straight home. It wouldn't take long—a couple of hours at most. She'd be back before dawn. No one would miss her. And she *wouldn't* get caught.

"Don't worry, Marcus. All will go well. I shall not fail you." But the man she held in her arms made no reply. She quickly felt for a pulse at his neck and expelled a breath of relief when she felt a fairly strong one. Marcus was unconscious but still alive.

Christa heard Ambrose and Hester returning to the cellar and hastily hid the dispatch packet in the side pocket of her long skirt before they could see it.

"Herman has gone to fetch the doctor, madam," Ambrose reported.

"Good. Mr. Desmond is unconscious from his wound," she explained, reaching for the medicine chest the cook held. "Help me bandage his leg, Hester. Then we'll move him upstairs."

The old butler and cook helped Christa carry Marcus Desmond's limp form from the cellar to a guest room on the second floor of the main house. After Christa sent Hester away, she confided a little in the trustworthy majordomo.

"Ambrose, I'll be going out for a short time tonight. There is something I must do for Mr. Desmond."

"But, madam, traveling alone at this late hour would be very dangerous."

"Perhaps, but it must be done. I'll return as quickly as possible. Now, I shall need some clothes for a disguise."

"A disguise?" the servant repeated, his eyes widening. "Oh, this does not sound good at all, madam. Please reconsider."

"It would be best if I didn't look like a woman in any way," Christa went on, thinking out loud and ignoring the old man's anxiety. "That new groom, Stewart, is about my size. Borrow a pair of dark-colored breeches from him, and a shirt and coat, but don't say for whom you need them. And get a hat of some sort if he has one. Hurry now. Time is of the essence."

The elderly majordomo rolled his eyes upward and shook his head as he left the bedchamber.

Christa quickly set about pinning up her thick black hair to facilitate hiding it under a hat. Then she removed the dispatch from the pocket of her skirt. Glancing over at Marcus on the bed, she remembered is warning of what might happen if she were caught with these papers on her person.

Christa was gifted with an extraordinary memory. Since childhood, she'd been able to accurately recall all that she'd read, seen, and experienced. Sometimes her ability was a curse, for it also prevented her from forgetting unhappy experiences. But tonight her gift would help her serve King George.

Untying the ribbon around the packet, she then broke the wax seal and took out the papers. She read each one carefully, committing names, numbers, artillery listings, and camp locations to memory. Most of the military information meant nothing to her.

When she finished, she took the papers over to the hearth and threw them into the low flames one by one, watching as the fire flared up with each addition.

Ambrose returned with the clothes she had requested. Again he tried to dissuade her from the action she seemed determined to take. "Please, madam, whatever it is you are doing—"

"Must be done, Ambrose. It is vitally important. Now please, no more words. Thank you for these." She took the small pile of clothing he held. "Go downstairs and wait for Doctor Hinton to arrive. And have one of the grooms saddle Moonstar for me." She thought again. "No, not Moonstar. She's too fine a mare. I could hardly pass for a servant riding on her. Prepare one of the grooms' horses for me. And no sidesaddle. I'll need to ride astride."

"Yes, madam, if that is your wish," the servant replied, resigned.

When he'd gone again, Christa hurried to her own room and quickly changed into the groom's garments. The white cotton shirt fit well, and the dark green breeches clung snugly to her trim figure. She was glad the coarse black wool jacket was a little too big and came down to the middle of her thighs, hiding the curve of her hips.

After tucking her hair under the knitted brown stocking hat, Christa pulled on an old pair of black riding boots and surveyed herself in the full-length mirror. With luck and the darkness, she just might pass for a servant boy. She could only hope so.

Chapter 3

At a British headquarters encampment commanded by General Fitzhugh Zachary, Trace Cavanaugh fought to hide his weariness as he crossed a clearing and made his way toward the general's tent. He ran a hand through his matted chestnut brown hair. Every inch of his six-foot frame ached with exhaustion. He thought longingly of seeking out his bedroll and becoming closely acquainted with it—for at least a week—but that wasn't possible. Getting a hot bath and a clean change of clothes for the buckskins he'd been wearing for almost ten days weren't likely possibilities either. Instead, he readied himself for another battle with Leland Garrett.

Not that Trace was adverse to the idea of confronting his nemesis. His turquoise eyes narrowed under sharply arched dark brows as he thought of this new chance to best Garrett. It was a ruthless contest between them, one Trace won more often than not. But Garrett was no fool, and he hated Trace bitterly for taking the general's favor from him. Garrett wanted that position again, no matter what the cost.

Trace hadn't slept in over two days—he'd been in the saddle most of that time—and his fatigue was certain to take the edge off his skill at verbal sparring with Garrett. He'd have to be very careful, for there was far more at stake than just a savage competition between two captains in King George's Royal Army. Only Trace knew the extent of the intrigue, or the degree to which it had become his overriding obsession.

A young private with carrot-colored hair and a face full of freckles fell into step beside Trace. "I'm glad to see you made it back all right, Captain Cavanaugh. We heard you took a big chance and went behind enemy lines to reconnoiter."

"It wasn't as dangerous as it sounds, Private," Trace assured him, smiling slightly. "The Continental forces are still scattered after that last rout we gave them. If they hadn't been, I wouldn't have gone."

"Ha, you don't fool me none, Captain," the young soldier replied with a grin. "I know you. We all do. That was just the kind of thing you like doin'—walkin' right under the rebels' noses and not gettin' caught. I sure wish I had your backbone.

"Well, I just wanted to say thanks for the leave you gave the platoon. I haven't been home to see my folks since I enlisted over ten months ago. I'll sure be glad to see them."

"Just don't forget to come back when your time is up, Dolby," Trace remarked jokingly. "I need good men like you."

"Oh, I'll be back all right, Captain. I wouldn't let you down. The rest of the boys and me intend to prove Captain Garrett dead wrong. He said we'd all desert when you gave us leave. I reckon he's in for a big surprise. I'd come back just to see the look on his face."

"I'll enjoy seeing that myself," Trace agreed. "Have a good visit home."

"That I will. Thank you, sir." After giving Trace a sharp salute, Dolby hurried away.

When Trace entered General Zachary's tent a few

minutes later, the general was ranting angrily at a dark-featured officer. "Damn it, Garrett! You let that blasted spy—the Scorpion—slip through your fingers again! I want him *caught!* We're on the verge of going into winter quarters, and I won't have him jeopardizing our supply lines. Those routes should have been completed by now. You were supposed to see to that as well."

The fifty-five-year-old British commander's steel-blue eyes glinted with anger as he turned to see who'd come in. His fierce expression softened somewhat when he saw Trace. "Good to see you back, Cavanaugh," he said, returning Trace's salute. "I hope your mission was more successful than Garrett's."

"Accomplished as ordered, sir," Trace assured him, stepping forward to place the papers he'd brought on the rough-hewn plank table. "It's all here in my report." He shot a look at Garrett, meeting his rival's cool gaze with an expression they both understood. Trace had come out on top again.

"Fine work. At least one of my officers is worth his mettle. Here, give me your best judgment on this matter again." The general thumped his index finger on a map spread out on the table. Red lines traced snakelike routes in several places. "Now that you've scouted the enemy's flank positions, which one of these supply routes do you think would be the most reliable?"

Trace studied the map, then pointed to the most northern red line. "I still say this way."

"Ridiculous!" Leland Garrett snapped, his brown eyes narrowing under black brows. "That way is beset with bogs and swampland!"

"And less likely to hide an ambush," Trace cut in confidently.

"And more likely to mire our wagons and aid sabotage!"

"Not if one knows precisely where to go," Trace parried.

"Oh, and you do, of course! You with your lowbred provincial expertise!"

"Be very careful, Garrett," Trace warned. His cool expression didn't change, but a slight twitch of his square jaw revealed that his teeth were clenched in growing anger.

"That's enough, Garrett," Zachary intervened sternly. "It's precisely Cavanaugh's expertise that makes him valuable to me and to His Majesty. You'd do well to emulate him. Now, about these supply lines . . ."

The general returned his attention to the map. Trace didn't try to keep a smirk of triumph from curling one lip.

"I agree with Cavanaugh about this route." Zachary tapped his finger on the line Trace had indicated. "But from your report, Garrett, the more eastern route you favor would have better access to merchants who are loyal to the king and would readily provide us with the supplies we'll need while we're in winter quarters."

"If I may speak, sir," Trace interjected. "I checked with the quartermaster before I reported here, and he gave me a list of the supplies he'll be requiring soon. I propose a test of both these routes. Captain Garrett will use his route and his suppliers. I'll do the same with mine. The results should speak for themselves."

Trace held Leland Garrett's gaze as he spoke. The gauntlet was thrown, the latest challenge issued.

"Well, I'm a sporting man," Zachary remarked. "That may just be the solution. Your orders, gentlemen, are to get the requisitions from the quartermaster and fill them. The man who returns first with the supplies will prove his route is the best. And see if you can find a source of gunpowder along the way.

Too many of His Majesty's munitions ships have been captured or destroyed of late. Our powder supplies are becoming dangerously depleted, and we'll need to replenish them while we're in winter quarters. Now, I suggest you both leave in the morning, after Cavanaugh's had a chance to rest from his last assignment. Carry on, men.''

Trace preceded Garrett out of the tent.

"You haven't a chance in hell of succeeding," Garrett stated arrogantly as soon as they were alone.

"As usual, you're mistaken, Captain." Trace's cool tone was tinged with sarcasm. "I'll succeed, no doubt about it. But to give you a sporting chance, I'll wish you luck. You'll need it to keep from making a fool of yourself.''

Garrett's hate-filled glare might have cowed a lesser man, but Trace only smiled, enjoying his opponent's wrath as he watched him stalk away. Both men knew there would be no waiting until morning to begin this contest.

Tired or not, Trace must leave immediately. But as he made his way toward the quartermaster's tent, he smiled again. Garrett had played right into his hands. He couldn't have planned it better.

Chapter 4

Darkness pressed ominously around Christa. Drizzling rain made traveling hazardous, and the threat of discovery seemed to loom around every corner. Again and again she had to fight down her fear.

As the rain fell harder, Christa guided her chestnut mare along nearly deserted avenues and back streets, hoping she was following the quickest route to the Wild Boar Alehouse. She was coated with spattered mud, and rain trickled down her neck. Cold and dampness penetrated her clothing. Her spirits flagged as she realized the task she'd agreed to do for Marcus wasn't proving as easy as she'd first thought. Nevertheless, she was determined to do what she'd promised.

She tried to skirt the main streets so there would be less likelihood of being seen. Each time she glimpsed someone en route, a chill of apprehension crept up her spine.

She was glad she'd brought Wolfgang with her. In the shadowy light coming from inside the homes she passed, the big mongrel looked more like his wolf father than his Great Dane mother.

As she neared her destination, Christa didn't like the appearance of the area in which she found herself. The shops and houses lining both sides of Sterling Street looked anything but reputable. Some buildings were dark, their occupants having gone either to bed or home from their workplaces. Christa slowed her horse's pace, trying to read the signs hanging outside the lighted buildings.

All at once, two British soldiers lurched arm in arm into the street from an alleyway, singing loudly and off tune. One of them stumbled and fell directly in front of Christa's horse, forcing her to pull up sharply to keep from riding into him.

" 'Ere, watch where you're goin', mate!'' his comrade shouted as he grabbed the mare's bridle. "Don't go runnin' down ol' Pike now.'' The smell of rum was strong around him.

"Unhand my horse at once!'' Christa ordered, momentarily forgetting her disguise.

"Well now, ain't you some upstart?'' the man replied, his slurred words growing angry. "Think you can order around two of King George's finest? Or maybe you're one of them rebel devils what's always sneakin' 'round hidin' instead of standin' out an' fightin' in formation like a proper soldier. Declare yourself! Be ye friend or foe?''

The soldier who'd fallen regained his feet, and both men stood at Christa's side. She swallowed hard and tried to think over the sound of her heart's wild pounding.

"Why, mates, I'm a friend, o' course. As loyal to good King George as you be,'' she answered hastily, trying to make her words match her servantboy disguise.

"Is that so?'' the one called Pike said drunkenly. "Well, I don't believe none of this tripe. I think this 'ere bloke needs to be taught not to run down the king's men.''

Before Christa could react, he grabbed her by the coat front and dragged her from her horse. The other man quickly took hold of her arms from behind while

Pike pulled back to swing a punch. Christa ducked his big fist, causing him to miss and make a full circle with his swing that sent him sprawling onto the street.

Christa kicked her right boot back with all her might, hitting her captor squarely in the shin. He let out a loud curse and slackened his grip enough so she could twist away from him. But before she could dart out of reach, Pike caught her around the waist.

"Let go of me, you big oaf!" she shouted as they both fell to the cobblestones.

"I got 'im, McDugal! Get over 'ere an 'elp me thrash 'im!" Pike called to his partner.

Suddenly a shadowy shape hurled itself at McDugal. With a gnash of vicious teeth, Wolfgang knocked down the British soldier and clamped his jaws fiercely onto his rear end. McDugal's scream of pain sounded over the whole neighborhood.

"Pike! Pike! 'Elp me, Pike! Get 'im off me! *Yow!*"

Pike pushed Christa aside and scrambled to his feet. As he hurried toward McDugal, he tried to draw his pistol, but as he did, his foot slipped on the wet cobblestones. Tripping, he plunged headfirst into McDugal and Wolfgang.

Christa watched fearfully as her courageous pet battled both men. She was searching desperately for a weapon with which to assist the dog when she was grabbed by the back of her jacket collar and yanked to her feet.

"Call off your hound!" a deep voice ordered sternly. When she hesitated, he gave her a rough shake, making her think better of defying his order.

"Down, Wolf! Stop, boy! To heel!" she called. Immediately, the big dog withdrew from the attack and padded over to her.

"Stay here and keep your beast with you," the man told her in a gruff voice that allowed no argument.

As the newcomer strode past Christa, she saw that he was tall and wore buckskins like a backwoodsman. He didn't hurry to where the two infantrymen lay moaning in a heap in the middle of the street.

"McDugal and Pike—I might have known." He stood over them with his hands on his hips. "And drunk again, by the smell of you. I should have let the lad's mongrel finish off both of you. You're little good to the regiment in this condition."

McDugal rose unsteadily to his feet, rubbing his backside. "Aw, Cap'n, we wasn't tryin' to make no trouble. 'Ad us a couple of rums, was all. Takes more'n that to get us unfit for duty."

"Save your breath, Corporal. I'm too tired to listen to your story. I don't know what this fracas was about, but it's finished now. Is that understood?"

"Yes, sir," both men said meekly.

"Now haul your carcasses out of here and get back to camp. If you're still on this street five minutes from now, I'll see that your next bunks are in the stockade."

The captain turned away and headed toward where Christa stood holding Wolfgang by the collar. The dog growled a warning deep in his throat that would have stopped most men, but the officer didn't seem the least bit intimidated. He didn't stop until he stood right in front of Christa. His broad shoulders blocked whatever light there was, casting his face in shadow.

"Get on your way, too, boy," he ordered with annoyance. "And don't be taking on men twice your size, if you know what's good for you."

"But they were the ones—" Christa started to protest, but the captain was already striding down the alley. She frowned, but decided it would be more prudent to let the matter drop. A few people had come out of a nearby tavern to see what all the commotion was about, and she didn't want to call more attention to herself. Better to depart quietly and get on with her errand before the two soldiers had time to consider her again. Even now, McDugal was helping Pike to his feet.

Though the rain had stopped, Christa felt wet and cold through and through, and bruised and dirty from her tussle with Pike. Somehow she still had to finish making the delivery for Marcus, preferably without getting jailed or murdered!

"Come on, Wolf," she said quietly. "We still have to find the Wild Boar."

Chapter 5

A block up the street Christa found her mount at a watering trough with several other horses. She tied the mare securely to the hitching rail, then searched the buildings around her, her attention drawn to a noisy establishment across the street. To her dismay, she saw that the sign nailed to the single-story building said "THE WILD BOAR."

A feeling of dread inched up her spine as she raised on tiptoes and looked though a dirty window into the low-class tavern. She'd never been in such a place in all her life, and she didn't relish the prospect now. But she couldn't turn back. Marcus was depending on her.

"Wolfgang, you come running if I shout for you, boy. Now sit and stay," she ordered.

The big gray-and-black animal sank to his haunches. Christa tucked a stray strand of dark hair under her knitted hat, took a deep breath to gather her courage, and walked through the open door of the Wild Boar.

The interior of the crowded, smoky alehouse proved even less inviting than the outside. The plastered walls were a dingy gray color, veined with numerous cracks. The customers appeared to be mostly scruffy-looking waterfront ruffians. Christa tried not to think about that fact as she swallowed back her fear and inched along the edge of the big open room, trying to find an inconspicuous place to sit. No one seemed to pay any attention to her as she moved to where a wide hearth held a welcome fire. But as she put out her hands to warm them, someone spoke.

"What can Bess be gettin' for you, ducks?"

Christa turned to find a tall young woman with braided blond hair standing next to her, holding a small tray. She wore a black skirt that was short enough to show her ankles and a tight-fitting gold blouse that clung to her very ample bosom.

"Well, if you got yourself a good enough look, maybe you'd care to order a mug of rum now," she remarked good-naturedly. "I ain't standin' here for my health, love."

"I, ah, that is . . . I can't," Christa stammered in confusion, trying to make her voice coincide with her disguise. Money. Why hadn't she thought to bring some with her?

"No coins, huh?" Bess went on. "I figured as much by the look of you. Well, you best be gettin' outta here. Duffy, the owner, don't like customers what can't pay. He'll be tossin' you out on your ear soon's he finds out." She started to turn away, but Christa touched her arm to stop her.

"Wait, please. I can't buy rum, but you look mighty kind. Real pretty, too. Could you be helpin' me to find somebody? It's real important. I don't want no trouble, honest." Christa put an urgency in her voice she hoped would gain the serving girl's sympathy.

"Well, long as you put it that way," Bess gave in, apparently pleased by the compliments. She smiled widely, not seeming at all put off by Christa's wet and dirty appearance. "Who'd you be lookin' for, ducks? I know most every bloke in here."

"Feller by the name of Trace Cavanaugh," Christa replied. "Is he somebody you'd be knowin'?" She looked at Bess hopefully.

"Ah yes, Trace . . ." Bess said his name wistfully, clutching the small tray she was carrying to her full breasts. "Best-lookin' piece of man a girl could ever hope to see, with blue-green eyes that look right into your soul. 'Course, you bein' a fella, you wouldn't see it that way, I reckon. But you're in luck. Trace's here tonight. That's him over there in the back corner. But don't you be stickin' around too long. I can get away from here in an hour, an' I'm aimin' to spend time with Trace. We won't want nobody botherin' us neither."

Bess pointed to a shadowy area where someone sat alone, slumped over the wedged-in table, then she walked away.

Christa's heart sank as she studied the figure. *That* was Trace Cavanaugh? From where she was, the man appeared to have passed out from drunkenness.

With disappointment, she realized she'd wanted Cavanaugh to be a dashing rake like Marcus, heroically serving his king on dangerous secret missions. Apparently that was not the case.

Reluctantly, Christa threaded her way through the crowd to the back corner. The man was sitting in a chair, but the upper half of his body was sprawled over the small round table. One arm lay straight out, the hand holding onto the handle of a tankard of ale. His other arm cushioned his head like a pillow. An offensive smell emanated from his wet and dirty buckskins. At least a week's growth of dark, scraggly whiskers covered what little Christa could see of his face. His dark brown hair was wet and matted with mud.

Was this the man she was supposed to find? Marcus must have been delirious from his wound when he'd told her about this man Cavanaugh.

Christa's apprehension peaked, making her stomach churn sickeningly when she realized she had to at least try to communicate with the man. Summoning her courage, she gingerly poked him in the shoulder, in a spot that didn't look quite as dirty as the rest of him.

"Trace Cavanaugh?" There was no response. "Wake up, Cavanaugh." This time she gave his shoulder a healthy shake and watched closely, ready to run for the door if he did anything threatening. Was there something slightly familiar about him?

"I hear you," the man on the table mumbled. One eye slowly opened halfway and looked in her direction, then closed again. "This better be important," he went on in a low voice.

Swallowing, Christa plunged forth, keeping her voice restrained so she wouldn't be overheard by the men at a nearby table. "The rook is the king's pawn." She held her breath, anxiously awaiting his answer to the code phrase.

Trace's senses were clouded by exhaustion, but he still heard the words. He opened his eyes and slowly raised himself to a sitting position to get a better look at who had spoken them. Though the light was dim, his eyes widened at the person standing before him.

Christa shared his surprise.

"You!" they both said at once as each recognized the other from the incident with McDugal and Pike out in the street.

"Who are you?" Trace demanded, fully alert now. He frowned menacingly, and Christa hastily stepped back, taking care to keep the table between them.

"The rook is the king's pawn," she repeated, eyeing him nervously. She wished the light were brighter so she could see his face better.

"Checkmate." Trace gave the correct response, but he, too, warily watched what appeared to be a boy.

Everything about the lad was so muddy that it was hard to tell how old he was or what he looked like.

Christa almost collapsed with relief. "Marcus Desmond sent me," she hastily explained. "I've somethin' important for you," she added in as gruff a voice as she could muster, glancing around quickly to make certain they weren't being overheard.

"Why didn't Marcus come?" Trace asked, motioning for her to take the chair on his right, closer to him.

"He was shot by a rebel patrol earlier tonight. His leg. Couldn't ride, so he sent me."

"I've been waiting for that information. Rode a long way to get it. Is Marcus all right?"

"Will be, I think."

"Good. Let me have the dispatch then. Time is important."

"It's in my head. Fetch me paper an' pen an' I'll write it down for you right quicklike," Christa replied, but Cavanaugh didn't appear to be listening to her. She turned sideways to follow his gaze to the front door, where three men had just entered.

The man in front was huge. His patched gray coat strained at the buttons over his fat stomach. All three men's faces were covered with scraggly beards, and their clothes looked as if they hadn't seen wash water in a good number of days. The big man's squinty-eyed gaze fell on Trace and Christa, and he scowled fiercely as he started toward them. The other two men followed.

"Damn," Trace muttered under his breath.

"Heard you was in town, Cavanaugh," the leader ground out in a gravelly voice when he reached their table, while the other two men spread out, one on either side of him. "We come to fetch you fer Daisy.

She ain't too happy with you, and when *she* ain't happy, *we* ain't happy. Right, boys?''

"Right, Ox," the two smaller men answered together, nodding and grinning in agreement.

"We're goin' to take you to her, so's you kin make up with her real nicelike, see," Ox informed Trace. "Now you kin come peaceablelike or you kin come beat to a pulp, but yer acomin'. So which way'll it be?"

"Now, Ox, I'm very sorry to hear Daisy's unhappy," Trace answered in a tone so casual that no one would have guessed his life had just been threatened. He leaned back leisurely in his chair. "She's a fine girl and very beautiful. It's hard to believe she's a sister to you three. But what was between us is over now and she knows it. You don't really want to get into a fight again, do you, boys?" He looked steadily in turn at each of the Bedlow brothers. "Clem? Harley?"

Ox's companions glanced dumbly at each other, looking a little doubtful.

Christa didn't know what to do. The tension was almost tangible. Her first instinct was to run, but the three men surrounded the small table, blocking all escape routes. She could only sit helplessly and watch what was happening.

"Shit! Enough of this jawin'!" Ox shouted in the next instant. He lunged, but Trace was a split second ahead of him. Rising swiftly to his feet, he grabbed the edge of the wooden table and flipped it over sideways so that Ox went sprawling to the floor.

Christa gasped and lurched backward. Her chair toppled over, taking her with it as it fell. With difficulty, she untangled herself from the broken chair and scrambled away just before Harley awkwardly careened toward her, propelled by one of Trace's well-placed punches. He hit headfirst with a terrible thud into the low stone mantel of the fireplace, and crumpled to the floor.

The patrons of the alehouse rose to their feet, calling out their enthusiasm for the fight, but no one offered assistance as Trace fought the three big men. Frantically, Christa turned to Bess, who had appeared beside her.

"Won't somebody help Cavanaugh? He's outnumbered!"

"With the Bedlows, that's about even for Trace," Bess explained with a wide smile, keeping her eyes on the fracas. "But he did seem pretty done in tonight. Might not be as good a fight as usual." She was clearly enjoying the spectacle as much as the others were, though she did wince when Trace hit Clem Bedlow, making him ricochet into a stout wooden support beam. He bounced off and crashed down hard on his back on a nearby table.

The brawl continued between Trace and Ox now, and Trace appeared to be in a bad way as the much larger man held him from behind in a crushing bear hug.

Christa gasped as Ox's thick arms squeezed tighter and tighter around Trace's chest. Suddenly Trace threw his head back, hitting Ox solidly on the nose. The obese man let out a howl of pain and released his quarry. Trace whirled and sank his fist deep into his adversary's ample belly. The blow barely fazed Ox, who only bellowed a laugh and swung his powerful fist like a deadly club. Trace ducked in time, but Harley and Clem grabbed him from both sides, pinning him between them. Ox moved in, hitting Trace hard in the midsection. The blow doubled him over. Ox brought his huge fists smashing down in a right and then a left cross on Trace's jaw, whipping his head from side to side.

Christa couldn't stand there watching any longer. She was certain Trace Cavanaugh was going to be beaten to death before her eyes! In panic, she snatched up a full pitcher of ale from a table close at hand and ran at Ox Bedlow. Wielding it with all her might, she hit him squarely on the back of the head. The pitcher shattered, covering him with ale and broken crockery. Christa froze stock-still, staring wide-eyed as she watched Ox straighten and put a hand to his head. He looked puzzled as he slowly turned toward her.

Trace used the few seconds Christa had gained for him to escape Harley and Clem's hold. Using the two brothers for leverage, he quickly swung his legs up and kicked out, catching Ox in the back and propelling him forward. Christa sidestepped just in time to avoid being knocked over as he crashed to the floor.

Trace threw himself sideways, taking the other Bedlows with him. They struggled on the sawdust-covered floor until Trace gained the upper hand by grabbing both men by the backs of their coat collars and knocking their heads together. When he released them, they slumped unconscious to the floor.

Ox was staggering to his feet as Trace turned and picked up a round-backed chair. He brought it down on the big man's head and shoulders with such bone-jarring force that the chair shattered. Ox grunted loudly and collapsed flat on the floor. He didn't move again.

"Is he dead?" Christa asked fearfully, staring at Ox's hulking form at her feet.

"No," Trace told her between gasps. He brushed at a trickle of blood on the side of his mouth. "It would take more than this fight to do in Ox and those two." He tilted his head toward Harley and Clem, then winced as if in pain. "A waste of good ale, though.

Thanks for your help. Come on, let's get out of here. We don't want to be around when they wake up.''

Cheers and applause erupted in the room as Trace stepped over the Bedlow brothers and headed for the door. Following, Christa almost crashed into him from behind when he stopped abruptly to take Bess into his arms and give her a lusty parting kiss.

"Next time, love," he promised, flashing a smile that clearly was balm for the serving girl's disappointment, judging by her dreamy-eyed expression. Then Trace disappeared through the door, Christa trailing behind him.

Chapter 6

"Do you have a horse?" Trace asked when he and Christa reached the street. At her answering nod, he added, "Get it and follow me."

"Come on, Wolf," she called to the dog, who was still waiting for her. He padded after her to her mount.

Trace had just joined Christa on his own horse when a rider approached and reined in his horse next to them. By the faint light in the street, Christa saw that he was an older man, perhaps in his early fifties, and small in stature. Like Cavanaugh, he wore buckskins.

"You comin' or goin'?" he asked, directing his question to Trace as he reached up and pushed an animal skin hat farther back on his head.

"Going," Trace replied. "Glad you got my message to come, Cabe. I had a run-in with the Bedlows in there. We're heading for Suko's. Ride along and I'll fill you in on what I need."

The newcomer nodded, but he looked back toward the alehouse and ran his tongue over his bottom lip as if he wished this meeting could be taking place in there.

"Cable Shipley, this is . . . What is your name, boy?" Trace turned to Christa.

"Uh, it's Chris," she told him, thinking fast. "Chris Kendall." Her maiden name would have to do for the moment.

34

"Cabe, meet Chris. He brought the dispatch we've been waiting for from Marcus Desmond."

Cable Shipley gave a quick nod, which Christa returned. Then the two men reined their horses down a side street. Christa followed.

They rode along several twisting, turning streets. Christa had no idea where she was, so she carefully stayed close to Cavanaugh and Shipley, hoping they didn't have far to go. The crisp night air penetrated her damp clothes, making her squirm uncomfortably in the saddle.

Finally they turned down an avenue of houses that looked considerably more substantial than those near the Wild Boar. Still, Christa noted this wasn't the affluent, fashionable part of the city where Haviland Court and Montclaire were located. They stopped before a two-story clapboard house.

"If'n you don't mind, I won't be goin' in there with you," Cabe Shipley remarked. "That Chinaman an' me don't git along none."

"He and Suko are from Japan, Cabe, not China," Trace corrected.

"Same difference. He's still a slanty-eyed devil what'd jist as soon cut yer gizzard out as give you the time of day. Always sharpenin' them swords of his'n." The backwoodsman shook his head with apparent disgust.

"All right, there's no need for you to come in anyway," Trace agreed. He reached inside his buckskin shirt and drew out several folded papers, handing them to Shipley. "Here's a list of the supplies I'll need as fast as you can get them. Zachary has me competing with Lee Garrett on this expedition. Nick Fletcher should be able to get most of them. You know where to find him."

Shipley nodded as he tucked the papers inside his

own deerhide shirt. "You an' Garrett sure do have yer go-rounds, don't you? But he's such a puff-chested rooster, it purely does my heart good to see you best him every time."

"And I intend to again with this supply route. Tell Nick that Zachary has us on the hunt for munitions, too—especially gunpowder."

"Will do." Shipley nodded and reined his horse around to ride away.

"Come with me, Chris," Trace directed then. "But leave your mongrel here with the horses."

Reluctantly, Christa ordered Wolfgang to stay. The mention of the name Garrett had caught her attention. Could Cavanaugh and Shipley have been talking about the Leland Garrett she knew? The man she wanted to forget, she reminded herself disparagingly. She hadn't let herself think about Lee in a long time, but now the mention of his name scraped an emotional wound, bringing back a sharp reminder of the old pain. Shrugging off the unpleasant memory, she hurried after Trace, worrying about what she might be getting herself into next. Cavanaugh and Shipley's conversation about the people who resided here hadn't been reassuring.

The night was very dark, but Cavanaugh seemed to have no difficulty seeing where he was going. Christa stayed close behind him. When they reached the backyard, she saw a candle burning at a window, its circle of light revealing a back entrance. Trace paused while entering the unlocked door and turned to Christa.

"Stay behind me, be quiet, and do exactly what I tell you," he said in the voice he probably used when giving orders to troops. Christa nodded, her apprehension mounting.

They entered a kitchen area. The candlelight reflected brightly off clean, whitewashed walls. Christa glanced around, noticing that the embers in the fireplace had been banked for the night. Everything in the kitchen looked orderly.

Trace picked up the pewter candleholder by the window and cocked his head to the side as if listening for something. Christa did the same, but she didn't hear a sound. The whole house was unnervingly quiet. She tensed, wishing she knew what was about to happen. Not knowing made it worse.

Trace put a finger to his lips, then motioned for her to follow him. He led the way around a baking table and through an archway to a narrow hall. A woven reed mat covered the floor of the corridor, muffling the sound of their boots. Christa sensed Trace's tense expectation. It matched her own.

Suddenly a bloodcurdling yell shattered the stillness. Christa screamed in fright as Trace spun around, caught her around the chest with his arm, and dragged her with him to the floor in an awkward tackle just as something swished past their heads. The candle went out, leaving them in darkness for several long seconds. Then someone lit a dragon-shaped lamp hanging from a wall sconce, and for the first time, Christa saw what had come at them making that terrifying sound.

A fierce-looking oriental man stood over them, legs wide apart, holding a deadly-looking curved sword toward her and Trace with both hands. His gray-streaked hair was pulled tightly away from his face and knotted at the top of his head. He wore a short, full-sleeved brown robe over matching wide-legged pantaloons. A black sash gathered the robe together at his waist and secured there another curved sword that was even longer than the one he held. A sinister smile of satisfaction curled his thin lips. Christa knew that the sword he held was what had swung so closely past their heads.

Trace rolled off her and sat up, resting his forearms on his bent knees. "Good to see you again, Tohashi," he remarked casually. "As usual, your welcome is a warm one."

"Yan-kee dog! Why have you come here? You are not worthy to enter this house!" The oriental spoke with such vehemence that Christa was certain they were about to be hacked to pieces.

"You're right about that at the moment," Trace went on with surprising calmness, glancing down at his dirty clothes and stroking his whiskered chin. "But I intend to remedy the situation with a good hot bath."

"You will not have it here!" the older man countered, scowling malevolently as he stepped closer. Christa gasped and instinctively pulled back, banging her head against the wall.

Trace rose slowly to his feet, keeping his eyes steadily locked on the other man, who he towered over when he was standing. "That will be for your mistress to decide, samurai," he stated, his tone much more serious. "I do not seek your approval. Tell the princess I am here."

For a moment neither man's gaze wavered. Christa held her breath. Her fate, her very life, was being decided in these tense seconds. Finally the oriental looked away, showing disgust as he lowered his sword and returned it smoothly to his sash. Turning, he strode to a set of double doors a few feet away. Sliding them apart, he waved his hand to indicate the room on the other side, then disappeared down the hallway.

Chapter 7

"Do you still have your wits, Chris?" Trace's manner lightened as he reached down to help Christa to her feet. "Are you hurt, lad?" he asked with concern when she staggered and caught hold of his arm to steady herself. Her legs felt as wobbly as a newborn colt's.

"He tried to kill us!"

"No, he didn't try, I assure you. If Tohashi had wanted us dead, we'd be in many precisely cut pieces right now. Just be glad he used the *wakizashi* and not the *katana*, the longer fighting sword he was carrying. A samurai uses that weapon when he really means business."

"Well, you mighta warned me." Christa used her boy's voice again and let a surge of anger toward Trace and the oriental man take the place of the nerve-racking fear she'd felt only moments ago. Frowning, she followed Trace down the hallway to the room the samurai had indicated.

Trace strode to a small table and turned up the wick of a beautifully designed double-globed glass lamp. The bright light revealed an enchanting room, and Christa forgot her anger as she gazed around her in wonder.

Large folding silk screens lined the four walls. Each screen consisted of three panels painted with exotic birds and flowers in delicate pastel colors. Never had Christa seen anything like them, or like the unusual furnishings.

There were no chairs. Instead, large silk cushions rested on woven reed mats on the floor around a low, black-lacquered table. The square cushions depicted nature scenes embroidered in a rainbow of vivid colors. A large cobalt-blue-and-white porcelain vase decorated with scenes from a Japanese emperor's court stood in the middle of the table.

The only large piece of furniture in the room was a rosewood cabinet near the entrance doors. Graceful white cranes and pink lotus blossoms decorated the wood. Two glass doors on the top half revealed lovely green figurines inside. Jade, Christa thought as she peered at them more closely. She'd read about such art objects, but had never imagined they'd be so lovely in actuality.

"Cavanaugh-san!" someone called joyfully from the doorway. Christa turned to see a petite woman of perhaps nineteen dressed in a bright green kimono. Her straight black hair fell to her shoulders and was adorned with jeweled combs. She ran to Trace with small, swift steps and threw her arms around his neck. Then she seemed to remember herself and quickly pulled back. Lowering her head shyly, she murmured, "Oh, I am so sorry."

Christa saw Trace smile just before he made a formal bow of respect in the oriental fashion. "Don't be sorry, Suko. I'm pleased you're happy to see me. It's been too long since I last visited you."

The woman also bowed, and she brightened again at Trace's words. Her dark, almond-shaped eyes sparkled in the lamplight as she gazed unwaveringly at him.

"So many months with not one word, Cavanaugh-san. I was so very worried about you."

"And that surely was what kept me safe, Suko. You must forgive me and my friend for coming like this, without notice and rather worse for the wear, I'm afraid. Princess Suko Yamagata, this is Chris Kendall."

"You are welcome," the princess replied shyly again. She lowered her eyes and bowed. Christa rather awkwardly did the same. "I am so very glad to have you both here. You may rest and refresh yourselves for as long as you wish. Anything I have is yours." Suko's smile held a special warmth as she bestowed it on Trace.

"I regret our stay must be a brief one," he explained. "May I trouble you for a bath and some food? It's been a while since I've had either."

"But, of course, Cavanaugh-san," Suko answered eagerly. "Your pardon for one moment." She bowed and went out to the hall, calling for Tohashi. The samurai appeared immediately, received instructions from his mistress, then departed, his expression still fierce.

"All will be made ready," Suko told them when she returned to the parlor. "Now, please to sit down." She delicately gestured a small hand toward the cushions on the floor. "You must tell me of all you have been experiencing since last I saw you, Cavanaugh-san."

Christa caught Trace's eye, hoping to remind him that they had urgent business to attend to. But he gave a slight shake of his head, then turned his attention to the lovely woman seated on her knees on one of the big square cushions. Trace joined her across the table, sitting cross-legged. Christa sat down, too. Though she was anxious to finish her business with Cavanaugh, she was curious to know more about this Japanese princess.

Christa noticed that the oriental woman gave her complete attention to Trace as he related his activities.

It didn't take a mind reader to tell that Suko held him in very high esteem. In fact, Christa judged the princess's feelings went much deeper than mere esteem. Her face held the same wistfully adoring expression Christa had seen on Bess, the serving girl at the Wild Boar. And apparently Daisy, that sister of the Bedlow brothers, had been enamored of Trace Cavanaugh as well. Amazing the effect he seemed to have on women. Christa was at a loss to explain it, for certainly he held no appeal for her whatsoever.

At last Tohashi came to the parlor.

"All is in readiness," Suko said. "Please to follow me."

She led the way down the hall to another room at the back of the house. This one was smaller than the parlor and very plain. It contained no oriental furnishings except a full-length mirror in a freestanding, black-lacquered wooden frame. Gold etchings of birds and flowers embellished the frame. The walls of the room were white and undecorated. A fire burned in the wide hearth. Several straight-backed wooden chairs had been arranged near one wall, and in the center of the room stood a large metal tub with a high back, from which clouds of steam were rising.

"That looks heavenly, Suko," Trace said with pleasure. "Thank Tohashi for its preparation."

"I am glad you are pleased, Cavanaugh-san." The young woman beamed. She reached over to a table, where soaps, towels, and other bathing articles were neatly arranged. "Now I shall assist you to bathe," she continued, reaching for a long-handled brush.

Christa's eyes widened. It was alarming enough to think that Trace Cavanaugh might intend to take a bath in front of her; she hardly wanted to be present while this oriental girl attended him. She could only guess what that might lead to between them!

"No, my little flower, you will not." Trace put his hands on Suko's shoulders and spoke gently. "You know I've told you our custom is different here in America. I'll bathe myself."

"But, Cavanaugh-san—"

"That's the way of it, Suko," Trace interrupted firmly. "Your illustrious father sent you here to America just before he was killed, so you'd be safe from his enemies. This is your home now. If you're to be schooled in the ways of my people, you must learn about propriety as we view it." He smiled. "Besides, take pity on me. I don't know all the ways of your culture. I've no desire to have a confrontation of honor with Tohashi if I inadvertently make a mistake in my actions. I value my head as it is—still connected to my neck."

Suko looked crestfallen, but she offered no more argument.

"As you wish, Cavanaugh-san. I shall return when you have finished and bring the food that is now being prepared. Tohashi will wait in the hall. If you need anything, you have only to tell him of it." With that she bowed and left the room, closing the door behind her.

Chapter 8

Christa had no intention of staying with Trace Cavanaugh while he took a bath. She was about to say she'd wait in the parlor, but Trace was already speaking.

"I may wed that girl one day, Chris," he said contemplatively. "She comes from highborn blood, yet she's been taught since birth to know her place and be everything a man could ever want in a woman—obedient, adoring, gentle, sweet in spirit. The princess is not at all like the so-called well-bred women in this country. They're pampered, selfish, temperamental—more trouble than they're worth, in most cases. In comparison Suko's like a rare flower among briers."

Briers, indeed! Forgetting the part she was playing, Christa took his words as a direct insult. Her quick temper flared. Without thinking, she was about to unleash it at him when she was halted by what he did next. He unlaced the rawhide ties on his buckskin shirt and drew the garment over his head.

"Now that we're alone, Chris, you can tell me the information in the dispatch. Start with the artillery assessment and locations." He pulled off his long-sleeved cotton undershirt as he spoke.

Trace had turned away from Christa. She swallowed hard and quickly measured the distance to the hall door with darting eyes, preparing to exit in a hurry, before he could undress any further. Two large oil lamps gave bright light to the room, and from where Christa stood, it was impossible not to see Trace's broad shoulders and the tanned expanse of his back, rippling with cords of muscles and ending in a narrow waist.

"Well, come on, out with it, boy," Trace instructed, turning toward her.

Christa saw something swing on a gold chain around his neck. Flashing in the lamplight, it appeared to be a piece of jewelry, a ring with a red gemstone in the center.

"Uh, it'd be best if I fetched paper an' pen an' wrote it all down for you." Christa averted her eyes from Trace and the ring, speaking too quickly as she headed for the door.

"I'd think twice before going out in the hall. Tohashi's there, and he can be very unfriendly when he wants to be, as I'm certain you recall. Just tell me what you know. I'll remember it. That is—if you do, in fact, have the information."

Christa was trapped. Cavanaugh sounded suspicious of her. If she made more of a fuss about leaving the room, he might press her further and discover her true identity. And she didn't want to face the samurai in any way whatsoever.

"I got the information, all right," she hastily assured him. "The artillery first."

She concentrated hard on reciting the figures and locations she'd committed to memory, and not on the fact that Trace Cavanaugh was watching her closely now. After a few moments, he seemed satisfied with what she was telling him and went to sit on one of the chairs while he listened.

"Here, lend a hand with these boots, will you?" he interrupted briefly. "I've yet to find a bootjack in this house. The Japanese don't use our kind of footgear."

When Christa hesitated again, he persisted. "You do know how to pull off a boot, don't you?"

Christa had never done the task herself, but she'd seen servants do it often enough. Resigning herself to the fact that she'd have to try, she came over to Trace, turned her back to him, and spread her legs apart. He lifted his right boot for her to pull. Though she took a firm grip on it and tugged hard, she barely budged it.

"Here, try again," Trace directed. This time he put his other foot on Christa's backside and pushed. She was so startled by the placement of his foot and by the force propelling her that she gasped and lunged forward, yanking off the boot as she went.

"There, that's got it, lad. Now the other one." Trace held up his left foot. Groaning inwardly, Christa reluctantly moved close to him again, straddled his outstretched leg, and grabbed the boot. Immediately, he gave her an assisting shove again. The boot came off, but Christa's dignity was considerably put out of place in the process.

Yet her perplexity with this situation was far from over. Trace stood up and began to untie the drawstring holding his buckskin pants around his waist. Christa's face flushed in dread over what she knew would follow. She turned swiftly away from him and went to the fireplace. There she unbuttoned her black wool jacket, opening it to let the welcome heat of the fire warm her through her wet, dirty clothes. She breathed only a little easier when she heard a splash of water. Daring to glance out of the corner of her eye, she saw Trace sink down into the tub. He sighed with pleasure as the hot water engulfed him.

Christa tried to keep on speaking, relating the details contained in the dispatch, but her words came falteringly. It was unnerving being in this small room with a virtual stranger, knowing he was lying quite naked in the short metal tub.

Trace asked several questions as he scrubbed the sweat and grime from his body. He was very pleased to hear what this messenger lad was relaying. It confirmed his suspicions about Boswell. He had to be the traitor among them. Otherwise, Marcus Desmond wouldn't have had this information.

The hot water was soaking some of the weariness out of his muscles. He felt more alert now, and relieved. Exposing Boswell could only help his own position. For the time being at least, he'd be safe from suspicion.

"You've done well, Chris," Trace said aloud, just before he splashed water over his face to rinse away the remains of shaving soap. "I see why Marcus had confidence in you. How about a bath for you to wash away the mud? It'll make you feel like a new man, I assure you. I'll have Tohashi refill the tub when I'm finished. This water isn't fit for anyone else to use."

Christa felt real panic now. She'd caught a glimpse of herself in the full-length mirror and knew she was, indeed, in need of washing. But while her wet, itchy clothes and muddy countenance made her long to soak in just such a tub of hot water, the thought of doing so here and now was completely out of the question!

"I, uh, I think maybe I'll do it later," she replied, still not looking in Trace's direction. "I been feelin' a might sickly for a spell an' don't want to catch no chill." She forced a pretend cough to confirm her story. "Besides, I need to be gettin' along home. I done what I come to do." She turned to start for the door.

"You'll stay a little while longer, lad," Trace informed her firmly. "The princess expects us to eat with her. The Japanese take the offering of hospitality very seriously. Not to remain and partake of what is being prepared for us would be an insult to the princess, causing her and her household to lose face, to be dishonored. So we'll be staying—*both* of us. And before you sit down to table, you'll make yourself presentable. There's water in that pitcher on the stand next to you. Use it to wash.''

Christa bristled at his stern tone. He was the commanding captain giving orders to an underling and he expected no argument, that was clear.

''Before you do that,'' Trace went on, ''fetch that bucket of clean water warming there at the fire and dump it over me to rinse off all this soap.''

Christa's eyes darted to the bucket he meant, but she didn't move.

''Come on, hop to it, Chris,'' Trace called with annoyance.

Christa was slow to bring the bucket over to the tub. She did *not* want to do it at all. Cavanaugh wasn't asking anything unreasonable of what he thought was a servant boy. His speech and demeanor were those of a man from the upper classes. He'd be accustomed to having servants attend him. And she mustn't arouse his suspicions again. If he discovered she'd lied about her identity, he might think she'd lied about the dispatch information, too. She could only hope the soap-filled water would cover those parts of Trace Cavanaugh that she did *not* want to see.

She had no such luck. When she tilted the bucket to let the water spill out in a slow, even stream, Trace remained sitting only long enough to rinse his hair and face. Then he stood up and turned, letting the flow spill over him. Christa's eyes widened and her mouth dropped open in shock at all she saw of him. She wasn't aware that she'd gasped out loud and dropped the bucket.

"Whoa, easy there, lad!" Trace swiftly caught the bucket and dumped what little water remained over himself to finish the rinsing. He seemed amused by his helper's obvious embarrassment.

Christa whirled around and hurried to the washstand. She knew her face must be scarlet.

Trace dried himself with a thick white towel and then wrapped it around his hips, tucking one corner in at his waist. The bath had cleared his dazed senses, leaving him contemplative as he watched the boy across the room. Something was amiss about Chris Kendall. Several details clicked into place. The vivid, long-lashed, blue-gray eyes seemed rather unusual for a lad. And they'd looked so stunned when he'd stood up in the tub just now. He also remembered what he'd felt when he'd grabbed Chris around the chest and tackled him to avoid Tohashi's blade.

Trace frowned. He leaned back against the oak table, folded his arms across his chest, and watched while the boy finished at the washstand.

At the same time, Christa realized that Trace had become very quiet. She turned, her gaze drawn to him. She could hardly believe the transformation in him now that the mud and grime were gone.

Clean-shaven, he appeared to be about thirty years old. The strong, chiseled lines of his square jaw and handsome face stood out strikingly. His powerful, muscular build emitted a bearing of confidence and control, an assurity in his ability to overcome any challenge. His dark brown hair was thick and wavy. Wet from the bath, it fell rakishly over his forehead. More dark hair thinly covered his wide chest, diminished to a line down his rippling, flat stomach, and disappeared into the top of the low-slung towel around his hips. Drops of water glistened against his flesh in the lamplight.

Christa continued to stare at Trace as he reached for a man's long kimono of turquoise silk decorated with a gold dragon, which Suko had left for him. He slipped his arms into the wide sleeves and tied the black sash at his waist.

Though he was well covered now, Christa still took an involuntary step back when he walked over to her. He stopped only an arm's length away, holding her gaze. She slowly drew in a breath to try to steady her racing pulse. Her legs felt weak.

His eyes were the same intense turquoise hue of the silk robe he wore, the brilliant blue-green of a tranquil tropical sea. Yet there was a hint of an undercurrent of danger in them and a penetrating magnetism that seemed to reach out and take hold of Christa, jolting her like a bolt of lightning.

"Well, I must say washing has improved your looks considerably, *Chris*," Trace noted, cocking an eyebrow. "All that remains now is to improve your manners. A gentleman does *not* dine with his hat on."

Before Christa could stop him, Trace pulled off her stocking hat. Freed from confinement, her black hair tumbled down about her shoulders in a tangled mass. In panic, she whirled to run, but Trace quickly grabbed her around the waist and pulled her down to the floor. He rolled her over onto her back and straddled her hips with his knees, holding her wrists against the floor on either side of her head. Christa tried hard to twist away from him. Her unbuttoned jacket parted down the front and her full breasts strained against the thin cotton material of her borrowed shirt. Trace's glance took in everything.

"Well, you most certainly are *not* a lad!" He frowned menacingly and his anger mounted at her deception. He didn't like being duped.

"Let go of me!" Christa demanded, outraged by his rough treatment.

"Not until I get an explanation, wench. Stop fighting, or I'll be forced to thrash some cooperation into you. And believe me, right now that's a very appealing idea."

"Release me, sir. I won't tell you anything until you do," Christa seethed at him, her eyes flashing to a darker shade of blue in her fury. "There's no need for such barbaric actions. Unhand me at once!"

Trace was surprised again, this time by his captive's vehement tirade. *She* was giving *him* orders! He was momentarily caught off guard by her show of spirit and the quality of her speech. She was an excellent actress with a talent for quickly changing characters, no doubting that. And she was beautiful as well. Exceedingly beautiful.

But he mustn't be distracted by her mesmerizing eyes or alluring body. He made himself set aside the temptation of her sensuous figure for the time being. He must discover who she really was and just what she was up to. Too many people's lives could be jeopardized, including his own. To that end, he pulled her by the wrists to a sitting position and let his ominous tone relay his serious intent.

"I don't know what game you're playing, woman, but let me assure you it's a most dangerous one. If I perceive you to be a threat to me in any way, I'll kill you here and now. So speak the truth and be quick about it!"

Fear caused Christa to cease struggling. The strength he used against her was far greater than hers, and his malevolent gaze revealed his capability to carry out his murderous threat. She was at his mercy, and she hated that helplessness. But she must do as he said, at least for now.

Chapter 9

Trace saw the intense malice in the blue-gray gaze of the woman he held pinned to the floor. Fear reflected in her eyes, too, but the hatred was stronger, thrusting into him like a razor-sharp sword. This woman had spirit, all right. He knew she was lying still now only because his superior strength had overpowered her. He could tell that her will remained undaunted. And judging by her black expression, she was planning a mean retribution. The thought flashed through his mind that he was glad no weapon was within her reach.

"Very well, Captain Cavanaugh," Christa scathingly conceded, "since you give me no other choice, I'll cooperate. I'm Christa Haviland, wife of Nevin Haviland."

Trace said nothing for a moment, surprised by her admission. He knew the Havilands. Orin Haviland was an outspoken loyalist who used his well-known name and vast fortune to thwart the American cause for independence whenever possible, especially if it meant a greater gain to his reputation and coffers. Trace knew Nevin somewhat as well. He served with General Howe as a captain whose duty post was a safe, behind-the-lines desk at Howe's headquarters here in New York.

"You don't expect me to believe you're a member

of that prestigious family,'' Trace replied finally, his voice unyielding. ''The wife of a Haviland doesn't go prancing about the city at night disguised as a lad.''

''I'm not in the habit of lying, Captain,'' Christa snapped, continuing to glare at him.

''You gave me a false name. What would you call that?''

''It wasn't false. Chris is part of my name and Kendall is my maiden name,'' she explained with some exasperation. ''I'm a Haviland by marriage, as I told you. Everything I related about Marcus Desmond and the dispatch is the truth. Marcus will verify what I've told you. He's recovering at Haviland Court. It was his idea that I wear a disguise. I was only trying to help him and our sovereign's cause.''

Trace watched Christa carefully, coming to a decision. He believed her. In his dangerous profession, his life often depended on his ability to read people quickly. But it would do no harm to have Marcus confirm her story. He needed to see him about several matters concerning the supply routes also.

''Very well, Mrs. Haviland, I'll take you back to Haviland Court as soon as we've finished our meal with Suko. For your sake, Marcus had better be there with the same version of your story.'' Trace's words carried a challenging undertone.

At that moment there was a quick knock on the hall door, and Suko entered, followed by her ever-diligent samurai.

''Cavanaugh-san, what has happened?'' The woman's dark eyes widened in surprise and alarm as she stopped abruptly and stared at Trace and Christa on the floor. Tohashi frowned fiercely, and his hand instantly moved to the hilt of his longer sword. He stood poised in readiness.

Trace eased his iron hold on his captive and got to

his feet, pulling Christa up roughly after him. "Nothing to be upset about, Suko. Seems we have a case of concealed identity here. But that's been remedied. This is Mrs. Christa Haviland. She'll need something suitable to wear while we're dining."

Suko's gaze went from Trace to Christa and back again before she seemed to comprehend his curt explanation. Clearing her throat, she lowered her eyes and bowed in acceptance.

"Of course, Cavanaugh-san," she acknowledged softly. She turned and hurried to the rosewood chest, from which she drew out a dark purple garment. "Will this humble robe be fitting?"

"Yes, Suko. Thank you." Trace took the robe and thrust it at Christa, addressing her sternly. "Get out of those wet clothes and make yourself presentable. We'll expect you in the parlor in five minutes. Tohashi will wait for you just outside the door. He'll see you don't lose your way."

Christa's spine stiffened at his terse orders, and for a split second she felt an angry impulse to throw the robe in his face. But Trace had already turned to go to Suko. In the next moments they left the room, the samurai in their wake.

Christa frowned and clenched her teeth as she threw the garment on a chair next to her. Rubbing her bruised wrists where Trace had so harshly handled her, she scowled as she decided she hated Captain Trace Cavanaugh and wasn't about to be dictated to by a bullying tyrant! Why, he'd threatened her life!

The thought suddenly doused her fury.

"My God, he did threaten to kill me . . ." she murmured, her voice trailing off on a fearful note as she stared at the door. Or he could have that bloodthirsty samurai murder her.

She had to get away from Trace Cavanaugh. But as

she glanced quickly around her, Christa saw with dismay that escape from this small room was impossible. There were no windows. The door to the hallway was the only exit, and a fierce Japanese warrior guarded that. She had to believe what Cavanaugh had said about taking her back to Haviland Court, and hope he meant *alive*!

Christa fumbled to get out of her wet clothes. After throwing them over a chair by the fire so they'd dry, she donned the amethyst silk robe Suko had provided, and tied the white sash tightly at her waist.

Christa had no time to admire the costly garment. Quickly taking up a brush from the table next to the tub, she ran it through her tangled hair and then left the bathing room.

Out in the hall, she managed a feeble half smile when she encountered the glaring samurai waiting for her. Reluctantly, she followed him along the corridor. At least his swords were still in his sash, she noted with relief, considering for a moment trying to make a run for it while his back was turned. But she quickly dismissed the thought, realizing the middle-aged warrior could likely move with a swiftness and agility that would prove most deadly for her.

Trace stood talking to Suko as Christa entered the parlor. His eyes flicked briefly over her in appraisal, but his expression revealed nothing of his thoughts. As they seated themselves on the square cushions around the low black table, he ignored Christa and gave his rapt attention to Suko, who expertly performed a Japanese tea ceremony. That was fine with Christa, for she had no desire to gain his interest again.

"As usual, your offering is bountiful, Suko," Trace said, complimenting the young princess with a smile. "My thanks for accommodating my tastes." Suko blushed and smiled with pleasure, shyly lowering her eyes.

Christa marveled that the food had been prepared so quickly. Sliced roast beef, broiled chicken, numerous cheeses, breads, boiled potatoes, and buttered squash were all heaped on fine china dishes. Only a large bowl of long-grained brown rice deviated from the American foods.

Trace usually found Suko's rendering of the tea ritual mesmerizing, for she performed it with grace and elegance, exemplifying an ancient culture that revered patience and ceremony. But now he found his gaze drawn to Christa Haviland. She intrigued him. Her behavior certainly didn't conform to that of the highborn ladies of quality he knew. It was difficult to believe she was the mud-spattered lad who'd fought McDugal and Pike and dazed Ox Bedlow with a crock of ale. Kneeling at the table as she was now, with her head held high and her shoulders back, she displayed the bearing of a lady well bred. Her beauty went beyond the delicate contours of her face. Trace was all too aware of the way the fine silk of the deep purple kimono clung to her body, outlining the gentle curves of her full breasts, her narrow waist, and softly rounded hips.

He frowned. Why hadn't he sensed something was amiss with her sooner? He must have been too preoccupied with foiling Garrett and trying to avoid a trouncing by the Bedlow brothers.

Christa hadn't realized she was hungry until the delicious aroma of the food reached her. She was aware, too, that Trace had begun watching her—keeping guard over her, no doubt. He had a way of making her feel very uncomfortable. It added to her extreme dislike of him. As much as she enjoyed the delicious food, she wished the meal would come to an end.

"I regret we must leave now, Suko," Trace said finally when he had finished the last of his food. "Perhaps the next time I come we can spend more time together."

"I would like that very much, Cavanaugh-san." Suko's face showed an eagerness that spoke volumes about her feelings for Trace. "Your horses have been fed and rested. They await you."

Tohashi guarded Christa outside the bathing room when she returned there to put on her boy's clothing. She hated to change from the soft, caressing silk of the kimono to the rough, dirty cotton and wool of the clothes in which she'd arrived. But at least they were dry now.

Trace changed elsewhere. When Christa rejoined him, she saw he'd discarded his buckskins for garments similar to hers—tight-fitting black breeches, a tan cotton shirt, and a short, dark blue seaman's jacket that came to his hips. His rakishly handsome features stood out sharply. Again Christa was surprised at how different he looked now from when they'd first met. She stared at him, noticing how his clothes fit perfectly over his tall, muscular body. She decided he must keep spare clothing with the princess. Perhaps he even lived here. That thought raised a question about his relationship with Suko. Christa was curious to know the answer, but she dismissed the thought as something she'd never discover. After tonight, she'd likely never see either one of them again.

"Good-bye, little flower," Trace said softly as he stood before Suko at the back door. She lowered her eyes and bowed. Trace bowed, too, then raised her delicate chin with his fingertips. "Have I not taught you the way of saying farewell in my country?" He bent his head to kiss Suko's cheek, but she quickly moved her head so that his lips covered hers.

"You learn quickly, little one," Trace noted with an amused smile. Suko blushed but showed no sign of regret for her action.

"Until we meet again, samurai." Trace's tone was stern as he gave a curt nod toward Tohashi, who still frowned menacingly and showed no sign of acknowledging Trace's parting words.

Chapter 10

The rain had ceased, but the threat that it might soon resume hung heavily in the moist night air. Wolfgang rose quickly to his feet when he caught sight of Christa. She gave him a pat on the head before reaching for the reins of her horse.

"Stay close behind me as we ride, Mrs. Haviland," Trace directed, helping her mount.

"Are you afraid I might try to escape, Captain?" she haughtily shot back.

"Actually, I'm more concerned about the enemy. Rebels could be anywhere. They've had enough trouble lately. To let you blunder into them as you did with McDugal and Pike could be disastrous to both sides. So keep up with me. I don't intend to coddle you just because you're a woman."

He pressed his heels to his horse's flanks before Christa could speak the scathing retort that sprang to her lips. The nerve of him! How she wished she knew the way back to Haviland Court from this part of the city so she wouldn't have to rely on this arrogant, overbearing officer to get her home.

"Come, Wolfgang," she called to her pet. "We must follow the captain. But after we reach Haviland Court, boy, you have my permission to make a meal of him!"

The crisp October wind tumbled the rain-laden

clouds overhead like a child wrestling playfully with downy pillows. The erratic illumination coming from the half-hidden moon made it difficult for Christa to see Trace and keep pace with him. He obviously knew well the lay of the land, while she didn't. Her annoyance with her taciturn escort escalated when more than once she was struck by low-hanging wet tree branches along the rough trail they followed.

After a while, Christa wondered why nothing around her looked familiar. When she'd come to the city earlier to find the Wild Boar Alehouse, she hadn't traveled through such a heavily wooded region. Fear knotted in her again as wild ideas raced in her head. Was Cavanaugh planning to kill her after all, in this dreadfully secluded place? Was she following him like a blind sheep to the slaughter? What did she know about Trace Cavanaugh anyway? He was virtually a stranger to her, and a dangerous one at that. Why had she trusted him when he'd said he was going to take her back to Haviland Court?

Christa pulled her horse up short, uncertain whether to go on with Trace or make a dash to escape him and try to find her own way home. Her mount neighed in protest at the sharp pull of the bit. Trace turned and brought his horse up beside her.

"Keep that mare quiet!" he ordered in an angry whisper. "There could be enemy patrols or camps anywhere around here. Why did you stop?"

"Where are we going?" Christa demanded with equal vehemence. She held herself tensely in the saddle, ready to spur her horse away.

"To Haviland Court, as I told you." Annoyance that she would question him sounded in Trace's stern tone.

"For some reason, I don't think this is the way, Captain. I'll go no farther until you explain yourself."

Christa hoped her fear didn't show in her words. She let her eyes dart around, searching for an escape.

"This is the way I have chosen to take, Mrs. Haviland. It's the safest route. Now do as you were told and stay behind me."

"Do not order me about, Captain Cavanaugh. I'm not one of your subordinates!" Christa glared at him.

"You'll follow my orders regardless, madam," Trace snapped. "I have no intention of letting you get us both captured or killed by the enemy. I told you they could be . . ."

Trace's voice trailed off as his eyes caught a flicker of light in the woods off to their right. Christa didn't notice his attention was no longer on her as she started to protest further.

"Silence!" he ground out in a harsh whisper. "Look there."

Christa frowned, turning in the saddle to look where he pointed. A campfire glowed through the distant, half-barren trees.

"Continentals?" she asked, her anger quickly changing to apprehension.

"Possibly. I'd better take a closer look. Stay—"

"Oh no, you're not leaving me here, Captain," Christa interrupted, afraid of being left alone to an unknown fate more than she feared remaining with him.

A ray of moonlight pierced the cloud cover, revealing Trace's scowl. But he didn't argue with her.

"Very well. But stay close and don't make a sound."

Trace and Christa tried to remain behind the cover of tall bushes and giant pine trees as they cautiously followed a circuitous route toward the campfire. When they approached a wooden footbridge spanning a narrow ravine, Trace guided the horses down the rocky hill to the dry creek bed at the bottom. With the bridge directly overhead for cover, he stopped and dismounted, handing the reins of both horses to Christa, then taking something from inside his sea jacket.

"Wait here for ten minutes," he instructed in a hushed voice as he gave her his gold pocket watch. "No matter what you hear, don't leave this spot, understand? Keep the horses and that mongrel of yours quiet. A sound now could be fatal to both of us. If I'm not back in that time, go to Haviland Court on your own. It's west—that direction." He pointed over the bridge. "These woods don't continue much farther. You can make it from here if you use caution. Tell Marcus what happened."

"But, Captain—"

"Don't argue with me, woman!"

Trace turned away from her to reach across his saddle for a pistol in a leather holster. He removed a spyglass from his saddlebag and hastily climbed the other side of the ravine, disappearing over the top.

Trace Cavanaugh never expected his orders to be questioned. Christa had learned that much about him. She also knew she must defer to his judgment now, for they could be in real danger.

With fear gnawing at her, she dismounted, putting herself between the two horses so she could hold on to both bridles. A shiver of dread crept up her spine as she murmured soothingly to the horses to keep them quiet.

"Stay still and keep a sharp watch, Wolf," she whispered to the dog when he came to stand in front of her, his tail wagging. "I've really gotten us into something this night, haven't I, boy?" Christa sighed with dismay as she thought about how, only a few short hours ago, she'd been in the music room at

Haviland Court playing the harpsichord. How she wished she were back there right now!

She strained to see the position of the hands on the watch. What if that campsite did belong to the rebels? Cavanaugh might be captured or even killed.

Christa wouldn't let herself think about those awful possibilities. She disliked Trace Cavanaugh with a vengeance, but she didn't want anything bad to happen to him. After all, King George needed all his loyal soldiers to win the war against the patriots. Cavanaugh must come back.

Biting her lip, Christa glanced to the top of the ravine, then back to the fine timepiece she held. With growing trepidation, she watched the hands slowly mark off the allotted minutes, one by one.

Chapter 11

Trace lay on his stomach in the wet grass at the top of a small rise. His arched brows nearly met in the middle of his forehead as he scowled at what he saw through the brass spyglass. A military encampment was located just below him, a sizable one with two formidable artillery guns in view. This close, he could see many more fires burning before orderly rows of canvas tents. A large platoon, Trace judged as he counted more than a score of the two-man shelters. British. The patrolling sentries' uniforms revealed that fact.

"Damn!" Trace murmured, rolling onto his back. "What in hell are they doing here?"

No troops were scheduled to be in this area. Who could be the commander? But, except for the short time he'd been at General Zachary's camp earlier, he'd been away from all headquarters for more than a week. New orders must have been issued while he was gone.

Whatever the reasons, the British were here. And they shouldn't be. Not with a force of patriot soldiers due within a day to march through these woods to Fort Washington.

Trace knew he had to do something to prevent this encampment from threatening the American troops. At least there was still time to come up with a plan.

But the headstrong Mrs. Haviland presented a

problem. She thought he was a loyal officer in King George's army.

I've worked hard to make a great many people believe that same thing, Mrs. Haviland, Trace thought, determined not to let her discover that he was actually loyal to the rebel cause and working secretly for George Washington, the commander of the patriot forces.

He rolled back onto his stomach and scanned the camp again with the spyglass, his mind working calculatingly. The hour was late. All was quiet. No double sentries had been posted. They weren't expecting trouble. He'd have the element of surprise on his side.

Trace looked around, trying to get his bearings. At the sound of moving water not far away, he knew exactly where he was—Hastings Hollow.

A plan began to materialize in his mind. The dam. The earthen structure three-quarters of a mile southwest of here held back the greatest portion of Cochoran Creek. If he could destroy the dam, the mighty force of the unleashed water would do what he alone couldn't do—eradicate this outpost in the hollow.

The plan was sound, but accomplishing it would be another matter. He'd need gunpowder, no small order in the middle of a forest. From what he remembered about the dam, he knew he'd need to set two charges that must detonate simultaneously. But he couldn't be in two places at once. Or could he? The thought of Christa Haviland flickered into his mind again. A diabolical smile turned up one corner of his mouth as he wondered just how much the loyal Mrs. Haviland would do for her king.

Trace swept the glass over the hollow below him once again. Two tents were larger than the others. One must belong to the commander. Trace moved his viewing instrument to the tent at the northernmost point of the camp, located away from the main body of men. Two sentries guarded it, one at the front and one at the back. That was where the munitions must be stored. The British could always be depended on to follow regulations. This outpost had been set up by the book.

Christa swung around in panic when she heard a commotion behind her. Wolfgang came to his feet and growled a warning. Relief flooded over her when she saw Trace hurrying down the embankment, loose stones and dirt following his steps.

"Everything all right here?" he asked in a low voice.

"Yes. Nothing seems to be stirring. Did you find anything?"

He chose his words carefully and avoided looking at her. "There's a camp all right. Rebels. And they're in an ideal position to jeopardize a movement of our troops scheduled for tomorrow. We must do something."

"We? What are you talking about?" Christa asked, not really wanting to know the answer.

"I have an idea, but I'll need your help."

"Now just a minute, Captain Cavanaugh. I—"

"You told me before that you are loyal to your king," Trace cut in, sounding impatient. "You risked danger in bringing the dispatch to me earlier tonight. There will be no more peril in helping me sabotage this outpost. Believe me, I wouldn't involve you if it weren't necessary. I don't like working with civilians. Being a woman makes you an even less appropriate choice. But you're all that's available at the moment, so I have to take a chance on you. Do you truly wish to help the cause, or were you just spouting words before?"

In the dim moonlight, Trace saw Christa's delicately arched dark brows dip into a frown.

"I meant what I said, Captain," she snapped. "Just tell me what I must do."

Trace hid his smile. "Mount up, then. There's no time to lose."

Trace had no intention of letting Christa get close enough to the encampment to see that it was filled with British troops, not Continentals. When they reached a small grove of thick pines, he dismounted and handed his reins to her.

"Stay here with the horses. Will that animal of yours attack on command?" He tilted his head toward Wolfgang.

"My command, yes."

"Good. Keep alert for patrolling sentries. It won't take me long to get gunpowder from the camp."

"You're going *into* the camp?" Christa couldn't believe her ears.

"Well, I don't happen to have two kegs of explosives in my saddlebags. And that's what we'll need to blow up the dam."

"Blow up the dam . . ." Christa's voice trailed off.

Trace was already gone, lost from view among the trees and undergrowth. To make matters worse, rain had started to fall again with a steady force.

Trace carefully circled around to the north end of the British camp. The wet ground helped muffle the sound of his movements as he worked his way close to the soldier on guard at the back of the munitions tent. He felt his body tense. All his senses were alert to the danger the next few minutes would bring.

He rummaged around in the wet leaves until he found two small rocks. Rising slightly, he pitched one into some bushes across from him. The guard looked toward the sound, taking his musket from his shoulder and pointing it in readiness. The second rock, thrown to nearly the same spot, brought the sentry cautiously forward to investigate. In an instant, Trace sprang to his feet, whirled the soldier around by the shoulder, and landed a bone-cracking blow to the startled man's jaw. He fell to the ground unconscious, without uttering a sound.

Trace ducked behind a tree and waited, listening intently for anyone who might have heard the slight commotion. When nothing else stirred, he crouched low and made his way to the back of the tent. Drawing a stiletto from his boot, he pierced the wet canvas and ran the sharp blade downward, making an opening just big enough to crawl through.

It was dark and musty-smelling inside the tent. Trace cautiously made his way along the dirt floor on his hands and knees until he felt the cold iron of a pyramid of cannonballs. He knew the kegs of gunpowder he sought would be close by. He quickly found them, along with a box containing ropes of fuse.

Trace stuffed a coil of fuse inside his jacket, then knelt to take a small keg of the explosive powder under each arm. Voices coming from the front of the tent stopped him dead still, his ears straining to listen.

"'Bout time you blokes got 'ere," a cockneyed voice said gruffly. "Either of you mates 'ave a chew on you?"

There was a mumbled reply, but Trace didn't stay around to hear more. The guard must be changing. The soldiers would soon discover the unconscious sentry and the slit canvas.

The alarm was raised before Trace managed to get halfway back to Christa. He didn't try to stay low now, as he ran through the hampering underbrush. Puffing for breath, he finally reached the grove of pines.

"Send the horses off and follow me," he called to Christa.

"What?" she asked, surprised by his sudden appearance.

"Do as I say and be quick about it! The camp's alerted!"

Christa slapped both mounts on the hindquarters, then stepped lively to follow Trace. Outside the grove, they ran full stride across a small clearing of flat ground. The wide, meandering path of Cochoran Creek was on their left as they entered the trees again and struggled up a rock-strewn hill to the top of the earthen dam. Wolfgang darted and circled around them. The rushing water of the creek drowned out the sound of his barking.

Panting for breath, Trace quickly fell to his knees and dug into the muddy soil with both hands.

"Your keg goes here," he hastily explained to Christa, glancing up at the sky. "This rain won't make it easy to light the fuses."

Thinking of a sudden solution to that problem, he pulled two thin cigars, then a small tinderbox, out of the breast pocket of his jacket. Leaning over to use his body as a shield against the rain, he struck flint to steel and used the tiny spark to light one of the cigars. In the next instant, the increasing rain doused the tinderbox, but the cigar glowed red as Trace drew on it.

"Captain, what are you doing? What's going to happen?" Christa demanded as her eyes went to the keg of gunpowder. She was frightened, certain she was in the presence of a madman who was about to blow them both up.

"Here, take this." Trace ignored her questions and stuck the end of the other cigar into her mouth.

"You'll have to light the fuse with this cigar. Inhale air through it to keep it burning."

Christa nearly gagged on the bitter taste of the rolled tobacco. She wanted to spit it out, but Trace was already leaning forward to touch the lighted end of his cigar to hers.

"Do it, damn it, Christa!" Trace ordered fiercely when she didn't respond. "If we don't blow up this dam in the next few minutes, we're going to have the enemy all over us!"

Alarmed by his words, Christa drew on the thin cigar as he'd told her. She choked as the putrid smoke filled her mouth and nose, but the end of the cigar began to glow red as the tobacco ignited.

"Now, keep it going. You won't die."

He turned to use the hilt of his knife to break a hole in the top of the wooden gunpowder keg. Then he took the coil of fuse out of his jacket, cut off a length of it, and jammed it through the hole into the black powder.

"Listen to me carefully." Keeping his cigar clenched in the corner of his mouth, Trace took hold of Christa by the shoulders. "Use my watch to mark off two minutes. I'll need that long to get my keg in place on the other side. Then light the fuse. You'll have about thirty seconds to hightail it away from here before the powder blows. Head straight across this hill to higher ground." He pointed in the direction he meant. "When the dam goes, you should be safe. I'll join you there. Understand?"

Christa could only nod in agreement, not trusting herself to speak. She felt too sick from fear and the foul-tasting cigar. Then Trace was gone, lost from sight in the rain and darkness.

Chapter 12

Christa kept the collar of her wool jacket pulled up around her ears, but still the chill of the night and the rain seeped into her clothing. The horrendous smell and taste of the cigar made her cough violently and feel sicker by the moment. But she struggled to keep puffing on the tobacco, using the glowing end to illuminate the face of Trace's pocket watch. The two minutes dragged by. The timepiece shook in her hand from her fearful trembling.

Suddenly Christa heard shouts in the distance. She squinted to see down the hill, trying to pierce the darkness. Bobbing lights that might be torches dotted the woods below her. Enemy soldiers were heading toward her!

Christa stared frantically at the watch, willing the minute hand to move faster and trying not to think about what might happen if the oncoming soldiers caught her or the gunpowder blew up too soon. Was Trace in position yet? Two minutes had passed.

Christa sucked in one more strong draw on the cigar. Coughing out the strangling smoke, she touched the cigar to the end of the fuse. The detonating coil flared to life in her hand, nearly burning her. Sparks sped rapidly toward the keg. Christa whirled around and dashed across the steep hill, calling for Wolfgang to follow.

The rain stopped, but the wet grass caused Christa to lose her footing. Twice, she nearly fell down the slope.

Suddenly, the deafening explosion shattered the air, followed quickly by another blast. Christa was thrown to the ground by the repercussions. She heard the unleashed water of Cochoran Creek thunder down the demolished side of the earthen dam, but she'd escaped far enough away so only a heavy spray of water and rubble reached her as she scrambled to the place where she was supposed to rendezvous with Trace.

"Well done!" he shouted above the roar of the water as he came up behind Christa and slapped her on the back. He was wet and muddy, but she could still make out the satisfied grin on his face as he added, "Mission accomplished. That camp will get a good dousing down. They'll be busy recovering for days. So much for one enemy outpost. I had my doubts about you, but you did well. Come on, time for us to take our leave."

"Will anyone be drowned?" Christa asked worriedly.

"Not likely. The main force of the water will be broken by the trees, causing the flood to lose much of its fury by the time it reaches the camp. But it'll still do plenty of damage and force the troops out of this area."

They reached the horses in the pine grove a few minutes later. Trace was helping Christa mount when she noticed that Wolfgang was nowhere in sight.

"Wolfgang!" she called, but not even whistling brought the huge dog into view.

"He's likely just off somewhere. He'll catch up with us," Trace assured her as he swung into the saddle.

Christa nodded in agreement, but still looked anxiously for some sign of him. Trace glimpsed the worry on her face . . . and the riders coming toward them.

"Come on!" he shouted, yanking on his horse's reins to turn in the opposite direction. But more riders were moving in from that side as well, cutting off their escape. Trace was forced to pull up his mount sharply to avoid colliding with them.

" 'Old up there, me buckos," the lead man ordered as he halted his own horse. The darkness made it difficult to see if they held weapons, but Trace heard the threatening click of hammers being pulled back on at least two pistols. He swore under his breath at his carelessness, at letting success with the dam lower his guard. Five men surrounded them now.

"Give us a light, Twigg," the same man said again. Someone produced a torch and lighted it while the leader added, "Well now, mates, you reckon these two 'ere was the ones what caused that ruckus just now that near got us all drowned?"

Deserters. Trace had a bad feeling that's who these men were. They wore only pieces of British infantry uniforms, along with other sundry makeshift garments. Such men were dangerous scavengers, holding no loyalties to anyone but themselves. They sometimes banded together to prey on any victims unfortunate enough to fall into their path. And he and Christa had done just that.

"Get down off them 'orses," the leader ordered gruffly in a heavy cockney accent. "You did us a favor doin' in that there camp, so maybe we won't kill you— maybe. But this 'ere rain puts us in a foul temper, ain't that right, boys? An' we ain't 'ad us much o' anythin' good to eat in a spell. You two got anythin' to offer that might keep us from wastin' lead on you?"

Trace knew he and Christa were trapped. His mind

raced to come up with a plan of escape, but he forced
his tone to be jovial as he slowly dismounted.

"Well now, gents, I may have something of interest
to you."

Christa's fear paralyzed her, for she knew they had
no food or other supplies that might appease these
desperate men. What could Trace be talking about?

"I might be willing to make a trade, boys," he
continued, stepping a little closer to the leader. "My
life in exchange for something I think you'll find much
more to your liking than mere food."

"We're listenin'," the big man answered.

"What would you boys say to having a woman to
warm up to on such a nasty night as this?"

Christa's blood ran cold. Dear God, Cavanaugh was
going to betray her to save himself!

"And a sweeter piece of womanflesh you'd be hard
put to find, lads," Trace went on, taking one more step
toward the leader. The other men began to murmur,
sounding very interested in Trace's offer.

"Keep talkin'. Where is she?" the man called Twigg
asked eagerly.

"Why, she's right here, lads." Trace had their rapt
attention as he pointed toward Christa. Then with
lightning swiftness, he brought his arm back and hit
out, catching the leader fully in the stomach with a
hard blow. The stocky man bent double, gasping for
breath.

"Ride, Christa!" Trace shouted, hitting another man
squarely in the jaw.

Christa was just as startled by Trace's actions as the
others, but she recovered quickly enough to dig her heels
into her horse's sides. The man nearest her stepped in
front of her mount and waved his arms wildly. Her mare
neighed in fright and reared, causing Christa to lose her
hold and tumble to the ground. In the same instant, the

butt of a musket caught Trace on the back of the head. He went down, stunned to unconsciousness by the blow. Rough hands grabbed Christa and yanked off her stocking cap.

"'Ey, Potts, I got me the wench!" the man holding Christa hollered to the leader.

"Looks like we struck it lucky tonight, boys," Potts declared, making his way over to Christa. "Don't worry about that bloke on the ground, Twigg. Whiskey's musket did 'im in fer sure. Bring the torch over 'ere so's we kin 'ave a look at this 'ere wench."

The four men joined the one holding Christa. Potts stepped forward and roughly gripped her chin.

"Well, she's a might dirty, but then we are, too, ain't we, boys?" Potts observed with a grin. "Let's see what the rest of 'er looks like."

With that, Potts pulled a knife out of a leather sheath hooked to his belt. In quick order, he slashed at the buttons of Christa's jacket, then pulled the wool fabric apart, revealing her white shirt underneath. Held as she was, with her arms pinned back painfully, her breasts strained against the shirt. Potts's knife again made quick work of the buttons holding the fabric together. Now only her thin chemise protected her from their lecherous gazes.

"Ain't 'ad me a woman in a long time. I'll 'ave at 'er first, boys, then you kin 'ave 'er. This 'ere's your lucky night, sweet thing."

Potts ran his tongue over his thick lips, looking as if he meant to devour her on the spot. Christa felt everything inside her go limp. She wanted to die like Trace Cavanaugh. She prayed she could die, for she knew that what was going to happen to her now would be worse than the most agonizing death.

"Boris, you an' Whiskey 'old 'er down. I ain't in no mood fer no fight fer what I'm after. Gag 'er, too.

I don't want 'er yellin' drawin' anybody 'ere,'' Potts directed.

Christa screamed and twisted and kicked before a dirty kerchief was stuffed into her mouth and two of her captors wrestled her to the wet ground, laughing at her futile efforts to resist them.

"Light another torch, Twigg, an' stick 'em both in the ground over 'ere. I don't want to miss seein' nothin' o' what she's goin' to show us.''

Potts's knife blade glinted in the torchlight as he knelt between Christa's outstretched legs. He was expert with the weapon, slashing the sharp point through the delicate silk fabric of her chemise without touching the skin underneath. The fullness of her breasts was exposed to their evil gazes now. Potts licked his lips again, all but drooling as he wiped the back of his hand across his mouth, then fumbled with the belt at his ample waist.

Trace heard Christa's screams, but he was fighting against overpowering blackness, and the struggle took all his strength and will. The excruciating pain in his head told him he wasn't dead. Something wet touched his face again and again. His senses stumbled back to him, until he realized the darkness he saw now was that of the night around him and not the oblivion of unconsciousness. He blinked to clear his blurry vision, staring toward the torches. The wetness touched his face once more, and Trace realized something was licking him. Wolfgang. The big dog lapped his tongue along Trace's cheek.

Knowing he must help Christa, Trace pushed the animal away and struggled to sit up. More alert now, he saw that no one was guarding him. He crawled to the horses and used the stirrup to pull himself upright. Ignoring the fierce pounding in his head, he removed his two-shot pistol from the saddle holster and cocked back both hammers.

Potts never knew what struck him. He died the same instant the sound of the pistol shot reached his ears, collapsing in a crushing heap on top of Christa.

Trace plunged into the circle of men, wielding his heavy weapon like a club. He caught Boris soundly on the side of the head, knocking him senseless. Wolfgang lunged at Whiskey, tearing at him with viciously gnashing teeth.

As Trace battled the other two cutthroats, Christa struggled to get out from under Potts's immense bulk. She wept with near hysteria as she knelt in the wet grass and clasped her jacket around her to hide her nakedness. Her eyes widened with fright at the desperate scene before her.

Trace tackled Twigg around the waist and forced him to the ground, landing a bone-cracking blow to his jaw that left him motionless under Trace. But the other man grabbed Trace around the neck in an iron hold that threatened to crush his windpipe. Whiskey threw off Wolfgang long enough to grab a knife out of his belt. Christa saw the blade glint in the torchlight just as the huge dog lunged again. A sickening yelp issued from the dog's throat, but the stalwart animal attacked again, this time going for his victim's throat. Whiskey fought no more.

In the same instant, Trace reached up, grabbed his attacker around the head, and twisted sideways, throwing them both to the muddy ground. But the outlaw suddenly loomed up over Trace, holding a large rock in his hands. Christa glimpsed what was happening. Boris's musket lay on the grass beside her. Swiftly, without stopping to consider, she raised it and squeezed the trigger. The violent kickback of the weapon knocked her backward, but the ball found its mark, sending Trace's opponent pitching over him in death.

It took Trace a few moments to catch his breath and let the dizziness in his throbbing head clear before he could get to his feet. Unsteadily, he made his way over to Christa.

"Are you all right?" he asked as he reached out a hand to help her up. For a moment, Christa didn't move. She only stared past him to where the deserter she'd shot lay unmoving on the ground.

"Christa, are you hurt?" Trace persisted, kneeling beside her.

"No!" she cried, turning panic-stricken eyes on him as she jumped back in fear.

"Christa, it's Trace Cavanaugh." He grabbed her shoulders to stop her from fleeing.

"Thank God!" she gasped in frantic relief, collapsing into his arms. He held her closely for a few moments, feeling strangely protective of her. Then he urged her to her feet.

"We can't stay here. Can you ride?"

She nodded, then looked frightened again. "Wolfgang!"

Turning, she ran to where the animal lay on his side next to Whiskey's body. The big black-and-gray animal raised his head and whimpered, but he couldn't get up.

"No . . ." Christa whispered as she knelt beside him and ran her hands over his furry side. Her palm touched something wet, and she knew it was blood. Hot tears stung her eyes and spilled over as she cradled the dog's head in her hands. "You'll be all right, boy. You'll be all right," she murmured, trying to swallow the painful sobs welling up in her throat.

Trace knelt on one knee next to Wolfgang and ignored the painful hammering in his head as he leaned down to study the wound. It was a long, deep knife cut into vital organs. The bleeding was heavy.

He expelled his breath. He hated what he had to do. Wolfgang had helped greatly in saving their lives.

"Christa, he's badly hurt," Trace said gently. "He's suffering."

"No, please, we can't," she pleaded, hugging the big dog's head and weeping openly. Wolfgang's wet tongue licked her cheek.

"There's nothing else to do." Trace forced a finality into his voice. "He fought bravely. He doesn't deserve a lingering death."

Christa knew he was right. She'd glimpsed the wound and knew Wolfgang must be in terrible pain.

"I'll do it, Christa," Trace offered quietly. "You go to the horses."

Christa nodded. She leaned over and buried her face in the thick fur just behind the big dog's head.

"Good-bye, Wolfgang," she whispered with a choked sob. He licked her face one last time.

Trace used his knife to carry out the grim task. The night remained gravely silent as, afterward, he walked quickly to where Christa waited with the horses.

They rode away into the darkness without looking back.

Chapter 13

As Trace and Christa resumed their journey to Haviland Court, the fickle storm unleashed its overburdened clouds once more. Trace soon realized they wouldn't get far. The deluging rain rendered the route nearly impassable, and his wound was giving him trouble. Dizziness and throbbing pain racked his head, making it difficult to stay seated on his mount. The dangerous drama that had been played out with such grisly results back at the grove was taking its toll on him. He wondered about Christa, following behind him. How was she holding up?

Christa felt numb. She closed off her mind, forcing herself to think only about the rain soaking her clothes, the wind biting her face—anything to keep from focusing on the horrible events she'd just experienced.

Trace pulled up his horse and studied the surrounding landscape. The cave. It wasn't far. There they could wait out the storm. He shook his head to try to clear it, then gritted his teeth against the shooting pain the movement caused, fighting to stay conscious.

A steep grade led up to the cave. Trace clutched a fistful of his horse's coarse mane to keep his seat as the animal lurched up the hill over the slippery, rock-strewn ground. The entrance to the cave was wide enough to allow Trace and Christa to ride their horses inside.

"We're staying here for the night. I've used this shelter before," Trace told her as he dismounted and fumbled to light a lantern hanging from a nail driven into the rock wall. The glow revealed a good-sized room carved out of the granite hillside.

When Christa didn't dismount, he came around to help her. "There are some blankets in the corner," he said, reaching up to take hold of her narrow waist. She looked bedraggled and beaten as he lifted her down and steadied her on her feet. She was trembling, but Trace couldn't be sure if it was from cold or shock. He felt a sudden urge to hold her, much as he might hold a child who'd had a terrible fright. But he resisted the feeling and instead led her over to the corner.

"Get out of your wet clothes and wrap up in one of those blankets." He pointed toward the supplies he'd stored there the last time he'd used the cave as a shelter. Christa's eyes sought his face as if she were hearing him speak for the first time.

"You must get out of those wet things before you catch a chill." He made his tone firmer now, sensing she was not comprehending all he was saying. "I'll tend to a fire. Do it now, Christa."

Christa didn't want the protective shroud she'd pulled over her thoughts to be taken away. But the authoritative note in Trace's voice moved her to obey him. She watched him walk to a pile of dry wood near the entrance and begin to construct a fire.

Christa slowly looked around her, clutching her cut clothing together with one hand. She recognized the man across the cave from her. Trace Cavanaugh. He'd told her to take off her clothes. His back was to her, but what did it matter if she undressed in front of him now? How could such an insignificant act matter when such horrors were clamoring in her mind?

She began to undress, but violent shaking overcame

her. She couldn't stop the sobs of anguish that rushed
forth, making her fall to her knees and bury her face
in her hands. Trace came to her at once and took her
in his arms.

"Here now, take it easy," he tried to soothe her.
But he wasn't sure what he should do to ease her
torment. Violence and death, fighting for survival, were
nothing new to him, though he never got used to them.
He knew it wasn't likely that Christa Haviland had ever
experienced a night like this in all her life. Yet he felt
helpless to do anything for her. It was a new and
unsettling feeling for him.

Christa clung to him, longing for the protection he
offered, hoping desperately he could somehow change
all that had happened this night. But she knew he
couldn't.

"I killed that man. And Wolfgang," she murmured,
her voice so hushed that Trace could barely hear her.

"Shooting that man saved my life," Trace told her
gently. "And the beast fought bravely to help us.
We're fortunate to be alive."

Christa nodded and tried to swallow back her sobs.
She didn't resist when Trace gently removed her jacket
and torn shirt. The silk chemise hung in tatters against
her breasts, barely covering her. Trace averted his eyes
as he slid the thin straps from her shoulders and let the
ruined garment slip to the floor with her other clothes.
Then he reached down for one of the folded blankets
on the pile of supplies and wrapped it around her.

"Get out of those breeches, too, while I see to the
horses."

When Trace finished unsaddling the horses, he saw
she'd taken off her wet trousers and laid them over
some rocks with her other clothes to dry. She came
over to the fire and sat down on one of the saddle
blankets Trace had spread on the ground. Her back was

to him as he went to the corner and removed his own clothes, spreading them out to dry.

He carried two more logs to the fire, but when he leaned over to add them to the flames, a wave of dizziness caused him to stagger. He leaned against the stone wall to keep from falling. Christa hurried to him.

"Here, let me help you, Trace." She wrapped his arm around her shoulders and eased him down to the blanket on the floor. "Where are you hurt?" She ran her gaze over him, looking for bleeding, a wound.

"It's only a cracked head. I've had worse. Nothing to worry about," he assured her with more nonchalance than he felt. He was tired, bone-weary. His arms and legs felt like lead weights attached to him. He had to fight to ward off the fog creeping into his consciousness.

"A head wound? Is it bleeding?" Worry showed in Christa's expression as she reached toward his hair.

"It's nothing, I said," Trace snapped, catching her hand in midair. He winced at the movement. Regretting his sharpness with her, he expelled his breath and spoke more gently. "I'm sorry, Christa. I haven't slept in days. My head's pounding like a herd of horses is stampeding inside it, but there's nothing you can do." He paused to look directly at her. Her large blue-gray eyes watched him intently. "We've had quite a night of it, haven't we?"

She nodded and lowered her head, clutching the coarse wool blanket tightly around her. Trace continued to hold her other hand, knowing she was wounded, too, though not in a way that showed outwardly. Again, he felt helpless to know what to do for her. In all his considerable experience with women, he'd never found himself in a situation like this one. It perplexed him, as did the fact that it seemed right to be touching her.

They both seemed to realize simultaneously what he was doing. Trace let go of her and Christa drew away at the same moment. She turned and busied herself putting logs on the fire.

Trace watched her as he shifted around to lean against the side of the cave for support. An unfamiliar feeling for her tugged at him. Was it compassion? Protectiveness? Perhaps it was just brotherly concern, he thought.

"Come here, Christa," he said finally. "There isn't a draft by this wall. You'll be warmer here."

Slowly, she sat down next to him.

"Do you think you can get some sleep?"

"No. But you must rest, Captain. I'll keep the fire going."

Trace couldn't keep her in focus. He was slipping into the oblivion of unconsciousness, and he couldn't fight it any longer. Closing his eyes, he surrendered to the welcome release.

Alarm sprang up in Christa when she saw Trace go limp. Oh, God, was he dead? But when she moved closer and touched the side of his neck, she could feel a strong pulse. Expelling her breath in relief, she pulled his blanket closer around him. He slumped over from his seated position, and Christa caught him, easing him down so that his head rested in her lap. Timidly, she touched his temple, brushing away the wet, tangled dark hair. She saw again the gold chain holding the ruby ring around his neck. She'd noticed it at Suko's, too, and wondered about it. But now her mind became occupied by more troubling thoughts.

What a strange and frightening night it had been. This man had saved her life, saved her from horrendous brutality at the hands of those vicious men. And she had saved his life by shooting one of them. They both might be dead right now. Pitted against life-threatening danger and violence, they'd survived. Together. She felt drawn to Trace by a special bond created during those horrible moments. How could two people go through something so terrible and not feel some linking inside, some joining of spirits?

Conflicting emotions jumbled together inside Christa—regret that she'd left Haviland Court at all tonight; sorrow for Wolfgang, yet gratitude for his courage; and gratitude for Trace Cavanaugh's courage.

Christa looked down at the man whose head she cradled in her lap. She barely knew him, but she trusted him with her life. He could have gotten away and left her to suffer at the hands of those men, but he hadn't. Even hurt, he'd come to help her.

She felt drained of strength and will. Leaning her head back against the cold stone wall, she listened to the rain outside. Soon she heard nothing more as a cloud of exhaustion settled over her, obliterating her awareness of everything around her.

Chapter 14

Trace opened his eyes. He felt warmth on his face. Sunshine beamed into the cave. The ray of light touched Christa Haviland as well. How had he come to be lying in her lap?

Even through the dirt streaking her face, Trace could see how lovely she was. Relaxed in sleep, with her head tilted to one side, she had a girllike innocence about her.

Taking care not to awaken her, Trace slowly got to his feet. His head still throbbed somewhat, but he'd had worse headaches from indulging in too much rum. He'd survive.

He glanced outside at the sky. Just past dawn, he judged by the sun's glowing half circle on the clear horizon. It was chilly in the cave. He swung the blanket off his shoulders and draped it gently over Christa, then dressed quickly and went to stir up the embers of the fire.

He was saddling the horses when Christa awakened with a start. Trace knelt down beside her, putting a hand on her shoulder.

"Don't be afraid," he tried to assure her when she turned her large blue-gray eyes on him. "Do you remember what happened last night?"

Christa stared at Trace for a long time, trying to focus on who he was and where she had been sleeping.

Then she sighed heavily and nodded as full recollection came to her.

"A—are you all right?" she asked haltingly. "I was so afraid last night when you seemed to lose consciousness."

"I'm better. Don't be concerned. But we must be going. It isn't safe to stay in one place too long. And I must get you back to Haviland Court."

"Haviland Court," Christa repeated, remembering her home with apprehension. "They'll be wondering what happened to me."

"What will you tell them?"

"I—I don't know . . ."

Isabelle and Winston would never let her hear the end of it if they found out all she'd done last night. Her acid-tongued sister-in-law and arrogant brother-in-law already made her life as miserable as they could at every opportunity. They must *not* find out about the sabotaging of the dam, those terrible men, the shooting . . . She could only thank heaven they'd been away from Haviland Court last night when Marcus had arrived.

And what would Nevin say? What would her husband think of her if he found out? He expected her to be a proper upper-class wife, as befitted his family and social position. Her actions last night would *not* meet with his approval, even if she tried to explain she'd only wanted to aid the king's cause.

Trace watched the play of emotions on Christa's face, but he could only imagine what was causing them. "Get dressed while I finish saddling the horses," he told her, standing up again. "I want to leave as soon as possible."

He was careful to keep his back to Christa so she'd have some privacy in dressing, but he couldn't keep from thinking that, under other circumstances, he'd be acting quite differently toward the beautiful, unclothed woman who had shared the cave with him all night.

"I'm sorry there's nothing to eat," he said a few moments later as he tightened the cinch of his horse's saddle.

"I'm not hungry," Christa told him, pulling on her shirt. The listlessness in her voice made Trace glance over to her.

"Are you feeling ill? Can you ride? Perhaps you caught a chill from the rain—"

"No, I'm all right. I can ride." There was little energy in her words.

Trace understood. He had little appetite himself. They were both still feeling some shock from all they'd been through last night. He was glad she appeared to be somewhat recovered from her near rape and the shootings. But then, Christa Haviland didn't strike him as the kind of woman who'd fall prey to hysteria. Last night would have certainly given her cause if she were prone to it. She was stouthearted, no denying that. Trace was glad she appeared calm. He didn't want a distraught woman on his hands.

A cloudless azure sky peeked through the bare treetops overhead as Trace and Christa silently rode through the forest toward Haviland Court. The clear October air had a crisp tang to it, hinting at winter lurking on the breeze.

When her imposing, three-story home came into view, Christa took the lead, riding on a little-used pathway to the back of the stables.

Trace had never been to Haviland Court, though he knew its location. He was impressed with the sprawling red-brick mansion and its many well-kept outbuildings. Someday he'd have such a home to mark the beginning of the Cavanaugh family line. All he'd been working for, all the wealth and influence he'd attained so far, and would yet gain, would be exemplified in such an estate as this one. He'd promised himself long ago that in America he'd fulfill his dream. A respected name, an honorable family, a prestigious place in society—it would all begin with him . . . him and the woman who would build it with him.

But first he must bury the bitter past that haunted him—bury Fitzhugh Zachary.

Christa's voice drew him back from his grim contemplation.

"Stable your horse here, Captain, while we talk to Marcus."

"There will be no need of that, Christa." Trace dismounted and came around to help her from her horse. He remained standing close to her even after she was firmly on the ground. His turquoise gaze lingered on her face.

"I can't tarry. I'm under orders to complete a supply route, and time is crucial. I'll see Marcus another time. Besides, I believe all you told me about him. There's no need to verify your story." He couldn't hold her gaze as he went on. "It would be best if you mentioned nothing about the sabotaging of the dam to Marcus or anyone else. The fewer people who know of it, the better, until I have a chance to make a proper report of the incident to General Zachary and we can assess the results."

"Yes, I understand," Christa replied, thinking about her husband and in-laws. Keeping last night's events a secret seemed the best idea.

"This is good-bye then," Trace told her in a low voice. "Will you be all right? Last night was harrowing. You faced it very bravely."

Christa could only nod. She was drawn by the warmth in his eyes, the compassion in his voice.

They were still standing very close. Trace knew he

should let go of her. He was not one to act rashly. He prided himself on his cunning and control, on thinking things through very carefully. Christa was another man's wife. She represented the enemy monarchy he continually risked his life to oppose. But despite these facts, he felt a sudden desire to kiss her.

Slowly, deliberately, he lowered his head and pressed his lips to hers. His arms encircled her, drawing her firmly against him.

Christa was too surprised to pull away. She was overwhelmed by sensation, by the taste of him, the strength of his embrace. Yet there was a gentleness in the way he kissed her. She dared not breathe even after he finally released her. She could only stare at him, her eyes wide with astonishment.

"I have a feeling we shall meet again, Christa Haviland," Trace said softly as he brushed his fingertips against her cheek. A slight smile touched his lips as he turned and mounted his horse to ride away.

Christa gazed after him in stunned confusion, unaware that a figure on horseback a short distance behind her had witnessed Trace's embrace.

Chapter 15

Christa gracefully descended the elegant main staircase of Haviland Court. She wanted to forgo this late afternoon meal, for she didn't feel up to facing the daily ordeal.

There wouldn't be many people at dinner. The war had separated the Haviland family, leaving few members to dwell within the walls of the huge house. When King George had begun his attempts to gain more strict control over his independent-minded colonies in North America by increasing taxes and creating laws regulating many phases of American life, industry, and trade, he had aroused a fiery discontent among the colonials. Anti-British radicals had gladly fanned this dissatisfaction into an outright revolution for independence that was dividing brothers, friends, and heretofore loyal citizens.

Christa wished Marcus felt up to attending the meal, but he was still very weak from loss of blood. She'd seen him earlier and told him she'd delivered the dispatch, but she hadn't mentioned anything more than that. He'd been unconscious all night and hadn't realized she'd returned only this morning. Could she get by with even less explanation to Isabelle, her irascible sister-in-law?

Trace Cavanaugh loomed into her thoughts as she reached the bottom of the winding mahogany staircase.

Everything they'd experienced in one brief night tumbled through her mind. But their last moments together in the stableyard haunted her. Even now, the thought of his kiss caused a twinge in her stomach and a quickening of her pulse. She touched her lips with her fingertips, remembering with distress how Trace's lips had felt on them.

I must not think of him, she told herself sternly. Pausing outside the dining room entrance, she forced Trace to the back of her mind, set a smile on her lips, and opened the door.

The spacious banquet hall of Haviland Court was paneled in rich cherry wood that was kept polished to a high sheen by the large housekeeping staff. Only three people would be dining at the long walnut table, which at other times could easily accommodate thirty guests. Dozens of white candles in three leaded crystal chandeliers suspended from the high ceiling remained unlighted for such a small gathering. Instead, candles in several silver candelabra illuminated the table and serving sideboards.

"We haven't seen much of you today, Christa," Isabelle Sheffield said by way of greeting as she glanced up from her place at the table. "That doesn't bother me, of course. The less I see of you, the better. But my breakfast was quite cold by the time that twit of a maid, Adelaide, brought it to me this morning. As mistress of the house, you shouldn't allow such blatant incompetence. But then, you're just as inadequate as mistress as she is as servant, so what else can I expect?"

"Good afternoon to you, too, Isabelle," Christa acknowledged, forcing herself to continue smiling. She gave a curt nod toward Winston Sheffield, who stood while she took her seat at the table. She didn't like Isabelle's husband. To her, his lean, dark-featured handsomeness was marred by the condescending air that was an habitual part of his demeanor. She felt uncomfortable now, as his cool hazel eyes followed her.

"I'm sorry you found your breakfast wanting, Isabelle," Christa replied, though she couldn't bring herself to sound sincere. "I'll speak to Adelaide. I was occupied elsewhere this morning. We had an exciting occurrence here last night while you were visiting the Hamptons, and as a result we now have a house-guest."

"What? Why am I never told about anything around here?" Isabelle demanded. "These miserable, ungrateful servants are all so absurdly loyal to you!"

Christa ignored her outburst and went on to explain. "Marcus Desmond was shot in the leg by a band of rebels last evening. He managed to reach the kitchen house, where we hid him when the rebels arrived and searched the estate."

"What? Rebels invaded Haviland Court!" Isabelle jumped to her feet. "That is an outrage!"

"Sit down, Isabelle. Don't excite yourself," Winston spoke up for the first time. "The rebels are no longer here, so it's apparent Christa was able to handle the situation." His eyes flickered with new interest as they sought Christa again.

"We kept Marcus hidden until the rebels decided to search elsewhere," she went on, avoiding Winston's gaze. "Marcus's wound has been attended to by a doctor. He's recovering in the green room."

"Well, of all things!" Isabelle declared as she tossed her thick auburn hair and resumed her seat. "General Howe and General Zachary are *both* going to hear about this! They must provide us with protection from these traitorous rebel swine. This war has become such a bore, with all these blockades and battles. I don't see why there is a war anyway. These are the king's colonies. We're the king's subjects. Our monarch must be obeyed without question. It's that simple. Every loyal subject of His Majesty knows that. There would be no war, no problems at all, if everyone just remembered those facts."

Isabelle paused to unfold her linen napkin and place it in her lap. Christa grew thoughtful. Was what her sister-in-law said true? Did His Majesty's subjects owe him unthinking obedience? For some reason, Christa cringed at the thought. Yet hadn't she done exactly that last night—blindly thought only of serving her king at all costs? A cost that had almost included her life! But was her loyalty really true? What did she actually know about the issues, the causes of this war?

"I wish all this ridiculous fighting would end," Isabelle went on, drawing Christa's attention. "Then we could have some decent food around here. Apparently, that's become impossible to acquire, judging by the pathetic fare we're forced to endure at this table. And I have not been able to have a new gown made in months because the only fabric the shops have is not fit for anything but rags. Not that there would be anywhere to go even if I had a new gown. Nearly all our social activities have been curtailed because of this outrageous war!" With disgust, she reached for her crystal wine goblet and downed a goodly portion of fine claret.

Christa's anger flared at her sister-in-law's callous words. "I'm certain General Howe and General Zachary will be distressed to learn how *inconvenient* the war is for you, Isabelle. Never mind that homes and property are being destroyed. Never mind that men are dying and being maimed on both sides each day that this terrible war continues!"

"It's not a woman's place to worry about such

distasteful events as killing and maiming," Isabelle countered haughtily. "I leave battles and destruction to men. Our king's loyal commanders are much better at it. I only care what happens in this house."

"And to *you*, of course," Christa added, keeping her tone level. "That's all you ever care about, Isabelle."

"In that you are correct for once, Christa." Isabelle's deep brown eyes narrowed. "I always have my best interests at heart. You'd do well to remember that."

"That's enough, Isabelle," Winston cut in, frowning a warning at his wife. "Ambrose, serve the meal," he directed the butler. "I don't like eating cold food."

Christa tried to eat, but the well-prepared roasted chicken, vegetables, breads, and cheeses had no appeal for her. Isabelle's acerbic tongue was something she'd thought she'd get used to—or at least be able to tolerate—when she'd first come to Haviland Court as Nevin's wife. But even after two years, she could still be upset by her husband's sister. Even worse, Christa realized that she herself was beginning to lash back with the same sharp sarcasm.

At that moment, Conway, Ambrose's assistant, entered the dining room and bowed. "Your pardon, but a visitor has arrived seeking an audience with Mr. Sheffield," he announced formally.

"A visitor?" Isabelle asked. "How unusual. Who is it, Conway?"

"Captain Garrett, Mrs. Sheffield."

"Lee? But how wonderful! Show him in at once."

"Yes, madam."

Christa was glad for the few moments it took Conway to show their guest to the dining room. She was upset enough without having to encounter Leland Garrett, and needed the time to gather her composure before facing him. All too soon she was watching his self-assured swagger as he followed Conway into the room. He looked tired and dirt-streaked, which was unusual for him.

"Your pardon, everyone. Forgive me for arriving without announcement and in such a sorry state of attire," Garrett declared. "You are looking lovely, as usual, Isabelle." He smiled charmingly at her as he took her outstretched hand. Then he turned to her husband. "Winston, good to see you again, old chap."

"Oh, Lee, you are a welcome sight indeed," Isabelle remarked. "We see practically no one these days. And it's been such an age since you last visited. Come, dine with us."

"My thanks. I'd be glad to share your table. I've been in the saddle most of the night, with little time to partake of food."

"Ambrose, fetch a place setting for Captain Garrett," Winston directed.

"Ah, Christa, how good to see you again after so long," Garrett commented with casual politeness. As he went around the table to where Ambrose was stoically setting the fine china for him, he stopped at Christa's chair. Although she didn't offer her hand, he reached for it anyway and held it longer than necessary. His brown eyes locked onto hers, and he smiled when he saw her delicately arched brows turn down in a frown.

Christa gritted her teeth to hold back her irritation, but she was determined to play the gracious hostess.

"Whatever are you up to that's kept you riding so hard, Lee?" Isabelle asked. "You look positively exhausted."

"The answer to that is also my main reason for coming here, aside from my desire to see all of you again, of course," Garrett explained. He swept a pointed glance toward Christa as he continued. "I'm on an important assignment for General Zachary. We're attempting to establish a network of suppliers along a safe route that can be used when our troops go into winter quarters. The general's expectations are high and I'm working against time. Winston, I'm hoping for your help.''

"What do you need, Lee?" Isabelle cut in. "I'm certain we can help you. Anything for you—and our king, of course," she added quickly.

"Thank you, Isabelle," Lee acknowledged. "I know your business interests are far-reaching. I'm depending on both of you, and Orin as well, for help.''

"My father has been in England for several months," Isabelle explained. "Our son, Harvard, is with him. I don't know when they'll return. However, Winston and I have full power—or rather, I should say, a good measure of control—over the Haviland interests," she corrected herself hastily, glancing at her husband.

"Very well then," Lee went on. "Can you supply tents, bedding, butchered meat, canned rations? Gunpowder is fast becoming scarce. We need a source of saltpeter to replenish our supplies of powder during winter quarters.''

Christa's attention was drawn at the mention of saltpeter. She forced herself to address Garrett. "Lee, I don't know if this will be of help to General Zachary or not, but when I was going through some of my father's papers not long ago, I came across a portfolio containing a deed for a saltpeter mine our family owns. The mine was closed down because there were several cave-ins, and repair and production costs had risen too high.''

"That would certainly bear investigating at any rate," Lee replied with interest. "I'll want to discuss it at length with you, Christa.''

She cringed at his smile of approval and was almost sorry she'd mentioned the mine, for she wanted to avoid Lee Garrett as much as possible. But she told herself she had to think beyond her own selfish preferences and consider that the mine might help the war effort.

"In the spring, when the campaign begins again, we'll need horses as well," Lee went on as he turned back to Winston and Isabelle. "There's profit to be had for all of us in supplies, my friends."

Christa tried to eat some of the food she knew Hester had worked hard to prepare, but Garrett's last words made her lose her appetite completely. The word *profit* would strike Isabelle and Winston's interest, she knew, and that realization sickened her. While men died, lost everything, others scavenged and grew wealthy from war.

Christa thought of Trace Cavanaugh. He'd talked to Cable Shipley about needed supplies last night, and even mentioned Lee. Were they pursuing the same goal? Was Cavanaugh as greedy as Leland for gain? The thought troubled her.

She pushed away her plate of half-eaten food, unable to make herself eat anything more. "If you'll excuse me, I'll retire and leave you to talk business," Christa said as she rose from her chair. The men stood also.

"Delightful," Isabelle agreed. "We'll be rid of your argumentativeness and sour expression." She turned back to Garrett as Christa walked hastily from the room.

"Lee, there's something quite distressing we must talk to you about as well," Isabelle went on. Her deep auburn brows dipped disapprovingly when she saw how Garrett's eyes had followed Christa's departure.

"Lee," she continued pointedly to draw his attention, "you must speak to General Zachary about protecting us. Haviland Court was invaded by rebels last night! Our dear friend, Marcus Desmond, was shot. At this very moment, he's in the guest wing recovering from his wound. It was an outrage!''

"Rebels? Here?" Lee frowned. "How many were there?"

"I don't know. Winston and I weren't here at the time. Christa was telling us about it just before you arrived."

"Then I must speak with her, and with Marcus Desmond, to get the details," Lee replied as he lowered his linen napkin. "The general will want to know of this incident. Pardon me."

Isabelle's mouth dropped open in surprise as she watched him leave the dining room.

"I wonder if the rebel patrol was his real reason for going after Christa," Winston speculated. "Do you suppose there's still something between them?"

"What do you mean?" Isabelle turned her brown eyes on her husband with acute interest. "There was never anything between Christa and Lee."

"Ah, but there was, my dear. As I heard it, he courted her several years ago, before she married your brother. That will be all, Ambrose," Winston said to the butler. "You're dismissed."

He waited until the elderly majordomo had exited before he addressed his wife again. "You must take better care to control your tongue, my dear. We don't want to ruin everything at this point. I've told you to try to keep Christa's goodwill so she doesn't become suspicious of our plans. And remember, as you said, the servants are very loyal to her. We must use care."

Isabelle brushed the back of her hand under the mass of auburn curls that tumbled around her shoulders. "I'm not worried. She's too stupid to ever suspect anything. How I abhor having her as mistress of

Haviland Court, just because she's married to that
worthless brother of mine. *I* should be mistress, and I
shall be one day. Then I'll replace all of these useless
servants. But I grow impatient with waiting. How I
wish our plans could move ahead more quickly. What
do you make of that jibberish Christa was saying about
a mine? From what Lee said, there could be great
profit in such a venture. And more profit would further
our plans more quickly.''

''But you heard her say the mine was probably
worthless.''

''What could she know?'' Isabelle snapped back.
''She has no interest in business. It's beyond her
capabilities. I'm going to do a little investigating of my
own. However, as usual, your counsel of caution in all
these matters is wise. I shall heed it.'' She leaned over
and ran her hand along her husband's arm. ''Could we
go upstairs soon, darling? Sparring with that inferior
Christa whetted my appetite for a more challenging and
enjoyable contest. Are you up to it?'' She regarded him
through long, auburn-tinged lashes.

''Always, my pet. And I've thought of something
I'm certain you will find arousingly different.'' Winston
entwined his hand roughly in her hair and drew her
closer. ''But what about Lee? He's our guest.''

''Lee made his choice of company. I want to be with
you.'' Isabelle smiled provocatively, knowing she
couldn't let her husband discover her inclinations
toward one Leland Garrett. That would be disastrous.
She ran a long, tapered fingertip teasingly over her
husband's thin black mustache and around his mouth.
''You're always full of such delightful surprises. Let's
hurry. I feel my pulse beginning to race just thinking
of what you will do to my body.''

Chapter 16

"Adelaide," Christa called as she left the dining room.

At the sound of her name, the young maid turned on the stairway. "Yes, Mrs. Haviland? Oh, I know what you're goin' to say, ma'am, an' I'm truly sorry about bein' late with Mrs. Sheffield's breakfast this mornin'. I overslept just a little again. I'll surely try not to let it happen tomorrow."

Adelaide was a dark-featured, merry girl who was often given to daydreaming, but she could work hard and was an asset to the household staff and Christa liked her happy spirit. It would have taken something far more serious than an incident that annoyed Isabelle for Christa to chastise Adelaide.

I should reward her for doing it, Christa thought sarcastically as she smiled at the girl.

"I know you'll try, Adelaide. Think nothing more about it. And don't forget about our music lesson this afternoon."

The maid looked vastly relieved. "Oh, I can't wait. I'll be up to the music room at the regular time, to be sure. Thank you, ma'am. I surely don't deserve all this time you've bin takin' teachin' me things."

"Of course you do, Adelaide. You're a bright girl, and I enjoy your company. I'll see you later then."

"Yes, ma'am," the maid replied, smiling widely as she bobbed a curtsy and hurried down the hall.

"Educating servants can be a dangerous hobby," a deep voice chided from behind Christa. She turned to see Lee Garrett standing in the shadows near the dining room entrance. He stepped forward, stopping only when he was directly in front of her. "You'll make that maid long for privileges she was never meant to have."

"I hope I do, Captain Garrett," Christa answered with cold formality, resenting his condescending attitude, which was so typical of him. "Contrary to what you may think, knowledge was not meant only for the privileged classes. We are all entitled to share it and create dreams from it."

"Ah yes, dreams. And what do those include for you, my lovely Christa?" Lee stepped still closer and took hold of her arms. "Do you still dream of me and long for what was once between us?"

Frowning, Christa twisted out of his hold. "Don't be ridiculous, Lee. Whatever was between us happened a long time ago and is certainly *not* something I care to remember. I'm married to Nevin, and I shouldn't have to remind you that you're married to Nedra."

"Our marital status is of no consequence," he replied lightly. "I've regretted that the war has kept me from renewing my . . . friendship . . . with you. I've always found it a curiosity that you tied yourself to Haviland. Surely he can't be man enough for you. You were always so fiery. And the simpering fool to whom I'm married is merely an annoyance to me. She served her purpose in the wealthy dowry she brought me, and she doesn't interfere in my life.

"In truth, I've always known it was the jilting I gave you for Nedra that drove you into Haviland's arms. It was cruel of me to do that to you, especially when your life was fraught with such distressing events. One brother lost at sea, the other made a useless invalid by a naval battle. Then your father committed suicide, leaving all those gambling debts and creditors clamoring to foreclose on Montclaire. Taking all that into account, it's no wonder you fled to Nevin Haviland's arms in wedlock.''

Christa was stunned by how close his deductions came to the actual truth about those horrible events. She was surprised he'd kept so closely informed about her life after their very unpleasant parting.

''I understand why you're angry with me,'' Lee went on. ''I'll admit I treated you badly. I was a fool to let you go. You're still the most beautiful woman in New York. How well I remember your warmth and passion. Perhaps in time your heart won't be so cold toward me. It would be an enjoyable challenge to try to thaw it. I'm going to be stationed here during winter quarters. We could see each other often.''

''No, we cannot see each other.'' Christa spoke firmly, trying hard not to let her growing anger get the best of her. ''It's a shame nothing has tempered your conceit, Lee. Let me assure you, I consider our past relationship to be a dreadful mistake I once made—one that I have no intention of repeating. Neither do I appreciate being reminded of it. As for my husband and my marriage, they are none of your concern. Now, if you'll excuse me, I must see to a guest.''

Christa turned toward the stairway, but Lee took hold of her arm to stop her. ''Very well then. For now, we'll leave it at that. But before you go, tell me about last night.''

''Last night?'' Christa's heart seemed to stop beating. Could he know about Trace Cavanaugh and all that had happened?

''Isabelle told me there was a problem with an

enemy patrol and Marcus Desmond was shot. The incident must be investigated, of course."

Christa almost laughed in relief. Apparently Lee didn't know about everything else that had occurred.

"I—I can't tell you very much," she began to explain, trying to keep her composure. "There were five or six men on horseback in the rebel patrol. A Lieutenant Cosgrove was their leader. Marcus arrived with a bad leg wound only moments before they burst in upon us. They searched the house looking for him, but we managed to keep him hidden. They left within minutes to continue the search elsewhere."

"Blast those riffraff Continentals!" Lee exclaimed vehemently. "What bloody audacity they have to trespass our battle lines when this city is indisputably held under British control! But this incident will give me good reason to spend more time here at Haviland Court. Citizens loyal to His Majesty must be protected. I'll see to it this estate is patrolled regularly when I can't be here. Now, show me to Desmond's room. I want to speak to him as well."

"He needs to rest, Lee. He's very weak from the vast amount of blood he lost," Christa said, trying to dissuade him. She didn't want anyone else to find out she'd delivered the dispatch.

"Then I'll stay only a few moments." He gestured toward the wide mahogany staircase that led to the second floor, and took hold of Christa's elbow. She had no choice but to show him the way.

In the green guest room, Christa walked around to the far side of the four-poster bed where Marcus Desmond lay sleeping. When she touched his forehead, checking for a sign of fever, he opened his eyes and smiled at her.

"Forgive me when I say I've dreamed of just such

a moment as this, Christa," he murmured. "Waking to have your loveliness be the first vision I see."

"Hush, Marcus. Don't exert yourself," Christa admonished, startled to hear him say such a thing. She considered him a dear friend whom she valued highly, but he'd never before said anything so intimate to her. Nor did she want him to. Was he delirious? His words upset her, as did the fact that Garrett was witness to them.

"Leland Garrett is here, Marcus," she went on, hoping Lee hadn't heard. "He wants to ask you about last night, if you're up to it."

"I feel stronger now, Christa. I'll speak with him, of course."

A little while later, Christa returned to her own room, relieved that her encounter with Lee Garrett was over. How glad she was that she'd earlier asked Marcus not to tell anyone about her part in delivering the dispatch. She'd told him only that she'd given it to Trace Cavanaugh at the Wild Boar Alehouse, as instructed. Marcus had therefore explained to Lee that he was a special courier and the information he'd been carrying had reached its destination, mentioning Christa not at all. Now she was free to forget all about last night.

She felt weary in body and spirit. Encounters with Isabelle and Winston usually left her angry and depressed. She'd tried so hard since her marriage to become a part of the Haviland family. But it increasingly seemed an exercise in futility. Isabelle, especially, seemed to resent her and went out of her way to make life unpleasant for her.

Seeing Lee Garrett again hadn't helped Christa's state of mind either.

Once, she had thought she loved him very much.

When she met Lee four years ago at her coming-out ball, she was a vulnerable, innocent girl of nineteen, just introduced to society after being educated at a private school for young ladies. She had been sheltered all her life and had little experience of men. And Lee Garrett was expert in his courtship. How easily her head was turned by his handsome good looks and dashing charm! He used her affections, then heartlessly cast her aside when he learned about her family's financial straits. Plain but wealthy Nedra Cummings quickly became the object of his attention.

Christa crossed her spacious bedroom and sat down at the maple writing desk in the corner. Her eyes drifted over the single vellum sheet of a letter she'd received from her husband two days before. As usual, Nevin's missive was formal and succinct, saying only that he was in good health and that his duty station was being changed to Kip's Bay on Manhattan Island.

Nevin. Their marriage had saved her and her family in many ways. She owed him so much.

"Miz Christa? Is you in there?"

"Yes, come in, Letty," she called.

A thin Negro woman who was three years older than Christa bustled into the bedchamber, closing the hall door behind her. "Mr. Ambrose don' tol' me to come up an' see if'n you'd be wantin' a food tray brung to you. Said you didn't eat hardly nothin' down at dinner jus' now. Miz Isabelle sour yer appetite agin?"

Christa didn't mind her personal maid's forward ways. She could be herself with Letty. And they shared a great dislike of Nevin's younger sister.

"I know I shouldn't let her bother me." Christa sighed in exasperation. "But her nastiness always sets me on edge. Why is she like that, Letty? She seems to have everything to make her happy. She's beautiful and intelligent. Winston is a handsome and attentive husband. She has a child, a life of ease.''

Letty was thoughtful for a moment. Finally she said, ''You ain't never asked me 'bout this b'fore, Miz Christa, so I ain't never mentioned it. We always bin forbid to talk 'bout it 'round here. So this here's fo' you to hear only.''

Letty went back to the door and opened it a crack to see out into the corridor. Satisfied that no one was listening, she closed the door again and rejoined Christa at the corner desk.

''I has lived here at Haviland Court all mah life. Mah mama was nursemaid to Miz Isabelle up 'til she was took with a fever an' died when I was fourteen. So I done growed up 'round Miz Isabelle.

''She weren't always a mean thing. She be only a year older'n me—twenty-seven now. I kin recall us havin' some mighty fine happy times aplayin' together when we was young'uns. But she would git powerful sad sometimes. She lost her mama when she were only eight years old. So she kinda turned all her lovin' feelin's to her papa, Mr. Orin. How she did try to please him, jus' to git a smile from him or a word o' praise. But Mr. Nevin were the apple o' Mr. Orin's eye, becuz of him bein' the son an' heir an' all. Po' Miz Isabelle done got pushed aside so often, I reckon she done jus' finally give up.

''Well, when Miz Isabelle were sixteen, she met Mr. Benjamin Blissfield. A light come on in them big brown eyes o' her'n, an' she really fell in love. An' a rightly nice young fella he were, too. But he didn't have no money. He were wantin' to be a doctor so's he could help people. Miz Isabelle said money never meant much to him.

''But it shor' 'nough did mean somethin' to Mr. Orin. When Miz Isabelle an' Mr. Benjamin wanted to be amarryin', he went into a fit o' rage that 'bout took the roof off'n this here fine dwellin'. Said he'd already choosed Miz Isabelle's man, one suited to her highborn station. That were Mr. Winston. Miz Isabelle weren't never to see Mr. Benjamin ever agin. Her yellin' an' cryin' over that there decree were pitiful. It broke her heart to pieces.

"But Mr. Orin's word 'round here is law. An' he be a right powerful man in many a way. Didn't none o' us ever see Mr. Benjamin agin. Nobody yet done know fo' shor' what really happen to him. It were said that Mr. Orin ruined Mr. Benjamin's chance to git into a doctor-learnin' school. Some said Mr. Benjamin sailed away to some other parts in the world after that.

"Finally, Miz Isabelle done like her papa said an' hitched up with Mr. Winston. But she ain't never bin quite the same since. It jus' seem like the sweetness died right outta her. Now she only seems to want to be mean to people, hurt 'em an' take from 'em, like she were hurt an' took from. It be truly sad."

Letty shook her head as she stopped speaking. Christa's heart was touched by the Negro woman's sad narrative. What must it be like to love a man that much? She didn't know. At one time she had thought she loved Leland Garrett. She was in love with Nevin now, wasn't she? And yet she'd never had a feeling so strong and consuming that the loss of it might change her life forever. Did she really *want* to know a love like that? It seemed to bring as much pain as joy.

Deep in thought, Christa picked up her husband's letter again. When she did, she saw a gold pocket watch on the desk. Trace Cavanaugh's watch. She'd forgotten to give it back to him.

Trace Cavanaugh. A fluttering sensation touched her stomach the same way it had when she'd been with him last night.

Suddenly Christa felt a strong urge to be with Nevin. Perhaps seeing her husband was all she needed to dispel her restless loneliness.

She'd read that the battle lines had been pushed farther north than Kip's Bay, to Pell's Point in Westchester. There shouldn't be any danger in going to the bay where Nevin was stationed. Many women were with their men, even at the battle lines. They cooked, nursed the wounded—did anything they could to help the cause.

Christa rose to her feet. "Letty, pack some of my things. Tomorrow I'm going to the Kip's Bay outpost to see Mr. Nevin."

Letty's jaw dropped open at her mistress's unexpected declaration, but Christa didn't notice. She was already going to the large oak wardrobe to pick out the clothing she wanted to take. She smiled as she imagined the happy look on her husband's face when he saw her tomorrow.

Chapter 17

At eight o'clock the next morning, Christa stood in the elegantly appointed coral-and-white front parlor of Haviland Court, pulling on kid gloves that perfectly matched her sapphire blue suede traveling ensemble. Nevin had always liked her in that outfit.

All was in readiness. A groom would momentarily take her three pieces of luggage to the waiting family carriage. Glancing at the maroon leather bags, she worried she might have packed too much. But she didn't know how long her visit with Nevin might last.

"Your pardon, madam," Ambrose said as he entered the parlor followed by a well-dressed woman who walked with an energetic step. "Mrs. Zachary is here to see you."

"Olivia," Christa acknowledged with surprise. Immediately her hand flew to her mouth as she remembered why her friend was there. "Goodness, I'm to hostess our sewing tea today!"

"I take it those plans have changed, my dear," the other woman replied, glancing at Christa's packed bags.

"I must confess it completely slipped my mind," Christa went on with dread. "Much has occurred in the last day or so."

"Has something happened to Nevin or someone in

your family, Christa?'' Olivia Zachary's face showed concern.

"No, they are all fine as far as I know. Let me explain.''

In a few minutes, Christa had related the story about the Continental patrol and Marcus Desmond, though she was careful to say little more than that.

"So you see, Olivia, my concern over Marcus's close brush with death made me long to see Nevin, to know he's all right. It's been months since he's had a leave to come home. I miss him so much.''

"I understand. It's been quite a while since I've seen Fitzhugh. Generals can never get away from wars, it seems. Perhaps with winter coming on the battles will cease for a while, and we'll be able to have our men home again. At least I'm here in America. I'm glad I was visiting the Colonies when the war broke out. I wouldn't want to be in England, an ocean away from my husband.''

"I knew you'd understand.'' Christa smiled warmly at her friend, envying the love she saw in the older woman's eyes when she spoke of her husband.

At age fifty-three, Olivia Zachary looked at least ten years younger. No graying marked her dark blond hair. Though small in stature, she had a quick intelligence that made her a force to be reckoned with when the occasion warranted it.

"When the other ladies arrive, I'll serve as hostess in your place,'' Olivia offered. "But please be certain you take several well-armed grooms with you.''

"Yes, yes, I shall,'' Christa replied eagerly, giving her friend a quick hug. "And thank you so much, Olivia. I'll repay you somehow for this kindness.''

The older woman smiled. "Only have a wonderful reunion with your husband, my dear, and I shall be repaid in full. If you should see my Hugh while you're there, please tell him I miss him very much.''

"I shall be happy to deliver that message," Christa assured her.

"Well then, get along now. I'll go to the kitchen to let Hester know twelve ladies will be arriving within the hour, expecting her best cakes and tea. I can't wait to see the look on her face when she hears *that!*"

Nevin Haviland smiled as he scanned the written reports he was filing. According to them, General William Howe had captured a large force of General Washington's Continentals here at Kip's Bay last month and forced the remaining rebel army to retreat northward the length of Manhattan Island. Intelligence accounts revealed that the patriots were short of food, equipment, and ammunition. Often in battle, they were outnumbered three-to-one by the British. The rate of desertion was high.

The tide of war seems to be turning in King George's favor, Nevin thought with satisfaction as he replaced the papers in the folders on his desk. And I'm well behind the front battle lines, thanks to the Haviland influence and money.

There was a chill in the October air as Nevin left the headquarters office and returned to the tent he shared with another officer. He unbuttoned the jacket of his uniform and stretched out his nearly six-foot length on his cot. His tired eyes felt the strain of filling out and reading reports hour after hour. But that was better than lugging around a rifle and heavy pack and getting shot at, he decided as he closed his eyes and massaged his temples with his fingertips. *That* was most distasteful.

The other occupant of the tent stirred on his cot

across from Nevin. "You're finally off duty, Nev?" he mumbled sleepily.

"Aye. I told the colonel my hand was so cramped from filling out his bloody reports that I was taking the remainder of the day off to rest."

The other man snorted. "I'll just bet you told Donaldson that. The old bastard's certainly taken the enjoyment out of this war since he was put in charge here."

"You have that right, Hyde," Nevin agreed. He hadn't minded playing at war. After a lifetime of being harassed and ordered about by his tyrannical father, he'd finally escaped his control and had the chance to similarly bully soldiers who outranked. He'd enjoyed his improved status for a while, but two years was enough.

Nevin thought momentarily of Charity, his sweet little mistress, who was always so willing to take his mind off tedious duties. He reached into the breast pocket of his jacket and took out a white embroidered handkerchief. The fragrance from it immediately reminded him of Charity. He'd given her the expensive perfume and taught her where to wear it on her voluptuous body to entice and excite him. She had quickly learned everything he taught her.

"That belong to your pretty little woman?" Hyde Osborne asked as he got to his feet and walked to the washstand at the back of the big tent. "The way you're smiling, you must be thinking about her."

Nevin's smile held a smirking confidence. "She's always a pleasant thought. She knows her place and happily waits on me hand and foot when we're together. She's like a piece of clay and I'm the fine sculptor molding her into the woman I want."

Hyde Osborne sighed. "You're a lucky bastard to

have such a wench. How're you planning to get out of camp to see her this time? Donaldson said no passes.''

''Yes, Donaldson.'' Nevin said the name contemptuously. ''He's become a problem, all right. He takes this war too damned seriously to my way of thinking, and I'm sick of it. I didn't expect to make a career out of this rebellion.'' Nevin lowered his voice as he went on. ''Just between us, Hyde, I've a plan for bringing my duty to an end.''

''Well, I wish you luck, Nev. You know your secret is safe with me. But if it works, I may just use it myself sometime soon.''

Chapter 18

"Mrs. Nevin Haviland to see you, General," the young corporal on sentry duty informed his commander.

"Christa here?" Fitzhugh Zachary cocked a graying eyebrow in surprise. "Well, send her in, Corporal."

Another soldier in the spacious command tent perked up at the mention of Christa's name. Trace wasn't expecting to see his partner from the other night's escapades again so soon. What was she doing here? Could he trust her to keep silent about their activities?

"I beg your pardon for this interruption, General Zachary," Christa said by way of greeting as soon as she entered the tent. "I'm very glad to see you. I had no idea you were at this outpost."

"I arrived only a little while ago myself, Christa. You're a delight for war-weary eyes, my dear." He took her outstretched hand and guided her farther inside the tent.

"I always appreciate your compliments, General," she replied, smiling at him. But her smile froze on her lips when she saw the other two men present.

"Allow me to make introductions," Zachary offered. "Gentlemen, this is Mrs. Haviland. Colonel Efrem Donaldson"—he gestured to his left toward a bewhiskered man in uniform—"and Captain Trace Cavanaugh, my aide-de-camp."

Both men gave nods of acknowledgment. Christa did likewise as she tried to quell the increased beating of her heart. Trace gave no indication of being acquainted with her, much to her relief.

"Well, Donaldson, from what you've told me, you seem to have everything under control here," Zachary continued. "Trace, I'll want to talk to you further about this saltpeter shortage. But for now, gentlemen, our meeting is concluded. You're dismissed."

Trace wanted to stay. He felt uneasy about what Christa might say, and he found it hard to draw his gaze away from her. She looked so different from when he'd last seen her. Before him stood a beautiful, composed woman, not the fighting, mud-spattered ragamuffin he'd first encountered on Sterling Street or the subdued, bedraggled woman he'd left at Haviland Court. The deep blue of her finely tailored traveling suit drew out the same hue in her large eyes. The alluring curves of her figure were flattered by the tight fit of her clothing. Every shining black curl of hair showing beneath her bonnet was perfectly in place.

But his commander had spoken, and there was nothing Trace could do but send a smart salute toward General Zachary and follow Colonel Donaldson from the tent.

"Now, my dear, what brings you here to Kip's Bay?" Zachary asked Christa when they were alone.

"I'm hoping to see my husband, General."

"Nevin's stationed here?"

"According to his last letter, yes. It's been a long time since I've seen him. I was hoping we could have a brief visit."

"I see. I'm not certain traveling was wise, Christa. Rebel infiltrators roam the countryside. You could have been in danger. But I understand how it is between two young people in love. The heart grows impatient, making it easy to overlook unknown perils.''

Christa kept silent about the rebel patrol that had invaded Haviland Court. She had decided to keep that night a secret from Nevin, and hoped Trace Cavanaugh would, too.

''I bring a message from your wife, General,'' she said, changing the subject.

''Olivia?'' The general brightened. ''She's well, I trust?''

''Yes, I saw her this morning. She said that, if I saw you, I was to say how much she misses you.''

Christa watched a gentleness come into the stern expression of the distinguished older man. He smiled, then seemed to remember himself. Clearing his throat, he said, ''Tell her I regret we've been apart so long. It's my hope I may be able to see her once we've settled into winter quarters. But right now, the offensive we're engaged in against the Continentals requires all my attention. We all wish for a speedy end to this rebellion, but I fear that won't happen. However, let's see about reuniting you with your husband.''

''Thank you. You're most kind, General.'' Then Christa voiced a thought that had come to her during Zachary's brief conversation with Trace Cavanaugh. She hadn't told Lee Garrett anything more about the saltpeter mine. It seemed appropriate to mention it to the general now.

''You mentioned saltpeter before. I understand that substance is in short supply.''

Zachary looked surprised. ''Saltpeter? Why, yes, that's right. It's potassium nitrate, used in making gunpowder. Our supplies are rapidly being depleted, since His Majesty's ships from England are too often intercepted by the enemy. We need to look for a supply source close at hand.''

"I may know of such a source. My family holds a deed to a saltpeter mine. However, the mine was closed down years ago and may be of no use."

"Then again, it might be." The older man sounded interested. "Do you remember where the mine is located?"

"I believe it's outside the small town of Wooster, about four hours' journey north from New York City. I mentioned the mine to Lee Garrett yesterday while he was visiting Haviland Court, but I didn't have a chance to give him the papers."

"Captain Garrett is on another assignment for me. I can send Captain Cavanaugh, whom you met just now. Our forces hold that area. It's certainly worth investigating. I'm due at another meeting right now, Christa, but I'll want to discuss this matter further with you later. For now, let's see about finding Nevin."

Zachary pulled back the canvas flap of the tent. "Corporal, do you know the whereabouts of Captain Nevin Haviland?"

"Yes, General. He's on duty at the quartermaster's office," the young guard answered smartly.

"I'm going in that direction now, sir," said another voice. "I'd be happy to show Mrs. Haviland the way."

Christa recognized Trace's deep voice even before he stepped into view.

"Fine," Zachary agreed, turning to her. "Captain Cavanaugh will help you. Tell him what you just related to me about the mine. I must caution you to make your visit with your husband brief, Christa. The battle front changes daily. You'd be safer at Haviland Court."

"Yes, General. I shall heed your advice. Thank you." She flashed him a warm smile, struggling to hide the strange turmoil she felt at seeing Trace again. Had he been waiting outside for her?''

"So we meet again, Christa," Trace said when they were out of earshot of the guard. "Have you recovered from the ordeal of the other night?"

Christa felt unsure of herself, confused by his nearness and how handsome he looked in his uniform. She didn't want to admit to herself that she'd thought about the possibility of seeing him here at the encampment.

"Y—yes, I think so," she managed to stammer.

"How is Marcus doing? Did you tell him or anyone else about everything that happened that night?" Trace didn't let her see how anxious he was to hear her answer.

"He's much better, but I thought it best not to tell him anything other than that I delivered the dispatch to you. I've told no one about the other occurrences, as you and I agreed." She looked directly at him. "Did you?"

"No, I report to General Zachary, and this is the first chance I've had to see him since the dam incident. I wasn't planning to mention your involvement in my report, if that's satisfactory with you."

He wasn't going to report anything at all about that night, he thought to himself. The Continentals were being blamed for the destruction of the British encampment, and that was just what he wanted.

"I'd appreciate that consideration very much, Captain," Christa answered with relief. "I'd just like to forget the whole night."

"What of the dog? Have you been asked about him?"

"In the past Wolfgang has gotten loose and run off at times. I simply explained that he'd done the same again. Only I know he won't return this time." Christa's voice dropped as she remembered her brave pet.

"I see," Trace replied, feeling some regret that he'd reminded her of Wolfgang's death. He changed the subject. "The quartermaster's office is just over there." He gestured to their left. "Now, what did the general mean about a mine?"

Christa repeated what she had told General Zachary about the saltpeter mine. At the mention of Lee Garrett's name, Trace's brow furrowed.

"But he doesn't know the location of the mine?" he asked.

"No. I left Haviland Court early this morning without speaking to him again."

Trace nodded and said nothing more as they continued to the quartermaster's office.

Christa was glad for his reticence. She felt uneasy being with him and hoped they'd find Nevin quickly. She couldn't wait to see her husband again, she told herself. She filled her mind with that thought as she carefully kept pace with Trace's steps across the slippery grass.

Chapter 19

"Cap'n Haviland ain't here," the sergeant manning a desk in the quartermaster's office said in answer to Trace's query. "He went off duty about fifteen minutes ago. He was plum tuckered out. Probably went right to his tent. It's the second to the last one in the officers' section."

"All right, Sergeant," Trace replied as he exchanged salutes with the enlisted man. "We'll look for him there."

"There is no need for you to trouble yourself further, Captain Cavanaugh," Christa told him when they were outside again. "I'm certain I can find my way from here."

"It's no trouble. And the last time we were together, I believe you were calling me Trace. I'd prefer that." He watched for her reaction.

"I think it best we keep our relationship on a formal basis, sir." Christa kept her tone cool so she wouldn't reveal how nervous he made her feel.

"Well, it's pleasant to know at least that we have a relationship," Trace answered, purposely misconstruing her words. "The officers' area is this way."

Christa frowned but kept silent as she went with him toward the long row of tents. How should she take his meaning? He seemed to be teasing her, yet there was a note of sincerity in his voice. His manner confused her.

"Captain Haviland, are you there?" Trace called when they reached Nevin's tent. He surprised himself by realizing he'd be glad if Christa's husband couldn't be found.

What sounded like a low mumble came from inside. Christa pushed aside the canvas flap to look in.

"He's here, Captain. Thank you. I won't be needing your help any longer."

"Very well, Christa." Trace didn't show his reluctance to leave as he touched a finger to the upturned brim of his black tricornered hat and gave a slight nod of his head.

The tent was large enough to allow Christa to stand. Two cots with thin mattresses, two trunks, a small writing desk, and a wooden washstand comprised the furnishings. Nevin lay asleep on his back on one of the cots.

"Nevin," Christa said softly as she bent over him and touched his shoulder. "Darling, it's Christa."

Her husband's hazel eyes flew open and he sat bolt upright.

"Christa! What the devil are you doing here?"

Those were not the words she had hoped to hear from him.

"I—I wanted to see you, Nevin. It's been so long."

"So you just arrive unexpectedly at a military post like some camp follower? My God, Christa, whatever possessed you to do it?" He was frowning fiercely.

"I only wanted to see if you were all right and be with you for a little while. General Zachary didn't seem to mind that—"

"Zachary is here?" Nevin interrupted sharply.

"Yes. I just spoke to him. Nevin, I'm very sorry if I've upset you."

The look of contrition on his wife's face made Nevin regret his brusqueness. Berating her wasn't the way to handle this situation. But Christa had caught him completely by surprise. She was the *last* person he wanted to see right now, when he was ready to put the plan he'd been telling Hyde Osborne about into play. And Zachary's arrival could mean the camp would be moving closer to the battle front. He wanted no part of *that*.

"It is I who am sorry, my dear," he said then, forcing a gentleness into his voice as he changed his approach. "Here, sit down. You must be fatigued from your journey."

He gestured toward Osborne's empty cot. Christa hesitantly sat down on the edge.

"I'm afraid the long hours of my duty have made me anxious," Nevin explained as he went to the washstand and poured some water from the china pitcher into the bowl. The few moments it took to wash his face and hands gave him time to think.

"This is a military camp," he went on, drying his hands with a towel. "There are few women here, and those who are are not ladies of genteel breeding. The men here haven't had much opportunity of late to see any woman, much less a woman of your beauty. Their actions might be anything but gentlemanly toward you."

"I might have known you'd only be concerned about my welfare," Christa replied with relief as she smiled at him. "You're so unselfish, Nevin. It's only one of the reasons why I love you."

Of course, I mean those words, she told herself as she rose to her feet again and came over to him. Reaching up, she touched the side of his face.

"How tired you look. Is there no one else who can take some of the burden of duty from you?"

"We're undermanned because the troops are needed at the front lines."

"I'm so glad you're not there." She reached up to put her arms around his neck. She knew he disapproved of such outward displays of emotion, but there was no one to see them here in the tent, and she needed to be near her husband, needed to feel his arms around her. They'd had so little intimate time together during their marriage. He was away so much fulfilling his army duty.

"Now that I'm here, can we not make the best of it?" she murmured softly. "Show me you're happy to see me."

Christa closed her eyes, and Nevin knew she was waiting to be kissed. She was beautiful and unsuspecting. Pathetically so. Her body molded along his. He felt her breasts pressing into his rumpled shirtfront. His lust for a woman—any woman—was aroused.

Nevin smiled to himself as he roughly lowered his mouth to Christa's. The memory of her sensuously curved body exploded in his mind. He wanted her. But here was not the place. He forced himself to break off the kiss.

"We can't do anything here, Christa." He held her away from him. "Another man shares this tent. He could return at any time."

Christa wasn't surprised by this change in him. She'd learned to almost expect it. One moment he acted impassive and unresponsive; the next, he could hardly check his desire for her.

"We must find a place for you to stay," Nevin went on. "I'm off duty until tomorrow. I know a boardinghouse located just beyond the camp. We'll go there."

"Well, this is certainly not as splendid as Haviland Court, but it will have to do for your short stay."

Nevin deposited Christa's bags near the door of the room he'd just rented.

"It's really very nice," Christa observed as she looked around the small room. It was painted a soft yellow that brightly reflected the autumn sunlight flooding through the two windows. The canopied bed, green-and-yellow wing-backed armchair, and small writing desk were all finely crafted.

"Mrs. Warwick, the proprietress, was once a wealthy woman," Nevin continued, "but the war has caused her fortunes to falter, and she, like many others, has been forced to open her home to strangers to keep food on the table." His tone was condescending, as though he found the idea of sheltering strangers repulsive.

Christa felt sad for the kindly older woman who'd been most gracious while she'd been showing them the room. She frowned slightly at her husband's lack of sympathy.

"Well, she said dinner wouldn't be ready for an hour yet," Nevin noted, coming over to Christa. A smug smile turned up one corner of his mouth in a way that was only too familiar to her. "Let's finish what we began back at my tent." He ran his hands along her arms.

"But you're exhausted from your long hours of duty, Nevin. And I'm rather tired from my journey as well. Perhaps later . . ." Why was she trying to deter him from taking her to bed? She'd longed to be with him. Wasn't that why she'd come?

"No, I want you now, Christa," Nevin insisted, his smile spreading fully over his thin lips as he began to unfasten the buttons down the front of her suede jacket. "You know my need of you will not take long. Then you'll have time to rest."

Christa nodded, hiding her reluctance to make love

with him. She stood perfectly still while he undressed her.

This was what she wanted, she convinced herself. She wanted to be close to her husband, please him, be a proper wife. It was her duty to submit to him. She owed Nevin so much. He'd saved Montclaire. Because of him her family still had a home. Her heritage wasn't lost.

He said nothing as he removed her clothing piece by piece. His hazel eyes narrowed as he gazed hungrily at her nakedness.

When he ran the tip of his tongue over his lips and began to fondle her breasts, Christa cringed inside with shock. Her husband reminded her of the horrible men who'd attacked her the other night!

When Nevin cupped a breast in one hand and lowered his mouth to suckle the nipple, Christa closed her eyes and bit her lip, making herself endure his caress. Over and over in her mind she repeated that this was Nevin, her husband. What he was doing to her was right. But should she tell him she'd almost been raped two nights ago? That terrifying experience must be why she felt such reluctance to be with him now. Surely he would understand.

But she knew him well. He'd be outraged to learn how she'd come to be in such a terrible circumstance. She hadn't acted as a proper, well-born wife should. He'd get very angry, and she didn't want that. And he'd become upset if she tried to stop his embraces now, for she could tell from his quickened breathing that he was becoming very aroused. She had to endure his fondling and anything else he wanted to do to her.

Nevin made her lie down on the bed. He stared at her while he removed his clothes.

"Your body is so beautiful, Christa. Touch yourself. Rub your hands over your breasts."

"Nevin, please. Not that—"

'Do it, Christa. Obey me!" His tone was urgent, demanding.

Resistance sparked again within her, but she forced it down and did what he wanted, knowing that watching her caress herself would excite him even more, and that this act of joining would be over quickly. It was all Christa wanted now.

"Yes, that's the way . . ." Nevin instructed in a raspy whisper as he watched her move her hands slowly over her breasts. Then he came to her and roughly fondled her himself. He kissed her mouth hard, bruising her lips, then loomed over her, forcing her legs apart with his knee so that he could plunge into her.

His entry hurt Christa, but she submitted to his harsh thrusts without making a sound. In a short time, he collapsed on her, panting after his swift climax. Christa felt crushed beneath his weight—crushed in both body and spirit. This joining with her husband was no different from any others they'd ever had.

Nevin grunted with satisfaction and rolled to the other side of the big bed, where he quickly dozed off. Christa covered herself with the blankets, wishing the simple gesture could cover her terrible disappointment as well. She felt so empty inside.

How she'd wished that this time with Nevin would be different. The war had separated her from him for so long. She'd hoped that if they were able to spend more time together, she'd grow to care deeply for her husband, that their lovemaking would bring her some of the pleasure he seemed to enjoy from it.

Stop it, Christa silently scolded herself. She knew she was being selfish. She received pleasure from making love with him, she was sure. She felt grateful

because he wanted to lie with her, wanted her body
Nevin held and caressed her a little. That part of their
intimacy would have to be enough, all she could ever
expect when she performed her duty to her husband.

Chapter 20

The next evening, Christa visited General Zachary again. Trace Cavanaugh was with him in the command tent.

"I'll be leaving tomorrow morning," Christa told the general, giving him her complete attention.

"I know your visit has been brief, my dear," Zachary replied, "but that can't be helped. I trust you've enjoyed your stay?"

"Yes, although Nevin and I haven't had much time together. Colonel Donaldson has assigned everyone to extended hours of duty."

"Yes, I regret that that step has been necessary. We're seriously short of men here."

"And Nevin would never shirk his responsibilities," Christa added. "He was most adamant in insisting it would be unfair to the other men if he were relieved of his duty so that he could spend time with me today."

"He's right, and most fortunate in having such an understanding wife. At times I wish my Olivia were of a similar mind regarding my responsibilities." Zachary gave her a fatherly smile as he went on. "But let's get to the business at hand. Captain Cavanaugh will be escorting you back to Haviland Court to obtain the information about the saltpeter mine. He'll be investigating its production potential. And I'll feel better knowing he'll be with you on your journey home. He's my best man, and you'll be thoroughly safe with him.''

"The general is too kind with his praise." Trace spoke for the first time, hiding a secret satisfaction. He'd worked hard to earn his commander's esteem, though for a reason known only to himself. But for now he put that thought aside and turned to Christa. "I deem it an honor to escort Mrs. Haviland home."

His turquoise eyes caught hers. During the moment that their gazes held, Christa began to feel uneasy about having Trace accompany her back to Haviland Court. She remembered his kiss of a few days ago. Would she really be safe with him?

"Thank you, Captain," she forced herself to say politely, knowing she had to agree to the general's plan or risk provoking his questions. But she couldn't hold Trace's gaze.

"You must excuse me now, gentlemen," she went on quickly, changing the subject. "My husband will be getting off duty soon, and he promised to share evening supper with me." She turned to Trace, keeping her tone casual. "I'll see you at the main gate at seven o'clock tomorrow morning, if that's convenient, sir."

"Most convenient," Trace acknowledged with a tilt of his head.

All at once an earsplitting explosion shattered the air.

"What the—!" Zachary exclaimed, hurrying to the tent entrance.

"Looks like the arms bunker just blew, sir!" the corporal on guard shouted as he pointed toward bright flames visible at the eastern end of the camp. More blasts rocked the air, and clouds of billowing smoke spewed from the fire.

"*Damn*! That's all we need!" Zachary declared as he squinted toward the burgeoning conflagration. "Let's get over there!" He turned quickly to Christa.

"You'd best stay—" he began, then stopped when he saw the stricken expression on her face.

Christa's hand flew to her throat. Her eyes widened in shock as she struggled to speak. "Th—the arms bunker . . . Nevin's working there, taking an inventory!"

"I'll find out," Zachary stated. "Trace, stay here with Mrs. Haviland."

"No, I must know," Christa insisted, and before any of them could stop her, she lifted her skirts and began running across the open field toward the fire.

The whole camp had been aroused. Chaos reigned around the flaming bunker. Men shouted orders and wielded buckets of water, trying to form a brigade line, but the wind threatened to spread the voracious flames.

Trace caught up with Christa and pulled her to a stop before she got too close to the fire. "You must stay back, Christa!" he shouted sternly, grabbing her arms in a tight grip.

Two more explosions suddenly rent the night, knocking Trace and Christa to the ground. Trace rolled on top of her to shield her from hazardous flying debris.

"Are you all right?" he asked when he could safely move away from her.

"Y—yes, I think so."

Trace got to his feet and pulled Christa up and away from the underground bunker. The intense heat of the fire drove everyone else away from the burning structure as well.

"We won't be able to find out anything about your husband until the flames die back. You must stay away, Christa." Trace held her by the arms in front of him, forcing her to listen. "I'm going to see what I can do to help.

"Private!" he called to a heavyset young man running past them.

The man stopped and saluted. "Sir?"

"Stay with this woman. Keep her out of danger."

"Yes, sir!"

Before Christa could protest, Trace disappeared into the melee. She wanted to do something, anything, to help fight the fire and learn more quickly of Nevin's fate. She started after Trace, but the private stopped her with a gentle pull on her arm.

"Please, ma'am, do like the cap'n says," he beseeched her. "When Cap'n Cavanaugh gives orders, he means for 'em to be carried out. If anythin' was to happen to you, ma'am, he'd have my hide."

A sudden gust of wind brought the intense heat from the inferno blasting at Christa and the soldier. They both instinctively stepped back and raised their arms to protect their faces. Christa let the young man draw her away, but her eyes never left the flames. Desperately she searched for some sign of Nevin.

Blinking against the glaring brightness, she tried to focus on the men working to combat the destructive fire. Trace was directing them. He stood silhouetted against the sky-reaching flames, his stance firm, his voice calling sharp orders. The men followed his commands unquestioningly, acknowledging his leadership.

Christa searched each man's face, hoping to see Nevin.

"Ma'am! Ma'am!" Another soldier ran to Christa. "Some men bin hurt. Kin you help?"

"Yes, of course," she agreed, forcing her attention to him. Here, at least, was something she could do. Lifting her skirts, she hurried to where three men lay on the wet grass. A fourth man knelt beside them.

"How badly are these men hurt?" Christa asked, stooping next to him.

"I don't know hardly nothin' about this, ma'am," the grisly looking soldier admitted. "I plugged up plenty 'o musketball holes in fellers in my day, but I ain't much fer knowin' what to do about burns like them two got." He jerked his head over his shoulder to indicate the other injured men. "This here one got somethin', maybe a chunk of wood or metal, drove clean through him in one o' the blasts. He's bleedin' real bad. It don't look good."

"We'll try to stop his bleeding," Christa replied, taking charge. "The other two will have to wait for now. Are there bandages?"

"Aye, ma'am, right here." The man handed her a leather satchel.

Suddenly the young man on the ground raised up and grabbed her arm, making her jump in shock.

"Don't let me die! Please, I don't wanna die!" he cried, his eyes wide with fear, his breath coming in harsh gasps.

"No, you're not going to die. We'll save you. Please lie down," Christa said, trying to assure him as she pressed her hands against his shoulders and lowered him to the grass. But as she examined the wound, she knew she hadn't spoken the truth. The gaping hole in his stomach was bleeding profusely. As she unwound a wad of bandages, she bit her lower lip to hold back the wave of nausea that welled up inside her at the sickening sight and smell of the wound. He was only a boy, not more than fifteen or sixteen years old, and he was going to die. As she fought to stop the flow of blood and her hands became wet and sticky, she knew with a terrible dread that these were his final moments.

"Hold this in place," she directed the soldier helping her. When he'd put his hand firmly on the thick wad of cloth covering the wound, Christa hastily wiped her hands on her suede skirt and lifted the young soldier's head into her lap. She pushed his dark, curly hair away from his face. His teeth were clenched, but he looked steadily up at her.

"Do you know this man's name?" Christa glanced toward the older man.

"Aye, ma'am. It's Robbie. Robbie Moore."

"Try to lie still, Robbie," Christa said softly to the injured soldier when he jerked and half turned in her lap. Blocking out everything around them, she focused solely on him.

"Do you have a girl back home, Robbie?" she asked, smiling. He gave a small nod. "Well, you'll be going home to see her soon. There's no need for you to be in the fighting anymore. You've done your part."

His eyes held Christa's for only a moment longer. A deep gasp for breath issued from his lips as he stiffened and his face twisted into a grimace. Then his eyes closed, and he went limp in Christa's arms. She knew he was dead.

"I reckon we ought to be seein' to the others, ma'am," the other soldier coaxed after a long moment. "Ain't nothin' more we kin do fer Robbie."

Christa clenched her teeth as sorrow welled up in her. He was so young. She hugged his head to her chest, rocking gently. "I'm sorry I couldn't do more, Robbie . . ."

Tears spilled from her eyes as she finally laid him aside. Forcing herself to turn away, she took the medical bag and went to the other two men.

Trace stood off to one side. Christa's courage and compassion for the young boy had touched him deeply, leaving him thoughtful as he watched her tend the other injured men.

Chapter 21

Nothing remained of the timber and earthen munitions bunker except a blackened, smoldering hole in the ground. Several other shelters had been destroyed as well, but most of the encampment was saved from ruin.

Christa stared down at the dark green wool blanket covering a body on the ground before her. A soldier held a lantern to light her circle of vision.

"Are you certain you feel up to this?" Trace asked gently, standing beside her. She nodded.

"Go ahead with your report, Lieutenant," he directed the tall young officer holding the light.

"Yes, sir. As I told you before, I worked on the arms inventory with Captain Haviland today. We finished just as it got dark. As we left to go off duty, Captain Haviland mentioned he was concerned because some of the figures we'd listed on our inventory didn't match the quartermaster's numbers. He said he was going back inside the bunker to recheck a few things, but it wouldn't take long, and I could go off duty."

"Did you see Captain Haviland go back inside the bunker?" Trace asked.

"Yes, sir. He took a lantern with him. I was on my way to the mess tent a minute or two later when I heard the first explosion."

"And neither you nor anyone else, to your knowledge, saw Captain Haviland come out of the bunker before or after the first explosion?'' Trace's voice was grave.

"No, sir. I didn't see him. I've asked around and haven't found anyone else who did either."

"This body was taken from the destroyed bunker. Do you believe it's Captain Haviland?'' Trace pointed toward the covered form on the ground, but he kept his eyes on Christa.

"Yes, sir. The captain must have stumbled with the lamp and accidentally started the fire."

"Do you wish to ask this officer any questions, Mrs. Haviland?'' Trace asked formally, though his tone was less stern than when he had addressed the lieutenant.

Christa shook her head and continued to stare at the shape on the ground.

"Thank you, Lieutenant. You're dismissed. Give your written report to General Zachary in the morning." Trace returned the other man's salute and took the lantern from him.

"I want to see his body,'' Christa said when they were alone, her voice hardly above a whisper.

"Christa—"

"I want to see his body,'' she repeated more firmly.

Against his better judgment, Trace set the lantern down on the scorched grass and bent to pull back the blanket. Christa wrapped her arms around herself to try to fortify herself against the sight.

The horribly burned corpse was Nevin's size in height and build, but no hair or facial features remained. The stiff limbs and torso were covered with charred flesh.

"My God . . .'' Christa gasped, swaying against Trace. He caught her in his arms just as she went limp, swept her up, and carried her away from the gruesome scene.

* * *

Christa didn't know how she would have managed without Trace's help. He arranged everything necessary to transport Nevin's body to Haviland Court and rode with her in the family carriage during the long journey from Kip's Bay. They spoke little, but having Trace seated across from her, exhibiting strength and calm control, helped her greatly.

When Isabelle, Winston, and all the household servants gathered in the main parlor to hear the story of Nevin's death, Christa faltered in her words, overcome by grief. Trace finished the narrative, easing even that burden for her.

Now he stood behind her, watching Nevin's body being laid to rest in the family cemetery on the small rise near the estate. Late afternoon sun cast long shadows behind the bleached stone markers of several generations of Havilands who'd already ended their sojourn in life.

A gentle breeze touched Christa's face and carried the Anglican priest's eulogy to the hundred people gathered together on the grassy knoll. The Havilands were an old and respected family. A son who died in the service of his king deserved an honorable and reverent funeral.

Tears spilled from Christa's eyes as she tried to concentrate on the priest's words. The protective numbness that had pervaded her being over the last two days was fading, letting disbelief, grief, confusion, and fear seep into her consciousness. So many emotions were jumbled together inside her. This funeral was all a bad dream. Soon she'd wake up and find none of it was happening. Nevin would be alive. She'd be his wife. Love would grow between them. They'd have children, a wonderful life together. This was just a nightmare.

Agony caused Christa's senses to reel. When she swayed and almost lost her balance, she felt an arm come around her. Glancing sideways, she saw that her mother was trying to help her bear up. Elspeth Kendall smiled meekly at her daughter as she held her around the waist.

Christa tried to smile back in gratitude. Her dear mother. Small in stature and grown plump with the passage of years, she was gentle and loving in nature. Sometimes it seemed to Christa that she'd changed places with her maternal parent—that it was her mother who was now the dependent child.

But Christa was glad for her mother's comforting arm. She mustn't lose her grip on her emotions for fear of upsetting her mother. She must be strong.

Olivia Zachary stood on Christa's other side. She, too, put a hand on Christa's arm in a supportive gesture.

Clothed in the black of mourning and standing sedately next to her husband with her head bowed, Isabelle Sheffield presented the picture of a grieving sister. Yet her eyes weren't on her deceased brother's wooden coffin. Through the thick black veil of her hat, she watched, undetected, the man who really interested her.

Captain Trace Cavanaugh looked ruggedly handsome in his dress uniform of the elite Royal Artillery. The dark blue knee-length flared coat with red-and-gold trimming contrasted boldly with the whiteness of the vest and breeches. Very tight-fitting breeches, Isabelle noted with a raised eyebrow.

They'd all seen a good bit of this dark-featured British captain since he'd arrived with Christa two days ago. With an authoritative efficiency, he'd seen to the details of arranging Nevin's burial. Isabelle was glad of that, since Christa seemed to be in such a grief-

tricken state. Isabelle herself didn't want to be
bothered with arranging anything. She found the whole
ceremony a distasteful annoyance and was having difficulty feigning bereavement over her brother's death
when she really felt overjoyed by the turn of events.

Isabelle studied Trace's broad shoulders, the chisled
line of his square jaw, the mesmerizing turquoise of
his eyes. She had been disappointed when her lover,
Lee Garrett, had departed from Haviland Court the
same morning Christa had traveled to Kip's Bay. But
here was handsome Captain Trace Cavanaugh to
consider. Winston was about to leave on an ocean
voyage to Spain on business, and Trace Cavanaugh
might be just the man to assuage her loneliness while
he was away.

Isabelle repressed her smile of anticipation as she
continued to watch Trace like a hawk circling its prey.

Chapter 22

By early evening, most of the guests had paid the respects to Christa and the rest of the family, an departed. Christa's mother and maiden aunt would b staying at Haviland Court for several days, and they' already retired to their rooms in the guest wing. Olivi Zachary was one of the last visitors to leave.

"You should try to get some rest, Christa," th older woman admonished with concern. "You've ha a terrible shock, yet you've borne up nobly. Please tak care of yourself, my dear. I'll stop by tomorrow."

Christa nodded in gratitude as Olivia bent and kisse her on the cheek before leaving the front parlor.

"Mrs. Zachary's advice is sound, Mrs. Haviland," Trace concurred. He kept his manner polite, as he ha during all the time he'd been spending with Christa but it was becoming increasingly difficult to maintai a formal demeanor. Looking at her sitting in the wing backed armchair, he noticed the lines of strain an fatigue on her lovely face and thought about how she'd, indeed, been strong these last two days. Sh hadn't wept in front of anyone, except briefly at th gravesite. He remembered seeing the liquid blue-gra of her eyes and the streaks on her cheeks from he tears. She must be terribly broken inside, yet she kep an outward control and dignity he couldn't help bu admire.

"Well, I agree," Isabelle exclaimed, rising from the divan. "We've all had a very long day. I'm glad it's over. Go up to bed now, Christa. Your bereavement has obviously drained you. You look terrible."

"We should retire as well, Isabelle," Winston stated, moving toward the double doors.

"In a few minutes, Winston. I wish to speak to Captain Cavanaugh." Isabelle kept her gaze on Trace, ignoring her husband's scowl. "I hope you'll be able to stay on for a day or two, Captain, so we might repay your kindness with hospitality." Keeping her back to her husband, Isabelle flashed Trace a provocative smile.

"I was glad to be of service, Mrs. Sheffield," he replied with polite formality, pretending not to notice her barely cloaked invitation. "I regret to say that I must leave at dawn tomorrow. My orders from General Zachary regarding Mrs. Haviland and her deceased husband have been fulfilled."

Isabelle fought to hide her disappointment. His coolness whetted her interest in him, but she took care not to reveal that fact in her husband's presence.

Christa also grew uneasy at Trace's words. He'd been such a source of strength during this agonizing time. What would she do when he was gone?

As if feeling her glance upon him, Trace turned to Christa. "I know this is a difficult time for you, Mrs. Haviland, but since I must leave first thing in the morning, may I trouble you for the information about the saltpeter mine?" He kept his gaze steadily on her, trying not to notice the gentle curve of her soft lips.

"Yes, of course. It's the least I can do in return for all you have done for me," Christa answered quietly, remembering the mine for the first time since she'd spoken of it to Trace at the encampment. "The information is in the study."

"I thought Lee Garrett was looking into the mine," Isabelle commented.

"I've been ordered to investigate that matter," Trace explained. "If I may, Mrs. Haviland, I'll accompany you to the study for those papers. Excuse us." He gave a curt nod toward the Sheffields, then left with Christa.

Isabelle stared after them, a thoughtful look on her face. "Our plans are progressing marvelously, Winston," she declared as she closed the parlor doors for privacy. "We're happily rid of that worthless brother of mine, yet we didn't have anything to do with his death. But I did want to have a hand in his destruction myself. I feel somehow cheated. Nevertheless, we must take such windfalls as they come. With Nevin out of the way, our plans to gain control of the Haviland holdings can move forward even more quickly. We must find out more about this mine business of Christa's."

"Yes," Winston agreed, coming over to her. "To find a good source of potassium nitrate now would, indeed, be most profitable."

"And that is my ultimate goal—to increase my fortune, to wield the power that money can buy. I want that more than anything else in the world."

"*We* want that, Isabelle," Winston reminded her, pulling her roughly to him. "Just remember, my dear, we're in this together. You can't accomplish all your goals without me. Never think you can, Isabelle. Don't even dream of taking other partners—in anything. I'm quite selfish in that. What's mine is mine. We'll succeed together—only together." He brought his mouth down hard over his wife's lips and pressed her to him so tightly that a gasp escaped her.

Christa and Trace stood alone in Orin Haviland's cherry-paneled study. Flickering lamplight cast wavering shadows over the book-lined walls and finely crafted furnishings of the spacious room.

"Please sit down, Captain," Christa said, gesturing toward a round-backed, black leather armchair as she went to a mahogany desk.

While Christa looked through the contents of a drawer, Trace watched her intently. Her back was to him, but he could see her lovely features reflected in an oval gilt-edged mirror hanging on the wall. The glow from the lamp wasn't bright enough to reveal the lines of strain that had shown on her face earlier in the parlor. Here, the light accentuated her delicate cheekbones, the fragile arch of her eyebrows, the appealing curve of her lips. Trace forced himself to stop staring when she turned and spoke to him.

"Yes, here is the portfolio about the mine." She handed Trace a thin, brown leather case tied with a cloth ribbon. "I brought my father's private papers here after he died, to facilitate execution of the estate."

"That would be Montclaire," Trace commented as he accepted the portfolio from her. At Christa's questioning look, he explained, "General Zachary told me something of your family, at my request."

"Then you must know my father took his life two years ago, leaving Montclaire steeped in debt. It's no secret." Christa spoke quietly and lowered her head. When she looked up again, Trace saw that her chin had risen and her shoulders had straightened.

"To speak honestly, Captain, many of those debts remain unpaid. My husband . . ." Her voice dropped, and she took a slow, fortifying breath before she could go on. "My husband helped, of course, but I'm no longer certain if that financial assistance will continue, now that . . . Now."

"I understand," Trace said gently. "I regret I had to remind you of these matters."

"No, it's all right, Captain. I must confide in someone, and you've been such a great help these past few days. I find it easy to talk with you. It's entirely up to me to save Montclaire. My brother, Myron, is my father's heir, but he is an incapacitated invalid. My dear mother and aunt have no understanding of such matters." Christa's chin rose a notch higher. "I *shall not* lose my family home, Captain. Since profit from the saltpeter mine would greatly help pay our debts, I must ask you to take the greatest of care in investigating the mine's potential. Of course, I hope to help our sovereign's cause as well."

Trace was mesmerized by the determination shining in Christa's glistening eyes. He knew what it meant to value a family heritage, knew why Christa wanted to preserve hers now.

Conflicting emotions twisted inside him. He had his own reasons for wanting this mine to be made workable, but they didn't include bringing profit to Christa Haviland or saltpeter to the British. The mine would help bring him closer to achieving the goal that had dominated his life for years, perhaps even precipitate the destructive climax he sought for his enemy, Fitzhugh Zachary. And he'd serve his country at the same time—the fledgling nation for which he fought in secret.

Still, Christa's expression held such trust and vulnerability. It aroused unexpected feelings in him—protectiveness, and a desire to help in any way he could, no matter what the consequences. Why was she affecting him so strongly? Where was his long-held focus on his ambitions?

Trace forced aside the impulse to go to her. He couldn't allow himself to become involved with a woman. Too much was at stake, his plans for vengeance at too crucial a point. He needed to keep his concentration fixed solidly on those efforts. And to do that, he had to get away from Christa Haviland—*now*.

He didn't like using her, deceiving her. But attaining his goal overrode all other considerations. He'd learned very early in life to use his intelligence and cunning to gain what he wanted, to take the upper hand before someone else stole the opportunity. That philosophy had gained him much in wealth and prestige.

He could no longer hold Christa's gaze. He made himself turn and pick up the leather case from the chair, tucking it under his arm. His uneasiness made his tone very formal as he spoke.

"I'm honored you feel you can confide in me, Mrs. Haviland. Be assured that I shall carry out this investigation to the best of my abilities. Now, since I'll be leaving Haviland Court at daybreak tomorrow and have no wish to disturb you then, I'll bid you farewell at this time."

Christa was confused by the sudden change in him. Had she misread the friendship and compassion she'd seen in his eyes over these last few days? Now he seemed to have withdrawn from her, to have put up an invisible barrier between them. She couldn't let him leave without trying to reestablish their earlier warmth.

"Captain Cavanaugh . . . Trace." She stepped forward and put a hand on his arm to stop him from turning toward the door. "Before you go, I must express my deep gratitude for all you've done for me during this very difficult period. I don't know how I could have managed without your help. You've given me strength. Your friendship is of great value to me. I . . . I shall miss you."

Trace tensed under her touch. He could feel the pressure of her hand on his coat sleeve as though she were touching his bare flesh. *Gratitude*, *friendship*— those were the words she used, the emotions she felt.

What else did he expect her to feel right now? What did *he* feel?

I wish to hell I knew, Trace cursed to himself, masking his own inner turmoil with a passive expression. He was so occupied by controlling his thoughts that he was barely aware that his other hand had moved to cover Christa's on his arm.

"I was glad to be of service," he replied awkwardly. "My condolences again for the loss of your husband."

Simultaneously they both seemed to realize they were touching each other. Christa looked down and slowly withdrew her hand.

"M—my thanks again," she stammered in confusion, glancing back up at him. "Godspeed and goodbye . . . Trace."

He held her gaze, wanting to say more to her, but the words wouldn't come. "Good-bye, Christa," he murmured finally.

The big room seemed strangely empty without Trace's presence. Christa absently rubbed her hand where he'd touched it and stared through the open doorway, watching Trace walk down the long hall. After a moment, he turned to go up the staircase. Not once did he look back.

Chapter 23

October and November of 1776 held few victories for the Continental army. General George Washington's rebel forces experienced defeats under British Generals William Howe and Charles Cornwallis in New York and in New Jersey, at Pell's Point, White Plains, Fort Washington, and Fort Lee. The rebels were driven out of Canada on the American northern front. At the Battle of Valcour Bay, the British swept General Benedict Arnold's American flotilla from Lake Champlain.

In early December, Howe declared his campaign at an end for the winter and sent the bulk of his forces back to New York, leaving garrisons at Trenton, Princeton, and Bordentown.

To avoid capture by the enemy, the Continental Congress moved from Philadelphia to Annapolis, Maryland. Washington's army was on the verge of collapse as morale plummeted with each defeat that forced the troops to retreat across New Jersey and into Pennsylvania. Disease, lack of supplies, desertions, and indifference on the part of the Congress and many people of the Colonies threatened to cause the army's undoing.

In a blinding snowstorm on Christmas night, General Washington attempted a bold retaliation by crossing the Delaware River with his Regulars and launching a surprise attack at Trenton, New Jersey, against an encampment of Hessian mercenaries, allies of the British. In the ensuing battle, the Americans defeated the hated Hessians. That victory brought a much-needed surge in enlistments in the Continental army.

A second victory over a British force, at Princeton in early January of 1777, further raised American spirits. Washington led his exhausted but heartened troops into winter quarters in the hills around Morristown, New Jersey.

"So His Majesty's much-touted easy victory over the Continentals has been stayed again," Christa murmured aloud as she put aside the newspaper from which she'd been reading the details of Washington's lastest triumph. She sighed, rising from the gold brocade divan to stretch her legs.

Her bedchamber had been a comforting haven during the three long months of her widowhood. The bright yellow silk wallpaper and white scalloped cornices and woodwork helped to dispel the gloom and heaviness of spirit she often felt.

Going to the corner desk, she picked up a printed pamphlet entitled *Common Sense*, which she'd read earlier. Its author, the firebrand journalist Thomas Paine, vehemently espoused the cause of American independence and freedom from British rule. The publication was only one of many writings Christa had read and contemplated over these past months. Such activities helped fill the empty hours that weren't occupied with supervising the household. The proprieties of widowhood required that she stay in relative seclusion while she struggled to bear the burden of a suitable mourning period.

Christa had a different view of the American cause now. She'd learned that the kings of the British Empire had given the Colonies a large measure of self-rule during the two hundred years since colonization was first established in the New World. The current ruler, King George III, was attempting to restrict the freedoms Americans had come to consider their inalienable rights. The king and the Parliament, the governing body in Great Britain, imposed heavy taxes and regulations on many aspects of American life and business without giving the Colonials a voice in Parliament. "No taxation without representation" was now the battle cry for the staunch advocates of independence.

Christa saw merit in the patriot cause, yet she felt pulled in two directions, for she still tended to be drawn to King George and the motherland by culture and family heritage.

Turning toward the window, she drew back a panel of the white velvet draperies and peered outside. Large white flakes floated peacefully down on the windless air. The ground was already covered with several inches of snow, leaving the landscape glistening and white.

Christa wished her darkened spirits could be brightened as easily. She felt a terrible void in her life. She told herself the loss of her husband had left her so empty inside, so lacking in direction. Yet in her heart, she knew the hollow feeling had existed in her even before Nevin's death.

"Miz Christa," a voice called from the hall.

"Come in, Letty."

The servant entered the bedchamber waving a cream-colored envelope in her hand.

"A letter done come fo' you. I think it be from that nice Mr. Desmond." Her pleased expression was topped by a wide grin as she handed the letter to Christa. "So you bin readin' these here newspapers agin, ah sees, tryin' to learn all 'bout this here war."

Letty bent to gather the papers into a neater pile. "Ah don' put no stock in areadin' all the time. That kin only git a body stirred up an' bothered. That be why ah ain't let you teach me readin' an' writin'. Ah gits in 'nough trouble 'round here as it is. An' readin' won' help git this here war done an' over. It's only the captains an' admiral an' such what kin shake hands an' say quits to all this here fightin'."

"Yes, Letty, you're so right. Only the leaders can finally end it," Christa replied absently as she broke the seal on the letter.

"Anythin' more in them papers 'bout that there gang o' rebel spies you was tellin' me 'bout?" Letty went on chattering. "Ah think it be downright excitin' how everythin's so secret an' all, an' they got all them code names. That there one what everybody's done callin' the Scorpion shor' must be a brassy sort. The scullery maids in the kitchen was jus' this mornin' talkin' 'bout him. They's imaginin' all sorts o' things—that he be han'some an' young an' brave. Ah done scolded 'em good 'bout it, tellin' 'em not to fo'git he's a enemy workin' agin the king. That put their flappin' jaws shut, ah'm tellin' you."

"No, there wasn't anything more in the newspapers about the Scorpion," Christa answered her, smiling a little at her maid's prattling.

Letty sidled up to Christa and peered over her shoulder. "Mr. Desmond shor' do write nice, don't he? What's he say?"

"Yes, he does have a fine hand, Miss Nosey." Christa smiled again at Letty's forwardness, but she was used to it. "He says he can't come for his visit on Sunday."

"Well, more's the pity. That be a real shame," Letty commented with real disappointment. "It be good company fo' you to have him comin' each week, Miz

Christa. Ah purely don' know how you stands it 'round
here these days. Miz Isabelle seems to be goin' out o'
her way even more'n usual to be mean to you.''

Christa didn't need to be reminded of her sister-in-
law's spitefulness. She experienced many examples of
it each day. She also felt disappointed because business
was taking Marcus out of the city, and he'd have to
miss their weekly visit.

He'd recovered quickly from his wound, but retained
a slight limp. He made it a point to visit each Sunday,
coming as a friend offering condolences and legal
advice. Christa's position in the Haviland family
remained tenuous, and she needed his support and
counsel.

"That nice Mr. Desmond," Letty was going on
wistfully. "Now it be purely plain fo' all o' us to see
that he do care 'bout you, Miz Christa. Ah kin see it
in his eyes whenever he look at you. Ah don' reckon
he's done said nothin' 'bout his feelin's to you yet,
'cuz of him bein' a real gentleman an' you bein' in
mournin' an' all. But the time's acomin' when you
should be thinkin' 'bout pickin' up yo' life agin. You
is a right beautiful woman, Miz Christa, an' only
twenty-three. You can't be mournin' Mr. Nevin
fo'ever.''

"Oh, Letty, I'm just not ready yet. It's too soon.''
Christa sighed heavily as she sat down in the straight-
backed desk chair. She knew Letty was right about
Marcus Desmond. He was always polite and restrained
in his manner, but Christa knew his feelings for her
were deepening. Yet she didn't know how she felt
about him. She was grateful for his friendship, his
caring. But so many emotions churned inside her
regarding her husband, feelings she was still trying to
sort out.

"Was there anything else in the post, Letty?"
Christa went on, trying to focus on a different subject.

"Jus' this other letter." Letty pulled a white
envelope out of her apron pocket. "Ah don' know who
it be from. The writin' weren't that o' anybody I
knows."

Christa used her silver letter opener on the waxed
seal. When she unfolded the single sheet of matching
paper inside, her heart gave a start. At the bottom of
the page, the signature of the sender seemed to jump
out at her. Trace Cavanaugh.

In all this time, she'd received only one brief letter
from him, stating that he'd located the potassium
nitrate mine and was hopeful as to its potential produc-
tivity. He'd expressed his condolences again, but in a
most formal manner.

Christa quickly read this latest missive from him.

Dear Mrs. Haviland,

This is to inform you that repairs to the shafting
structure of the mine are progressing well. Ample
evidence indicates the existence of potassium nitrate
deposits.

Legal documents must be executed authorizing
production. In one week's time, I shall send said
documents to you for the proper signatures.

                        Respectfully,
                        Trace Cavanaugh
                        Captain, Royal Artillery

Sending the papers, not bringing them himself.
Christa was startled by the disappointment she felt. She
didn't like admitting there was another reason for her
recent turmoil, yet Trace Cavanaugh often stole into
her thoughts. She couldn't forget all they'd been
through during those few short days back in October.

How well she remembered his patriotism, his courage, his kindness toward her. His handsomeness . . .

Christa blinked in surprise. Sometimes she hated her perfect memory. Now it caused Trace's rugged features to come into sharp focus in her mind's eye. She had to wipe them away, for whenever she thought about him, a baffling perplexity came over her.

"Now who could that be?" Letty perked up at a sound coming from outside and went to the window to pull back the drapes. "Why, it be a coach down in the drive. Somebody's done come avisitin'. Wonder who it could be?"

Suddenly she gasped.

"Lord a'mighty, Miz Christa, it's the master!" The woman's dark eyes were wide with dismay when she looked back at her mistress. "Lord have mercy on us, Mr. Orin done come home!"

Chapter 24

Christa tried to sit perfectly still in the round-backed black leather armchair, but doing so was very difficult. The mid-morning sunlight of the January day filtered through the long, narrow windows across the room, but didn't reach Christa, who would have welcomed its warmth to ease her pangs of apprehension. Her hands felt clammy and fidgety as she clutched them together in her lap. The master's study, with its rich cherry paneling and sturdy furnishings, usually gave her a sense of solidness and security, but she experienced no such feelings as she sat opposite Orin Haviland on this day. Her formidable father-in-law paid her no heed for the moment, as he gave his attention to some documents in his hand. His three-hundred-pound bulk seemed to dwarf the mahogany desk at which he sat.

The patriarch of the Haviland family had returned from England only yesterday, but already his intimidating presence had changed the atmosphere of the household. The servants went quickly and quietly about their tasks, giving more than the usual effort to each labor. They spoke in whispers behind their hands, their eyes darting in furtive glances.

Christa shared their uneasiness. She, too, had been glad of Orin Haviland's absence from the estate during the months he'd remained in England overseeing the Haviland shipping enterprises there. He'd taken Isabelle and Winston's eight-year-old son, Harvard, with him to arrange for the boy's education at a prestigious English boarding school. But Orin Haviland was never away from Haviland Court any longer than necessary. Christa felt he didn't trust other people to manage his affairs.

Winston's trip to Spain had also made for more tranquil conditions around the estate, although Isabelle's tyrannical behavior had often made up for both men's absences.

Christa gathered her courage to face this meeting called by her father-in-law, knowing that her future and the fate of her family and Montclaire might be determined in the next hour.

She tried to distract herself while she waited. Moving her hands to the curved arms of the leather chair, she suddenly pictured Trace Cavanaugh sitting in exactly the same chair three months ago. She remembered how he'd helped her then, when Nevin's death was so new and painful. Trace had shared his strength and compassion and given her courage to endure those terrible first days. Perhaps thinking of him now would help her.

In her mind, she pictured him so clearly. His muscularly powerful six-foot frame, which she'd seen all too completely at Suko Yamagata's. The ruby ring hanging from the gold chain around his neck. His wavy chestnut-colored hair damp with rain. And his haunting turquoise eyes overshadowing his ruggedly handsome features.

Unexpectedly, she remembered, too, the feel of his lips on hers just before they'd parted in the stableyard. The vividness of the memory startled her, making her grip the leather armrests and wish her memory were not so flawless. She was glad when Isabelle entered the study just then, followed by Ambrose.

"A messenger arrived very early, madam," the elderly majordomo was saying as he trailed after Isabelle. "It seems that Captain Garrett will be delayed in his arrival until later this morning."

Christa cringed. This was the first she'd heard that Lee Garrett was expected at Haviland Court. They hadn't seen much of him during the last month, and Christa had been glad of that.

"Very well," Isabelle acknowledged with her usual curtness as she put the fine porcelain teacup she'd carried in with her on the edge of a round maple table. "You're dismissed, Ambrose. Heavens, Father, couldn't we have had this meeting later? Why, I've barely had a chance to drink my morning tea, let alone eat breakfast. You've only just arrived home after all these months away. Must you think of business already?" She offered no greeting to Christa.

Orin Haviland stood to his full six-foot-five-inch height as he turned toward his daughter. He was a huge man who, at the age of fifty-six, carried a significant position of his weight in a well-rounded stomach and rolling layers of jowls about the neck. His face was set in an habitually stern expression.

"You know I am *always* thinking of business, Isabelle." His deep voice boomed over the spacious room. "This damned war has made a shambles of too many enterprises. But because of my foresight and diligence, the many Haviland interests in England haven't been adversely affected yet. I trust that's been the case here as well."

"There have been some difficulties, Father," Isabelle said nonchalantly, though she shifted her gaze away. "After all, the war is taking place *here*, not in England. Many things have been affected by it."

"But, as you well know from my tutelage," Orin

continued, "there is always profit to be gained from such circumstances."

"And that's exactly what you'll find I've tried to accomplish, with Winston's help, of course. He's still away in Spain trying to negotiate agreements with new buyers for our textiles." Isabelle picked up four leather-bound books from the table and handed them to her father. "You'll want to see these ledgers, I'm certain. In your absence, Winston and I and your barristers were careful guardians of the Haviland enterprises here. We did find opportunities for profit and pursued them, as you allowed."

"That sounds reassuring enough." Orin Haviland's steel blue gaze held his daughter's unwaveringly. "But I'll give very careful scrutiny to these accounting books nonetheless."

"I expected no less," Isabelle replied, showing no sign of being intimidated by her father. "Winston and I did everything," she went on haughtily. "Nevin gave us no assistance whatsoever when he was alive. He cared nothing about what happened to the Haviland fortunes. Instead, he wanted to play soldier. And look what that got him—quite dead. Your heir is gone. You only have my Harvard for a blood heir now. You see, Father, I've always done what's best for you and the family."

"Unless Christa is pregnant." Orin Haviland spoke the startling statement so unexpectedly, it was a second or two before Christa even realized that his attention had shifted to her.

"She can't be pregnant!" Isabelle blurted angrily, rising to her feet. "Nevin was gone most of the time. And he showed very little interest in her when he *was* here. How could *she* ever satisfy a man, let alone a Haviland? You know fully well, Father, Nevin only married her to please you. We all knew Nevin required new women all the time to satisfy him. Why, how many servant girls have we had to dismiss over the years because of his indiscretions? That Maxwell girl—that insipid Charity—was trouble enough before you got rid of her. Nevin seemed to be particularly taken with that little tart of a maid. You didn't know, Father, but he continued to carry on with her—expressly against your wishes—even after he married Christa. We all knew it. It was a joke to him, a way to defy you. He made no secret of it, except to you. And to Christa, who was too stupid to see what was happening right under her nose." She turned her cold, dark eyes on Christa in a disdainful look.

The cutting edge of Isabelle's cruel tirade slashed into Christa with a force as powerful as a blow. She stared at her sister-in-law in shock. She'd heard murmurings among the household servants about Nevin's interest in other women, but she'd always dismissed such talk as groundless gossip.

"But perhaps Christa was aware of Nevin's sexual exploits," Isabelle continued with a note of triumph, "and she chose to overlook them because she had lovers of her own. If she does claim to be pregnant, you can't believe it's Nevin's child, Father. She likely doesn't know who the father is herself. She's had many lovers. Winston saw her behind the stables blatantly kissing one of them when she returned from a tryst one morning a few months ago. And that was when Nevin was still alive!" Isabelle smiled and folded her arms across her chest.

"Well, speak up, Christa. How do you answer my daughter's accusations?" Orin demanded, aiming his frowning gaze directly at her.

Christa was speechless. Her mind whirled in confusion under Isabelle's vicious verbal attack. She was innocent, she knew. Isabelle was lying, but how could she explain what Winston had witnessed? He must have seen Trace's farewell kiss the morning they returned from the cave. How could she explain herself?

Isabelle's cruel barbs stabbed at Christa. Had Nevin betrayed her with other women? She didn't remember the Maxwell girl.

"See, she doesn't even try to deny anything because she knows it's all true!" Isabelle stated, smug with satisfaction. "Pregnant, indeed! Just let her try to claim she carries a Haviland heir in her belly."

Christa tried to get a grip on herself, but she couldn't with Orin and Isabelle staring at her so menacingly. She felt trapped. Summoning up a reserve of courage, she rose to her feet and stubbornly lifted her chin.

"Your accusations are outrageous. I shall not dignify them with an explanation."

Then she turned on her heel and walked swiftly from the study, slamming the door shut behind her. Lifting her skirts, she ran up the wide, winding staircase and didn't stop until she reached her bedroom. Locking the door securely behind her, she leaned against it for support. She knew she'd escaped Orin and Isabelle only temporarily. She'd have to answer their cruel accusations eventually. But she needed time to think first. After she'd had a chance to calm down and gain her composure, she'd try to talk to her father-in-law alone—without the presence of malicious Isabelle.

How could she gain Orin Haviland's good graces? She wasn't pregnant, that she knew. Her father-in-law was a hard man. He'd wanted her to produce Haviland heirs from the very beginning of her marriage to Nevin. Now that there was no chance that a child would be conceived, he'd have no further use for her, no reason to let her stay at Haviland Court. What would become of her? What would happen to her mother, her aunt? Her invalid brother? Orin would discover Nevin had been giving her money to meet her family's many debts and would withdraw that support. And without Haviland money Montclaire would be lost.

The stirring of air she'd caused by bursting into the bedchamber had sent several papers fluttering off her writing desk. Sighing deeply in despair, Christa went to where they'd fallen to the hardwood floor and gathered them up. Marcus's letter was on top.

Christa thought of her dear friend. Perhaps she could turn to him for help. He'd offered it often enough. But would accepting his assistance obligate her to give him more than just gratitude? She knew Marcus wanted a wife.

"No, not marriage. Not another man, not yet," Christa murmured aloud to the empty room. She was more confused than ever about her feelings, especially those concerning her dead husband. Isabelle's terrible words must be lies, but in her heart Christa wondered.

She and Nevin had never been close. They had shared a marriage bed, but he had given her only his body, never his heart. She realized that now. Perhaps she'd been guilty of the same thing. They'd never shared their innermost selves with each other, their hopes, fears, dreams. Was that estrangement the reason for the nagging emptiness she had always felt, the feeling that something wasn't right between them? Had she really known her husband? Had Nevin ever had any ambitions besides getting the upper hand over his domineering father? He'd spoken of that often enough—of besting his father in some way.

Christa sat down on the divan, trying to sort out her thoughts. Her glance fell on the second letter she'd received yesterday. Trace Cavanaugh's.

Christa studied the precise script. His confidence and boldness showed in the strong, unwavering strokes across the vellum. Trace. He was at the mine.

The potassium nitrate mine would be going into production soon, Trace had said in his letter. Christa's heart began to pound faster as she made a decision. She'd leave Haviland Court and go to the mine to sign the papers Trace needed. That would save time and might allow production to begin sooner. And she would get away from Orin and Isabelle. If she left for a few days, she could delay the inevitable confrontation with Orin Haviland until she was better prepared to answer him. And she could also avoid seeing Lee Garrett.

Christa gave a hard yank on the bell cord to summon Letty to pack. Then she opened the wardrobe and took out a maroon riding skirt and fur-lined jacket. While she decided what clothing to take on the journey, she didn't let herself think about the fact that going to the mine to sign the documents would bring her face to face with Trace Cavanaugh once again.

Chapter 25

Christa was ready to leave within an hour. "Where are my leather gloves, Letty?" she asked with impatience as she took a last-minute inventory of what she needed.

"Ah declare, but you is purely outta yo' wits to think o' doin' this," Letty exclaimed, shaking her head as she retrieved the gloves Christa wanted. "Mr. Orin's goin' to have a fit o' apoplexy when he done hear 'bout this. It be purely dangerous fo' you to be ridin' 'bout the countryside. An' a mine ain't no place fo' a lady no how."

"This is business, Letty. I'll be fine. The war's at a standstill. Both sides are in winter quarters. There are no battles. Now stop clucking at me like a mother hen and close that valise."

As Christa swung her fur-lined maroon cloak around her shoulders and slipped her fingers into her matching gloves, she hoped she sounded confident. She told herself there wouldn't be any danger, but just as a precaution, she hid a small, two-shot pistol in the side pocket of her riding skirt.

"I'll return tomorrow or the day after at the latest," she went on as she took the tapestry valise from her maid.

"Miz Christa, please—" Letty began to protest again, but Christa stopped her.

"I'm going, Letty. No more arguments. Now don't worry, please. I'll be all right." Christa gave her maid a quick, affectionate hug, then she left the bedchamber.

Abel Sherwood, the stockily built twenty-year-old groom who accompanied Christa on riding excursions, had Moonstar and his own mount waiting. As he secured Christa's valise on his saddle, he coughed several times.

"Are you ill, Abel?" Christa asked with concern.

"It ain't nothin', ma'am."

"Very well, if you're certain. Let's be on our way."

The morning was crisply cold, pristinely clear. Christa reined Moonstar out of the stableyard and deeply inhaled the sharp January air, smiling. It felt wonderful to be outdoors with her fine mare beneath her. They should reach their destination in about four hours, if her memory of the route served her well. She had no map. She'd given the only one to Trace.

Isabelle frowned as she watched Christa's departure from her second-story bedroom window.

"Now what are you up to?" she murmured as she held back the green drapery. "I thought you gave up riding while you were in mourning for my worthless brother."

Isabelle was still pleased with herself for the way the session in the study had gone with her father.

"You're no match for me at all, sweet sister-in-law," she went on aloud, smiling with satisfaction as she recalled how easily Christa had been cowed. "Your days at Haviland Court are numbered, you wretched creature. I've had to endure your irksome presence in this house long enough. A few more sessions with Father like the one we just had, and we'll soon see you gone for good." Isabelle tossed back her long auburn hair and gave a short laugh. "I'll add Montclaire to my holdings, too, as soon as I've procured all the notes of credit against it.''

Everything was going so well—the business acquisitions, the treachery. She hated sharing her wealth and power with Winston, but it was necessary. He was helping her accomplish what she wanted most—to take over her father's financial empire. But she hadn't missed Winston while he was in Spain these last few months. Lee was keeping her most satisfied. But Winston would be returning soon. In fact, he should have been back by now. She and Lee would have to be more discreet about seeing each other.

Yes, everything was progressing wonderfully well. Nevin was dead. Christa would be out of the way soon. Isabelle smiled again. Her plan of revenge against her domineering father for all the cruel hurt he'd inflicted on her over the years was nearly ready to be executed. She must not let her impatience and hatred cloud her judgment now.

Isabelle squinted out the window again to try to follow Christa's course, but she was no longer in sight. She must know what Christa was doing, so that nothing would jeopardize her plans.

Crossing the spacious bedchamber, Isabelle went to the door of the dressing room. A young maid was cleaning the bathing tub.

''Aren't you finished with that yet, Dulcie?'' Isabelle demanded with annoyance. The eighteen-year-old girl jumped at the sound of her mistress's stern voice, spilling a tray of colognes and lotions with a clatter.

''You stupid girl! Why are you so clumsy?'' Isabelle's anger was only too apparent in her black look.

''I'm sorry, Miss Isabelle. Truly I am.'' The girl cowered under her mistress's reprimand.

''Oh, never mind. You can clean that up later. Go

find Letty, and send her to me immediately. Then wait downstairs for Captain Garrett's arrival. I want to know the minute he gets here. Well, don't just stand there! Hurry, you ninny.''

Dulcie jumped again at Isabelle's sharp tone, bobbed a quick curtsy, and hurried from the dressing room.

Chapter 26

Christa pulled her fur-lined cloak tighter around her to ward off the sharp wind as she reined in Moonstar at the top of a wooded rise and studied her surroundings for familiar landmarks. She was alone now. Abel's cold had worsened after they departed from Haviland Court, so she had insisted he stay and rest at an inn in Wooster. The mine was located not far from the small town. She'd set out to find it herself.

She spied a narrow stream below her, in a clearing. With a gentle urging, she guided Moonstar down the rocky slope, then dismounted to let the mare go to the water.

Christa was glad for the chance to stretch her legs. She hadn't ridden since Nevin's death, and she'd lost her fitness for it. The hours on horseback today were already making her stiff and sore.

As she rubbed the small of her back, a sound carrying on the wind caught her attention, arousing her concern. Approaching horses. Several of them pounding the ground. She was off the main road. No houses were anywhere in sight. This place was so isolated . . .

Sudden fear gripped her, making her go quickly to Moonstar. Taking up the loose reins, she led her horse behind an outcropping of high boulders. Holding Moonstar's muzzle, she stroked the mare's head, hoping to keep her quiet as the other horses came closer.

Six men topped the rise, then guided their mounts down the slope to the stream's edge a short distance away from Christa's hiding place.

"We ain't goin' to have no luck anymore t'day, Sergeant. Can't we head back to camp? At least there be a warm fire awaitin' there," bemoaned the first man to dismount.

"But nothin' to fill me empty innards or anybody else's either. You wanna go back to camp an' face Gen'r'l Washington with that news?" came the gruff reply from a bushy-bearded man who had stayed on his horse. The others grumbled their agreement. "Then we best get on with the foragin' after we water up here. I know of a farmhouse jus' north of here. Maybe we kin commandeer somethin' there."

Cold fear crept up Christa's spine as she watched and listened to the Continentals from her hiding place. If she were discovered now . . .

She'd forced herself to forget the horrible night when she and Trace had been captured by the deserters. Now the terrible memory came only too readily to mind. Her hand crept to the side pocket of her riding skirt and closed over the cold metal of the pistol she'd brought, but it gave her little courage, for she knew the weapon wouldn't be of much use against so many. With a further sinking feeling, she realized that this time there would be no Trace Cavanaugh or Wolfgang to save her.

"We best be gittin' to that farm," the sergeant urged, glancing at the sky. "Looks to be a storm abrewin'."

Christa was overcome with relief when the men remounted and started to leave. But at that moment, Moonstar snorted and tossed her head. Christa frantically grabbed the bridle and held the mare's nose to silence her.

"You hear somethin'?" The sergeant pulled up his horse and twisted around. The other five men reined in as well. Christa's heart almost stopped with fright. For a long moment, none of the men moved as they watched and listened.

"It weren't nothin', I guess, jus' the wind. C'mon, let's git movin'," the sergeant finally decided, spurring his horse up the hill. One man stayed a few seconds longer, scanning the woods around him, but then he, too, turned his horse to follow the others.

Christa's legs were shaking too hard to support her any longer. With her back pressed against the cold, hard stone, she slowly sank to the ground. Her mouth was dry and her heart was beating frantically as she closed her eyes and pressed a hand to her mouth in relief. So close. Such danger. How foolish she'd been to come alone.

"You're one *damned* fortunate woman!"

At the sound of the deep-timbred voice cutting sharply through the air, Christa's eyes flew wide in fright. Instinctively, she jumped to her feet, but slipped on the icy snow and fell hard on her backside. Wincing with pain, she glanced up to see a man reining in his horse. *Trace Cavanaugh!* He scowled menacingly at her as he jammed his pistol into his saddle holster and swung down from his mount.

"What the hell do you think you're doing riding out here alone?" he demanded as he impatiently thrust out a hand to help her up.

Feeling foolish, Christa let her temper flare. "I don't have to account for my actions to you, Captain Cavanaugh," she snapped, returning his glare.

Trace saw the defiance in Christa's smoke-blue eyes and had to fight to control his own temper. With forced calm, he answered, "That's quite true. You have every right to be as foolhardy as you wish. Please be about it. Good day." With that, he turned on his heel and strode to his horse, swinging up into the saddle with practiced ease.

Christa's mouth dropped open in surprise, then she paniced as she saw Trace turning his mount away to leave. With sudden fear, she found her voice. "Captain! Trace! Wait . . . please."

Trace pulled up his horse and looked back at her. "Yes, Mrs. Haviland?"

His manner was chillingly polite, making Christa feel like a child who'd been reprimanded.

"If you must know, I had a groom with me, but he was taken ill back in town. I was coming to the mine to see how the repairs were progressing and to sign the documents you told me about in your letter."

"I see. As owner, you have that right, of course. The mine is ahead on this road about three miles. I'm returning there now. Follow me and make haste. A storm's brewing."

Christa cringed at his superior tone. How she wished she could have mounted Moonstar and ridden in *any* direction other than to the mine. Her forehead creased in a deep frown as she saw Trace spur his horse to leave, showing no intention of coming to help her mount. A sudden gust of frigid wind whipped her cloak around her. She glanced at the churning sky. Its ominous grayness made her swallow her pride and anger and hurry to Moonstar. Mounting hastily, she gave the mare her head in trailing after Trace, and they soon left the stream and clearing behind them.

Chapter 27

Darkness had descended, and a sleeting rain had begun to fall, when Christa and Trace reached the mining site. Trace led the way to a small cabin, where he dismounted and came around to help Christa down from her horse.

"Go inside," he told her, speaking for the first time since they'd left the clearing, shouting above the sound of the wind. "I'll see to bedding down the horses." He turned to lead the animals away.

Christa hurried to the log house. Inside, she stumbled around in the dark until she finally found a candle and tinderbox. It was almost as cold inside as it had been outdoors. She kept her fur-lined cloak hugged tightly around her as she went to the hearth to start a fire. It was too cold to wait for Trace to come back and do it. Besides, she knew he'd expect her to tend to it.

The flame from the dry kindling was licking over the three birch logs stacked on the grate when Trace entered the cabin. Stomping his snow-covered riding boots by the door, he quickly removed his wet gloves and tricorn hat and came over to the fire to warm his hands.

"Are the horses all right?" Christa asked to fill the awkward silence.

"Yes. I gave them oats and water. The shed's small, but dry." His tone was curt.

"My thanks for seeing to Moonstar," Christa said sincerely. He gave a sharp nod as he held his hands over the growing flames.

Christa knew he was still angry at her brashness in coming to the mine camp. She, too, wished she hadn't acted so impulsively, for now, because of the storm, she must remain here with Trace.

Sighing in defeat, she looked around her. By the light of the fire, she could see the crude cabin more clearly now. There were few furnishings—only a narrow bed next to the fireplace, a rough-hewn wooden table, and three chairs in the middle of the room. A cooking stove and a tall wooden cupboard that had seen better days filled the far corner. Ragged remains of red curtains hung at the two windows.

Trace followed her gaze. "Hardly Haviland Court, is it?" he stated, sounding annoyed. "There are no other accommodations here, except for the bunkhouse where the men stay. I gave them all time off to go to town. Several necessary pieces of equipment haven't arrived, so we can't go ahead with the work."

"What needs to be done?" she managed to ask, forcing down her uneasiness at being alone with Trace.

"We still have one shaft to open and secure, but I anticipate that will take only two weeks to complete. Then we can start production. Damn it, Christa," Trace swore suddenly, grabbing her by the arms as he lost patience with the drivel of conversation, "why did you come here? Didn't you realize how dangerous such a venture could be? My God, don't you remember what nearly happened last autumn? You might have been brutally used by those men, or even killed!"

She was too surprised to do anything except instinctively try to pull away from his grasp and thunderous look.

"Y—yes, I remember," she stammered, held by his gaze. "I had to get away from Haviland Court. I just didn't think . . ." Her voice trailed off.

"You didn't think!" Trace echoed her words with exasperation. He wasn't thinking too clearly at the moment himself, he realized, because all he could visualize was the danger Christa had been in at the clearing. And the delicate line of her small chin as she stood so close to him now, her lips slightly parted . . .

"It was damned foolishness, woman!"

"I know. I realize that now." She lowered her eyes.

"Don't look contrite. I'm not finished bellowing at you yet!"

Christa raised her gaze to meet his again. He was still holding her arms.

"There's no need to continue yelling at me, Trace. I was frightened to death by the stream. I didn't know you were nearby. I've learned my lesson."

She'd called him "Trace." Not "Captain" or "Captain Cavanaugh," as she usually did. He liked hearing the sound of his Christian name on her lips.

"And if you'd known I was nearby?"

"I—I would've been less afraid. While I was hiding, I thought of how you saved me from those horrible deserters last fall."

"You seem to think me an extraordinary man to be able to take on a half-dozen armed soldiers single-handedly whenever you need to be rescued."

"And yet you would have done just that, wouldn't you?" Her liquid blue-gray eyes held his.

"Fool that I am . . . yes." Trace tried to sound scornful of himself, but the words came out much less severe. If only she'd stop looking at him like that—so steadily, so appealingly.

Christa saw that his face was wet from the sleet, his chestnut brown hair touseled over his forehead. The firelight flickered over his handsomely chiseled features and lighted his compelling eyes.

"No, not a fool, Trace," she whispered, stepping instinctively closer. "Never a fool."

Trace drew her to him and leaned down to meet her lips. The kiss was hesitant at first, exploring. The gentle pressure of his mouth caused wonderful new sensations to come to life in Christa. A warmth began to uncurl in her stomach and spread through every part of her.

Her nearness sent Trace's pulse racing. As the taste of her soft lips aroused a hunger in him for more of her, his kiss became more fervent. His senses were filled with her. He slid his hand along her back up to the damp tangles of her hair, and felt her tremble. Pressing his body against hers, he thought of nothing except the woman in his arms.

Chapter 28

Christa was breathless when she and Trace finally parted. Slowly she lifted her long, black-lashed eyes to look at him. They were still standing very close, encircled in each other's arms. She took a deep breath to ease her aching lungs and try to slow the rapid beating of her heart.

"You are an impetuous one, aren't you?" Trace murmured softly as a small smile touched the corners of his mouth.

Christa blushed with shame as the reality of what had just happened between them struck her. She desperately wanted to stay in Trace's strong, protective arms, but her conscience warned her of the impropriety, of the wantonness of being with him like this. Yet their kiss seemed so right, filled with a shared longing. She was surprised by the unfamiliar excitement it had aroused, and a little frightened, too.

Trace saw the flicker of changing emotions cross her features and wondered what she was thinking. His reason questioned his own potent reaction to their kiss, but he wouldn't listen to it. He wanted to savor these moments, draw them out.

"Christa . . ." He spoke her name gently as he started to draw her close again. But she pressed her hands against his chest to hold him at bay.

"No, Trace, please don't." As she tried to pull back

om him, she couldn't meet his gaze. "Please let me
)."

He released her, though he didn't want to. For
onths, Christa had filled his thoughts. His mind's eye
uld conjure up her lovely face in a moment. He'd
smissed his preoccupation with her as only a passing
ncy, knowing he'd desired many other women before
r. He'd stolen countless kisses as impulsively as he'd
ne just now with Christa. But something he couldn't
npoint made this kiss different. The uncertainty left
m guarded.

Christa sat down on the edge of the bed and stared
to the flames of the fire. "I shouldn't have come."

"You're right in that. It was very dangerous," he
;reed.

She peered at him over her shoulder. "In more ways
an I could have possibly imagined."

Trace ran a hand through his hair. "It was only a
ss, Christa. Just a crazy impulse. It meant nothing."
e couldn't meet her gaze.

"Yes, I know." She looked back at the flames again
 that he wouldn't see the hurt she knew shone in her
es. Of course, kissing her would mean nothing to
race. That's all their embrace would be for her, too—
 impulse, a mistake she wouldn't repeat, for she
dn't want to feel anything for him, or for any other
an.

She rose to her feet. "I can't stay here." She
utched her cloak around her and started to walk to
e door, but Trace grabbed her arm.

"Don't be absurd. You can't go out in the storm.
ou're staying here with me." His grip was firm and
s tone left no room for argument.

"I don't think I should, Trace," she told him,
nsure of herself. "My reason is telling me to part
om you."

"Do you fear me, Christa?" His eyes held hers.

"No. But I don't know what I feel about you. We've passed in and out of each other's lives so fleet ingly, and under such extraordinary circumstances. It' all so bewildering."

Trace understood what she was saying. His ow thoughts matched her words.

Christa sighed and went on, trying to sort out he thoughts. "Being with you here, alone, is wrong, know. I admit I didn't think of these circumstances thi morning when I decided to leave Haviland Cour Everything seems to be falling to pieces there Nothing's certain. I don't like being at the mercy c the Havilands, their hatreds, their selfishness. I hav my own family to think of, too. As you know, m father left Montclaire deeply in debt. The decisions make affect so many people. Yesterday, I received you letter about the mine. Profit from the saltpeter coul solve so many burdensome financial difficulties, so wanted to see the mine for myself."

"Your husband didn't make adequate provision fc you?" Trace kept his voice businesslike, devoid c emotion. What had he expected her to say, after all That she'd come to see him, be with him? He tol himself he was glad she was keeping him at a distanc now. He was too close to the goal he'd sought for s long. This mine was important to him, too. But fc reasons very different from Christa's, reasons involvin Fitzhugh Zachary.

"My husband was very much under the control c his father," Christa answered. "Orin Haviland returne to Haviland Court last night after a long stay i England. He has little use for me now, since I can n longer be of service to the family by breeding Havilan heirs."

Trace didn't miss the note of bitterness in her voice. It became stronger with her next words.

"Being a man, you can't know a woman's feeling of dependency. She's secondary to a man in every way, subject to his whims, his magnanimity, what he feels is best for her, what use he wants to make of her. So often she's looked upon as being frivolous, inconsequential, a mere pawn. Her dreams must be limited to running a household and bearing and raising children, while men decide and accomplish what they consider to be the more significant ventures in life."

The bright golden flames of the fire silhouetted Christa's lovely face. Trace saw her hands clench into fists. He sympathized with what she was saying.

"Sometimes a man faces conditions that aren't to his liking," he said. "He doesn't always choose the circumstances in which he finds himself. He can be unfairly judged because of his name—or the lack of one—instead of according to his abilities and achievements. The anger and bitterness grow each time he must prove his worth."

Christa gazed at him in surprise. He did know how she felt. And he was talking about himself, she knew. Her heart was touched by the pain his words revealed.

As if realizing he'd said too much, Trace cleared his throat and started to unlace the ties of his buckskin jacket.

"You'll stay here, Christa," he said firmly, slipping the jacket off and throwing it across the bed. "Perhaps you're hungry from your journey. I think there's some food in the cupboard. It won't be very fancy fare, I regret to say."

"It will do," Christa replied, not wanting to argue with him.

Trace and Christa said little as they put together a rudimentary meal of salt pork, biscuits from a tin, and cheese and apples Trace had brought with him from town.

"So you feel the mine might start to be workable in a fortnight?" Christa asked to make conversation when they were seated across from each other at the plank table. It seemed easier to talk of business.

"Yes, barring any more unforeseen delays," Trace replied, matching her casualness. "The bad weather has delayed our getting equipment here to aid in the work, but General Zachary has given his full support in men and supplies. There are many who wish to see the potassium nitrate made available."

Many, indeed, he thought, recalling how easily he'd manipulated Zachary into taking responsibility for the mine. The potassium nitrate compound would benefit one side in the war, but not King George's side. And Fitzhugh Zachary's downfall would be one step closer.

"Where is your home, Captain, your family?" The question was out before Christa realized she'd spoken. She blushed and lowered her eyes to her chipped plate. "I'm sorry. I don't know why I asked that."

"You called me Trace before. Can you not continue the practice?"

Her gaze met his, but she could only nod in answer.

"Unlike you," he began to explain, "I have no family ties. I've traveled a great deal to accomplish the goals I've set for myself. I own a house and several shipping enterprises in Albany, but I'm seldom there. My military duties require me to follow the changing battle lines with my regiment."

"You have no parents, brothers, or sisters?" Again the question was out before Christa thought better of it. Only at the last second did she keep from adding the word *wife* to the list.

"No one. That's the way I prefer it." Trace regarded her steadily. "There was only my mother, and she died when I was fourteen. I want no ties and am bound by none."

"Is that not a lonely life, Cap—, Trace?"

"It's a free life, and one I gladly choose. I have much to do yet. The name of Cavanaugh will someday be one my descendants are proud to bear. This country offers bountiful opportunities for a man to realize his aspirations. And I intend to take full advantage of that freedom."

Trace got up from the table and went to the cookstove, where a pot of tea boiled. Christa watched as he poured the steaming, dark liquid into two crockery mugs.

If only Nevin had had Trace Cavanaugh's determination, his drive to be his own man, she thought sadly, how much he could have accomplished. She admired Trace as she never had her husband. She respected his ambitions, his striving to better himself, build something of which he could be proud, instead of living off the accomplishments of others as Nevin had done. And Trace would do what he'd said, she had no doubt. A fixity of purpose was reflected in his haunted eyes; his confidence rang in his voice. He would succeed. She found herself wanting to hear more about his dreams, his aspirations. Wanting to know more about him.

Trace took his time getting the tea. He was surprised by how much he'd told Christa. He hadn't meant to. He'd never shared those thoughts with anyone. Yet it hadn't been hard to reveal them to Christa.

His hand accidentally brushed hers when he handed the mug of tea to her. Their eyes caught for a quick moment before she murmured a thank you and looked away toward the fireplace, where a log hissed and broke apart as the flames consumed it. Her glance fell across the bed in the corner by the hearth. Trace followed her gaze.

"I suppose we should discuss what the sleeping arrangements will be tonight," he said abruptly. His own thoughts followed that same path, but he was sure his ideas were quite different from Christa's.

"Is there any place where I might sleep other than this cabin?" Christa asked as she busied herself gathering up the dishes.

"The miners' bunkhouse is about a quarter of a mile away, but it's hardly fit for a lady. May I remind you that this isn't the first time we've been alone together for the night?"

"That's true, but you were half out of your senses from a head wound and spent most of the night unconscious. You're not in that condition now," she noted, watching him carefully.

He walked over to her, stopping directly in front of her. His voice was marked by gentleness when he spoke. "You have nothing to fear from me, Christa. I'd never force you to do anything against your will, you must know that. We both have reasons for keeping a distance between us. You take the bed. I'll take the floor. That way I can keep the fire going all night."

"Thank you, Trace," Christa murmured, grateful for his understanding.

Their gazes held for a moment longer, then they each turned away to prepare to sleep.

Chapter 29

Christa awakened to the smell of salt pork frying. A healthy fire blazed on the hearth, but Trace was nowhere to be seen. For a moment a feeling of panic surged through her. Something might have happened to him. Then she relaxed, realizing the food and the fire indicated he was around somewhere.

Christa didn't want to move from her warm spot. She'd spent the night on the narrow bed wrapped tightly in a blanket and her fur-lined cloak.

She had lain awake for a long time after she and Trace had taken their agreed-upon places for the night. She'd watched him long after he'd settled on the floor before the fire. She knew she could trust him, that he'd never hurt her. Perhaps she'd kept watch because she hadn't trusted herself. She felt strangely drawn to Trace. He was handsome, of course. But she felt more than just a physical attraction. He had a kind of presence about him, an inner strength, a surety about himself.

Christa winced as she got out of bed and pulled the blanket around her like a makeshift robe to hide her nightclothes. Her body was still protesting the hours of riding yesterday. Every muscle ached, it seemed.

Trace returned to the cabin carrying a bucket of water. "Good morning," he said with a smile as he poured some of the water into a pottery basin. "Here's water for washing. I trust you slept well." He added boiling water from the steaming teakettle.

"Yes, I did. Has the storm ended?" She watched Trace take off his jacket and hat, noticing that a shadow of a beard darkened his jaw.

"Yes, the storm's passed. The sleet turned to snow sometime during the night. There must be three inches on the ground now." He went to the stove. "Sit down. Breakfast is ready. You'll have to pretend it's not the same food we had last night."

Christa had to smile. This whole situation was so crazy—being here in this ramshackle cabin alone with Trace, sleeping together but not together, eating fried salt pork and stale biscuits. Quite a contrast with the way she'd spent breakfast at Haviland Court only yesterday. Yet she did not find these circumstances unpleasant.

"You needn't have done so much," she said, taking a chair at the table. "Why didn't you wake me to help you?"

Trace carried their filled plates over to the table and sat down across from Christa. "A pampered lady from Haviland Court capable of frying salt pork? Will wonders never cease? And yet I must say I've come to realize you seem capable of doing whatever you set your mind to. I didn't wake you because I thought you needed the sleep. You tossed and turned for quite a while last night."

Christa grew uncomfortable under his gaze.

"I'm sorry if I kept you awake."

"It wasn't your tossing and turning that kept me awake." His eyes met hers levelly.

Christa looked away, knowing only too well what he meant.

"As soon as we've finished eating, I'll take you to the mine," Trace went on. "You can see for yourself the progress we've been making, sign the papers I need from you, and be on your way back to Haviland Court before mid-morning. I'll see you as far as Wooster, and make sure your servant is fit to take you back to New York. I'm expecting that overdue equipment today, and I must be here to supervise its installation. Shall I saddle the horses, or do you think you can manage the half mile to the mine on foot?''

"Walking is fine." Christa didn't contradict his plan. She was getting to know him. He was accustomed to giving orders, and while she was not afraid to stand up to him if the situation warranted it, this time she saw no need to do so.

A short time later, Christa hugged her heavy cloak around her as she walked outside with Trace. Her mood was lighter now. It was a glorious morning, crisp and cold and blanketed in the fresh white snow that had fallen during the night. No wind disturbed the silence. The snow muffled their footsteps. Then a lone bird broke the quiet by chirping a fragile song.

As Trace and Christa made their way to the mine, they were unaware that two figures watched them from a hidden vantage point among a grove of pine trees.

"So they're together," Isabelle Sheffield observed, cocking an eyebrow. "And no one else appears to be around. That's interesting. I can't say much for the captain's taste."

She hid some of her jealous anger from the man with her. She had plans for Trace Cavanaugh, and she resented the fact that Christa had gotten him first. Christa, of all women. There would be other men, of course, but had she underestimated her sister-in-law? While she happily accused Christa of having lovers to discredit her to her father, she really hadn't thought Christa capable of promiscuity.

Lee Garrett said nothing, but his expression was

malevolent as he kept his gaze on Trace and Christa.
Cavanaugh with Christa. The thought of it was despicable. His hated enemy was with a woman he
wanted . . .

"I'm glad you knew where the mine was located,
Lee, after I made Letty tell me where Christa was
going," Isabelle went on. "I knew coming here would
be worthwhile, even though we did get caught in the
blizzard last night and had to stay in that wretched inn
back in town. I know exactly what we must do now,
my love. It's all so simple."

Her brown eyes narrowed and took on a glint that
matched the frigidity of the winter air. "They've
played right into our hands. You and I both want this
mine. The profits could be enormous. I have a plan to
make that happen, which will also rid me of Christa
once and for all. Then we can easily obtain the rights
to the mine from her stupid mother. And you can
finally best your arch enemy, Trace Cavanaugh, as
well."

Garrett turned to look at his mistress with interest.
"And just what do you have in mind, Isabelle? Your
plan sounds too perfect."

"You said this mine is being worked by soldiers and
that this area is a military camp. Therefore, there must
be gunpowder stored somewhere. No one's around. All
we have to do is lure Christa and Cavanaugh into the
mine and blow up the entrance."

"What?" Lee's eyes widened with shock. He
couldn't believe what he was hearing. He knew Isabelle
was calculating and ambitious. Those qualities had
been part of her appeal when they'd first become
lovers. She could do much to advance his career. And
she was a tigress in bed, a challenge he enjoyed. But
murder?

"You're talking about killing two people, Isabelle."

"It all depends on your perspective, darling. You kill the enemy for some lofty cause in war, don't you? Do you call that murder? I consider Christa and Cavanaugh enemies to my cause, which is gaining everything I can in any way I can. That's been your goal, as well, Lee. At least that's what you've told me. We can make the explosion look like an accident, a cave-in. It happens all the time in mines. Don't think of this scheme as murder, if the thought bothers you. We're only going to seal them in the shaft. Perhaps there's another way out, and they'll escape."

"Cavanaugh's no problem," Lee agreed. "I'd welcome being rid of him. But Christa . . ."

Isabelle stepped closer to Garrett. "She's nothing compared to me and what I can offer you, darling. Never forget that fact. Think of my body coupled with yours during the wonderful, exciting nights we've had together."

She put her arms around his neck and kissed him hard, letting her tongue dart into his mouth. She smiled to herself when he let out a small moan and pulled her roughly against him. Lee was so easy to manipulate. All men were. They were slaves to their animal needs. And she'd long ago learned how to use her beauty and that need to her advantage and pleasure. She'd have her way in everything. Nothing would stop her. Nothing!

Lee was breathing jaggedly when Isabelle finally pulled away from him. "Patience, my love," she told him sweetly. "You'll have me later—all night, again and again, just as it was between us last night. I'm eager to feel you inside me. But for now you must wait until after we carry out our plan."

Lee nodded, spellbound by her gaze. Isabelle's kiss, her words, her wild passion, set him on fire. How he wanted her. He'd do anything to have her.

Chapter 30

Trace lighted a lantern and led the way into the main shaft of the mine.

"We had to do a good deal of work shoring up these old timbers," he explained to Christa, pointing overhead to the cross sections of thick wooden beams supporting the ceiling. "Many of them were rotted through from age."

Christa stayed close to Trace, inside the circle of light cast by the lantern. When the burning wick flickered unsteadily as they walked, eerie shadows danced on the rock walls around them. The deeper they went, the more damp and stale-smelling the air became. From somewhere nearby they heard the sound of water trickling over rocks.

"The main shaft branches into two others here." Trace held the lantern high and pointed to his right. "That one opens into a large natural cavern. We've found some deposits of potassium nitrate there. This shaft"—he gestured toward the other side—"shows more promise for a larger yield of the compound. We'll know more when we get it completely open. The beams in that part of the mine were rotted away in places by water. There were several cave-ins when we first started work in that area."

"No one was hurt, I hope." Christa looked at him with concern.

"No, everyone managed to escape."

She shivered in the heavy, dank air. She remembered how frightened she'd been the one other time she'd been here as a child. Her father had chided her for her timidity and forced her to go deeper into the mine with him. Finally the rough stone walls had seemed to be pressing in on her from all sides, and she'd run from the mine as fast as she could. The closed-in feeling was easier to control now while she was standing with Trace in this wider main shaft, but just the thought of going into one of the off-shooting shafts made her stomach queasy and her hands clammy inside her fur-lined gloves.

The merest trembling of their rocky footing was the only warning they had of the explosion. The concussion knocked Trace and Christa to the hard-packed ground and showered them with dust, dirt, and rock fragments.

The acrid air choked Trace. He coughed violently and struggled to his knees to crawl to Christa. She wasn't moving. With an effort, Trace picked her up and carried her away from the fire that was starting to consume the wooden beams near the caved-in entrance. At the back of the main shaft, the air was more breathable.

"Christa," Trace called as he gently put her down on the ground, gasping in the clearer air. Quickly, he went back for the lantern. Looking Christa over, he could see no visible injuries. At that moment, she moaned and stirred.

"Trace?" She blinked several times before his face came into focus.

"Lie still, Christa. Are you hurt?"

"I—I don't think so." She struggled to sit up. "What happened?"

"An explosion," he explained, his voice grim. "The entrance appears to be blocked."

Christa's eyes widened. "Blocked? You mean we can't get out?"

"I'm not certain. If you're all right, I'll go back to look."

"Yes, I'm fine. Let me come with you."

Trace would have argued with her, but Christa was already on her feet.

Using his jacket and her cloak, they beat out the fire edging along some of the support timbers. When the smoke and dust settled, Trace tried to move some of the boulders piled in front of the entrance. Christa helped with some of the smaller rocks.

"It's no use," Trace said finally, as he wiped his smoke-smudged shirtsleeve across his sweaty brow. "We're not getting anywhere. There's too much."

They both sat down on the dirt floor with their backs against the rubble.

"Is there another way out?" Christa was afraid to hear his reply.

"Not that I know of."

His simple answer sent a terrible dread through her. She got to her feet, pacing nervously.

"What caused the explosion? We can't be trapped in here. We must try to get out!" She started to feverishly pull at the rocks again. Trace stood up and grabbed her arm to stop her.

"Christa, keep your head! Half the hill could have come down to block that entrance. It could take weeks for my entire crew to clear it—*if* they were in camp to start now and *if* they knew we were in here. We have to think.

"Sometimes there are dangerous gases in mines that can cause explosions. But I've been in enough battles to know the sound of gunpowder igniting. There's powder in the munitions supply shed, but the shed's nowhere near the mine, for safety reasons. That explosion was deliberately set. Do you have any idea who might have done it?''

"Do I—? Trace, no, I can't imagine who would do such a terrible thing." Christa put her hand to her forehead in distress as she tried to think. Who could hate her enough to want to kill her?

Watching Christa, Trace saw the dawning realization in her eyes, just as she denied it.

"No, she couldn't do it. She's cold and cruel at times, but she'd never—"

"Who, Christa?" Trace interrupted, frowning as he took hold of her arms.

"Who?" She looked at him in confusion, still trying to reason why Isabelle's name had even come to her.

"What woman do you mean?"

"Isabelle. Nevin's sister. But this is murderous. She wouldn't gain anything by my death. Besides, she was still at Haviland Court when I left yesterday to come here. She wasn't planning on going anywhere I know of, because she was anxious for Lee to arrive for his visit."

"Lee?"

"Leland Garrett."

Trace's frown deepened into a fierce scowl. He let go of Christa and ran a hand through his hair.

"There's no love lost between Garrett and me. He was enraged when I was given command of the operation of this mine, especially since you'd told him about it first. He's been here. He knows the location. And he's fully capable of conceiving and executing such a deadly plan to get rid of me."

Trace was livid with anger. He should have foreseen something like this happening. And now Christa was endangered because of him and his vendettas against

Garrett and Zachary. What a fool he'd been to underestimate Garrett.

"And Isabelle could have helped him." Christa made the statement quietly, wishing she didn't feel such conviction. Deep down she knew her sister-in-law was a cold, heartless woman of great ambition. Isabelle had changed greatly in the last two years, become more cruel and ruthless. But Isabelle and Lee? Could they work together to do something as evil as attempted murder?

Surely Lee wouldn't want to kill me, Christa reasoned. But I spurned his advances. Was the explosion revenge for that? No, these thoughts were too confusing, too ridiculous. There had to be another explanation.

"Perhaps we're wrong," she told Trace, her frown matching his. "Perhaps an enemy patrol set the charge. The Continentals wouldn't want this mine to go into operation and provide His Majesty's forces with saltpeter."

"That's a possibility," Trace acknowledged, but he knew the truth. He had access to both sides' plans for this mine and knew that neither the Americans nor the British wanted it sabotaged. "We'll figure out an explanation later," he continued. "First we have to find a way out of here. Perhaps there's some other exit."

He picked up the lantern and motioned for Christa to follow him deeper into the mine. "I know the cavern shaft is a dead end," he explained, "but the other shaft we were still opening may offer an escape."

Trace led the way. As they moved through the tunnel, Christa heard the sound of running water getting louder.

"Be careful not to touch any of these support beams," Trace warned as they ducked through a low area. "They aren't stable, and there's no telling what the vibrations from the explosion might have done to them."

As if to verify Trace's words, the old beams creaked and shifted, sending a small cloud of dirt and pebbles down on them. They hurried on.

"This is as far as I've been," Trace said as they came to a pile of rubble left by a long-ago cave-in. "We were working to shore up the ceiling and support beams before we tried to remove all this debris. I don't know what's on the other side, but I think now is a good time to find out. Do you think you can get through there?" He pointed to an opening in the pile of rocks near the hard-packed dirt floor.

The narrowness of the opening made Christa's stomach lurch, as did the thought of having all those tons of rock and dirt suspended over her when she crawled through it. But she forced down the frightening feeling, took a deep breath, and nodded, determined to try. There was no other choice.

Trace was squatting beside the opening with the lantern to try to see to the other side. "I'll go first. When I get through, hand the lantern to me."

Christa nodded again and took the light from him.

"Be careful, Trace," she said, barely above a whisper. She nervously bit her lower lip as she watched him get down on his hands and knees and crawl through.

"I'm on the other side, Christa," he called, making her jump. "Come ahead."

She pushed the lantern through the opening and was very glad to see it light Trace's dirt-smudged face. Taking a deep breath, she got down on her hands and knees to follow him, concentrating on Trace waiting for her on the other side of the three-foot-long opening. But as she made her way through, one of her boots scraped against the pile of rubble, dislodging a good-sized rock. Christa cried out in panic and tried to cover her head with one arm as dirt and smaller stones showered down on her. Her heart pounded wildly, for she was certain the huge pile of rock was about to bury her. Terrible fear overwhelmed her.

"Hurry, Christa! Keep coming!" Trace called. He quickly crawled to her from his side of the opening. Taking her hand in a firm grasp, he worked his way back out, pulling her with him.

"Thank you for helping me," Christa said gratefully when they were standing on the other side.

Trace nodded. "Are you all right?"

"Yes."

Trace held up the lantern to survey their surroundings. The shaft ended on this side of the rubble. Before them was a spacious, naturally formed open cavern. Jagged rock walls rose up on all sides to a height of at least fifty feet, by Trace's calculation. In front of them was a wide pool of water. And the water in the pool was rising. Even while Trace and Christa watched, the water inched its way along the dirt floor, coming closer to them.

"This isn't what I was hoping for." Trace tried to make his tone light as he took in the situation, but Christa's heart sank at his words.

Trace's anger returned. Damn, but he hated Garrett! There had to be a way out of this mine. He'd find a way or *make* one, if for no other reason than to live to exact his revenge on the bastard!

Slowly he circled the pool, scanning the walls and outcroppings of rock. Christa shivered and pulled her dirty cloak more tightly around her to ward off the cold. She was very frightened and had to force down the panic threatening to overwhelm her. Trace looked calm and controlled. She would be, too, she vowed silently.

"There isn't any way out down here, and we're going to have to get away from this water," Trace explained. The wide pool was clearly flooding over what little ground they had. And the place in the rubble that they'd crawled through only a few minutes before was filled with water now. They couldn't go back that way.

"The explosion must have done something to make the water flow increase," Trace continued. "There might be a way out up there."

Christa looked to where Trace pointed, and her heart sank further. About thirty feet up the rock wall was some kind of opening. A small stream of water flowed over the edge of it, falling down to the pool.

Trace turned to her, his dirt-streaked face grave.

"That may be our only chance, Christa, and it's a slim one at best. But we have to try it. You'd better get out of that skirt, so it doesn't hamper your climbing. Leave your cloak here, too."

Hot tears stung Christa's eyes, but she blinked them back as she nodded and stepped away from Trace to take off her riding skirt, leaving only her pantaloons. He took off his own bulky jacket.

"Follow me and take care," Trace said as he took up the lantern and started for the wall. "The rocks will be slippery from the dampness."

Trace climbed cautiously, testing each handhold and bootstep before putting his full weight on the rocky ledges. When he needed to use both hands, he hooked the lantern to his belt. Once he passed a solid section, he encouraged Christa to follow. With nerve-racking slowness, they climbed the jagged rock wall. The clammy granite was sharp in places, and it cut into Christa's hands as she clung to it. About halfway up, a wider ledge enabled Trace to stop and wait for her. Christa had almost reached it when the rock under her left boot gave way.

"Trace!" Her frantic cry alerted him just in time to grasp her hand as she clutched the edge of the slippery ledge.

"I have you!" He hauled her up in one powerful pull and took her in his arms, stroking her tangled hair. "You're all right, Christa. You're doing fine. We can make it the rest of the way to that opening. Have courage."

She nodded, but she was very frightened. She clung to Trace, trying to gain some of his courage. She wouldn't think about how high up they had to go or about falling. Or that once they did reach the opening, it might not provide a way out.

"Ready to go on?"

"Yes."

The wall got steeper the higher they went, but the granite still offered juttings at regular enough intervals for Trace and Christa to finally reach a narrow ledge next to the oval-shaped opening they were seeking. Trace got down on his hands and knees. Holding the lantern out as far as he could, he leaned over and peered into the opening.

"I think I see some light!" His voice rang with excitement. "It must be from a surface opening where this water is coming in. Come on."

Very carefully, Trace moved to the edge of the opening. He had to bend down low to get inside it. He waited until Christa had joined him, then led the way through the shallow water toward the small speck of daylight. They found a hole overhead just wide enough for one person to climb through at a time. After he climbed out, Trace reached down and helped Christa through.

Together they stood outside the mine on the steep, snow-covered hill overlooking the bunkhouse and the cabin a little farther away.

"We made it! Oh, Trace, we made it!" Christa cried as she hugged him, crying with relief.

"Of course, we did," he replied with more assurance than he felt. "Come on, it's freezing out here. We have to get inside."

Taking Christa's hand, he led the way down the slope, keeping a sharp eye out for anyone who might still wish to harm them.

Chapter 31

Christa was trembling and her legs felt weak as she struggled toward the cabin with Trace. The cold air cut into her riding jacket and clinging pantaloons like shards of ice. With a cry, she tripped over a fallen, snow-covered branch and fell.

"Christa!" Trace bent to gather her into his arms. "Are you hurt?" he asked worriedly.

"No," she answered, grateful for his strength. She put her arms around his neck to hold on while he carried her.

Trace kicked the cabin door open and took her over to the bed. When he put her down on it, his own shaking made it difficult for him to wrap a blanket around her. Then he went to the hearth to bring the banked coals of the morning fire to life again, clutching a blanket around him as he waited anxiously for the kindling to catch.

"Come over by the fire," Trace urged. When Christa stood up, he pulled the narrow, straw-filled mattress from the bed and put it on the floor before the hearth. "We can sit here where it's warmer."

As she settled before the fire, a paralyzing weakness overwhelmed Christa, making her continue to tremble. It wasn't caused only by the cold. Shock was setting in in the aftermath of their life-threatening struggle to escape the mine. Tears welled up in her eyes as she stared fixedly at the flames.

Trace noticed her trembling and the way she wrapped her arms protectively around herself. "It's over, Christa," he said gently as he put his arm around her shoulders. "We're safe."

She looked at him intently and leaned closer against him. "Are you all right, Trace?" She felt him shaking, too. His lips were tinged with blue from the cold. She wanted to reach out to him, to warm him somehow.

"I'm fine, Christa," he assured her, wanting to ease her concern. Her eyes drew him to her, just as the heat of the fire urged his cold body toward it.

"I—I'm grateful for what you did back at the mine," she stammered. "You saved us. I was so frightened we were going to die. If you hadn't found a way out . . ." Her voice trailed off.

"Don't think about what might have happened. We did escape. You don't have to be afraid now," he murmured, pressing his chin against her hair and tightening his arm around her. Her hair was damp but very soft against his face. He wanted to go on comforting her, protecting her. He was shaken himself by how close they'd come to being fatally trapped in the mine. What if Christa had been badly injured or even killed?

He frowned, troubled by the thought. The reality of the danger they'd been in made him want to hold her closer. He drew her chin around so that she had to look at him.

Christa searched his face with tear-filled eyes. Her heart began to beat faster as an unspoken understanding passed between them. She knew she could trust him, knew he was reaching out to her.

"Trace . . ." she whispered, bringing her arms up to encircle his neck. She closed her eyes and touched her lips to his. The tenderness of the kiss sent a tremor through her body. A small cry caught in her throat as she clung to him.

Slowly, still held by the kiss, they lay down together on the mattress. Trace held her close in his arms even after the kiss ended. For a long time, they didn't move or speak. Then he brushed her tangled hair back from her face with his fingertips. His thumb wiped at a smudge of dirt on her cheek.

Christa touched his face where a small scratch ran to the crease at the side of his mouth. Not a word was spoken between them, but much was said by look, by touch.

Trace's fingers moved from her cheek down the side of her slim neck, over her shoulder, and along her arm until he reached her hand. This he lifted to his lips and kissed gently. All the while, his compelling turquoise eyes never left hers. They held Christa transfixed, spellbound.

Outwardly, she remained very still, but inside her body was slowly coming to life. The essence of her being opened deep within her and sent out a new and hesitant pulsation of feeling.

An intense warmth radiated from the fire and from the two people lying entwined before it. Trace kissed Christa again, letting his mouth linger on hers, exploring its softness and taste. She hardly moved beneath him, yet just by lying in his arms, so close, so willingly, she awakened an overwhelming desire within him. It set his pulse to a rapid pace. His desire was interwoven with a wanting to know her, to give her all of himself—his body, his being. And he wanted all of her in return, wanted to taste her sweetness, hear her murmurings of ecstasy, feel her body quickening with need for him.

He pressed his lips to hers with a growing ardor that took both their breaths away. He stopped just long

nough to undress her and remove his own clothes.
'hen he set his hand to movement. With one fingertip,
e traced the delicate line of her lips, her chin, down
er neck again to her naked breasts. With a touch as
ght as a downy feather, he played over and around
ae voluptuous pale mounds, exquisitely tormenting the
p of each to a straining peak. With deliberate
lowness, he let his lips follow the same path his
ngers had just explored.

The reaction within Christa was tumultuous. She
aurmured softly with shock and rapturous pleasure. A
embling swept through her, but it was not from cold
r fear, as it had been before. Now it was caused by
  heretofore unfulfilled yearning that began to rise
aside her, setting her heart to pounding a wild cadence
nd igniting a fiery excitement that spread to every
ber of her body. She wanted more of Trace. She had
  touch him, feel the rippling muscles of his powerful
rms and back beneath her impatient fingers, let the
atense heat of his body flow to her as they pressed
gether, length to length. She began to move with
im, wanting to anticipate where his next kiss would
e. Her hands sought to learn every part of him.

She drew Trace's head back from its bold journey
ver the curves and hollows of her flesh so her gaze
ould find his handsome face and search his eyes. The
enderness was there again, rendering her helpless.
Drawing his lips to hers, she let the fervor in her kiss
peak to him of her rising passion. His reply was to
evour her lips. How glad she was when his touch
ecame more demanding, when he asked even more
rom her. Gladly she gave it. His hand, playing over
er breasts and along her body to the inside of her
highs, became too much to bear. A tremendous
rgency rose in her.

Trace wanted to keep touching her, exploring her,

but he couldn't hold back his own need any longer. His
blood was on fire, his breath coming in small, jagged
gasps as desire welled up in him like a mounting tidal
wave.

Christa's legs parted to receive him, and her hips
arched to meet him as he moved over her. In a
moment, he was within her, and they became one body
and spirit, welded by the inferno of passion raging
between them. Give. Receive. Cling. Release—blessed
magnificent release. It came simultaneously to both of
them in an overpowering, pulsating surge.

Suspend. Hold the rapturous moments of climax.
Make everything else disappear out of consciousness.
Trace and Christa willed that. Without speaking a
word, each knew the other's heart and desire.

It took so long for the heat to fade, for pulse and
breathing to slow, for calm to return. Christa kept her
eyes tightly closed, trying to sort through the jumble
of sensations and emotions she'd just experienced.
Never had she known such wonder and pleasure when
she'd joined with Nevin. Never had she felt so spent,
yet so awed, contented, fulfilled. Trace awakened her
need, her passion, and touched the depths of her
womanhood.

She opened her eyes and looked at him. His head
was resting on his arm while he continued to hold her
close against him. His gaze met hers.

Did she know what she had just done to him? Did
he know yet the true depth and meaning of what he
was feeling for her? He wanted her to be just another
woman with whom he'd shared some pleasurable
moments, like so many others he'd known. He didn't
like what she stirred in him—the need to give, to share.
He felt open, vulnerable, and resisted those feelings.
He was in control of himself, his life. But the need to
kiss Christa, to touch her, to make her his, greatly

tested his control. Instead of being satisfied with what he'd just had of her, his hunger for her grew by the moment. He wanted her again. Not just the joining of her body with his, but the closeness, the sharing. For a few precious moments, his loneliness had fled.

Trace put a stop to his thoughts. No, he wouldn't let her reach him again. He had to pull back, keep his inner self hidden as he'd done all his life. He couldn't get close to anyone. Doing so would only bring pain. He wouldn't let Christa be part of his life. Getting further involved with her could threaten the plans for vengeance he'd worked so hard to accomplish.

"What's happening between us, Trace?" Christa murmured hesitantly. "A little while ago, we were almost strangers, yet we shared this magnificent joining. I'm so confused. Tell me what you're feeling. I must know." She raised her hand and touched the side of his face.

Trace sat up and rested an elbow on a propped-up knee. He looked away into the fire, steeling himself to say his next harsh words.

"It's better that you don't know, Christa. You wouldn't like what you heard. Don't make more of what just happened than it really was. We had a close brush with death back at the mine. Something like that can make people act irrationally. We were carried away by the moment, by the relief of coming through the danger in one piece. That's all it was."

Christa was stung. How could he be so cold after what they'd just shared?

"I don't believe you, Trace." She hid her hurt by letting her anger at his cruelty speak for her. "Something passed between us just now. You felt it, I know you did. Perhaps we acted impulsively, but our need for each other was real. Why do you deny it now? Are you afraid to admit you might need me?"

His head swung around as his wrath flared. "I'm afraid of nothing and I need no one. I never have. Needing makes you dependent on someone else, and I'll never let that happen! Do you see this?" He snatched up the ruby-and-gold ring on the chain around his neck. "It belonged to my father. He gave it to my mother a long time ago. She needed him. I don't know who my father was, because she would never speak his name. But with all her heart she loved him and wanted only to be loved by him in return. That could never be, for he was killed not long after I was born." Trace's eyes took on a glacial glint of hatred. "I've sworn vengeance on his murderer, whom my mother named with her dying breath. And I won't rest until that revenge is complete, for he left my mother with nothing but this ring and a son with no legitimate name. The heartache of losing him weakened her will to live. She died when I was fourteen years old. I swore then I'd never need anyone as much as she needed my father, and I never will."

Christa heard the pain in his voice and her heart went out to him. She came around in front of him to see his face. "How lonely you must be. Please don't do this, Trace. Don't push me away. I have so much to give you." She leaned forward to hug him and felt him tense.

"I can't give you anything in return, Christa." Cold control marked his words.

"Then just take what I freely offer . . ." She looked into his eyes for a long moment before she leaned forward to kiss him.

Trace resisted her embrace. He wanted to remain impervious to her, but the passion they'd shared earlier lurked too near the surface. It easily ignited in him again. Angrily, he pulled her to him and kept his mouth pressed hard against hers. He'd take everything from her and give only his body in return, nothing more.

Christa was startled by his sudden roughness, but she made no attempt to stop him. She wanted to help him, but didn't know how. Perhaps by giving herself completely, she could touch his heart, soften his resolve. She had to try. She sank into his arms and let him lower her back to the mattress.

Trace's lips found her breasts, while his hands moved over her body, claiming her as his own once again. And she did the same to him. Kissed him, caressed him. They became intimately entwined. Arching her hips, she met him. Inside. Within. Reaching to the depth, to the core of their beings.

Christa clung to Trace. Tears filled her eyes and overflowed. Were they tears of joy, wonder, confusion, fear? All of those things. Her overpowering feelings flowed for the man in her arms, the man who had touched her heart.

What was she experiencing? Was she falling in love with Trace Cavanaugh?

Chapter 32

Trace was certain his reason had failed him. What other explanation could there be for what had happened between him and Christa? He'd never intended to make love to her. Yet their lives kept crossing. What gods or fates or devils were drawing them together, controlling their destinies?

He frowned. No, he controlled his *own* fate, his *own* destiny. Why then didn't he feel his usual confidence when it came to Christa? Somehow she got past his hard-practiced self-control to the part of him he always kept protected, hidden from everyone. How had she gotten him to talk about his parents and his vengeance against his father's murderer? She seemed to understand the pain inside him, perhaps even better than he did himself. She knew about the loneliness, and willingly came to him, opened herself to share the emptiness with him. He'd never before experienced this joining of spirits. Having it happen with Christa scared the hell out of him!

Lying on his side, he opened his eyes to find her watching him. If only she weren't so beautiful, so desirable. He knew her will and courage were strong, yet he glimpsed gentleness and vulnerability in her haunting blue-gray eyes. Against his better judgment, he realized he cared for her. Too much. He couldn't allow his growing feelings to cloud his reason. For so many reasons he must close his heart. His life was fraught with intrigue and danger. He was walking a very perilous path, one he must travel alone, as he always had. He must separate himself from Christa. He couldn't jeopardize her life.

Trace sighed heavily and sat up. Leaning forward, he reached for another log from the dwindling pile on the floor and tossed it into the diminishing fire. Christa sat up next to him and quietly broke the tense silence.

"Please tell me what you're feeling, Trace. Tell me what's in your heart."

Slowly he turned to face her and saw her heart reflected in her eyes. His resolve weakened when she touched his bare shoulder. The warmth of her hand seemed to burn into his flesh. He couldn't hold her beseeching gaze.

Looking back at the flickering flames of the fire, he made himself put her at a distance in his mind. He chose his words carefully, regretting the pain he was about to inflict on her.

"I can't tell you what you want to hear, Christa. We come from different worlds. You were born to wealth and prestige. I was not. I aspire to that world and I'll attain it, but now I'm a soldier at war. And a soldier can't have a heart. There can be nothing more between us."

Christa felt the blood drain from her face. His cold words were like a deadly, double-edged sword slashing cruelly at her fragile new feelings. She dropped her hand from his shoulder and fought to hide her hurt.

"You are unyielding in this decision?" She forced her voice to sound calm.

"Yes."

"Then we must part. Forever, if that's possible." She rose quickly, wrapping the crumpled blanket around her as she went to the bed to get her clothes. Trace followed her.

"I won't let you leave, Christa." He pulled her around to face him. "If Garrett and your sister-in-law did have something to do with the explosion, it's too dangerous for you to return to Haviland Court."

At that moment, the sound of horses reached them from outside. Trace tensed and took his pistol from its holster hanging over the back of a chair. Cocking back the hammer, he went quickly to the window and peered outside. Christa held her breath, anxious with fear.

"It's only some of the mine crew returning from town," Trace explained, putting down the weapon. He went to the trunk near the door and dressed rapidly in black woolen breeches, a white cotton shirt, and calf-high boots. "I must see to getting the men checked in and working on the cave-in as soon as possible."

He pulled a black seaman's jacket out of the trunk and shrugged into it as he went to the door. "Stay here, Christa. We'll discuss this matter further when I return." Then he was gone.

"Damn you, Trace. Damn you . . ." Christa murmured the curses at the closed door. She wished she'd never laid eyes on him, never let him kiss her, never let him touch her . . .

She must get away from Trace, sort out her feelings alone, out of his reach. And without his help she'd find out if Isabelle and Lee Garrett were the saboteurs.

When Trace returned to the cabin several hours later, he found it empty. Christa was gone.

Chapter 33

Christa departed from the mine camp and returned to Wooster where she found Abel Sherwood improved in health. She and the groom journeyed to Haviland Court without encountering any danger from enemy patrols. While riding, Christa had a great deal of time to think about everything that had taken place with Trace. Too much time. He loomed relentlessly in her mind. She was glad she'd left the cabin without seeing him again. He had a way of overpowering her senses, her reason, her conscious will . . . and her body.

Thinking about that only further tortured her troubled mind. She wished she could forget the wondrous feelings and sensations Trace had awakened in her. She wanted to make her stomach stop churning and her pulse cease racing at the mere thought of being in his arms, of having his lips, hands, and body claim her intimately. Why did Trace have to be the one to make her feel this way?

If only she'd felt so much with her husband. But Nevin had cared only about his own pleasure, satisfying his own needs. She had never been sorry when her intimacy with him had quickly ended. Nevin had never taken time to coax her to the magnificient, exhilarating climax she'd known with Trace. She longed to experience again the closeness she'd had with Trace, share with him the blessed feeling of being wanted, needed.

Christa knew she was falling in love with him. The painful realization that he didn't love her in return kept her upset and silent during most of the trip back to Haviland Court.

When Christa reached the estate, she forced those disturbing thoughts to the back of her mind and concentrated on the sabotage that had occurred at the mine. The explosion had been no accident. Trace had been certain of that fact.

Christa knew her sister-in-law was acutely interested in the mine for its money-making potential. She was ruthlessly ambitious and greedy and didn't bother to try to hide those traits. Lee Garrett was ambitious, too, Christa remembered from the past. Had they worked together on a scheme to gain control of the mine by trying to kill her?

There was only one way to find the answer to that question. Christa wasn't versed in the strategies of subterfuge and deception; she decided to use a direct approach and confront Isabelle—Lee, too, if he was at Haviland Court.

She summoned Letty to her bedroom.

"Oh, Miz Christa, ah is so glad you is back," Letty gushed with relief when she saw her mistress. "Ah was worried to death when you went off so sudden like that."

Christa opened her valise for Letty to unpack. "I wasn't gone long, was I?" Only long enough to be nearly killed and fall in love, she added to herself. "Is Miss Isabelle here?"

"Why, yes'm, her an' Cap'n Garrett done come in jus' a little while ago. They left yesterday to do some business o' some sort."

Christa's knees went weak and she had to reach for

the high footboard on her bed to steady herself. Isabelle and Lee . . . away together yesterday. The words echoed loudly in her mind, pointing to the truth of her suspicions. But she still must go through with the confrontation, somehow gain some proof of their treachery. Hopefully, with all the servants about, there would be no chance of harm coming to her here at Haviland Court.

"Ambrose," Christa addressed the elderly major-domo when she came downstairs later in the evening, "where are Miss Isabelle and Captain Garrett?"

"Miss Isabelle is alone in the front parlor. Captain Garrett has departed."

Christa looked toward the double sliding doors. "Thank you, Ambrose," she said. "Miss Isabelle and I have something to discuss. Would you mind staying close by in case we should need anything?"

"Not at all, madam. I shall listen for your summons."

"That will be fine. Thank you, Ambrose."

Knowing she could call the butler for help made Christa feel more courageous as she walked with him to the parlor doors. She straightened her shoulders and held her head high as Ambrose slid the heavy doors apart for her to enter the room.

Isabelle glanced up from the book she was reading. Christa watched her reaction. She wasn't disappointed. Isabelle's eyes widened in surprise and her mouth dropped open as her face visibly blanched.

"W—why, Christa, you've returned," she stammered.

Christa saw all she needed. Anger churned inside her, but she kept her outward appearance cool and controlled. "You seem shocked to see me, Isabelle, and I don't wonder at that."

"I—I haven't the faintest idea what you're talking

about.'' Isabelle came to her feet, dropping her book as Christa walked slowly toward her. Her obvious nervousness made Christa bolder. She'd never before had such an advantage over her sister-in-law.

"Of course you know to what I'm referring, Isabelle. Perhaps you should sit down again. The shock of seeing me may be too much for you, for I know you weren't expecting me to be alive."

"You're speaking gibberish!" Isabelle snapped, turning her back on Christa. But Christa reached out and caught Isabelle by the arm, forcing her around to face her.

"Call it what you will. The fact remains that I know what you and Lee Garrett tried to do to me and Captain Cavanaugh this morning." Isabelle's increasingly pale features made Christa press on. "Such a vile, criminal act cannot go unpunished. You will *not* get away with it, Isabelle.''

The other woman sank to the divan, stunned, and Christa knew her bravado had worked. Isabelle's facial expression declared her guilt as surely as a spoken confession.

But Isabelle Sheffield was not a woman to be easily defeated. She sat up straight on the peach-shaded couch and regarded Christa defiantly.

"You can prove nothing. It's your word against ours. You're no threat to us. You're nothing around here now, since my stupid brother got himself blown to pieces.''

"Then why did you try to kill me?" Christa shot back.

"You really don't know, do you?" Isabelle's smile looked purely evil. "You're such a stupid creature, Christa. I want the mine, of course. There's great profit to be made from it. With you out of the way, I could easily have obtained ownership from that imbecile

mother of yours. She'll sign anything. She already has.
It's just a matter of time before I possess Montclaire
completely as well. It will make such a nice addition
to my holdings.

"I always get what I want, Christa. I never let
anything or anyone stand in my way. Your days as
mistress here at Haviland Court are numbered. Father
will be throwing you out soon enough. You're worthless to him. Actually, I must admit I shouldn't have
been so anxious to rush your death at the mine.
Winston always tells me patience is not one of my
virtues. It's really much better this way. I'm glad
you're still alive. Now I can enjoy seeing the look on
your face when Montclaire becomes mine and you're
helpless to do anything about it."

She took a step forward, and Christa retreated in
kind. Now it was she who was stunned. The cold,
ruthless calculation in her sister-in-law's cruel words
and expression frightened her. Could Isabelle be
insane, crazed with the greed, power, and hatred she'd
increasingly shown over the last two years?

Christa was afraid, but anger surged through her,
too. Her blood pounded in her temples. She hated
being thought of as inconsequential, as something
easily discarded. She considered Montclaire, her
family's home for generations. It meant everything to
her. It was her history, her heritage. She'd fought long
to save it, sacrificed so much. Montclaire was the
reason she'd married Nevin and tried to be a good wife
to him. She would *not* let Isabelle steal her home.
Somehow she'd find a way to stop her, Winston, Lee—
anyone who threatened her!

Christa raised her chin and regarded her adversary
squarely. She let no fear show in her expression as she
spoke with seething contempt. "You're insane,

Isabelle. Montclaire will never be yours. I'll see to that. Do not underestimate me as an enemy.''

The two women locked gazes in a battle of wills. Finally, Isabelle gave a diabolical laugh. But she was the first to look away.

"You are truly ridiculous, Christa. You can't begin to be a match for me. We'll soon see just who will be victorious.''

"Rest assured I'll do everything in my power to keep you from carrying out any more of your evil plans, Isabelle.''

Both women knew there was nothing more to say. Christa turned on her heel and left the parlor, holding her head high.

Chapter 34

Christa paced nervously in her bedchamber. It was well past midnight, and she was weary to the bone from all she'd been through in the last day, but she couldn't rest.

She was leaving Haviland Court. Her belongings were packed. Ambrose and his son had just taken the last of her trunks down a rear staircase and out to the waiting carriage in the stable. She was going to Montclaire . . . and safety, she hoped. Certainly she couldn't stay here any longer. While she'd put up a bold front to Isabelle earlier in the parlor, in truth, she feared for her life. She'd fight Isabelle, but on her own territory, not here.

"Miz Christa?" Letty came into the bedroom.

"Yes, Letty, what is it? I sent you to bed."

"Oh, Miz Christa, you has gots to take me with you," the Negro woman beseeched as she clung to a black wool cloak and a faded brocade valise. "Ah can't stay here. Miz Isabelle hates me. She'll be makin' my life plum miserable. An' I'd be amissin' you so. Please, Miz Christa."

"Oh, Letty, I can't involve you in this difficulty with Miss Isabelle. There could be danger."

"Please, Miz Christa. Ah gots to come with you." Letty sank to her knees before her mistress and took her hand.

213

Christa couldn't bear the anguish in her servant's shiny face. She helped her to her feet.

"All right, Letty. I'd like you to be with me. You're a dear friend."

"Oh, thank you, ma'am."

"Very well then, go down the back way to the stables. And be very quiet. I don't want anyone to know we're leaving. I'll join you shortly. I just want to make a last check to see if we packed everything I wanted."

"Yes'm."

Letty's departure left the room ominously quiet. Christa swung her navy blue wool cloak over her shoulders and glanced around, sadly taking in the details of her beautiful room for perhaps the last time. She had the feeling she'd never return to Haviland Court.

She walked to the small bathing room located between her bedchamber and her husband's room. She wanted to be certain Letty had packed her silver brush and mirror set. The pieces had been a wedding gift from her mother and had great sentimental value to her.

Christa put down the candleholder she was carrying and checked the top of the small vanity. No grooming set was in sight.

Suddenly a sound caught her attention, making her tense. She strained to listen. There it was again. Coming from Nevin's room. Someone was moving around in there!

Christa's heart beat faster. Who could it be? A servant? A thief? What was the person doing? Possibilities streaked through her mind as fear gripped her. Could it be Isabelle or Lee Garrett sneaking about, furtively planning to reach her room by this indirect way to finish the heinous crime they hadn't accomplished at the mine?

Blowing out the candle, Christa quickly returned to her room, making no sound. Should she rouse the household? What if she were wrong in thinking those sounds meant danger to her? No, better to wait a little.

A weapon. She might need something for defense. She'd already packed her small pistol. In desperation, she glanced around her bedchamber. The fireplace tools!

She ran on tiptoe to the wide hearth, grabbed the brass poker, then hurried to the tall wardrobe to hide in the shadows to one side of it. Holding her breath, she fearfully watched the open doorway of the bathing room.

A long minute went by. Then another. Christa knew the fast beating of her heart far surpassed the speed of the ticking of the clock on the mantel. Her grip tightened on the cold metal of the poker, whitening her knuckles.

Another minute inched by. Christa breathed jaggedly, trying to control her taut nerves. Still no one came through the doorway. She frowned, feeling her fear subside a fraction. Why weren't they coming to kill her?

All was quiet now except for the sound of the fire crackling in the hearth across the room. Christa began to think she might have imagined the sounds. Perhaps her fatigued senses were playing tricks on her. But she had to know for certain.

Silently she inched around the wardrobe, keeping to the shadows at the edge of the room. When she reached her writing desk, she picked up the oil lamp in one hand, still gripping the poker tightly in the other. Cautiously she entered the bathing room.

The door to Nevin's room was still closed. Christa put an ear against the wooden panel. No sounds came from the other side, as they had before. She swallowed hard. Should she go in?

Her nerves tensed again. Tucking the poker under her arm, she slowly moved her hand to the round brass doorknob and turned it. The door made no noise as she opened it just enough to see into the other bedchamber. That limited view revealed nothing, so she nudged the door open all the way.

She saw him across the room. His back was to her, his lanky frame silhouetted by the light from an overhead oil lamp. His head was down, as if he was reading something.

Suddenly he swung around. For a brief moment his features were revealed in the lamplight. Christa gasped in shock, so stunned that she dropped both the lamp and the poker. The glass globe shattered loudly as it hit the hardwood floor. Instantly, the spilled oil was ignited by the still-burning wick. Christa gave a cry of alarm and jumped back from the burst of flames. She tore the cloak from around her shoulders and threw it over the small pool of fire, stomping on the material to smother the flames.

She sensed the man's swift movement away from her to another part of the room, but putting out the fire took her attention for a few seconds longer. Coughing from the smoke, she finally swung her head around to search for him, but he was nowhere in sight. She saw two panels of the wall come together near the fireplace. He must have disappeared through some secret exit.

Still coughing, she staggered over to the fireplace and pounded on the panels, but they remained firmly in place. In the dim light, she couldn't see any means of making them open, no button or lever to trip.

Christa sank down in an armchair, shocked by what she'd seen. It couldn't possibly have been him. Yet she knew her eyes hadn't deceived her. She'd seen her husband. Her *dead* husband. Nevin Haviland.

Chapter 35

"Christa, dear, whatever are you doing here?" Elspeth Kendall asked with delight as she entered her daughter's bedroom the next morning. "Crothers just told me you arrived late last night. What's happened, dear? Are you all right?"

Christa's mother had been petite and thin in her young womanhood. Now increased weight rounded her figure to plumpness. Her black hair, thick and full like Christa's, showed only a few signs of gray in its chignon. And her smile was as Christa had always remembered it—full of genuine concern and caring.

Christa got up from her dressing table and hugged her mother. "I'm fine, Mother. Don't worry. Isabelle and I had a . . . falling out, and it became necessary for me to leave Haviland Court. I hope my being here with Letty will not be an inconvenience."

"Of course not, dear. Don't be ridiculous. This is your home. And we were due for a visit. But I'm sorry to hear you and Isabelle are not getting along. She's your family, too."

Christa didn't say anything more about her sister-in-law for fear of upsetting her mother. Her maternal parent was a gentle, trusting woman who looked to others to take care of her and orchestrate her life. She didn't adapt well to conflict and change.

"You and Aunt Matilda and Myron are well, I

trust?'' Christa went on as she sat down next to her mother on the worn rose-colored sofa. The bright daylight streaming through the long windows revealed the growing shabbiness of the old furnishings and draperies. The room had been beautiful once. That memory saddened Christa. Still, she was glad to be home.

"Oh yes, we're all fine," her mother answered. "This cold spell has been hard on your Aunt Matilda's joints. They get so stiff, you know. Myron does so like to gaze out the windows whenever it snows. I wonder if there is somewhere in his poor, hurt mind that remembers when you and he and Julius were all children and you played so happily in the snow. Do you remember those times, dear?"

"Yes, Mother," Christa replied, gazing out the window.

She didn't know how much to tell her mother about what had happened. How could she explain about the mine and Trace and Isabelle? How could she say she'd seen Nevin alive? Her mother would think she was insane.

Christa knew she had to find out how her husband could still be alive and where he was now. And all the while, she must protect herself from Isabelle's treachery.

"Mother." She turned to face her parent now. "Has anyone asked you to sign some papers or documents recently?"

"Why, yes, dear. Isabelle was here last week with a Mr. Pemberton. He was such a nice man. They spoke of some legal matters that meant absolutely nothing to me. You know how difficult it is for me to understand such things. But he was so kind, saying he'd see to all the details. All I had to do was sign two documents he'd brought with him. Isabelle assured me that doing so was in all of our best interests."

Of course she did, Christa thought with a sinking heart. She knew no Mr. Pemberton. He was not the barrister with whom they usually dealt.

"Since he seemed so concerned and competent," her mother continued, "and Isabelle assured me of his reliability, I didn't see the need to consult you on the matter as I usually do. I didn't want to bother you, for I know you're still mourning your dear, departed Nevin." She patted Christa's arm.

Nevin departed, indeed. Christa forced herself to concentrate on the matter at hand. "What did you sign, Mother? Do you remember? Do you have a copy of it?"

"Mr. Pemberton said he'd have the papers properly executed and then send copies to me. But I must say I haven't received them yet, and it's been over a week, I think. But I'm certain the delay is nothing to worry about. I trust him. At any rate, the documents pertained to our gristmill. Mr. Pemberton, and Isabelle, too, felt it hasn't been managed as well as it could be under old Mr. Dorrity's supervision. They're right, of course. The poor man is getting so feeble, and his sons seem to be rather a shiftless pair. They do not assist him much in running our mill. That was Isabelle's observation, too. She's very astute in business. I don't think that's appropriate for a woman, but we must all use our talents as we see fit, I suppose."

"Did you sign the mill over to Mr. Pemberton, Mother?" Christa was afraid to hear the answer. The gristmill was one source of the badly needed income for the estate.

"Yes, dear, I think that's what I did. Mr. Pemberton assured me he knew someone who would run it far more efficiently and gain us a larger amount of profit.

And you know how badly we need that money. Also, he said he'd see that Mr. Dorrity was given a small pension when he was replaced. Wasn't that kind of him? We certainly don't have the money to do that.''

Christa's spirits sank further with each word her mother spoke. Gaining the mill must be part of Isabelle's scheme to attain Montclaire. Somehow Christa had to get the mill back. And track down Nevin. Neither task would be easy.

''Well, I came up here to fetch you for breakfast, dear,'' her mother went on, getting to her feet. ''We can talk more down in the dining room.''

''Yes, all right, Mother. But you go ahead. I'll finish dressing, then be down shortly.''

''All right, dear.''

When she was alone again, Christa tried to make a plan. She worried about what other treachery Isabelle might be planning. With so many of the estate's debts outstanding and grown delinquent, it would be easy for anyone with the financial means to negotiate for all the notes her father had signed when he was gambling so much and in such a state of melancholy before his suicide. Isabelle and Winston possessed both the money and the influence necessary to gain control of the debts.

Christa looked around the room. Her home. Her family's home for over three generations. Was it lost?

She sank down on the edge of the bed and buried her face in the pillow. Tears came easily, spurred by the pull of her emotions in so many directions. Trace, her family, Nevin, Isabelle. She felt overwhelmed. And dreadfully uncertain of what the future would bring.

Chapter 36

"Sit down, Letty. I must talk to you." Christa gestured the servant woman to the rose-colored sofa.

Christa no longer felt sorry for herself as she had earlier in the morning. She'd spent the afternoon in her room thinking of ways to find Nevin. Only one possibility came to her.

Christa came right to the point as she sat down next to the maid. "Letty, tell me about Charity Maxwell."

"What do you mean, Miz Christa?" Letty hedged.

"I want to know about Charity and . . ." Christa's voice faltered, reflecting the pain of what she had to say. But she persisted with determined resolve, recalling again Isabelle's nasty comments about her husband and the housemaid. "I want to know about Charity and my husband."

"Oh." Letty's voice was quiet and she dropped her gaze to her lap. "Ah really don' know nothin' 'bout that."

"Yes, you do, Letty. Your face reads like an open book. Now, please, you must tell me anything you know. It's very important. Were Charity and my husband lovers while he was married to me, before he died?"

"Oh, Miz Christa, don' make me talk 'bout this," Letty beseeched, raising dark eyes to her mistress's face. "It'll only be ahurtin' you so, an' ah don' want to do that. It be all over an' done with, 'cause Mr. Nevin is gone now. It won' do no good to be talkin' 'bout it."

"Just tell me what you know, Letty, please."

Letty sighed heavily in defeat, then nodded.

"Charity were a good girl, Miz Christa, truly she were. She didn't want no part o' Mr. Nevin when he first begun makin' . . . his attentions knowed to her. But he kep' after her, bein' charmin' an' actin' so sincerelike. He jus' plumb wore her down. She begun lovin' him with all her po' heart. An' he was aseemin' to care 'bout her, too. We all thought so. Treated her real nicelike and took her out of the scullery. He made her a upstairs maid, but she didn't have no duties really after that. Except to the master." Letty lowered her eyes again.

Christa didn't want to hear any more, but she had to know the truth. It might lead her to Nevin now, and that was what she had to focus on.

"Go on, Letty, please."

"Well," Letty continued reluctantly, "Mr. Orin finally found out 'bout what was agoin' on. Whew, but there were a real explosion then. Charity were pregnant, an' Mr. Orin got in a fearsome rage 'bout how he wouldn't have no son o' his'n carryin' on under his roof with no scullery maid. He wouldn't be ahavin' no bastard whelps at Haviland Court. Them was his exact words. We all heared 'em, he were ayellin' so loud. An' he said if'n Mr. Nevin didn't git rid of Charity, throw her right out'n the gutter where she belong, he says, he were agoin' to disinherit Mr. Nevin altogether. He wouldn't give him not a penny never. Charity were gone the next day. Ah don' know what happened to her nor her wee one. It weren't long after that but Mr. Nevin done took you fo' his wife. There were talk agoin' 'round that he were still aseein' Charity somewheres after that, but that be all ah ever heared. Ah don' know nothin' else, Miz Christa, ah purely don'.''

"You have no idea where Charity is now?" Christa felt her one lead slipping away.

"No, ma'am, ah don'.''

"Did she have any relatives? Parents? Brothers or sisters?''

"No, none that ah kin recalls.'' Letty frowned, appearing to be thinking hard. "Charity were a orphan. No, wait! Ah remembers she tol' me once she had a aunt. Now where were it she lived?'' Letty tapped a long brown finger against the side of her chin. "Ah think it were somewheres 'round the fish market. An' her aunt's name were Maxwell, too, like Charity's. Do that help, Miz Christa?''

"Yes, it does, Letty. Thank you. Now perhaps I can find Charity.''

"Oh, why would you be awantin' to do that, Miz Christa?'' Letty's look was compassionate. "There ain't no mo' to be done 'bout it now. Mr. Nevin's dead. Let it be.''

Nevin's dead. The words echoed like crashed cymbals in Christa's mind. No, no, he isn't. She wanted to tell Letty, tell *anyone*, to make it seem more real. She knew she'd seen her husband. Now she had to find him so she could prove to everyone else that he was alive.

"I must see Charity's aunt, Letty. Fetch my cloak, please. I'm leaving immediately.''

Christa had never been to the fish market district of the city. While she waited in the closed carriage, she let Benten, Montclaire's burly, middle-aged coachman, make inquiries about the Maxwells at some of the run-down row houses around the area. Finally, he was directed to a dilapidated clapboard house whose paint had long ago peeled away. Several shutters on the windows hung askew on their hinges.

There was nothing inviting about the house, but Christa made herself get out of the carriage and approach it. She kept her cloak pulled tightly around her and gained courage by having Benten follow several steps behind her. The scraggly haired older woman who answered her knock was almost as big as the coachman.

"Yeah? What do you be wantin'?" she demanded gruffly, letting her dark-circled eyes sweep over Christa in appraisal.

"Are you Mrs. Maxwell, aunt to one Charity Maxwell?" Christa asked, showing no intimidation.

"Maybe. Who wants to know?"

Before Christa could introduce herself, a young woman a year or two younger than she was came up beside the heavyset woman. She was very fair of skin, with a rough-edged natural beauty, long red hair, and a buxom figure that strained at the low-cut white blouse she was wearing.

"What is it, Aunt Ida? Who's here?"

"Shut up, girl. That's what I'm atryin' to find out."

Christa watched the smaller woman intently while she told them who she was. "I'm Mrs. Nevin Haviland."

The young woman blanched white and clutched her aunt's arm for support. The stricken look on her face told Christa she must be Charity. But the middle-aged woman only shrugged off her niece's hand and frowned.

"What do you want? You ain't got no right abotherin' us. We don't like you high-falutins comin' 'round here. Stick where you belong an' leave us alone, you hear?" She started to close the weather-beaten door, but Christa put out her booted foot to stop her.

"Just a minute," Christa demanded, making her voice more stern. Benten stepped forward and pushed the door wide open again. "I came here for information about my husband, and I intend to get it."

"Yer husband's dead! We don't know nothin' more about him," the aunt snapped at her, though she took a step farther back into the house when faced with the looming Benten.

Christa knew the woman was lying. Charity's fearful expression told Christa more than any words could convey.

"I don't believe you," Christa went on, frowning menacingly. "My husband is alive and I want to see him. Tell him I'm at Montclaire. If he doesn't meet me there very soon, I'll come back here with the authorities to have you both arrested and him hunted down. Mark my words. I mean them!"

"There ain't no call to do that," Ida Maxwell offered quickly. Apparently, the mention of the authorities made her feel more cooperative. A calculating gleam came into her deep-set blue eyes. "Maybe we do know how to reach him."

"Aunt Ida, no!" Charity blurted, clutching her aunt's arm again.

"Shut up, you worthless slut! Why're you protectin' him? He ain't done nothin' but use you. He only comes to you when he's got a itch in his man parts,

wantin' you to breed his bastards so's he kin flaunt 'em
to that high an' mighty father of his'n.''

"But he loves me. He *married* me, Aunt Ida!"
Charity cried forlornly. "Our baby died, but he weren't
no bastard!" The young woman buried her face in her
hands.

"Love—bah! He don't love you none. An' how
could he of wed with you if'n he was hitched with
her?" She stabbed a fat finger in Christa's direction.
"He likely only pretended to wed you. He tol' me
once he enjoyed the idea of aflauntin' a gutter-born
scullery maid as a high-falutin Haviland, that he were
jus' awaitin' fer the right time to do it. It's all a jest
to him, you dim-witted fool, a sick-headed game rich
folk like him plays with the likes o' us. Whilst he were
apayin' our keep, I didn't give much of a care for what
he were adoin' to you or why. But now it looks like
his little game of aplayin' dead is up, so's we'll be
plumb outta luck." She turned back to Christa.
"What's it worth to you, missy, if'n we see that he
gits yer message?"

Christa was too stunned to speak. All the aunt and
Charity had said bombarded her reason. They knew
where Nevin was. Charity's child by him was dead.
Nevin had married Charity. It was all too confusing.
She had to find Nevin and make him explain his
actions.

"Well, how much coin will you be agivin' us to git
in touch with him?" Ida persisted.

Christa blinked. Money. The woman wanted money.
But Christa had none. Yet she knew she couldn't let
Ida Maxwell know of her destitute state. She wouldn't
be blackmailed by the old hag either.

"There will be no coin, Mistress Maxwell," Christa
said sternly. "What you'll gain by delivering my

message to my husband is to *avoid* being prosecuted by the authorities for fraudulent practices!''

Christa turned on her heel and returned to the carriage, hoping her bluff had worked and that she might somehow flush Nevin out of hiding.

Chapter 37

When Christa returned to Montclaire from her
startling visit to the Maxwells, she was too
overwrought to see anyone. She paced her bedchamber,
trying to make sense out of the crazy jumble of her
thoughts.

"Pieces," she murmured in frustration. "So many
pieces of some bizarre puzzle and none of them fitting
together!"

What was Nevin doing? And Isabelle? Was everyone
in the Haviland family going mad? Christa hated not
knowing, hated being deceived, threatened, betrayed.

She knew Nevin despised his father with a passion,
yet up to now, he'd never done anything Christa was
aware of to defy the domineering patriarch of the
Haviland family. Orin Haviland held strict control over
his son and daughter, over the whole household. Intimidation seemed to be his manner of dealing with
everyone.

And Christa was tangled up in the web of hatred and
intrigue—of lunacy—with them. Her own life was in
peril, and her home, her family.

Then there was Trace Cavanaugh to further compli-
cate her life. In vain, she tried to put him out of her
mind. She couldn't forget how she'd felt while making
love with him at the cabin. Her body ached for him.

Her pulse quickened and a shiver of excitement raced through her just thinking about him.

She rubbed her pounding temples with her fingertips. She couldn't reason anymore. Nothing made any sense.

Letty knocked at the hall door and entered the bedroom at Christa's beckoning. "Ah brung you some supper, Miz Christa," she said, carrying a silver tray to the bed.

"I'm not hungry, Letty."

"You has got to eat somethin' or you'll be awastin' away to nothin'." She put the tray down on the night table. "You be lookin' so peaked an' tired lately." She reached over and gently pushed back a tendril of Christa's hair.

"You fuss over me too much," Christa told her affectionately, wishing she could confide all the burdens plaguing her mind and heart to her loyal maid. But Letty couldn't help, and Christa didn't want to worry her.

"Will you be afeelin' up to goin' to General Zachary's dinner party tomorrow evenin'?" Letty asked. "Ah'll need to be knowin' so's ah kin git one o' yo' fine gowns all pressed up an' prettylike."

"The dinner party . . ." Christa echoed the words. She'd forgotten about Olivia's party. The invitation had arrived weeks ago. She hadn't planned on going, out of respect for her husband's death, but that no longer applied, did it? Christa thought to herself with a cold anger.

Olivia Zachary was a dear friend, and Christa knew the older woman returned her affection. Perhaps she could confide in the general's wife about Nevin. Fitzhugh Zachary certainly would have more resources at his disposal for finding Nevin than Christa did. If she could only convince Olivia to enlist his aid . . .

"Yes, Letty, I'll be attending the party," Christa replied determinedly. "And I'll wear my blue silk gown with the ivory lace trim."

"Yes, ma'am. That be a perfect choice." Letty gave a nod and smiled broadly as she went to the bedchamber closet for the gown Christa had chosen.

"Christa! And Elspeth and Matilda, how good of you to come! Don't you all look lovely." Olivia Zachary greeted the three women with genuine pleasure when they arrived at the party. "Christa, that gown is stunning. The color matches your eyes perfectly. I'm so happy you've come, my child, and discarded your widow's weeds. I feel mourning is often observed too long. Life must go on." She gave Christa a hug. "Thank heaven for winter and its hampering effects on this terrible war. At least we can observe some of the civilized social amenities."

"Thank you for inviting us, Olivia," Christa's mother said.

While the older women continued chatting, Christa made her way to the spacious ballroom of the house the Zacharys had been renting since the war had brought them to America. The two-story room, decorated in bright green wallpaper, was elegantly offset by a finely detailed white ceiling. White wainscoting covered the walls from floor to midway, and white cornices framed the tall, many-paned windows draped in green satin. Two large, candleladen crystal chandeliers suspended from the ceiling cast bright light over the room. Many guests stood talking together in small groups while a string quartet played in one corner of the ballroom.

"Christa!"

She turned at the sound of her name to find Marcus Desmond coming toward her.

"I never dreamed you might attend this affair," he said as he raised her hand to his lips. There was such pleasure in his expression that Christa had to smile.

"Marcus, it's so good to see you."

"Are you alone? I could have escorted you, had I known you were coming."

"I accompanied Mother and Aunt Matilda," Christa answered as she gently withdrew the hand he still held. "And I decided to attend only last night. I couldn't bother you at such short notice."

"Now I'm crushed. You know you could never do anything that would be a bother to me."

"Thank you, Marcus. I'll remember that. How's the leg?"

"This cold winter weather gives it a twinge or two once in a while, but otherwise it seems to be all right. I've discovered that favoring it from time to time when I'm defending one of my woebegotten clients gains me favor with the judge. Not that I would ever take advantage of such a tactic."

"No, never. You're too scrupulous for that," Christa teased.

"But enough of me. Will you allow me to escort you to the refreshment table? I'd enjoy making every man present green with envy because I'm with the most beautiful woman here." He broke into a hopeful smile as he made a slight bow and extended his elbow to her.

"You're too gallant, sir," Christa replied, laughing and taking his arm. She was glad to be with Marcus. He was a friend with whom she always felt at ease. And he was very good-looking in his purple knee-length coat of corded silk, with matching knee trousers and silver brocade vest.

She knew she could call on him for help. He would assist her gladly. Yet it was Trace who came to her mind now. Always Trace.

Would he be here tonight with General Zachary's other officers? Christa scanned the many faces in the crowd as she crossed the room with Marcus, not pleased to admit to herself that she secretly hoped Trace would be in attendance.

Then she changed her mind and hoped she wouldn't see him, for she knew her knees would weaken and her pulse would speed up if she did. Her stomach twinged just thinking about him. She was glad to be with Marcus, but he didn't make her feel this excitement. It only happened with Trace. No, she wouldn't allow it! She'd stay with Marcus. He was safe. Yes, she hoped Trace wasn't there.

But he was.

When Christa and Marcus reached the long table filled with appetizers and beverages, she saw him standing by the raised musicians' platform with several other people. Christa's breath caught in her throat. He was strikingly handsome in his dress uniform. The scarlet coat faced in black with gold trimmings, the white vest and matching tight breeches gave him a commanding appearance. Christa's gaze swept over every detail, from his white-powdered wig down to his black leather shoes.

Against her will, her heart had leaped at the sight of him, but now it sank with an almost audible thud when she saw who was with him. Suko Yamagata, the beautiful Japaneses princess Trace had once told her he might wish to wed someday. Suko looked up adoringly at Trace, giving her rapt attention to whatever he was saying. She looked like an exquisite, fine porcelain figurine, fragile and breathtakingly lovely. Her salmon-colored kimono detailed with black and green lotus blossoms was caught by a white silk sash at her small waist. Her coal-black hair, done in a traditional

Japanese style, glistened with silver combs and bejeweled ornaments as she turned her head.

Her samurai was also in attendance. Tohashi stood a respectful distance away from his mistress, but his eyes were constantly on her and her companions. In his black, full-sleeved ceremonial robe, his legs spread apart and his arms crossed over his chest, he presented an imposing figure. His very stance emitted unfriendliness, suggested a threat. He was garnering considerable attention, as was Suko.

"I see you've noticed the princess," Marcus commented next to Christa.

"Who is she?" she asked, pretending ignorance.

"Princess Suko Yamagata from the very distant land of Japan. Her father was an important man in the emperor's royal court. She was betrothed to one of the emperor's sons at birth, making her a royal personage. They do that sort of thing in Japan—betrothing infants. It's an ancient custom."

"Then she's married?" Christa wasn't certain why she hoped that was true.

"No. From what I hear," Marcus went on, "her husband-to-be died in a provincial war before they could wed. The princess's father and the rest of her family were killed as well. She barely managed to escape Japan with her own life, bringing with her considerable wealth in precious gems and that ferocious feudal warrior you see standing most protectively by her. He's the consummate samurai, all the way to the hilt of those two very formidable battle swords he's wearing in his sash. And he doesn't like Americans. He'd as soon split you down the middle as look at you, is my feeling."

Mine, too, Christa added silently, remembering too well her first meeting with Tohashi.

"Isn't that Captain Cavanaugh with her?" she went on aloud, trying to sound nonchalant.

"Yes. Trace met the princess's father while traveling in his youth. Miss Yamagata sought him out when she reached our country about a year ago. He's been her mentor and guardian ever since. And that's no easy task with the samauri around."

"I should imagine not," Christa agreed. "Then the princess is perhaps the captain's ward?"

"Not legally, but he makes no secret of his unofficial protection of her. And she makes no secret of her willingness to accept it." Marcus leaned closer and spoke more quietly behind his hand. "It's said she's in love with Trace, but that's no surprise. Most of the women here are in love with him. I don't know what it is about him, but you ladies seem to find him irresistible. The lucky bloke. He's never without a lovely companion. But then, neither am I." He smiled and patted Christa's hand on his arm.

Christa forced herself to return his smile, but as she took up a plate from the table to fill with the wide array of taste-tempting foods, her thoughts drifted from Marcus. She surreptitiously scanned the room and saw many of the younger ladies present sending covert glances in Trace's direction. It wasn't just Suko they were looking at. Marcus was right. Trace emanated a magnetism few women could resist. He was easy to fall in love with. Too easy.

She frowned, angry with herself. Did she love him? How stupid that would be. He'd clearly told her he didn't want her to be involved in his life. She must forget him, forget his courage, his bold self-assurance, his possessive hands and passionate caresses . . . But tormentingly, Christa remembered them all vividly. She was further tortured by the thought that he'd likely made love to many women. She was only one of them.

And besides, nothing could exist between them now, not with Nevin, her lawful husband, still alive.

Suko was the woman Trace evidently wanted. That night at her house he'd said she was a more favorable choice than a Western-cultured woman because she knew the ancient skills of pleasing a man. Something I'm obviously not well versed in, Christa thought to herself with anger and hurt as she drank a healthy portion of wine from her crystal goblet. The fine claret spread warmly through her, making her flush. And on her empty stomach, Christa knew it would soon have the effect of softening her surroundings, making reality seem less harsh. She took another sip.

Trace watched Christa chatting with Marcus Desmond. Her sapphire blue gown highlighted all he remembered of her sensuous beauty. The white lace edging the deeply cut neckline matched the creamy paleness of her skin. Her breasts were little revealed. Only the tempting tops showed with a small amount of cleavage. But his imagination could fill in the rest, and in his mind's eye, she wore no elegant silk gown. So easily he saw her, felt her in his arms before the blazing fire at the cabin, a fire that still seemed to burn inside him. Her powdered white wig was perfectly coiffured in deep waves and coils of curls, but he knew how her real black hair looked, how the thick, silky tresses felt entangled in his fingers.

Damn her! Trace cursed inwardly. Why did she have to be so desirable? She aroused him more than any other woman, made him feel a passion no woman had previously ignited. But he was sure his attraction was just physical, his man-need for a woman. He wouldn't let himself think he might be falling in love with her. Yet he realized he was drawn not only by her sensuous body but also by her strength of will, her loyalty, her spirit.

A servant passed carrying a silver tray laden with long-stemmed glasses filled with champagne. Trace took a glass in each hand, intending to give one of them to Suko. But when he heard the sound of Christa's light laughter float to him just then, he frowned and gulped down the contents of both glasses in quick succession.

Chapter 38

Many people in attendance at the Zacharys' dinner gathering were friends who Christa hadn't seen during the months of her mourning.

"Christa, my dear, it's so good to see you." The heavyset dowager, Mrs. Alvera Johnston, descended on her just as she and Marcus were going into the dining room. "You're looking so well, child." She said the words almost as an accusation.

"Thank you, Mrs. Johnston," Christa acknowledged with a wan smile.

"You're looking exceedingly lovely tonight yourself, Widow Johnston," Marcus complimented. The older woman looked pleased as she turned her attention to him.

"Why, thank you, Mr. Desmond. It's always nice to have one's appearance noticed favorably by a gentleman."

While Marcus was held in conversation with the dowager, Christa took the opportunity to move a little away and study some of the other guests. It was then she saw Orin Haviland arrive, accompanied by Isabelle. Impeccably dressed as usual, the Haviland patriarch carried his bulk well. He was immediately surrounded by a number of people seeking his attention.

Isabelle held her head high as she entered the ballroom. She was stunningly dressed in a bright red silk gown. Her hair was powdered white and piled high on her head in ringlets. Many male guests turned appreciative eyes in her direction.

Christa had no desire to confront any of the Haviland family members, and since Marcus was still detained by the Widow Johnston, she decided to seek out Olivia Zachary. When she finally found her friend, she saw, to her dismay, that Trace and Suko were with Olivia and her husband.

Christa decided not to join them. She could see Trace clearly from where she stood behind a shoulder-high pedestal displaying an elegant procelain vase. Trace was very handsome. She saw him flash a quick half smile. It gave his chiseled features such animation.

Christa's heart turned over, and an ache throbbed deep within her that she knew she wouldn't be able to overcome for a long time. She shouldn't have come tonight. It would have been better if she hadn't seen Trace again.

Keep your mind on why you came, she scolded herself. She had to speak to Olivia about enlisting General Zachary's aid in finding Nevin.

She looked at Fitzhugh Zachary as he spoke to Suko. In his military uniform, he cut a distinguished figure for a man in his mid-fifties. He hadn't let middle age widen his girth, as Orin Haviland had. Trace was speaking to him now, and for a moment Christa watched the two men, noticing for the first time that there were similarities in their features—the square jawline, the straight nose, the sharply arched dark brows. Yet the likeness ended with those attributes. The general had blue eyes to Trace's turquoise and his hair was black with streaks of gray at the temples to Trace's dark brown. Trace was also taller than his commander.

Christa couldn't help thinking it was curious how features could be randomly blended to create such resemblances in people who weren't related. Madeline Scarbrough, her best friend at finishing school, had looked so much like Christa that people had often mistaken them for sisters.

"There you are."

Christa turned as Marcus moved next to her.

"Did you finally escape Widow Johnston?" Christa asked with amusement. "Thank you for drawing her attention from me. I don't think she approves of my socializing so soon."

"Well, I do. And my opinion is the only one I ever consider." Marcus's brown eyes were warm. "But I swear that woman could talk a leg off a tall giraffe. So, since I rescued you from her, you must now repay me by accompanying me to dinner." He held out his arm and Christa took it.

"My pleasure, sir."

Trace didn't realize he was frowning as he watched Christa leave the ballroom. Her radiant smile irritated him greatly.

"Cavanaugh-san, what is it?" Suko asked at his side. "You look so displeased."

"It's nothing, Suko," Trace replied, quickly masking his annoyance. "Shall we go to the dining room?"

He felt a small twinge of guilt when he saw his companion's warm smile. She wore her heart in her dark eyes. He knew what her feelings were for him, and until recently he hadn't been averse to them. He'd even thought he was beginning to feel something special, something other than friendship, for Suko. But that was before. Before Christa . . .

Later in the evening, Christa finally approached her busy hostess. "The party is a great success, Olivia," she complimented her friend as they sat together on a small green brocade sofa.

"Thank you, dear. I'm pleased you think so. We've had so little chance for such social gatherings because of the war. I'm glad when the troops are in winter quarters and there are no battles."

"Yes, I agree," Christa replied. Taking a deep breath, she plunged into her real reason for needing to spend time with her friend.

"Olivia, I must speak to you about a most unusual but exceedingly important matter."

"Why, yes, of course, my dear, what is it? You look so serious."

"What I'm about to tell you will sound bizarre, even unbelievable. But I swear to you it is the complete truth." She paused for a moment, gathering her courage. "Nevin is alive, Olivia."

"What? What are you saying? Nevin, your husband?" The older woman looked incredulous.

"Yes. Last night at Haviland Court, I heard a noise in his bedchamber, and when I went to investigate . . . Oh, Olivia, I swear what I'm saying is the truth! Nevin is *alive*. I saw him and he saw me. But before I could approach him, he escaped through a secret panel in the wall. I couldn't find a way to follow him. But I know it was Nevin. I know he's alive! You must help me!"

"There, there, dear, calm yourself." Olivia took Christa's hand and patted it, a slight frown creasing her brow. "While this revelation, indeed, sounds quite extraordinary, I know you are not one who's given to hysterical imaginings. Dear me, but this situation does pose several most distressing questions. How can Nevin be alive when he was in that terrible explosion? Where is he now? What is he doing?"

"And how can I find him?" Christa interjected.

"That's why I need your help, Olivia—and your husband's. The general has more means of making an investigation than I. Could you prevail upon him to help me?"

"Of course, my dear. Hugh will be able to help, I'm certain. Come, we'll find him right now."

"Thank you, Olivia." Christa took hold of the older woman's hand. "Thank you for believing me."

Chapter 39

"Why, Captain Cavanaugh, how good to see you again," Isabelle exclaimed as she approached Trace and Suko at the buffet table. "We haven't seen you at Haviland Court of late."

"I've been occupied at your sister-in-law's potassium nitrate mine, Mrs. Sheffield. It's going to be of great benefit to His Majesty for the production of saltpeter. However, we've had a small setback because of a mysterious explosion that recently occurred." Trace kept his tone conversational, but he stared pointedly at her.

"Really? How dreadful." Isabelle blinked once, but otherwise showed no sign that she knew what Trace was talking about. "This must be the princess about whom I've been hearing so much," she continued, focusing her attention on his companion.

"Princess Suko Yamagata, Mrs. Sheffield," Trace said, introducing them. Suko gave a small smile and bowed.

"Why, she's perfectly delightful, Captain," Isabelle observed. "And so lovely, too. She hardly looks real. It's surprising what can come from a savage foreign land. Does she have the ability to speak English?"

Trace replied with cool disdain, "Suko's homeland has a history and a culture that are centuries older than even Great Britain's, Mrs. Sheffield. By Japanese

243

standards, we are the primitive savages. But, unlike you, Suko is too polite to make any such reference. You may speak directly to her. Not only does she speak English quite well, she is also fluent in five other languages. How many languages do you speak, Mrs. Sheffield?''

''Well, I—I speak French,'' Isabelle stammered.

''How limited. But please excuse us, Mrs. Sheffield. The princess and I were just going to dine.'' Trace gave a curt nod and led Suko away, leaving Isabelle standing alone with her mouth open.

''Why did Mrs. Sheffield not like me, Cavanaugh-san?'' Suko asked when they were far enough away not to be heard.

''Because next to you, my lovely lotus blossom, Isabelle Sheffield is a poisonous weed.'' Trace smiled down at Suko. ''I apologize for her rudeness. Think no more about her. Let's enjoy dinner.''

Christa had little appetite for the lavish banquet of meats and vegetables, fruits and delicate pastries. She realized she should try to eat, for she was feeling light-headed from drinking claret on an empty stomach. Fatigue crept in to make her eyes heavy. The hour was growing late. Those guests not staying the night were beginning to depart.

A short while later, Christa left the dining room to seek the haven of the room Olivia had assigned to her. She smiled, thinking of Marcus's crestfallen expression when she told him she was going to retire. Dear Marcus. He was a good friend, but she felt nothing more than fondness for him. His attentiveness hadn't lagged all evening. She'd welcomed it at first, but later had felt pressed in by his continuous presence. Avoiding Isabelle, Orin, and Trace had proved to be a strain on her, too. But at least she had acquired General

Zachary's cooperation in finding Nevin. He'd promised to begin an investigation immediately.

Christa kicked off her blue silk shoes and sank her toes into the hooked rug on the floor, relishing its soft comfort. A crackling fire warmed the room. For a few moments, she watched the flames cast dancing shadows over the beige walls. Her thoughts drifted to Trace. All evening, she'd been torn by a need to avoid him and a stronger desire to be with him. Several times she'd caught herself staring at him from across the room. She hated herself for longing for him.

An unexpected knock at the door made her jump. Her eyes widened when she answered it. "Trace . . ." she murmured in surprise.

"You looked very pale when you left the dining room just now, Christa. Are you ill?" His tone was formal.

"I—I'm only fatigued, Captain." Her heart beat faster when he made no move to leave.

"You avoided me all evening."

His steady turquoise gaze seemed to have the power to look right into her. The feeling unnerved her.

"I had no reason to speak to you," she explained defensively. "You were well occupied with the princess."

"As were you with Marcus Desmond."

"I'm surprised you noticed. Please don't worry about me, Captain Cavanaugh. I'll be fine after a good night's rest. Return to Miss Yamagata. I'm certain she needs your attention more than I."

"Suko decided to leave a while ago. She'd had enough narrow-minded snubbing for one night. I saw her home and returned just now at the general's request."

Christa relented her sharp words, feeling sympathy for the young Japanese woman. "I'm sorry Suko didn't enjoy herself. She must be very lonely in our country, away from all she once knew. Living here must be difficult for her.''

Damn! Trace cursed inwardly. Why wasn't Christa rude and aloof like Isabelle Sheffield and several others had been toward Suko tonight? Then he could be furious with her and rebuke her with scathing words as he had the others. But Christa was kind and caring.

''Yes, Suko misses her home in Japan very much,'' he replied, just to say something.

An awkward silence fell between them.

''I—I'm very tired, Captain,'' Christa said finally, her voice hesitant.

''You were calling me Trace at one time. Why did you leave the cabin?'' he asked suddenly.

''The cabin?'' She frowned, startled by his shift in topic. ''I had to leave. You gave me no reason to stay.'' Uncomfortably, she lowered her eyes from his steady gaze. ''I don't like what you do to me, Trace. You confuse me, torment my thoughts, make me angry. I don't like those feelings.''

She couldn't disguise the hurt that welled up inside her. To hide it from him, she turned away and wrapped her arms around herself. She heard the door close behind her, then felt his hands touch her shoulders. Her whole body tensed.

''I know those feelings as well,'' Trace whispered close to her ear. ''And others. What do you feel when I'm close to you like this? Tell me, Christa.''

He kissed the back of her neck. A shiver went through her. She closed her eyes and bit her lower lip to try to will her body to resist the urgent excitement that suddenly exploded to life in the pit of her stomach and raced to all her senses.

Trace felt her tremble. The heat of her body radiated through his hands. He couldn't pull them away. Too late, he realized his mistake in touching Christa at all. Her nearness overruled his reason. He couldn't keep from stepping closer and moving his hands down her arms to her waist. Slowly, he turned her around to face him. She kept her head down until he lifted her chin with his fingertips.

"Look at me, Christa," he murmured softly. Her beauty in the firelight was almost more than he could bear. She looked so troubled that he longed to hold her, keep the world at bay so he wouldn't have to see such pain on her lovely face.

Trace didn't know why he'd felt compelled to follow her when she left the dining room. She was wrong for him, an aristocrat, a loyalist. Reason told him to fight the overwhelming need she ignited in him. She haunted him. She was the forbidden fruit, everything he'd struggled against all his life while he sought to educate himself and gain wealth and influence by his own merit. And yet he had to have her. Had to taste her, feel her close to him again. Nothing else mattered.

"Trace, please don't do this," Christa pleaded. Her blue-gray eyes met his. "Don't hold me. Don't touch me. I can't let you. This can't be."

"Hush, Christa. It can be . . ."

She wanted to tell him about Nevin, wanted to say her husband was alive. Or was he? Hadn't she buried him? Was the man at Haviland Court last night really Nevin? Was he even her husband? Had he ever been? Terrible confusion blurred her reason.

Trace ended the desperate turmoil of her thoughts by covering her lips with his, silencing any protest she might have tried to make.

The kiss was deep . . . long . . . breathtaking. Christa tried to remain impervious to it. She made her hands stay at her sides when she wanted to encircle his neck with her arms. She kept her eyes open, forcing herself to think about the room, the fire, anything that might prevent her from being caught in the web of his desire.

Trace sensed her holding back and would have none of it. He released her lips only long enough to take a breath, then he kissed her again, more fervently. His arms pulled her hard against him.

Christa felt her will being snatched from her control. Trace's mouth possessed hers with a demand that overpowered her judgment, her fears, her conscious resistance. His tempestuous kiss caused a river of excitement to flow through every part of her being. She must give in. She sensed he was holding back, waiting for her to surrender so he could give her more. And she wanted more. She longed for him with all her heart.

She forced her troubling thoughts aside. This room could be their hiding place, where nothing reached them.

Christa moaned softly. Trace lifted her in his arms and carried her to the bed. He hated the formal clothing they wore—his uniform, her cumbersome gown. It took too long to get out of them when he was anxious to hold Christa, caress her, make love to her.

At last they lay naked in each other's arms. Trace checked his fiery hunger while he used his lips to explore and memorize every curve of Christa's quivering flesh. His hands caressed her—her shoulders, a soft, straining breast.

Christa wanted him to go on touching her, kissing her again and again. An urgency rose within her, making her long for the magnificent pinnacle of climax she'd known before with him. A scalding heat spread through her. Trace's lips found every point where her racing pulse strained close to the surface of her skin. His fingertips ran along the sensitive insides of her arms, to her thighs, and back to her passion-swollen breasts. And then his mouth and tongue followed the same path. Christa gasped and writhed beneath the wondrous torture, trying to anticipate where he would touch her next. Her fingers entwined in his hair, forcing his lips to remain on her breast. She knew by his jagged breathing and tense muscles that his excitement matched the heights of hers. She loved him for waiting, for caring about her pleasure as much as his own.

"Now, Trace, please . . ." she murmured. "I need you. I want you inside me. Now, please . . ."

He moved over her. Now he could know her completely, feel her consume him with all her womanliness. Her legs parted and she arched her hips to meet him, gasping and giving a low cry of pleasure when he entered her. They moved in perfect rhythm, he thrusting deeper, she opening, receiving, welcoming him. Then they froze in their movements as the shock of powerful pulsations exploded with full, overwhelming force and spread from him to her and back again.

Christa was limp with exhaustion. She closed her eyes and lay still beneath Trace, basking in the afterglow of their passionate lovemaking, in awe of what had passed between them, of what he'd made her feel. Had his pleasure matched hers? Yes, she knew it had.

Trace made no move to leave her. He wanted to stay intimately close to Christa, remain in her even now after the fierce explosion had subsided. He shifted sideways a little to ease the press of his weight from her. He let his hand slowly move over her, drawing out her pleasure. With the most tender of touches he stroked her body, over her stomach and rounded hips, up the gentle curve of her waist to her full breasts. Gently, softly his fingertips caressed the tips. Then he bent his head and used his lips and tongue to do the same.

Christa closed her eyes and moaned with dreamy contentment. She hugged him to her and ran her hands over his muscular shoulders, back, and arms.

"I can't bear this, Trace," she murmured happily.

"You don't find my caresses pleasing?" A slight smile touched the corners of his mouth before he leaned down to kiss her neck.

"Oh, yes, too pleasing. You make me want you brazenly."

"Then you've discovered my goal, fair lady."

Trace, too, was basking in a contentment he hadn't known so intensely with any other woman. He'd given all of himself to Christa, held nothing back, and taken all from her. He was spent, yet he knew he'd want her again very soon. Already he felt his need for her stirring anew.

He wouldn't let himself think beyond his physical desire. He convinced himself he wanted her so intensely because she was still new to him. Her body was warm and giving, so quick to respond to his touch. He hadn't had his fill of her yet. But he would. He always did. When he felt such a strong attraction to a woman, he pursued her until the conquest was made, the need gratified. But he eventually lost interest and moved on to someone else. The same would happen with Christa, he was certain.

He leaned down to kiss her softly again. She answered his kiss fervently and kept moving her hands over his body, exploring it, igniting it. With a slow deliberateness she kissed his mouth, then his rough cheek, his eyelids, his forehead. One finger played with a stray strand of his dark brown hair at his temple, then moved to trace the shape of his ear. The effect on Trace was immediate. The fire of his need grew hotter with each kiss, each movement of Christa's hands. He felt himself growing hard within her again. She felt it, too, and smiled with pleasure as she moved her hips to align with him once more. The rhythm began again. The compelling back-and-forth movement excited them both to the frenzied zenith of shared rapture.

Chapter 40

Christa drifted slowly to wakefulness, a persistent knocking pulling her back from the realm of dreams—dreams filled with enchantment, excitement, wonder. And one man—Trace.

"Come in," she called without thinking. Then, in panic, she sat up with a start and quickly pulled the quilts up to cover herself and Trace.

"Good mornin', Miz Christa," Letty sang out as she sailed into the room.

Christa didn't pay any attention to her. She was staring at the empty place next to her where Trace should have been lying. Where was he?

"Is somethin' wrong, Miz Christa?"

"No, Letty, nothing's wrong." Christa turned to the woman and tried to hide her confusion. "What time is it?"

"Why, 'tis near half pas' nine. Ah thought you was agoin' to sleep the whole day away. Late breakfast is bein' served in the dinin' room in a hour. But don't worry 'bout hurryin' none. You ain't the only one what's slept in latelike. That were some party last night. Did you have a good time?"

Letty sat on the edge of the bed, eager to hear details about the ball. She'd come to the Zacharys' to attend Christa and help with kitchen chores for the party.

"My, but you had a restless sleep last night," she went on, glancing at the tangled sheets and quilts.

Christa blushed with embarrassment as she pulled the quilt tighter around her to hide her nakedness.

"Can you have a bath drawn for me, Letty?" she asked. "I'll manage it and dress by myself this morning. Why don't you tend Mother and Aunt Matilda?"

Letty looked a little confused by Christa's change in routine, but she didn't question it.

"Well, if'n that be what you want. Yer mama were askin' me to help her with her hair." She stood up and walked toward the door. "I'll be sendin' up a couple of kitchen boys with the hot water."

After her servant had left the bedchamber, Christa lay back against the pillows, expelling her breath in relief. She did *not* want to explain last night to anyone, much less to her well-meaning but talkative maid. She just wanted to bask in the remembrance of her torrid and wondrous night making love with Trace.

A smile touched the corners of Christa's mouth. She became conscious of her body, of its stiffness and sensitivity caused from that unaccustomed activity. Even the soft quilt around her registered sharply on her flesh, which was still tingling from Trace's fervent lovemaking. The way his lips and hands could make her body come completely alive was unbelievable.

She hugged Trace's pillow. A happy feeling surged through her. This bedchamber was the most beautiful room she'd ever seen—her haven with Trace. Even the sunlight shining in the windows seemed brighter this morning because of the joy and contentment she felt.

Trace most likely had gone back to his room early to avoid being discovered by the servants, Christa reasoned, pleased that he cared about her reputation. But she couldn't help wondering what it would have been like to awaken next to him, to welcome the new day in his arms. The thought made her smile widen.

"What a wanton you are, Christa," she chided herself with a sigh. Never could she have imagined being so carried away by a man. Their joinings filled her with an excitement and awe that left her amazed and longing for more. She knew that what she felt for Trace could have only one explanation. She was in love with him. Irrationally. Desperately. Completely.

The realization filled her with both exultation and dread. Loving him was insane. It was wrong. Heaven help her, for she couldn't help herself. What would come of this love for Trace? Did he love her in return? Last night when they were together, so close, so completely united, she would have shouted to the heavens that he did. But now, when she found herself alone, everything seemed different. Thoughts of Nevin crept in to torment her. And Isabelle. Montclaire. Her family. Her ponderings sobered her, snatching away much of the joy she'd felt only moments before.

When Christa entered the dining room an hour later, she found her hosts already in attendance with two other guests she recognized, Major Torrence Stanton and Lieutenant Anthony Brigham. They were seated at the elegant dining table, about to be served the combination of breakfast and luncheon dishes waiting on the sideboard—eggs prepared in several ways, fried potatoes, porridge, breads, cheeses, sliced cold meats and poultry, and fruits. The array looked sumptuous, indeed.

Christa quickly scanned the room for Trace, but to her disappointment, she saw he wasn't present.

"Good morning, Christa," Olivia Zachary greeted her. "Come join us. Are you feeling all right, child? You look a bit flushed."

Embarrassment heated Christa's face and spread over her whole body, but she reminded herself that no one at the table could possibly know that the unusual pinkness in her cheeks had been caused by Trace's whisker stubble rubbing over her skin all night.

"I feel fine, Olivia," she assured the older woman as she took a place at the table.

Christa chatted with Major Stanton and Lieutenant Brigham during most of the meal. She was nearly finished eating when the men's conversation turned to military matters.

"Thanks to Captain Cavanaugh's successful supply route, we haven't experienced a serious lack of foodstuffs and equipment," Stanton related to Fitzhugh Zachary.

"I'm glad to hear that," the general replied. He turned to Christa. "Speaking of Captain Cavanaugh, I discussed the matter of that missing person with him early this morning. He's en route to Kip's Bay now to begin an investigation. If anyone can get to the bottom of the matter, he can. I've come to have a high regard for Trace. He's almost like the son Olivia and I lost. He's a man of extraordinary talents."

"Thank you, General. I'm certain you're right."

Christa saw a shadow fall over Olivia Zachary's features at her husband's words. She knew the sad story of the Zacharys' son, how he'd died of a consumption in the lungs as a young child. They had never had any other children. Christa's heart went out to her friend.

At least she knew the reason for Trace's absence. But now he knew that her husband was still alive. How would that fact affect his feelings for her?

Major Stanton continued speaking. "We've encountered nearly constant trouble from that network of rebel spies headed by the traitor we know only as the

Scorpion. The bounties you put on him and his coconspirators haven't gained us one shred of information of any value. The Scorpion is always one step ahead of us. Even while both sides are sequestered in winter quarters, he's found ways of undermining our plans.''

"Forgive me, Fitzhugh," Olivia said, addressing her husband. "I see Christa is finished eating, so I think she and I shall retire to the parlor and leave you men to talk business."

"Very well, my dear," Zachary replied, rising to his feet. The other two officers did the same.

"We should have your mother and aunt join us for some sewing in the parlor, Christa," Olivia suggested when they reached the hall.

"Yes, I'm certain they'd like that activity," Christa agreed. Then she stopped walking. "Oh dear, I forgot that Mother asked me to have a breakfast tray sent up to her. I'll only be a moment while I tell one of the servants."

Olivia nodded and Christa returned to the dining room.

Not wishing to disturb the men, she stayed near the door and motioned for the butler to come over to her. While she asked for the food tray, she only half listened to their conversation.

"We must take extra care in guarding and routing the special payroll wagon we're expecting, General," Stanton suggested. "It's been months since the men received compensation. This delay is severely undermining morale."

"I'm aware of that, Major," Zachary replied, his tone solemn.

"These Continentals are uncivilized rabble, undisciplined provincials, not honorable professional soldiers and loyal subjects of His Majesty," Lieutenant Brigham piped in, sounding angry. "We should have brought this Scorpion character to heel and destroyed the ring of spies he commands long before now.''

Christa glanced toward the young officer, offended by his insulting remarks. She resented his reference to Americans as being uncivilized rabble. She was an American, after all, and felt a sudden pang of allegiance to her homeland.

"Cool your indignation, Lieutenant," Zachary advised. "We sorely underestimated the Continentals, and paid dearly for that short-sightedness. They also have the strategic advantage of fighting on their home soil. Hopefully, we'll overcome these problems when the spring campaign begins. I, for one, take the rebels very seriously. I don't intend to repeat past mistakes. I'm still stinging from the blow of having that vital encampment at Hastings Hollow destroyed by infiltrators who sabotaged the dam. Our forces were made to look like bloody fools that day. But that incident is behind us. Now we must . . .''

Christa was too stunned to listen further. Her legs felt weak as she hastily excused herself to the butler and slipped out of the dining room. Sitting down hard on an upholstered bench in the hallway, she tried to fathom what she'd just heard. How could General Zachary's words be true? She'd been at Hastings Hollow. *Continental* forces had been camped there. Trace had said . . .

Christa's thoughts froze. The terrible feeling twisting in the pit of her stomach was nothing compared to what she felt in her heart. She hadn't seen the camp herself. She'd taken Trace's word that it was manned by rebels. But now she knew she'd helped him blow up a dam that had destroyed an important *British* fortification. Could Trace have made a mistake?

With a sinking heart, she realized the answer to that

question. Trace Cavanaugh wasn't the kind of man who made mistakes.

The Scorpion. She remembered Stanton's words about the ruthless spy whose cunning had foiled the British repeatedly. Could Trace and the Scorpion be one and the same? No, that was absurd, she argued with herself. Yet was it? A spy might pretend to be a loyal British officer in order to gain crucial information. Stanton had said the Scorpion always seemed able to anticipate their strategies.

Christa felt sick. Had Trace lied to her all along about everything? She didn't want to believe that. He couldn't be so devious, so ruthless, could he? But she didn't really know much about him. She had let her heart rule her feelings. Now a nagging inner voice told her to believe her suspicions.

She closed her eyes to hold back hot tears. She felt as if her heart had been torn from her. How stupid she'd been to trust Trace, to fall in love with him.

She must tell General Zachary all she knew, even if doing so required her to admit her criminal part in sabotaging the encampment. Trace must be stopped. Somehow there had to be a way.

Chapter 41

Christa sought out Fitzhugh Zachary later that afternoon and found him alone in his study.

"Come in, Christa," he said when he saw her at the door.

"I'm sorry to disturb you, General, but there is something very urgent I must discuss with you."

"You look so serious, my dear," he observed, coming around from behind his desk and motioning her to the sofa. "I'd be glad to listen."

"I'm not certain how to begin, sir." She hesitated a moment to let her anger give her courage to reveal her suspicions. "I heard you discussing the rebel spies with Major Stanton and Lieutenant Brigham earlier. I may know the identity of the leader of the infiltrators."

"What?" The general looked astonished. "You know who the Scorpion is?"

Christa chose her words carefully. "Yes, General. I suspect Trace Cavanaugh to be the Scorpion."

"What are you saying, Christa? That statement is ridiculous!" He frowned, revealing his disbelief.

"I helped him destroy the dam at Hastings Hollow last October." Christa spoke slowly, letting the impact of her words sink in.

"I believe you'd better start at the beginning and tell me everything," Zachary directed.

* * *

Two weeks later, Christa was deeply embroiled in a plan to capture Trace. She found herself hidden in the woods miles from New York City. The sharp, late January wind whipped at the edges of her black wool cloak. She pulled the wrap around her more tightly. Torrence Stanton was with her, along with thirty of King George's best infantrymen, all of them as carefully concealed in the trees as she was.

Marcus Desmond rode up. "Everything's ready," he reported to Stanton.

"Good. Now we wait and see if our trap can snare a scoundrel." Stanton pressed his tricorn firmer on his head to secure it against the wind.

"Do you feel it's wise to have Mrs. Haviland here, Major?"

"No, Desmond, I don't think it's wise. It's bloody dangerous. But she's aware of the risks involved. Without her information, we wouldn't be in a position to try to capture this important enemy of the Crown. General Zachary gave express orders allowing her to accompany us."

Marcus reined around and brought his mount to a halt beside Christa. "You're sure you know what you're doing?" he asked, a concerned look on his face.

"Yes, Marcus. I want to be here when Trace Cavanaugh is captured and exposed as the Scorpion." There wasn't a shred of emotion in Christa's voice. She felt as cold inside as the winter air was outside. Her heart had died when she'd learned of Trace's treachery. Why shouldn't he die as well?

When she had confessed to Fitzhugh Zachary about sabotaging the dam, she gave him only the facts concerning that night and revealed nothing about her personal involvement with Trace. She wanted to forget she'd ever felt anything for him, wanted to obliterate her love from her memory. Zachary had been willing to overlook her lack of judgment in helping Trace in exchange for the information she provided concerning his true identity and activities. The general chose to ignore the smaller fish to hook the more threatening shark.

At first, Zachary had rejected her suspicions. But on reconsideration, he had admitted they were plausible and explained many incidents involving the passing of intelligence information. Christa had caught a glimpse of hurt in his eyes before he'd masked it with rage over being duped. She understood his reaction completely.

After her meeting with Zachary, she'd returned to Montclaire. For days, she'd wept out her hurt and anger, until not an agonizing tear remained. Then she made herself close off the part of her that felt the knifing pain of Trace's betrayal and set her mind on a single purpose—to wreak a terrible revenge on him for his cruel use of her. She wouldn't rest until she succeeded.

Marcus Desmond drew her attention back to the present when he continued speaking. "I don't mind telling you I didn't like being the one who gave Trace the false information about this payroll shipment. If he is the spy we're after, well then, I have to admit I admire his intelligence and shrewdness in eluding us for so long."

Christa didn't share his feelings, but she said nothing.

The trap was set. The prey was being lured by the payroll shipment—gold coins Trace needed to help his patriot cause. To make the temptation even greater, Zachary had instructed Marcus Desmond to inform Trace that Lee Garrett would be in charge of the shipment. The general knew about the intense rivalry between the two men. If Trace was the Scorpion, he'd surely try for the gold.

Garrett and his detail of twelve dragoons would be guarding a decoy wagon filled with lead bars. The actual gold was still in New York City, aboard the British ship that had transported it from England.

The place where Christa and the others hid was ideal for an ambush. Thick pines and dense undergrowth lined the sides of the road, concealing them. If the attack came, Garrett and his men were to make a run for the woods, pretending to try to escape. When the enemy gave pursuit, the trap with its iron jaws made of loaded muskets would snap with deadly force and capture them.

Enough light remained in the twilight sky to see the payroll wagon when it suddenly swerved around the bend and thundered toward the ambush point where Stanton's three squads waited. Lee Garrett and his men were returning gunfire while they tried to keep up with the wagon. Suddenly they left the road and scattered into the woods to join the infantrymen. The wagon rumbled past.

"At least two squads!" Garrett shouted as he jumped from his horse.

The hooded attackers were coming fast, but they, too, scattered. Only a handful kept to the dirt road, while the rest of the twenty-odd men plunged through the trees and underbrush for cover.

Struggling to control her nervous horse, Christa saw the first man of the attacking force round the bend and tumble to the ground, shot from his horse. The battle quickly changed from horseback to hand-to-hand combat, with the British infantrymen fighting with swords and bayonets against the Continentals. Sporadic musketfire mixed with the clash of steel. Battle cries and shouts of pain and death filled the air. Horses screamed and thrashed. Men clutched each other in death grips and tumbled about, fighting desperately for their lives. Blood flowed freely, covering sword and bayonet blades, spilling from fallen bodies.

Right before her eyes, Christa saw a man's throat slashed. His eyes bulged and blood gushed forth as he sank to his knees, hung motionless for a second, then pitched forward, crumpling in death.

She screamed in horror, pressing the palm of her hand against her mouth and twisting away from the awful sight. Suddenly, her horse reared and plunged through the undergrowth, onto the road, and into the thick of battle. Hands grabbed at Christa, but she fought them off with kicks and flailing fists. Then a man spurred his horse into hers and thrust a powerful arm around her waist, sweeping her from her mount to his.

"Let me go!" she screamed, pounding him with her fists and clawing at his covered face. The black hood came off in her grasp, revealing his identity to everyone. *Trace!*

For an instant, Christa saw the look of thunderous rage on his face, then his fist hit her on the chin and knocked her senseless.

"Retreat!" Trace shouted to his men as he spurred his mount and plunged away down the road, carrying Christa with him.

Chapter 42

Christa regained consciousness just as she was tossed roughly onto a bed. She suppressed a moan as she lay perfectly still, trying to gather her dazed senses. Her head throbbed and her jaw ached.

"Don't worry," she heard a woman's voice say. "Nick will have us under way soon enough, and we'll leave those redcoats far behind. You'd better let me have a look at that wound, Trace."

Without moving, Christa looked over to where Trace was sitting in a straight-backed chair. A beautiful, auburn-haired woman of about her own age was bent over him. Christa let her glance sweep the room. She didn't know where she was, but she'd traveled enough to recognize a ship's cabin. And the ship was getting under way, as the woman had said. Christa heard the sound of shouted orders and running feet overhead.

"Go tend to the others, Kate. I can take care of this shot," Trace said. "Some of my men are badly hurt."

"All right, but I'll be back to check on you as soon as I can. What about the lady there?" The woman cocked her head in Christa's direction.

"Leave her to me," Trace answered. "She's my responsibility." His voice sounded tight with anger.

After the woman departed, Christa surreptitiously followed Trace's movements, fearing he might harm her. Everything she'd suspected about him was true. He was a liar and a traitor. And she was his captive.

None of these thoughts gave Christa comfort. Instead, they made her ache inside as much as her jaw ached outwardly. But she mustered her courage. She hated Trace. He was her enemy. While she still had breath in her body, she'd use it to fight him.

She quickly clamped her eyes closed again as Trace turned toward her. In the next instant, she felt the shock of cold water hitting her face. Sputtering in indignation, she sat up with a jerk. The quick movement made her head pound even harder.

"I thought you might be awake. Come here and make yourself useful." Trace's voice matched his rough manner as he grabbed her by the arm and yanked her off the bed.

Christa scowled as she steadied herself before him. Their gazes locked and the depth of emotion in their expressions contained the power of a lightning bolt. Anger and hatred flashed between them like a tangible force.

"What the hell were you doing in the middle of that ambush?" Trace ground out the words with barely checked control.

"I helped plan the ambush. I discovered your treachery in getting me to help you sabotage the *British* encampment at Hastings Hollow, so I did all I could to help General Zachary capture a vicious enemy, traitor, spy, and liar—*you!*"

"That depends on your point of view, doesn't it?" Trace stated with calculated coolness. "I consider myself a loyal patriot fighting for freedom and independence for my country, the United States of America. It's your country, too. You were born here. You're an American by birthright. So *you* could be considered the enemy, the traitor."

"That's ridiculous! I honor my king and his sovereign powers. These colonies belong to King George."

"Rubbish! We *were* King George's colonies. He made the mistake of letting us know a measure of independence and freedom in governing ourselves, which we came to value. We believe government is created by the people to serve the people. We don't exist to serve a king or a government. To show our strong belief in those ideals, we choose to fight to become a separate nation, duly declared and—"

"You mean *illegally* declared, don't you, Captain? You speak of ideals and freedoms, when you really mean treason and revolution!"

"Damn it, Christa—" Trace was frowning menacingly as he started toward her, but then he flinched.

"What is it?" Christa's tone was curt.

"Nothing. Don't concern yourself," he answered sarcastically. "It's just that while I'm standing here like an idiot arguing with a stubborn, narrow-sighted female, I also happen to be bleeding like a butchered sow!"

He gingerly lifted his left arm, which he'd kept tucked tightly against his side, and for the first time Christa saw the large bloodstain on his navy uniform jacket. Her stomach turned over at the sight of the bright red stain spreading rapidly down the side of his buff-colored breeches.

"If I may be so fortunate as to have your assistance in attending to this wound, I'd greatly appreciate it," Trace continued in the same flippant tone, though he steadied himself on the footboard of the bed. "Think of it as a service to King George. If I bleed to death, His Majesty will miss the supreme pleasure of watching me swing from the gallows."

For some reason, that thought didn't sit well with Christa. She noticed how pale Trace's face had become and felt a sudden impulse to help him. But then she remembered how he'd deceived her, and her anger hardened her heart.

"Tend to it yourself, Captain. I have no sympathy for traitors!"

Trace's temper flared at her stubbornness. He'd be damned if he'd ask her for help again. Nor would he let her know how weak he was from loss of blood.

With considerable effort, he managed to shrug out of his jacket and remove his bloody waistcoat and white shirt. Those actions took some time to accomplish, and he was sweating profusely from the exertion when he examined his wound. A musketball had ripped through his left midsection, entering from the front and going straight through. He judged that a rib or two might have been grazed, but didn't think any vital organs were injured.

Christa watched Trace try to clean the wound with soap and water while leaning on the wooden washstand for support. The injury did look nasty. It was still bleeding profusely. The urge to help him twinged in her again. She fought giving in to it, but after a few minutes, relented impatiently.

"Here, let me do it. Your fumbling is pathetic!"

"As is your compassion."

"I have no compassion for—"

"For traitors, I know," Trace finished with exasperation, but he stepped aside so she could reach the soap and water.

Christa carefully washed the shredded and bruised flesh. Trace said nothing more, but she saw the tightness in his clenched jaw and the beads of perspiration on his forehead.

She told herself it was only the ugliness of the wound, the sight of the mutilated skin, that affected her stomach and pulse rate, and not the close contact with

Trace. He handed her a jar of yellow salve and flinched when she applied it to the wound a little too vigorously.

"Does it hurt?" Stupid question to ask, she realized.

"It hurts like hell. That should delight you to no end."

"Yes, it does," she stated more haughtily than she really felt. As she wrapped a bandage around his midsection, she had to keep thinking hard that she hated him, that he was a spy, a traitor. Don't think about his pain, she ordered herself sternly. Or how handsome he is or how pale and weakened he looks from his wound. Don't think at all!

Trace was almost glad for the throbbing soreness in his side and the lightness in his head, for these things kept him from thinking about Christa's nearness, her beauty. He wanted to remain furious with her, but he felt his wrath ebbing with his strength. They were enemies. She hated him. Suddenly, those two thoughts gave him more pain than his wound.

"Do you wish me dead, Christa?"

She was startled by his words. "Y—yes."

"I don't believe you." His gaze focused steadily on her as his arm encircled her waist. "Look at me and say you wish me dead, Christa. Tell me you feel nothing when we're close like this. Tell me . . ."

Christa opened her mouth, but no words came out. His penetrating turquoise eyes seemed able to search her very soul and see the truth, the truth she wished she could deny.

"Damn you . . ." she whispered in agony as she pressed her forehead against his chin and put her hands on his bare chest. Her reason, her heart, her body were waging a terrible battle that kept her unmoving in his arms.

"I want you, Christa," he murmured softly.

"There's something very strong between us. I can't explain what it is, but it draws us together and holds us fast, even when we're apart."

Christa slowly raised her head until her eyes met his. Her feelings clashed mercilessly within her. She knew what he said was true, but she couldn't give in to her heart. Too many forces were acting against her and Trace. War, treachery, the evil of others, vows made—hers to a husband, Trace's to a vengeance that drove him. They would destroy each other.

At that moment, a sharp knock at the cabin door startled her, making her step away from Trace.

"Come," he called.

A tall, blond man in a seaman's jacket stepped into the cabin, ducking his head to miss hitting the low doorframe.

"I don't mean to interrupt," he said, "but Kate sent me to see how you are, Trace, and I'm anxious for your report on what happened. I've news for you as well."

Trace nodded as he shook hands with his friend. Then he sat down on the corner of the sturdy oak table as he felt a wave of weakness wash over him.

"You look as though you'd best get in that berth, Trace," the man stated, coming toward him to help, but Trace waved him away.

"I'll be all right. Christa Haviland, this is Nick Fletcher, a close friend of mine and captain of the *Sea Mist*, the stout ship on which you now find yourself."

"Mrs. Haviland." Fletcher gave a curt nod in her direction, then turned back to Trace. "You're right, old man, she is a beauty. But what happened with Garrett? I've only gotten a few details from the other men."

"How bad are the casualties? I had twenty-two men with me."

"Fourteen made it back, counting you. Five of those

are in bad condition. The rest look as if they've been in a good fight.''

"We were. There was an ambush." Trace's expression was grim as he contemplated the toll to his men.

"What kind of shape are you in?" Nick asked. "You look like hell."

"I'll be ready to fight soon enough. How went your part of the mission?"

"So well the bloody redcoats will be days figuring out what hit them. The ship was totally unprepared for our boarding. King George's gold now glistens in my hold below, bound not for General Zachary's unpaid battalions but for the needy palms of loyal Continental troops."

"B—but how did you know the gold was aboard the *Wentworth*?" Christa asked in confusion.

"We didn't know for a certainty," Nick answered, "but I've learned to trust Trace's instincts. He suspected Garrett's wagon might be a decoy. So he attacked Garrett while I invaded the ship with my men."

"So you're among this pack of spying traitors as well, Captain Fletcher?" Christa let her anger at their astuteness tell in her accusing tone.

"Be careful how you answer, Nick," Trace cautioned sardonically. "Admitting that will not put you on Christa's good side."

"That's a pity. I'm sorry you see our patriotic duty to our country in that light, Mrs. Haviland." He turned back to Trace. "General Washington will be pleased with you, as usual, my friend."

"And with you, Nick." Trace's voice grew grave. "I want some of the gold to go to the families of the men who died today. They fought bravely for the cause. I'll give you a list of names." He stood up and went for paper and quill at a writing desk, but stopped halfway to lean against a vertical support beam. Nick hurried to him.

"I'll see to it, Trace. You need rest or you won't be any good to Washington or anything else."

"Later. What of the Zachary matter in England?" Trace persisted, gritting his teeth against the pain from his wound.

"I took care of it. Heard from my man there just two days ago. You can trust he did everything as you instructed."

Trace's eyes narrowed. "Good. The secret bank accounts and fraudulent business enterprises to discredit him have been arranged here, too. We need wait only a little longer."

"I know, my friend. Soon you'll have your just revenge for the wrong he did to you so long ago. If I can be of further help, you need only ask."

"I know, Nick. Thanks. I'm going topside to see my men."

But as Trace turned toward the cabin door, he felt a sharp pain in his side. He clutched at the thick bandage and felt the hot stickiness of blood seep through his fingers. The cabin began to spin around him and his senses drifted away into oblivion.

Chapter 43

Hours later, Trace regained consciousness. Kate Fletcher was removing yet another set of bloodied bandages from his bullet wound.

"We're going to have to cauterize those two holes, Trace," Nick explained as he bent over his wife to examine the injury. The ugly discoloration and pus of infection was beginning to show in the mutilated flesh.

"Do what you have to, Nick," Trace told him.

Christa wondered where Trace found the strength to speak at all. During the hours of his unconsciousness, she'd assisted Kate Fletcher in tending him. Kate had resisted her help at first, then relented when Christa had pleaded with her.

Christa cringed as she watched Nick heat the long, wide blade of a hunting knife in the cabin's pot-bellied stove until it was white-hot.

"Hold him down," Nick ordered two crewmen who were also present, but Trace refused.

"No need. Just get it done, Nick," he said, clenching his jaws together.

"Come with me," Kate urged, taking Christa's arm.

"I'm staying," Christa replied firmly, pulling away.

She shouldn't have. She was certain she felt the excruciating pain caused by the hot blade when Nick Fletcher pressed it into Trace's wound. She saw Trace's body tense hard from it, heard his sharp gasp of breath, one that matched her own as the back of her hand flew to her mouth. The smell of scorched flesh was overpowering, twisting her stomach sickeningly. She started to go to Trace, but Kate stopped her with an arm around her waist. Trace's eyes met Christa's, then they slowly closed as he lost consciousness again.

For two days he lay in the berth, unaware of her presence or that of the friends who quietly slipped into the cabin to check on him.

Christa stared down at Trace now. How she longed to see his turquoise eyes open. She'd hardly moved from the chair she was sitting in next to where he lay. Something drove her to keep this vigil. She couldn't explain why. She only knew his pain and sickness had wiped away all the anger and hatred she'd thought she felt for him. She must be with him, near him, no matter what happened. Seeing Trace like this, in a nether world of delirium and fever, brought her more anguish than everything she'd discovered about him.

She longed to do something more to help, but she could only watch, bathe the perspiration from his body, change the dressing of his wound, and pray. Pray to God that the man she'd wished dead two days ago would live and be whole again.

In his delirium, he sometimes spoke. Most of his words were incoherent, but he called Christa's name clearly several times. She stroked his forehead and spoke soothingly to quiet him. His pain and suffering tore at her heart. She blamed herself.

"If only things could be different, Trace," she whispered, her eyes wet with tears. They were alone in the cabin. Kate had gone to help with the evening meal in the galley. "If only there were no war, no conflicts, no obstacles separating us."

Dreams. Foolish dreams, she chided herself. Life wasn't that simple.

She fell asleep with her head resting on the side of the bed, but awoke abruptly sometime later when Kate entered the cabin.

"I didn't mean to wake you," Kate apologized, putting down the tray of food she'd brought. "You need your rest, or I'll have another patient to tend to."

"Thank you for letting me stay with Trace. I'm grateful for your trust. I know you hate me as an enemy." Christa's voice was hushed with remorse.

"No, I don't hate you. And we're only enemies if you want to be," Kate answered. "Right now, I don't think much of war and fighting, for whatever causes. I wonder if the pain and destruction are ever worth it."

Christa nodded her agreement and returned her gaze to Trace.

"You're in love with him." Kate's words were a statement, not a question. Christa turned slowly toward her.

"How did you know when I've hardly realized it myself?"

"By your eyes when you look at him. By his pain, which I see reflected there. You'd take his hurt onto yourself if you could, wouldn't you?"

Christa nodded and lowered her head to gaze at her hands folded in her lap.

"I've felt the same for my husband," Kate went on. "When Nick and I first met, I hated him. I thought we were enemies and I wished him dead many times. We fought and argued. And made love. Being with him was both ecstasy and agony. We tried to leave each other, deny what we felt. I almost lost him when he was captured and tortured by a ruthless British officer. Seeing him so battered, so hurt, made my pride, my fight, my anger disappear. Almost too late, I realized I loved him more than life itself.

"After he recovered, we were married. I'll never be

parted from Nick again. Our love is a magnificent force, so hard to describe, yet very real. Do you know what I mean?''

"Yes." Christa nodded, amazed that Kate Fletcher could voice her own feelings so exactly. The love and hate, the need to be with Trace, yet fighting that need. Feeling the overpowering pull of a mysterious and wondrous force drawing her to him even when reason called it wrong.

"Trace loves you," Kate continued. "I'm not certain he realizes it fully himself yet, but I recognized the look on his face when he spoke about you. He set himself a direction for his life and I think you caused him to detour from it. He's fighting his feelings for you. If I may give you some advice, I'd say the two of you should try to resolve what's between you, before you destroy each other.''

"Perhaps I've caused his death already." Christa's heart shone in her eyes as her gaze drifted to Trace's face. "What am I going to do? If I lose him now . . .''

She was silent for a while, then she looked at Kate again. "Can you tell me some things about Trace? He's only told me a little about his life.''

Kate nodded and pulled another of the straight-backed table chairs beside Christa.

"Trace has no family. He knew only his mother. His parents were never wed. He hated his illegitimacy and vowed when he was only a boy to have a name of honor, to build a family and heritage of which he could be proud. He's worked very hard toward that goal, educated himself, taken chances, risked his life. America is the place to fulfill great ambitions. In our country a man is judged by what he is and what he does, not by his past or social class. Trace is fiercely loyal to the United States for the opportunities he has here, the freedom.

"He's driven by another ambition as well, one that Nick and I have tried to dissuade him from many times. He seeks revenge against a man who wronged him—General Fitzhugh Zachary. He's planned Zachary's ruin for years and is about to achieve it."

"But why? What has General Zachary done to Trace?" Christa asked. She knew Fitzhugh Zachary to be a stern commander, but he was also a brave soldier and a man of honor.

"He killed his father, the father Trace longed all his life to know. On her deathbed, Trace's mother named Zachary a murderer."

Christa's eyes drifted to the ruby ring on the gold chain around Trace's neck, and she remembered what he'd told her at the mine cabin about his mother and her love for his father.

"Will he kill Zachary?" Christa spoke barely above a whisper. Olivia Zachary loomed in her mind.

"Perhaps," Kate answered. "But Trace told me once that death would be too quick an end to his enemy. He seems more bent on destroying Zachary by bringing disgrace to his reputation, his honor, and good name. He says that, to Zachary, dishonor would be a fate worse than death."

"Yes, he's right," Christa murmured.

"I brought some food," Kate said. "You should try to eat to keep up your strength. Do you wish me to stay with you?"

"I'd like to be alone with Trace, if I may."

"I understand. I'll have Nick's brother, Jason, wait outside. If you need anything, just let me know." She moved toward the door.

"Mrs. Fletcher—Kate," Christa called to her. "Thank you."

Kate smiled and nodded, then left the cabin.

Christa bathed Trace's face with a wet cloth, letting her hand linger on his bare chest. Would he ever touch her again as she was touching him now, tenderly, longingly?

"Oh, Trace . . ." With her fingertips, Christa caressed the side of his face, feeling the rough stubble of his beard. She wished with all her heart that her touch had a magical power to heal, to make everything right. But she knew it didn't. And the heaviness in her heart made her lower her head to the bed and weep out her sorrow.

Chapter 44

Christa stood at the closed porthole window with her arms wrapped around her. Through the thick pane of glass she watched the moon paint the tips of the churning winter sea with touches of silver light. She thought of Trace still unconscious on the berth across the cabin from her. She was bone-weary from worry, but she knew she couldn't sleep. She must keep watch over him. Only he mattered now—not Nevin, Isabelle, Montclaire. Only Trace . . .

Her thoughts tortured her with memories of all they'd shared—the danger, the anger, the compassion, the desire. She sighed deeply and closed her eyes. Trace lingered between life and death because of her. The ache of regret overwhelmed her.

"Christa."

She jumped at the sound of her name and quickly crossed the room to go to Trace's side. At last he was awake. In the lamplight, Christa could see that his eyes were clear as they met hers.

"Yes, I'm here, Trace." Overcome with joy, she smiled as she touched his forehead, feeling that his skin was cooler now. The fever had broken. She took the wet cloth from the shallow pan of water and bathed his face again.

"How do you feel, Trace?"

"As if I just rowed this ship across the ocean single-handedly."

Her smile widened at his quip.

"How long have I been unconscious?"

"Over two days. You lost so much blood, and you were fighting infection and fever. I need to change the dressing on your wound, Trace. Kate and I have been doing it every couple of hours."

He nodded and said nothing more while she removed the wads of bandages covering the two holes in his side. She could now look at the bruised and decaying flesh without having nausea inch up her throat. While the wound was still ugly and blackened in places, no pus from infection showed on the bandages, and she could see small spots of pink where the mutilated skin was just beginning to show signs of healing.

"What is the prognosis, madam doctor?" Trace asked.

"I think you will live to plague the British yet another day or two."

"And how does that news strike Christa Haviland?" Trace was looking at her, his eyes reflecting his weariness but still alert. She felt the magnetic power of them drawing her.

"I'm glad, Trace." She spoke softly, but with firm conviction, meeting his eyes. She thought she saw a flicker of relief cross his face.

"Are you hungry?" she went on quickly, feeling unsure of what to do next. "Kate brought some food."

"Christa." She stopped midway to the table when he called to her. "I need you here."

He held out his hand and Christa came to the bed and took his fingers in hers. His blue-green eyes held her mesmerized.

"Lie with me, Christa," he whispered. "I need to feel you close to me. I need your strength . . ."

She didn't hesitate, for being with him was what she wanted with all her heart.

Kate had given her a loose-fitting morning dress so she didn't have to wear her riding clothes. She slipped out of the dress and her underclothes and went around the bed so she could lie next to Trace's uninjured side.

He watched her every movement. He knew he didn't have the strength to do anything but gaze at Christa and hold her close, but it would be enough.

The flickering lamplight touched the lovely, sensuous curves and hollows of her body as she came to him. He could feel her life, her vitality flowing into him. As he closed his eyes and let her fill his senses, a great tranquility settled over him. He could stop fighting now and rest. His strong will to live had seen him through once more. And Christa had helped him. During his delirium, he had known she was with him. He'd seen her sitting at his side when he drifted in and out of consciousness. Then she'd faded out of view as the fever claimed him again, but his will had struggled to be with her again.

Christa curled her body close against Trace. She slowly ran her hand over his chest to soothe him, feeling the dark hair soft under her palm. She saw his pulse beating at the base of his neck and lifted a silent prayer of thanks for his life, for the chance to lie with him, share her being with him.

After a little while, his chest rose and fell with the regularity of sleep. Christa sighed and softly kissed his cheek. She drew up a linen sheet and quilt to cover them, then settled back down contentedly at Trace's side and let her own exhaustion bring on the oblivion of sleep.

Chapter 45

Trace nuzzled Christa's throat. He relished watching her waken, all soft and warm and relaxed. She shifted under his tickling kiss and pretended to be still asleep, but Trace wasn't fooled. He knew what she wanted. Hadn't they awakened like this every day for the last three weeks, while he recovered from his wound?

Under Christa's solicitous care, his injury was healing well. He'd regained his strength quickly after his dangerous bout with infection.

Trace let his hand start to drift over Christa's nakedness the way a gentle summer breeze touches a fragile blossom, lightly, gently. And yet he knew she was very aware of his caresses, for her skin roughened with the momentary gooseflesh of excitement and the voluptuous swells of her nipples quickly strained to sharp peaks. Her eyes were still closed, but Trace saw the beginning of a smile twitch at the corners of her mouth.

"How long must I caress you like this before you awaken, m'lady?" he whispered, nibbling her ear.

"An hour or two at least, sir, for I feel very sleepy this morning."

"I think not, my beauty. You're very much awake and so am I, as I'll soon show you!"

He pulled her into his arms and kissed her possessively, entwining his fingers in her tangled black tresses and molding his naked body to hers.

Christa moaned softly and sank into his embrace, his passion. Trace knew her body so well now, but he seemed never to tire of exploring it, tasting and caressing her, bringing her to the height of excitement again and again. And she'd learned so quickly how to do the same to him.

She let her hands rub over him now, feeling the hard muscles of his arms and chest, down the rippling tautness of his flat stomach, and beyond. His sharp intake of breath and low murmur of her name told her she was bringing him pleasure. She concentrated fully on the exciting task, marveling that by giving she received so much in return. She gave him more than just her body. She gave her heart, the very essence of herself. Completely, unconditionally. The chalice of her being had long been empty before she knew Trace. She let him fill it to overflowing with his strength, his passion, his great need for her.

Perhaps she knew his need even more than he did himself. Trace, who was so fearless in the face of battle and danger, so expert in the physical aspects of making love, was most unsure of himself in learning the feelings of love. She saw it in his eyes when he gazed at her after yet another wondrous fulfillment between them. She knew he was fighting against falling in love with her, and losing that fight. Over these three weeks on the *Sea Mist* she'd slowly tried to coax his heart open, just as she coaxed his body to the brink of climax now.

"Christa . . ." he whispered in a voice husky with desire as he tried to move her hips to the right place atop him.

She let him enter her, gasping at the powerfully

ready feel of him inside her and the compelling sensations that surged through her.

"Wait, my love," she murmured. "You must wait a little longer while I pleasure you."

She forced herself to remain unmoving over him while she brought his hands to her breasts and placed tiny, tormenting kisses over his chest, his face, and lips.

For a few moments, he endured this sweet torture, then no more. Grasping her hips, he rolled with her until she was on her back and he loomed over her. Together they moved in perfect rhythm, she arching her hips and he bearing down more deeply and forcefully. And then the magnificent pulsations throbbed through them, seizing and holding them motionless for the explosive, overpowering moments of the ultimate climax.

It took a long time for pulse and breath to know a normal rhythm again. Entwined in each other's arms, Trace and Christa basked in the afterglow of completion and momentary exhaustion. She reveled in the heat of Trace's body against hers. If only there were a way to hold onto the enchantment, keep the world at bay. Let nothing separate her from Trace, the man she loved with all her heart and being.

Trace closed his eyes and sank into the hazy half slumber that crept over him while his body floated from the soaring height it had just known yet another time with Christa. How could he want her so much? No matter how often they made love, he felt content only for a little while. Then he had to have her again, longed to be in her, with her, taking from her, giving to her. He'd awaken in the middle of the night needing her, and she'd be there beside him. He could reach out his hand and touch the assurance of her soft, warm flesh. Never did she refuse him, for she seemed to have the same need to be close to him.

He relished the quiet, contented moments like this when they were lying in each other's arms. He'd come to truly enjoy all the time he spent with her. They talked for hours about many things—his dreams of a heritage like hers, his passion for independence for the United States.

He'd been so sure he'd get his fill of Christa and be done with her. But she'd reached inside him, stealthily come into his heart when he was unaware, and stayed there. And it was there he wanted her. His dreams seemed more real, more attainable with her in them. He wanted to fulfill them not just for himself now, but for her, for them together. Christa was strong. She would stand beside him, not meekly behind him as Suko had been taught. Somehow he would make Christa his wife. There had to be a way.

But Trace knew this idyllic interlude couldn't go on, even if he wished it. He was a soldier serving his country. His wound was nearly healed. He must return to his duty.

He thought about the visit they'd had late yesterday. General Washington himself had come aboard the *Sea Mist* from another ship.

Over six feet tall, with reddish hair, the Commander in Chief of the Continental army had a somber air about him. His strong features reflected the heavy burden of the rank he held, but his blue eyes flashed with a determined vitality as he gripped Trace's hand in a powerful handshake.

"I'm glad to see you're recovering from your wound, Major," Washington said, addressing Trace by the rank he held in the American army. "Good men such as yourself are hard to come by. Your intelligence work against the enemy has been of great value to our cause. Gaining the gold shipment was an important achievement. The coins are badly needed to purchase food, guns, and other supplies for our loyal troops, since our Congress has such an absurd apathy to such necessities." Washington's features looked even more severe for a moment.

"I'm grateful to be able to serve you and my country, General, and for your trust in me," Trace assured him.

"I've already given thought to the matter of your next assignment," Washington continued. "I want you on my advisory staff to assist me in planning the spring campaign. We've gotten wind of a strong, three-pronged plan the British might be working on, and we must devise a counterstrategy that can defeat it. Will you have recovered enough to join me at my headquarters in two weeks' time?"

"Most assuredly, General."

"Good. Then we'll meet again at that time."

Trace brought his thoughts back to the present and Christa in his arms.

"What are you thinking about?" she murmured, touching his cheek.

"My meeting with General Washington yesterday."

"I was thinking of that, too. I know you're anxious to return to duty, my love. Your patriotism is strong. I've come to feel it, too. I think it started when I read Thomas Paine's works months ago. A small conviction began to murmur at the back of my mind that he was right, that there is justice in the cause for independence. And when we've talked since then, you've made me see we're a new people—Americans. This is our country. It doesn't belong to Englishmen or Frenchmen or Hessians who come to our shores only to fight a war. They have no stake in the land. Now I understand your desire to have a fair voice in the government, a voice denied us by King George. As a woman, I've known only too well what it's like to be controlled by others, to have little say in determining what you can and cannot do. I feel your anger and your need to do whatever you can to help the cause. But I'll hate being parted from you.''

Trace took her hand and pressed her fingertips to his lips. ''I know,'' he whispered. ''I feel torn by what I must do. I'll find a way for us to be together after I join Washington. Until then, I want you to stay at my house in Albany. I want us to have a life together, Christa.''

''But how can we, Trace?'' Despair touched her voice. ''Nevin is still alive. He's my husband.''

She couldn't speak more because of the tightness in her throat. She didn't want to think of Nevin or parting from Trace. But she must now. The world always had a way of pushing its terrible reality into dreams. These wonderful weeks with Trace were about to end. She had to face the truth. They both did.

''To the world, Nevin Haviland is dead, Christa. Let him remain so. I love you. Nothing else matters. Let the past be buried. We have only now and the future. And I want to face them together.''

Christa sat up in bed and closed her eyes to fight back hot tears. She lowered her head to her arms crossed over her bent knees.

''I must know the truth, Trace,'' she said in a hushed voice. ''I want nothing more than to be with you for the rest of my life, any way you'll have me. But how can we know happiness when ghosts of the past would surely rear their cruel heads to haunt us? I'd always fear that.''

Though Trace tried to convince himself otherwise, he knew he had to resolve the situation with Nevin Haviland, just as Christa did. He wanted her and they would be together. Somehow he'd make that happen. But there could be no shadows over their love, no threads of doubt tied to the past.

He sat up next to Christa and gathered her into his arms.

"We have two weeks until I report to General Washington. We'll find the answers we seek, I promise you. And until we do, wear this." He unfastened the gold chain from around his neck, removed the ruby ring, and slipped it onto Christa's finger. It fit perfectly, just as it had fit his mother's finger. "This ring has great meaning to me, my love. I haven't taken it off since my mother gave it to me on the night she died. It symbolizes the great love she had for my father, and he for her. Now it expresses my love for you."

Trace kissed her softly. Christa clung to him, feeling her heart meeting and joining his.

"I love you, Trace," she murmured against his mouth. "My heart I give to you, and my body. All that I am. Please make love to me. I want to forget everything except what we are to each other now, in this place."

No more words passed between them as Trace lay Christa back against the pillows and leaned down to cover her lips with his, poising them both on the mounting tidal wave that would send them crashing into the glorious sea of overwhelming passion.

Chapter 46

Usually the sight of Montclaire brought a feeling of joy and pride to Christa, but not tonight. As the last rays of twilight faded behind the slate roof of her home, she felt a foreboding that chilled her beneath her warm black wool coat.

"Don't take too long, Christa," Trace cautioned as they pulled their horses into a glade edged by tall, barren oaks. "It's dangerous to tarry."

"I know. I'll only speak to Mother to let her know I'm all right and find out if Nevin's tried to contact me."

"Be sure you tell your mother about Cromwell, my barrister. I'll keep watch and wait for you where the trees offer a thicker cover. If you need me, signal with a candle at a window."

"Yes, all right. There at that lower window on the left." Christa pointed to where she meant. "That's a small music room no one uses now. Keep a careful watch, my love. If you should be found in the city, with General Howe's main winter headquarters here . . ." She couldn't finish the sentence. They both knew what Trace's capture would mean.

They exchanged a quick kiss, and Christa spurred her horse to a canter, glad for the few inches of snow that quieted the sound of her mount's hooves. She wanted to ride at full gallop, but knew it would be better to take her time, to act as if she were a messenger. She was disguised as a boy in breeches and jacket, with her hair hidden beneath a stocking cap.

"Why, madam, is that you? Whatever are you doing dressed like that and coming to the back door?" Crothers, the butler, questioned her in surprise when he opened the door to find her standing on the slushy steps.

"I can't explain now, Crothers." Christa brushed past him and pulled off her cap, letting her long hair fall free. "I must see my mother at once. And send for Letty as well. I'll be in the front parlor."

"Yes, madam."

"Christa, dear, you're here!" Elspeth Kendall exclaimed a few moments later when she joined her daughter. "We were so worried. Where have you been? Why are you dressed that way? We were told you were kidnapped by the enemy!"

"Mother, please calm yourself," Christa replied. She guided her to the rose-colored sofa and sat down next to her. "I'm all right. Much has happened, but I've been safe with friends. I came only to tell you I must go away for a while. I don't know for how long, and I can't tell you where, but it's for my safety. It's better if you know little about my plans. When I can, I'll let you know through a messenger that I'm safe."

"Oh dear, you frighten me with such talk. This all sounds so mysterious and dangerous."

Christa's heart went out to her mother. How she loved her and regretted having to leave her now. Her mother was gentle and childlike, always thinking well of everyone.

"I can't explain much more, Mother. Just listen to me very carefully. A man by the name of Jacob Cromwell will be contacting you. He'll be making some financial arrangements for us. Montclaire, the mill, everything will be out of debt. Father's saltpeter mine will soon be providing you with a steady income. Don't listen to Isabelle or that Mr. Pemberton again. We have a benefactor who's going to see to everything. You'll never have to worry about losing Montclaire again. There will even be money to open the old rooms and hire more servants.''

"But, Christa, can this be true? Who is this benefactor?''

How she wished she could tell her mother more about Trace's generosity—his giving in so many ways.

"I can't tell you now, Mother. Only trust me when I say he's very wonderful.''

Her mother patted Christa's hand. "I think he's more than just a generous friend, dear, and I'm very happy for you. I've worried so about you since your widowhood.''

The reminder of Nevin sobered Christa. She remembered her other reason for coming to Montclaire tonight.

"Mother, I want you to think carefully. Have any messages arrived for me during these weeks while I've been gone?''

"Messages, dear? Well, let me see.'' Elspeth tapped a plump finger against her chin and frowned slightly. "There was an invitation to Elvinia Stewart's wedding. It was addressed to your aunt and to me as well. It's to be a small affair. I really don't know what I shall wear.''

"No, Mother,'' Christa interrupted, trying to curb her impatience. "Were there any other letters or notes addressed just to me?''

"Why, yes, I believe there was. It came, oh, it must be at least three weeks ago. I gave it to Letty to keep for when you returned. I didn't open it, dear. I never read anyone else's postings.''

"I know, Mother. That's an admirable trait. Now, please excuse me. I must find Letty and have her pack a few things for me."

"Are you hungry, dear? I can have cook make up something for you."

"Yes, that would be fine. Please have it sent up to my room." Christa smiled, overwhelmed by the love and concern in her mother's eyes.

"Miz Christa, you is back! Ah could hardly believe Crothers when he said you was." Letty impulsively threw her arms around her mistress. "We all thought you was dead fer sure. Why, they said you was carried off by them enemy soldiers what robbed the payroll wagon. When we didn't hear nothin' more, we was all sure you was murdered! Ah'm so powerful glad you ain't. What happened to you? Where you bin all this time? What was you adoin' with them redcoats in a ambush anyway?"

Christa gave a little laugh. "One question at a time, please, Letty, but I can't tell you much. I've been safe, but I must leave Montclaire tonight, and I don't know when I'll return."

"Oh, you does have my curiosity stirred up, but ah knows you has to do what you think's best. Here, let me help you with them things." She started to fold a morning dress to put into the leather valise on the bed.

"Thank you, Letty. But now you must tell me something. Mother said a letter arrived for me, and she gave it to you. Where is it? It could be very important."

"Well, yes, one surely did. Ah didn't recognize the handwritin' either. It were wrote kind of crookedlike, not fine like Mr. Desmond's hand. Ah put it on yer desk." She went for the envelope and handed it to Christa, who quickly tore it open.

It was from Nevin. He'd disguised his handwriting.

The contents of the message revealed only that he'd meet with her alone at the gristmill. She was to send him word through Charity as to when.

This message was dated weeks ago. He must have sent it soon after she'd visited Charity and her aunt. She had to hope he'd still meet her at the mill.

"Letty, send Benten to me. I want him to deliver a message for me tonight."

"Yes, Miz Christa. Ah'll see to it right off."

Chapter 47

Trace fed several more logs to the fire in the wide hearth of the gristmill's main room. The flames clawed at the bricks of the chimney, sending heat and light out into the low-ceilinged room. But the fire couldn't overcome the cold of the late winter night creeping through cracks and crevices in the old stone building.

Christa sat at a rough-hewn wooden table, absently studying the different-sized drive wheels, belts, and pulleys that formed the internal workings of the gristmill. Nothing moved now. She and Trace were alone. Even the big mill wheel was still and silent at this time of year, for the creek that powered it was frozen, its force held suspended by nature's frigid temperatures.

"Do you think he'll come?" Christa asked with nervous trepidation.

"He has to. You know too much. There's been enough time for him to receive your message. I'm going to take my position behind those sacks of grain. I'll have my pistol on him at all times. But take care, Christa. If he even begins to make a threatening movement, fall to the floor out of the way so I can get a clear shot at him."

"But we need him alive, Trace, to get to the bottom of the mystery." Her large blue-gray eyes reflected worry as they met his.

"And I need *you* safe more than anything. It goes against my better judgment having you here at all."

"I know, but I couldn't stay at the house wondering what might be happening here."

Trace understood her feelings. He, too, wanted to confront Christa's disappearing husband. His inclination was to make certain she truly became a widow tonight. He felt a strong loathing for cowardly deserters, be they from the military or from their families, and Haviland was *both!*

Trace cocked back the hammer on his pistol and crouched behind the five-foot-high pile of grain sacks. Only the crackling of the roaring fire broke the stillness. With Trace out of sight, Christa felt very much alone. Her courage lessened with each moment that passed.

She jumped to her feet when the front door of the mill was suddenly thrown open so hard that it crashed back against the stone wall. A man rushed in, crouching low, a pistol at the ready. When he saw only Christa in sight, he slowly rose to his full height and lowered his weapon. But he didn't uncock it.

"Nevin." Christa leaned a hand on the table for support, hardly believing he was really here.

"In the flesh, my dear." He slammed the rickety door closed, shutting out the wind and swirling flakes of snow that were beginning to fall. "You came alone, I see. I'm glad of that for both our sakes."

He came across the room to stand directly in front of her. "You're looking well, Christa. Beautiful as usual, even in those unbecoming boy's clothes. Whyever are you wearing them? But they do serve to show the curves of your lovely body quite nicely." He put out a hand to touch her cheek and she recoiled from contact with him, taking a step backward. He smiled.

"Come, come, my dear, why so standoffish? We've shared everything together, the most intimate moments a man and woman can have. And they were quite pleasurable, I assure you, Christa. As a woman, you should be gratified I found you pleasing in that regard. I enjoyed having your body. You were soft and warm and totally submissive, just like a wife should be."

"Stop it, Nevin! It sickens me to hear you speak like that. I did only what I had to do, what it was my *duty* to do as your wife. But I never felt any pleasure in lying with you. I never enjoyed it."

"Where is it written a woman is to enjoy coupling? I hold a firm belief that the female gender was put on this earth solely for a man's use. You obliged me well in that capacity."

"As did Charity Maxwell?" Christa forced herself to refrain from lunging at him.

"Ah yes, sweet Charity. And quite a few others as well, I can confess now. I'm afraid I don't find one woman satisfying for very long. There are so many of you lovely creatures, and so little time."

"You're despicable." Christa's voice seethed with contempt.

"Decidedly." Nevin smiled snidely. "And I'll likely remain so. Charity is a delightful creature. I must admit she captured my fancy and has held it longer than any other woman I've met so far, including you, my dear. It started as a lark with her—a lowly scullery maid and all. I enjoyed bedding her, and it drove my father to distraction. She was beneath me, he raged, and I had to laugh in his face and agree that, indeed, she was beneath me—often.

"At times when he stormed at me, I feared he might be overcome with an attack of apoplexy. Or rather, I *hoped* he would be. All my life he's made me miserable with his bullying demands that I follow exactly in his footsteps. The Haviland heir must be this, this, and this, he drummed into me, until I was sick to death of hearing it. So I plotted a way to get even. Little Charity was my revenge for all the misery he'd caused in my life. You should have seen my father's face when I told him I'd married my little scullery maid and she had a son by me who bore the precious Haviland name. Of course, I never told him the little brat died.

"But I fear I did push Father to the brink with all that news. He didn't appreciate the joke. Why, he even threatened to disinherit me. I certainly didn't want *that* to happen. So I told him everything about Charity and the child was all a lie. To prove it, he required me to marry at once someone of a worthy family background and social position. You, dear Christa. Though you had little money, you did have Montclaire and a once-prestigious name. Your father needed cash to pay some of his gambling debts; I needed a wife to please my father. We struck an arrangement for you, my dear. I really bought you at a bargain price. You were beautiful and came from sturdy stock, as my father put it. He admired your sweet femininity—more to the point, those fine round breasts and hips of yours—and was certain you'd bear me many fine sons, legitimate Haviland heirs.

"So we had a lovely wedding, didn't we, darling? And a blissful two years together. But no heirs. What a pity. Father was not pleased. I delighted in foiling him again in his own plan. I was the obedient son fighting for our king, trying to produce heirs, doing everything he wanted, so I wouldn't lose my fortune. I hated my father, but I wasn't stupid. I loved my life of leisure. I decided I'd wait and hope nature took its course early with him and killed him off before too long. He's grossly oversized in weight. That must tax his heart exceedingly.

"Unfortunately, he made my life miserable whenever he could. And I came dangerously close to getting shot several times while I was doing my loyal military duty. I couldn't have that. So I devised the plan of blowing myself up. I could disappear indefinitely, have Charity and any other wench who caught my eye, and no longer endure Father's bullying, or Isabelle's jealous rages. She's quite mad, you know—greedy for power and even more wealth than we have already. She was always insanely jealous because I was Father's heir. I didn't doubt for a minute that she might try to kill me one day, when it suited her purposes. So I deemed it more prudent to wait for Father's demise safely hidden away, then come forward with a story about having a loss of memory or something, and claim my rightful inheritance right out from under Isabelle's nose. Quite ingenious, don't you think?"

"Who did die in the explosion, Nevin?" Christa asked coldly. "A body was found. Men were hurt in the blast. A young soldier died in my arms from his injuries. Your actions could be deemed murder."

"Such a pity." Nevin said the words, but there was no remorse in his voice. "The body was that of a corporal who died at the camp hospital. He was about my size. I dragged him into the storehouse just before I detonated the explosion. It all worked out so well. No one suspected anything, until you happened to see me at Haviland Court the night I returned for an important financial document I needed. Some time has passed since you made that discovery, yet no one else seems to know I'm still alive. Have you told anyone, Christa?"

She purposely avoided answering him, determined to ask the question foremost in her mind. "To whom are you wed, Nevin—Charity or me?" Her eyes narrowed as she waited for his answer.

"That is a bother to you, isn't it, my sweet?" His face wore a sneer. "I'm sure you'll be sorry to learn you were never legally my wife, Christa, though as I said before, I did enjoy our connubial bliss. I was legally married to Charity when I went through the motions of wedding you. I only pretended to placate my father's demands until I could create another life for myself in the very style to which I'd become accustomed. I fooled you and everyone else so easily. You never were a Haviland."

"Thank God . . ." Christa murmured in relief.

"But as I asked before, who else knows I'm alive besides you, Christa?" Suddenly his condescending tone became threatening as he raised his pistol and pointed it at her. Christa took a step back in sudden fear.

"I do, Haviland."

Nevin whirled around at the sound of Trace's deep voice. He crouched and took quick aim, but Trace was faster. His pistol exploded. The bullet struck Nevin's gun hand, sending his weapon flying and causing him to cry out with pain and clutch at his bleeding hand.

"Don't move, Haviland," Trace warned fiercely, "or the next bullet will be between your eyes. Believe me, I'd relish making that shot, you bastard. But I'd rather see you hanged for a deserter during wartime."

"Cavanaugh!" Nevin recognized Trace. "You're one to accuse me! You're wanted yourself for treason and espionage. We'll hang together!"

Suddenly the doors at each end of the room burst open. Before anyone could react, a squad of ten scarlet-coated dragoons rushed into the mill, wielding primed muskets with bayonets at the ready. Trace felt the deadly points of two blades poke sharply into his back.

"Drop the pistol!" came a rough command.

It would have been suicide to disobey when they

were so outnumbered. With one arm raised, Trace slowly leaned down and put his weapon on the dirt floor.

"Well, well, now, this is my lucky night," a familiar voice noted with gloating satisfaction. The speaker walked farther into the room, past the poised soldiers. Lee Garrett!

Trace cringed. He was caught and Christa was in the thick of it, too. Damn!

"My God, Haviland, I thought you were blown to bits," Garrett exclaimed as he recognized the third person he'd entrapped. "I knew having Montclaire watched might yield me a fine reward, but I never dreamed I'd skim such cream. What an interesting assemblage. A dead man who's alive. A traitorous double spy. And a lovely, but dangerous woman who deceptively misled the king's royal forces so her treasonous cohorts could steal a valuable shipment of gold."

"Lee, no, that wasn't—" Christa started to protest.

"Silence, Mrs. Haviland! There will be time enough for you to speak during your interrogation. And I assure you, I'll enjoy that session immensely. Sergeant, restrain the prisoners with—"

Before Garrett could finish his order, a loud cry sounded from behind him. He whirled around to see Isabelle enter the mill. She'd insisted on coming with him tonight, but he'd told her to wait outside for safety. Now he saw her stricken face as she recognized her brother.

"You! No!" she screamed hysterically. A soldier stood next to her holding a pistol. Before anyone could stop her, she grabbed it out of his hand and ran wildly at Nevin.

"You're dead! You must be dead!" She pointed the weapon directly at his chest. Nevin sprang at her, catching her around the waist and falling with her to the floor.

"Stop them, you fools!" Garrett commanded as everyone stood frozen, watching Nevin and Isabelle struggle over the pistol.

Three soldiers started to move in, but the sister and brother were locked together, rolling from side to side. The metal barrel of the weapon glinted in the lamplight and then disappeared from view as Nevin tried to use his one good hand to wrestle it away from Isabelle.

Suddenly a muffled shot was heard. For a shocking, suspended moment no one moved. All eyes watched them. Then Nevin rolled away from his sister. Isabelle lay on the hard ground, her eyes staring fixedly at the beamed ceiling. The pistol remained clutched in her hand, pointing to the bloody place near her heart where the bullet had entered and stilled her life.

Chapter 48

"You'll tell me what I want to know eventually, Cavanaugh," Lee Garrett stated vindictively, coiling the whip in his hand. "But I don't want to break you too quickly. Repaying you for all the trouble you've caused me is very enjoyable, I assure you. I want to prolong the task."

"Take your sick pleasure while you can, Garrett," Trace seethed through clenched teeth. "A day of reckoning will come for us. And on that day, I'll kill you."

"Bravely spoken words." Garrett snorted with a snide smile toward the two seamen assisting him. "But you'll never see that day." He drew back his arm and let go with the whip again.

Trace flinched but made no sound as he tried to block out the excruciating pain that shot through him when the whip ripped into his naked back. He was manacled in a cell in the confinement compartment of the *Wentworth*. He hardly noticed the ship's dull gray walls as he grasped the chains attached to the shackles and braced himself for another strike. His hatred for Garrett gave him strength. He focused on only one thought—the revenge he'd somehow exact.

He'd never tell Garrett the information he sought— the identities and locations of other agents in the

American intelligence network. He'd die first. Each cut of the whip into his flesh only hardened his resolve.

"What's the meaning of this, Garrett?" a fierce voice suddenly called out. "Open this door at once!"

Fitzhugh Zachary frowned as he waited for one of the seamen to open the cell door. The whip stilled in Garrett's hand.

"Are you a blithering idiot, Garrett?" Zachary raged. "Why are you using the lash on Cavanaugh?"

Garrett remained at attention and kept his eyes straight ahead. "You ordered me to interrogate the prisoner regarding his activities as the Scorpion, sir. When normal questioning garnered nothing from him, I thought a taste of the whip might loosen his tongue. May I remind the general of the vital importance of the intelligence information Cavanaugh possesses?"

"I'm well aware of everything concerning Cavanaugh, Captain. And I'll remind *you* it's not your place to take action on your own initiative! Your duty is to follow my commands. I ordered you to question the prisoner, not whip him to death! My orders from General Howe are to see Cavanaugh brought to trial for treason. He'll be of little use to His Majesty's purposes if he's dead from the lash or infection! Now, get him down from there and see to his cuts. Then report to me in my cabin." Zachary turned and stalked out of the cell.

Lee Garrett's face twisted in a grimace of rage as he wound the whip in his hand again. "You heard the general!" he snapped at the seamen. "Remove his shackles and get the ship's doctor in here. But don't take your eyes off the prisoner for an instant!"

During the early months of 1777, the British command located its winter headquarters in New York City. Buildings were commandeered for the housing of military personnel, the storage of supplies, and the confinement of prisoners.

After Christa's arrest at the gristmill, she was brought to a room in the basement storage area of an old winery that had been converted into a prison. A heavy weight of gloom pressed down on her as she sat on the old straw mattress that served as a bed. Sunlight coming through four small dirt-streaked windows near the ceiling gave her some light by which to study her surroundings.

She shared the narrow space with three dozen wooden wine barrels. She knew exactly how many barrels there were, for she counted them again and again, trying to keep from worrying about her terrible plight and what might be happening to Trace. She hadn't had a chance to speak with him before they'd been separated by their captors. She didn't know where he was, or where Nevin was either for that matter.

She tucked her legs under her. A shiver of dread swept through her as she heard something skitter around the barrels. Her ears strained for all the sounds around her, especially the tap of footsteps on the stone steps outside her cell. She dreaded the moment when Lee Garrett would arrive to interrogate her.

She began to nervously pace the short length of the brick-walled room. The stale-smelling air filled her nostrils and the dampness seemed to reach easily inside her seaman's jacket to chill her. Over and over she thought about the horrors of the night before—Nevin's cruel confessions, Isabelle's violent death, Trace's capture—and her own.

Suddenly, Christa heard the murmur of voices coming from beyond the low door of her cell. Hurrying to it, she pressed an eye to a crack in the rough planking, hoping to see who was speaking. A woman wrapped in a dark blue cloak was addressing the burly corporal on guard. Earlier, Christa had seen him dozing in a straight-backed chair propped back against the wall. Now he stood at strict attention.

"My husband will not be pleased to learn you've been napping on duty, Corporal," the woman reprimanded. "But I'm sure you won't do it again, so I'll overlook your negligence this time if you will let me see the prisoner Christa Haviland at once."

Olivia Zachary. Christa recognized her friend's voice, though she couldn't see her face behind the ruffled edge of her dark blue bonnet.

"Yes, ma'am, Mrs. Zachary, ma'am," the corporal hurriedly agreed.

Christa moved away from the door when she heard the key turning in the lock.

"Now, leave the door open, Corporal, and stay alert. I've no desire to be locked in this terrible place with such a desperate criminal as I'm told this woman is. I only wish to see if she needs anything, as I normally do with all of our prisoners here at the compound."

"Yes, Mrs. Zachary." The round-bellied soldier nodded quickly and backed away from the opening.

Olivia held up her hand to keep Christa from speaking. As she drew the door partially closed, she spoke louder than necessary, for the corporal's benefit.

"Now, young woman, don't try anything, or I'll summon the guard." She stepped farther into the dank room and drew Christa to the opposite end.

"Olivia! How glad I am to see you!"

"My heavens, dear, so much has happened. Hugh told me you've been accused of spying for the enemy, along with Trace Cavanaugh. He also said Nevin is alive and accused of murder and desertion. And Isabelle is dead. How did you get involved in these dreadful circumstances?"

Christa hastily told her the story.

"I wasn't spying for the enemy. I didn't even know Trace was the Scorpion until the morning after your dinner party," she ended her narrative. "I wanted to destroy him. I thought I hated him. But in truth, I've fallen in love with him, Olivia, and I've caused his capture." She lowered her head in anguish.

"My, but this is a terrible mess." Olivia took Christa's hand and patted it to soothe her. "I wish there were something I could do to help. I must talk with my husband about these charges against you. And I'll prevail upon him to have you removed from this place to more decent facilities." She glanced around, frowning. "This room is dreadful, so dirty and damp. You're so cold, dear. Here, let me try to warm you." She looked down as she began to massage Christa's left hand. Then she gasped.

"Where did you get this ring?" Olivia asked in a hushed voice.

"I . . . Trace gave it to me. It belonged to his mother," Christa stammered, confused by the stricken look on her friend's face.

"Dear God . . ." Olivia Zachary swayed on her feet so that Christa had to put an arm around her for support.

"Come, sit down here," Christa said, leading the older woman over to a wine barrel turned on its end.

"This cannot be," Olivia murmured as she pressed her hand to her chest.

"What, Olivia? What are you talking about?"

"You're certain you received this ruby ring from Trace Cavanaugh? And he told you it belonged to his mother, Constance?" Olivia persisted.

"Constance? How do you know that was his mother's name?"

Olivia sighed deeply and straightened her shoulders,

looking as if she was gathering her fortitude to do something she didn't want to do.

"Hugh has a ring just like the one you're wearing, Christa. He hasn't worn it for a very long time, but I know he still has it. The two rings formed a set, a family heirloom from his great-grandparents. He gave the woman's ring to Constance Lloyd."

The older woman paused, a faraway look coming into her light blue eyes. Christa waited for her to continue.

Finally, Olivia blinked, drawing herself back from the past to look at Christa. "We haven't much time, so I must speak quickly. As you know, Hugh and I had a son, Merrill. I was very sickly throughout my pregnancy and even afterward, so we hired a beautiful young local girl, Constance Lloyd, to serve as nursemaid. She was near to my own age and became like a sister to me. We were a very happy family.

"When Merrill became ill during the severe winter when he was not quite two years old, we were helpless to save him. He died so quickly. Losing him devastated me. Merrill was Hugh's pride and joy, his heir to the wealthy and respected Zachary peerage. He was heartbroken, too.

"We grieved in different ways, he and I. I withdrew from my husband, let my shock and bitterness become a barrier between us. I wanted to close out the world. Hugh needed someone to share his pain and help him bear it. Constance reached out to him from her grief. Only later did I learn they had found solace in each other.

"About a year after Merrill's death, Hugh left on a long sea voyage for the king. Constance left our home suddenly. A woman I knew cruelly took it upon herself to inform me that Constance was pregnant with Hugh's child.

"When he returned from his journey, I confronted him with his adultery. He said nothing, only turned and walked out of the room—to go to her. Their son was born shortly thereafter.

"I thought I'd lost my husband forever, but he came back and told me Constance had disappeared, taking with her the son he'd seen only once, on the night he was born. He confessed everything, including that he'd given Constance the ring as a token of his love for her. He thought I'd hate him, but I didn't. I understood what drew them together. If anything, I hated myself for my own selfishness, for closing him out and not seeing his need. We forgave each other.

"Hugh was injured in a battle on his next military assignment, and it rendered him incapable of fathering any other children. Perhaps that's been our penance for the sins we committed. But we've had a good life together all these many years. Our love has grown.

"Hugh tried to find Constance and their son, I know, but he could only learn she'd changed her name and gone to America. His attempts to find them yielded nothing.

"I realize now that Trace has his mother's turquoise eyes. And there is much of Hugh in him as well. Perhaps that's why my husband was so drawn to him. What cruel tricks Fate plays on us—that general and captain do not know they are, in fact, father and son. And now the son may be hanged for treason, sent to the gallows by the testimony of his own father."

"No!" Christa cried, jumping to her feet. "We can't let that happen! Trace hates your husband. He thinks the general killed his real father. For years, he's plotted revenge. Trace told me his plans are almost complete. Olivia, please, you must help me! We can't let them destroy each other!"

"You're right, of course, Christa, but what can we do? Oh, it's so hard to think. So much has happened."

Christa forced herself to concentrate. "I must escape from here, Olivia, and somehow find Trace. I have friends who will help me."

"But I know where Trace is. He's being held under heavy guard on a ship in the harbor, the *Wentworth*, due to sail for England the day after tomorrow. Because he's such an important political prisoner, he's to be tried in England before King George himself. There's so little time!"

"But time enough. We can't wait a moment longer. Perhaps if we lure the guard in here, I can use one of these barrels to disable him somehow." She went to the three stacked rows and tried to lift first one barrel and then another, but they were all too heavy.

Then she spied a wooden post, one of three driven into the dirt floor at the end of the rows to keep the barrels in place. The one closest to her no longer stood straight, and when she pushed it, she found that it moved.

"Stand against the wall, Olivia, out of the way. I have an idea."

Christa looked toward the cell door and back to the barrels, gauging the distance. She used all her might to grasp the round post and yank on it. With a splintering crack, the rotted wood let go and the row of stacked barrels tumbled down, making a loud clatter as they hit the floor. Holding the post, Christa ran up to the cell door, pressing her back against the cold bricks of the wall. The guard burst in a second later.

"What the bloody 'ell's goin' on in 'ere?" he demanded, but it was the last thing he said, for Christa swung the post like a club and caught him a solid blow on the back of the head. He pitched forward, hitting the dirt floor with a hard thud. Christa stood frozen, waiting anxiously to see if he'd get up, but he remained motionless. With relief, she saw his shoulders rise and fall slightly, so she knew he wasn't dead.

"Come, Olivia, we must get out quickly!"

The two women ran from the prison room and up the stone stairs to the main floor of the winery. Hiding behind the huge wooden processing vats and stacks of barrels, they cautiously wove their way past two other guard stations to the rear of the building. Olivia had to rest once to regain her breath, but otherwise she kept up with Christa.

The outer door creaked on its hinges when Christa opened it. Cold air hit her lungs, making her gasp for breath. Her heart beat wildly as she glanced about her. A little distance away, a soldier walked his guard round, his musket propped against his shoulder. His back was to them for the moment. Christa motioned for Olivia to follow her. The two women dashed across a narrow alley and were swallowed up by the shadows of an adjacent building just before the guard spun on his heels and marched back.

Chapter 49

"I still say it's too dangerous for you to be here!" Nick Fletcher exclaimed as he looked from his wife to Christa to Olivia Zachary. They were all huddled next to a sturdy piling supporting the wharf overhead. The murky water of New York Harbor lapped over the pebble-strewn bank at their feet. Moonlight penetrated the hidden place only enough to dimly reveal the grim features of those gathered there.

"But we are here, Nick," Christa argued, "and the plan is set. We can't let the *Wentworth* sail on the morning tide."

"Agreed," Nick said. "Is everyone clear on what's to be done?" All three women nodded. "Then let's be about it. Take care, my love." He gave Kate a quick kiss. "Good luck."

He walked away, raising his hand to signal to his waiting men.

"Are you certain you know how to use that pistol, Olivia?" Christa asked, watching her friend check the priming.

"Yes, dear. I'm not a general's wife for nothing. Hugh taught me to use firearms long ago, so I could protect myself when he was away."

"All right then, let's go."

Christa led the way out from under the dock to where stone steps wound up the muddy bank to the street level. The three women stayed out of sight in the shadows of an unused freight wagon. Christa surveyed the long wooden pier, her vision aided by the faint moonlight.

She couldn't see any of Nick Fletcher's crewmen from the *Sea Mist*, but she knew they were hidden behind the many crates and piles of merchandise lining the pier. On signal, the men would attack the double guard patrolling the wharf and the gangplank leading to the *Wentworth*.

Olivia squatted next to the tongue of the wagon and nodded her readiness to cover Christa and Kate. Christa gained courage from the older woman's feisty determination, but her pulse was racing and she trembled with fear as she returned Olivia's nod and stood up with Kate. Straightening her gray cloak and taking a fortifying breath, she wrapped her fingers more tightly around the smooth butt of the loaded pistol she held concealed at her side.

A few people were about, mostly sailors on their way to nearby taverns. They cast interested glances toward Christa and Kate, but the two women were after different prey.

Laughing and pretending to chat behind their hands, Christa and Kate crossed the dock toward the two guards stationed at the foot of the gangplank, calling cheery greetings to the other soldiers. When they came abreast of the men at the ramp, Christa pretended to stumble.

"Ow, blimey I've stoved me toe, Kate!" she wailed, hopping gingerly on one foot. "See if you kin tell if I broke me shoe, too."

She pulled up her plaid tavern-maid's skirt to show a good portion of stocking-clad leg and leaned over so her cloak fell open, revealing the low neckline of her blouse.

"'Ere now, what's goin' on there?" the taller of the two soldiers demanded sharply as he strolled over to them, followed closely by the other guard. Though he was frowning, Christa saw that her actions were not wasted on him. His eyes lingered on the full mounds of her breasts.

"Well now, Kate, ain't these two blokes a sight fer our sore eyes?" Christa exclaimed.

Kate nodded and smiled beguilingly. "Just the ones to 'elp a lady in distress. 'Ere, ducks, could you be 'elpin' me friend? She's 'urt 'er toe on one o' these 'ere broke plankin's."

"Well, ain't that a shame, sweets," the second guard observed with leering interest. "A maid what's as pretty as you shouldn't be 'avin' that 'appen to 'er. Maybe I kin take yer mind off'n that there toe." He lowered his musket from his shoulder and started toward Christa, but the other guard hauled him up short by the shoulder.

"'Old up there, Cobbs. Don't fergit yer duty. The General'll 'ave our 'ides if'n we tarry about with these 'ere wenches."

"Aw, but, Sarge, I ain't 'ad me arms about a perty thing like this in such a long time. I fergit what they feels like."

"It'll be the whip you'll be afeelin'. Now, git back to yer post!"

Christa moved closer to the men. "Speakin' o' feelin', ducks, what do you think of the feel o' this in yer belly?" She pulled aside her cloak and jabbed her cocked pistol into the sergeant's paunch. Kate did the same with Cobbs.

"All right, gentlemen, listen carefully," Christa went on, dropping the fake accent and keeping her voice low. "If you don't want holes shot through your middles, you'd better do exactly as you're told.

Sergeant, call over the rest of the men in the guard detail. *Do it!*'' she ordered fiercely when he kept staring at her in surprise. She pressed the pistol harder into his flabby stomach, and he seemed to realize she meant business.

"'Ere, you lads!'' he called out. "Front and center, in formation!''

The other British soldiers on the dock stepped lively to obey the sergeant's order. They formed two straight lines before him, shoulders back and bracing their muskets in attention stance.

"Tell them to drop their weapons,'' Christa murmured under her breath.

"Drop yer weapons, men!''

In the next instant, Nick's men poured from their hiding places, overtaking the soldiers on the dock. Nick and several others raced up the gangplank to capture the guards on the ship's main deck.

"Luck is with us,'' Nick observed softly when Christa, Kate, and Olivia joined him. "Not a shot's been fired. You were right, Christa, in thinking the British wouldn't expect another attack to follow so quickly after the last one when we relieved them of the gold. You women stay here while we go below and roust the rest of them out of their berths.''

At that moment, a British soldier who'd been knocked unconscious to the deck suddenly rose and pointed a musket directly at Nick. Christa caught the movement out of the corner of her eye and screamed. Nick dropped to one knee and fired his pistol just as the man's musket went off. Christa heard the ball whiz past and watched in horror as the soldier clutched his chest and fell backward.

The element of surprise was gone.

"Below decks, lads!'' Nick shouted as he waved his men to follow him to the main companionway.

Within moments, the crewmen of the *Wentworth* were engaged in a battle for their lives above and below decks. Huddled out of the way near the gangplank, Christa, Kate, and Olivia watched the intense drama being played out so violently before them on the torch-lit deck. Gunshots rang out sporadically, but the main fight was hand-to-hand, with swords, knives, and bayonets. The clash of metal on metal rang in the air, along with bloodthirsty battle yells and cries of agony.

Christa couldn't stay where she was and watch the holocaust. She had to find Trace.

"Come back!" Kate cried as Christa jumped to her feet.

But Christa didn't listen. She concentrated on staying close to the side of the ship as she made her way to a companionway near the bow. Screaming, she ducked just in time to avoid the slash of a bloody cutlass as it whizzed past her head. Kicking upward with her foot, she caught the British sailor fully between the legs. He gasped and fell to the foredeck, clutching his groin, momentarily helpless. Christa snatched up the cutlass he'd dropped and dashed onto the stairway.

"Trace!" she cried at the top of her voice in an effort to be heard above the pandemonium occurring below decks. Pushing her way past battling men, she hurried along the corridor, continuing to call out Trace's name.

Suddenly a huge seaman in a striped shirt loomed in front of her. For an instant, he seemed surprised to confront a woman, but then he swiftly raised his musket bayonet. Christa instinctively dropped to one knee and grasped her cutlass in both hands just as the man lunged at her. With all her might, she thrust the weapon upward, catching the man full in the stomach.

The blade was wrenched from her hand as he pitched sideways and fell like a lead weight to the deck.

Christa gasped for breath, hysteria welling up inside her as she stared in shock at the man she'd just killed. At that instant, Jason Fletcher, Nick's younger brother, crashed into her, bowling her over as he recoiled from a powerful hit in the jaw. Without stopping to help her up, he jumped to his feet and dove at his opponent, taking the man down with a flying tackle.

Christa crawled away on her hands and knees, staying close to the floor, trying to keep out of the way. Where could Trace be? Was he even on the ship? What if Olivia had been wrong? That terrible thought made Christa cry out his name again.

"Here! I'm here!" she heard someone shout. *Trace!* With a cry of relief, she stumbled to her feet, pulling at her hindering skirt, and pushed at a wooden door with a small barred window near the top. But a padlock secured the door in place.

In desperation, Christa sought something with which to break the lock. She spied a pistol stuck in the waistband of the breeches of a man who'd been killed. Averting her eyes, she ran to his still body and grabbed the weapon. Cocking back the hammer, she pointed it at the lock and pulled the trigger. The gun exploded, leaving a hole where the lock had been. The door gave way easily to her push.

Barred cells lined both sides of the long, narrow room in which Christa found herself.

"Christa!" Trace shouted from the cell closest to her.

"Trace!" She ran to him, clutching the hands he thrust through the bars. Her eyes darted to the bloodstained, shredded shirt hanging around his waist. "You're hurt!" she cried, frantic with fear.

"No, it's nothing. Get the key—there!" He pointed to a wooden peg on the wall across the room.

Christa ran to it and yanked off the ring of iron keys, then hurried back to Trace. In the next moment, the cell door was open. Trace took her hand and together they ran out to the corridor. Nick Fletcher met them there. His clothes were bloodstained and he had a deep slash across his upper arm, but he paid no heed to it.

"Trace! Good to see you, old boy!" He grinned and tossed Trace a sword, then turned just in time to land a jaw-cracking blow to a man who came at him from the side.

"Let's get the hell out of here, lads!" Nick shouted to the men around him. "The alarm's surely been raised by now. These decks'll be swarming with redcoats! We'll fight another day! Abandon ship! To the horses!"

It was the order the Americans had been waiting for. As suddenly as they'd launched the attack, they broke it off and headed topside, helping their comrades fend off a final quarry when necessary.

The British had been caught off-guard, and they'd taken the worst of the fight. Bleeding and dying men in scarlet uniforms lay strewn over the main deck. But a few were still battling Nick's men.

"Garrett!" Trace exclaimed when he spotted his enemy on the quarterdeck.

Lee Garrett swung around to face Trace. "Defend yourself, Cavanaugh. I've waited a long time to fight you!"

"So have I, Garrett," Trace shot back, swiftly raising his sword to parry Garrett's thrust.

The two men circled the small deck in a violent life-and-death struggle. Christa pressed a hand to her mouth to keep from crying out loud. Her eyes widened with fear as she intently watched each man's movements.

How could Trace show such strength? Surely he must be hampered by his wounded back. She cringed at the sight of the raw lash marks revealed by the torchlight.

Yet something seemed to be driving him, for he was gradually gaining the upper hand in the fight. Garrett backed away again and again, trying to fend off Trace's expert slashes. Both men were panting for breath. Trace's jaw was set in a sharp line and his dark brows nearly met from the fierceness of his frown as he concentrated on defeating Garrett.

Suddenly, Garrett stumbled over a coil of rope and fell backward. Trace could have finished him off easily with one more thrust, but he stepped back.

"Get up, Garrett," he said from between clenched teeth. "I'll see you eye-to-eye when I kill you!"

The hate in Lee Garrett's expression was almost tangible. He quickly regained his footing and lunged. Trace sidestepped just in time and brought his arm up to plunge his sword deep into his adversary's chest. Garrett appeared stunned for a suspended moment as he looked down at the blood spurting from the wound. Then his eyes rolled back and he collapsed, falling limp at Trace's feet.

"Come on, Christa. We have to get out of here," Trace directed, taking no time to consider his triumph. He grabbed her hand again and led the way toward the stern of the *Wentworth*.

Nick and most of his men were already off the ship, waiting on horseback at the far end of the wharf. Trace and Christa ran to reach them. From a nearby church tower they could hear the urgent peal of a bell.

"That's the alarm, Trace!" Nick shouted as he held two horses for them to mount, then threw Trace a jacket like his own. "I heard the assembly bugle, too. The pier'll be swarming with redcoats any minute now."

"Then let's be off, Nick!" Trace exclaimed as he quickly shrugged into the black jacket, ignoring the painful rubbing of the wool cloth over the welts on his back, and lifted Christa up into the saddle of her mount. He swung up onto his own horse, frowning when he saw who was mounted on the other side of Nick. Jason Fletcher held a pistol on the prisoner.

"What's *he* doing here?" Trace demanded, glaring at Fitzhugh Zachary, who returned his hate-filled look with equal fierceness.

"The general here tried to run me through in the fight just now," Nick explained. "He's bloody good with a sword. But I managed to best him, and thought it might be prudent to bring him along as a little insurance toward reaching the *Sea Mist*. Our pass through enemy lines, so to speak, if we need it." He raised up in the stirrups and shouted orders to his men. "You know the plan, lads. Split up. Head for the cove. And don't dally!"

"Wait for me! Wait for me!" someone called, and Christa turned to see Olivia Zachary running toward them.

"Here, Olivia!" she directed. "Up behind me!"

"Good God, Olivia! What are you doing here?" Hugh Zachary stared in astonishment at his wife.

"Oh dear, Hugh, you weren't supposed to find me here. I can explain everything. You must listen—"

"No time for that," Nick cut in. "Right now we ride!"

Chapter 50

"Think we're being followed?" Nick asked as he reined in his mount. The horse snorted and shied, its sides heaving. Billowing clouds that obscured the moon cast shadows over the riders.

Trace tightened his grip on the reins of his prancing roan. "Can't be sure, but we'd best assume we do have dragoons after us."

"Aye, that's my thought, too," Nick agreed. "The *Sea Mist*'s at Duncan's Cove and ready to weigh anchor as soon as we're all aboard." He pointed toward a thick grove of pines to their right.

"Then this is where we part company, my friend. I have orders to report to General Washington in New Jersey. I'm going to try to make it to Hattie's now, but I want you to take Christa with you, Nick. Will you have someone take her to my house in Albany? She'll be safe there."

"Aye, consider it done."

"No, Trace, I'm coming with you," Christa stated firmly as she spurred her horse up beside him. "I won't be parted from you now. There's something I must tell you."

"Sounds like Christa has as much of a mind of her own as my Kate does," Nick observed, grinning. "You have my sympathies, old man! But we don't have time to argue the point now. That sounds like horses coming fast behind us!''

"You're right. Jason, your pistol!'' Trace called. He caught it and aimed it at Hugh Zachary. "I'll take the general with me as a trophy for Washington. My thanks for what you did tonight, Nick.'' He clasped his friend's hand.

"Any time, Trace. You've saved my neck often enough. Until we meet again, my friend.'' He touched two fingers to his tricorn hat in a quick salute and spurred his horse away, followed by Kate, Jason, and two of his men.

"Mrs. Zachary, can you keep up?'' Trace hastily addressed the older woman. "You could stay behind and wait for the dragoons, tell them you were our hostage but you escaped.''

"No, Captain, I'm coming with you. If my husband's to be a prisoner, then I shall be, too. I've come too far to turn back now. But you both must listen—''

"As you choose, but hold what you want to say,'' Trace cut in as he leaned over and grabbed Hugh Zachary's reins out of his hands. "Don't try to escape General. It's not my plan to kill you, but rest assured I'll do precisely that if you give me provocation. Follow me!''

Not waiting for Zachary's reply, he grasped both horses' reins and dug his heels into his mount's sides. The roan plunged down the road.

The eastern horizon was lightening as they rode on, making the road easier to see. But the first rays of the crimson dawn also revealed an unwelcome sight to Trace. He sharply pulled up his galloping mount. They'd come to a long bridge spanning a deep gorge. Over a hundred feet below them raged murky, swift moving Cochoran Creek, which an early thaw had left as wide and deep as a river. At the far end of the bridge, Trace saw the torchlights and cook fires of a camp.

"What is it, Trace?" Christa asked, following his gaze.

"A British outpost, I'll wager, established to guard this strategic bridge."

"You're caught now, Cavanaugh!" Zachary gloated. "Dragoons behind, infantry in front. Surrender while you can!"

Trace ignored Zachary's taunt, except to send him a hate-filled glance. He whipped around in his saddle, searching for a side path or hiding place, but the hills to their left rose at too steep an angle for the horses to negotiate, and on the other side, just beyond the edge of the dirt road, the ground dropped sharply away, too steeply to be used as an escape route.

Trace's expression became grim as he realized they were, indeed, trapped. He racked his mind trying to think of something, knowing he had only minutes to decide. One possibility came to him. It was perilous, perhaps even suicidal, but what choice did he have? If only he didn't have to endanger Christa and Olivia Zachary as well.

As if reading his thoughts, Zachary taunted him. "Give up, Cavanaugh. I know you won't jeopardize the women's safety. You'd risk your own neck, but not theirs. You're finished!"

"When you find I've no breath left in my body, then you'll know I'm finished, Zachary!" Trace's turquoise eyes flashed as cold as ice. "But before that happens, I'll take you with me to Hell!"

He started to draw his sword and Christa screamed.

"Trace, no, please! You can't kill him!" She forced her horse between the two men. Zachary's mount reared. Zachary clutched the sorrel's mane and barely kept his seat as the animal plunged ahead onto the bridge.

"Damn!" Trace cursed fiercely as he whirled his own mount to go after the general. Still riding double, Christa and Olivia galloped after the men.

Trace was quickly abreast of Zachary. Lunging, he knocked the general from his horse, and the two men tumbled sideways, landing hard on the wooden bridge. Trace instantly jumped to his feet and drew his sword.

"Trace! Stop, please! *Trace!*" Christa screamed, spurring her horse to block his path.

"Get out of my way, Christa!" Trace scowled in fury, pushing her mount aside. He took a threatening step toward Zachary, who was still lying on the bridge clutching his left leg.

"Trace, stop! Listen to me! He's your father! Do you hear me? *Fitzhugh Zachary is your father!*" Christa pounded the words at him like blows, but he still advanced on his quarry.

"It's true, Captain!" Olivia Zachary cried. "Christa's telling you the truth! My husband is your father. He doesn't even know it himself."

Trace stopped and stared at the two women.

"It's true, my love. You must believe us," Christa beseeched when she saw the doubt in his eyes.

Olivia Zachary dismounted and ran to her husband, kneeling down beside him. "Is your leg broken, Hugh?" she asked, seeing it was bent at an unnatural angle.

Zachary's face was twisted with pain, but he gritted his teeth as he challenged his wife. "Have you gone mad, woman? What lies are these? I have no son! Our son died as a babe!"

"Our son, yes, but not *your* son by Constance."

Hugh Zachary stared at his wife and then at Trace. For a long moment, the two men were silent.

"Dear God, Hugh, look at him!" Olivia pleaded. "Can't you see yourself in him? And he has his mother's eyes. Christa showed me a ring he gave her. Hugh, it's the family ruby that matches yours, the ring you gave Constance. Trace is your son."

"Yes, see, here it is." Christa stepped forward and held out her left hand.

"No! You're lying!" Trace accused furiously. "He killed my true father! My mother told me on her deathbed. With her last breath, she . . ."

He stopped, shocked to silence by a sudden realization.

"Trace, what is it?" Christa saw the doubt, the confusion on his face.

"She was so ill, so weak . . ." he murmured.

"And you were just a boy," Christa went on, realizing what he might be thinking. "You must have been so frightened, so alone."

"I thought she said . . ." Trace stopped, his forehead deeply furrowed by a frown of painful concentration. It still hurt to remember his mother's death. He'd buried the memory deep inside sixteen years ago and set his sight on one goal—revenge against Fitzhugh Zachary. But now he forced himself to recall that terrible scene.

His mother's dying words had become rambling, disconnected, broken by harsh coughing spasms. The effort to speak had drained her last strength. He'd tried to grasp her words, their meaning, but now he knew he'd made a mistake. A terrible mistake.

"My God . . ." Zachary murmured, his features softening though he was still gripped by pain. "My son . . ."

So many questions flashed through Trace's mind as he stared at his father. But there would be no asking them now, for at that very moment, the scarlet-coated

British dragoons thundered around the bend in the road and came to a halt at the edge of the bridge. At the same time, soldiers from the British encampment at the far end of the bridge began to advance slowly toward them.

Trace stepped swiftly to Zachary and pressed the tip of his sword to the older man's chest, raising his other hand toward the cavalrymen.

"Halt where you are or I will pierce General Zachary's heart!" he shouted.

An unseen commander gave the order and the troops halted.

"Trace, no!" Christa cried in alarm.

"Be still, Christa!" Trace ordered fiercely in a low voice, his mind racing.

"It seems we're doomed to have a brief relationship as father and son, General," he said finally, "for despite everything else, I'm still the Scorpion. We're sworn enemies, fighting on opposite sides. I won't be taken and hanged. If you could ride, I'd keep you hostage, but from the look of that leg, I don't think you'll be sitting a horse for some time. That leaves just one alternative."

He turned to Christa, his expression grim. "There's not much chance we'll make it."

"I'm with you, Trace, no matter what."

"Then follow me. Until we meet another day, General." He nodded sharply in Zachary's direction, and, taking Christa's hand ran to the middle of the bridge.

"It's a bloody good morning for an invigorating swim, wouldn't you say, my love?"

"W—what?" Christa stared at him in disbelief as he unbuckled his sword belt and shrugged off Nick's jacket.

"You *can* swim?"

"Yes, but—"

"No time for arguments, Christa. Get out of that skirt." He yanked on the strings of her cloak and let it fall to her feet. She loosened the drawstring at her waist, and her plaid skirt quickly followed.

"I'll give you a lift up." Trace waved toward the three-foot-high wooden railing that ran along both sides of the bridge, then he grabbed Christa around the waist and hoisted her rump up on it and swung her legs over the top.

Christa's heart leaped into her throat. She sucked in her breath in a gasp of fear and swayed dangerously as she looked down. In the crisp cold air, the light of full dawn revealed churning Cochoran Creek far below. Her mind barely registered the sound of horses' hooves as the British soldiers closed in on them from both ends of the bridge. Trace swung up beside her on the railing and gripped her hand.

"You said you were with me no matter what, Christa. This feat will test our mettle! Swim for the right bank. If God wills, I'll see you there!"

He squeezed her hand for encouragement and plunged from the rail, taking Christa with him.

Chapter 51

Christa lost her hold on Trace and hit the frigid water with a bone-jarring impact. As the icy flow engulfed her, she fought back overwhelming panic and kicked her legs as hard as she could in an effort to reach the surface. Excruciating pain constricted her chest as she struggled upward, her lungs screaming for air, her limbs so numb from the cold that they seemed to be moving in slow motion. An eternity of seconds ticked by, until she was sure she wasn't going to make it. Then, all at once, her head burst through the choppy water and she was sucking in great lungfuls of precious air.

Thrashing around in a circle, she searched for Trace, but he wasn't there. The sound of musket shots made her glance upward to where soldiers on the bridge were firing over the side of the wall. Some of the balls hit the surface close beside her, showering her with icy spray.

Desperate with fear, she struggled to swim toward the far bank, but the strong current was carrying her farther and farther downstream. Already she was shaking uncontrollably from the cold. She had to get out soon or she'd freeze to death!

Where was Trace? Had one of the musket shots hit him? Had he been hurt in the fall and drowned? Christa tried to block out the terrifying possibilities.

Just then a familiar voice called, "Here, Christa, hurry! Keep swimming! You can make it!"

Trace! He was standing in waist-deep water near the bank, waving to her. She longed to reach him, but her arms were giving out.

"I can't make it, Trace!"

Immediately he realized she was going to be swept past him just out of reach. Spurred into action, he spotted a dead log lying higher on the bank. He sprang up the slope and heaved the log down to the water, then splashed in after it.

"Grab hold, Christa!" he shouted, pushing the floating wood toward her.

Gratefully, she clutched the protruding end of a gnarled root. Her hands were so cold she could barely hold on, but somehow she made her numb fingers curl around the rough wood. Trace did likewise, working his way down the length of the log until he was close to her.

"Try to hang on," he told her through chattering teeth. "Keep kicking. We'll have to ride downstream until we can work our way close to shore. At least we've escaped the shooting."

Christa could only nod in agreement. She needed all her strength to kick and hang on. But she couldn't help wondering which would be worse—dying from a musket shot or becoming paralyzed in the cold water and drowning. Both awful thoughts spurred her to hold on more tightly. She glanced over her shoulder and saw they'd drifted a good distance from the bridge. Would the soldiers try to follow them on shore?

"Kick for those rocks, Christa!" Trace called, pointing to a narrow peninsula jutting out from the shoreline.

A few seconds later, the log bumped onto the bank.

Christa felt for the bottom and almost wept with relief when her feet touched solid ground.

"This way." Trace pulled her after him as he waded to dry ground, and they both collapsed on the bank gasping for breath. The winter air felt warm on Christa's skin after the icy cold of the water.

"We must keep moving," Trace told her, forcing himself to his feet. "We'll catch our deaths out here— if the dragoons don't find us first. There's a place not far from here where we can hide." He pulled her to her feet.

Trace's lips were tinged with blue and his hand was shaking as it held hers. His tattered shirt was gone, leaving his chest and back completely exposed to the elements. Christa knew she wasn't much better off in her soaked blouse and pantaloons.

Trace must feel as cold and exhausted as she was, yet the determination in his voice proved he hadn't given up fighting. Though she felt dazed and sapped of energy, she willed herself to push harder, just as Trace was doing.

"Show me the way," she urged, trying to control her own trembling. His quick smile sent a surge of warmth through her as she hurried to follow his lead.

They stayed close to the bank, half walking, half running. In her weakness Christa stumbled several times, but Trace was always there to help her up again.

"It's not much farther now," he encouraged. "Just beyond those trees ahead. There'll be a warm fire waiting. Think of that."

She nodded, fighting back tears of exhaustion and despair. Trace pulled her into his arms for a moment.

"Have courage, my love. We can make it," he said gently before releasing her to continue toward the grove of barren oaks.

When a log farmhouse loomed into sight, Christa

gave a cry of relief. Smoke curled from a stone chimney, and all was quiet. Trace paused at the edge of the clearing and glanced around cautiously, then he swept Christa up in his arms and carried her across a dirt road and the remains of a garden.

"Hattie! Hattie Gillis, it's Trace! Open up!" he called, pounding on the door with his booted foot.

"Land 'o Goshen, if'n it ain't you!" exclaimed a gray-haired woman well into her sixties as she opened the door, holding a musket. "Good Lord, Trace lad, come in, come in." She propped the weapon against the wall and waved them inside.

"Come to the fire, both of you. Why, you look half froze to death! And, Trace, you with no shirt on!"

The hearth across the room blazed with a roaring fire. Smells of baking bread and cooking porridge filled the air.

Hattie Gillis hurriedly grabbed two quilts from the bed and wrapped them around her shivering guests. Then she went to a trunk in a corner and rummaged inside, bringing out several pieces of clothing.

"Here now, these ought to do. You git out of them wet things right quick. Trace, you change in the back room. I'll help yer friend.

"What's yer name, child?" she asked as she took Christa's wet clothes and handed her a faded print dress.

"C—Christa," she managed to reply through chattering teeth.

"Hattie's my name. Come back over to the fire, dearie, while I git you somethin' hot to drink."

Trace joined them dressed in a white cotton shirt and brown breeches.

"You be gittin' this here hot tea in you," Hattie directed, handing Trace and Christa each a steaming mug. "I make it good an' strong, don't I, Trace boy?"

"That you do, Hattie, and it tastes mighty fine right now, believe me," he assured her, smiling. "You're a fetching angel of mercy."

"Oh, go on now, you smooth-tongued devil," their plump hostess chided, but she blushed and grinned with pleasure. "Christa and me already met, but I still don't know what happened to turn the two 'o you into a couple 'o half-froze, drowned rats." She pulled up a three-legged stool and sat down next to Trace.

"We had to jump from the creek bridge to escape a pack of redcoats who were after us," Trace explained.

"Jumped from the bridge!" Hattie rolled her brown eyes toward the wood-beamed ceiling. "Are you daft? Why, you mighta bin killed by the fall alone."

"There was no choice, Hattie. Even now, the soldiers might be tracking us."

"Well, I kin hide you if they show up, like I done b'fore," she replied, getting to her feet. "Let me git some hot breakfast in the two o' you quicklike, then you kin take to the loft."

Hattie served up the hearty breakfast with a speed and efficiency that belied her age.

"I saw Ralph just a month ago," Trace told her as he finished the last of the thick porridge. "He's fine, but says he misses your cooking."

Hattie was clearly pleased to hear the news. "Said that, did he, now? Well, when he comes home from the war, I'll be amakin' all his favorites. You tell that boy o' mine I said so, next time you lay eyes on him."

"I'll do that, Hattie. Are you getting along all right here alone?"

"Oh, go on, you ask me that every danged time yer here, Trace. An' don't I always tell you the same thing? I'm fine. I got my animals fer company, an'—"

The sound of galloping horses made her halt in mid-sentence. Trace strode to the front window and carefully peered through the curtain.

"Five dragoons," he reported. "This way, Christa." He led her to a wooden ladder against the back wall.

The older woman hurried to her gun propped by the door.

"Don't shoot anyone, Hattie," Trace warned. "Just act like a peaceable citizen. I don't want anything to happen to you."

She looked disappointed. "Well, all right. I won't be afillin' 'em full o' holes if I kin help it. Git to hidin' now, the both o' you."

Hattie bustled to the door while Trace and Christa climbed into the loft. Going quickly to the far end, Trace reached up and opened a concealed trapdoor in the sharply slanting ceiling, then climbed through it to a narrow wooden platform suspended between two gables in the roof and almost invisible from the ground. When he'd helped Christa up beside him, he replaced the hidden door and motioned for her to lie down next to him on the boards. The roofline shielded them completely from view from the front of the house but if one of the soldiers studied the rear view of the roof very carefully, he might detect their hiding place. Christa's heart pounded as she heard Hattie speak to the patrol.

"Well now, Captain, 'tis a fine day, ain't it? What brings you to these parts?"

"My rank is lieutenant, old woman," the officer retorted. "We're searching for two fugitives on foot, a man and a woman. They're escaped criminals and highly dangerous."

"Lordy, Lieutenant, ain't nobody come by this way in quite a spell, 'ceptin' you blokes now."

"Nonetheless, we will search these premises. Stand aside, woman. Private, you search inside. The rest of you take the barn and immediate grounds. And remember, General Zachary's orders are to take the fugitives alive."

It seemed to Christa as if an eternity inched past as she and Trace remained huddled together waiting for the soldiers to complete their search. Shivering from the crisp cold, she pressed close to Trace, feeling the tension in his body and noticing that he kept his eyes steadily on the trapdoor. But no one opened it, and though they heard a single horse circle the farmhouse very slowly, no cry of alarm was sounded. Finally, the lieutenant called his men together.

"Your report, Private."

"No sign of the fugitives, sir."

"I doubted they could survive that water," the lieutenant said. "We could find no tracks to show where they came out of the creek. Mount up, men. We're returning to camp."

When she heard the horses galloping away, Christa, vastly relieved, immediately started to get up, but Trace pulled her back.

"Wait a little longer," he whispered.

A few minutes later they heard Hattie call from below, "All's clear, Trace!" On shaky limbs Christa followed Trace back inside and met Hattie by the fireplace.

"Thanks, Hattie. Sorry to put you in danger," Trace said with a grin, holding his hands over the fire to warm them and pulling Christa close to his side.

"Aw, go on, you know I love to git the best o' the British every chance I kin. I just hope that danged patrol ain't scared my cows outta their milk. I best be seein' to 'em."

"I'll help you."

"No, you won't, lad. My girls don't like no one 'ceptin' me amilkin' 'em. You an' Miz Christa hide yerselves upstairs. Git some rest. You'll be needin' it if yer goin' to leave at nightfall.''

Hattie left the house, and Trace and Christa returned to the loft, where a thick mattress near the chimney, topped with several layers of neatly folded quilts, afforded a snug sleeping area. A flat-topped trunk holding an oil lamp provided the only other furnishing.

Trace drew Christa down on the mattress and pulled her close. "Are you all right?" he asked gently. "You looked frightened to death while we were hiding.''

"I was," she admitted, glad to be alone with him, to have his arms around her. "Will the soldiers return, do you think?"

"No. I think we're finally safe.''

"It's hard to believe we've actually escaped the British. Mrs. Gillis showed such bravery in facing the patrol.''

"Yes, Hattie has courage, all right, but so do you, Christa. Taking part in Nick's attack on the *Wentworth* to free me was no small matter. You might have been killed." His turquoise eyes held hers and his voice became hushed. "I thank God nothing happened to you there or when we escaped from the bridge. My life would mean nothing without you. I love you, Christa.''

"Oh, Trace," she whispered, overcome with emotion. "I love you with all my heart." She kissed him lingeringly and snuggled deeper into his arms.

"So much has happened," she murmured when they separated a little to catch their breath. "What will you do now? How do you feel about Fitzhugh Zachary?"

"How could I have been so wrong about him? For so long I was obsessed with exacting revenge. And it was all a mistake." His voice trailed off as he shook his head in regret. "I must stop all I've done to try to ruin him. I established secret bank funds and bogus business enterprises in his name here and in England, all to make him appear to be betraying the king and profitting illegally from the war. I sought to destroy his reputation and see him stripped of his rank and peerage in the realm.''

"Can you prevent his ruin now?"

"Yes. It'll take some doing, and I'll need Nick's help, but I can remedy the damage.''

Christa glimpsed the pain and regret in his eyes. She hoped her next words would help him.

"Olivia told me he loved your mother very much. Friendship and grief drew them together after your half brother died. Olivia was nearly out of her mind with her own bereavement and turned away from her husband. Your mother was a servant in the household. The wrenching pain of the terrible loss of the boy caused Fitzhugh to turn to her. They fell in love, but your mother left him after you were born. He tried to find you both after you came to the Colonies, but his efforts were in vain.''

Trace nodded. "My mother must have changed her name to Cavanaugh when we came to America to ensure that my father wouldn't find us.''

Christa held him close and rested her head on his shoulder, trying to share his hurt.

"How I wish I could take away the loneliness you must have felt as a young boy, your fears, your anger. But I can't change the past. We must both look to the future now. You have a father and the proud lineage you've wanted so much.''

"Yes, I've longed for both. Perhaps once the war ends, I can meet my father on different terms. But now it seems more important to make my own way, to continue to build my own heritage here in America.''

Trace drew away a little to look at Christa. "What did I do to deserve you?" he murmured, gently touching her cheek. "I love you with all my heart,

Christa. When we're together, everything seems possible. With you at my side, all my dreams can come true. I have so much to do, to build. I feel new-born, like our nation, ready to spread my wings and soar. America offers so many opportunities just waiting to be grasped. Will you marry me and share them with me?''

"Oh, yes, Trace. I could want nothing more than to share my life with you. Yes, I will be your wife.''

He said nothing more, but his loving smile filled Christa with boundless joy. When they kissed again, it was as if a powerful, unseen strand had bound their hearts together. Their lips, their bodies, spoke the language of love as no words ever could. The past lay behind them, its dark desires and painful secrets exposed and conquered. Ahead, the dawning future glowed with the bright promise of everlasting love.

Epilogue

Christa slipped out of her nightgown and climbed
into bed with her husband, snuggling close against him.
She smiled in the darkness as she felt the warmth of
his naked body touch hers.

"Are the children finally asleep?" Trace asked,
gathering her in his arms.

"Yes. They were just too excited about our trip
tomorrow to settle down. Sailing across an ocean is
quite an adventure for a six-year-old and a four-year-
old. Nathaniel is acting every bit the worldly older
brother to Millicent, expounding fact after fact to her
about the voyage, the ship we'll be on, England—
everything he's heard from us over the past month.
Millicent giggles a lot, but she hangs on his every
word."

"We have wonderful children, Christa. Have I told
you lately how much I love them and you?" Trace
asked tenderly.

"You mentioned it a few hours ago, my love, but I
don't mind hearing it again." She put her arm across
his chest and hugged him tightly. "Oh, Trace, we're
so blessed. I'm the happiest woman in the world. And

336

I'm just as excited about our trip to England as the children are.''

Trace sighed in contentment. ''I'm looking forward to it, too. It's been a long time since I've seen London. I'm glad the war is finally over and the British are no longer the enemy.''

Christa felt something wet and cold touch her elbow.

''Don't worry, Prince Lanyard, you'll be coming with us.'' She laughed as she reached out to pat the tawny Great Dane's head.

''That should produce utter chaos on the ship,'' Trace observed wryly.

''Perhaps, but I can't leave him here for the months we'll be away. We haven't been separated since you gave him to me as a tiny pup on our wedding day. He'd be so lonely.''

''And we couldn't have that.''

''No, we couldn't.'' Christa smiled, knowing Trace's attachment to the big dog was as strong as hers.

''It will be good to see Olivia again. I've missed her these seven years since she returned to England. Nathaniel and Millicent are so anxious to meet their grandparents. I know Olivia will spoil them terribly. And Fitzhugh likely will, as well. For all his rough general's exterior, I think there's a gentle, loving man inside. Are you still apprehensive about seeing him again?'' Christa asked quietly.

''No, he's my father. I've wanted to know him for a long time. Now the opportunity is here. But I'm glad you'll be with me.''

''Will you let Fitzhugh acknowledge you publicly as his son, as he offered in his letter?''

''Yes, if that pleases him. But I won't change my name. My mother gave me the name Cavanaugh, and

I'm known in my own right by it. I bear it with pride."

"As do I, my dearest husband." She kissed him softly and murmured with contentment as he began to stroke her hair.

"Do you think you've packed enough of our possessions for this trip?" Trace said on a lighter note. "You're taking nearly the whole house, aren't you?"

"You told me the *Freedom* was a stout vessel, a fine addition to our shipping line," Christa teased. "I felt it could endure the weight of all our trunks. But if you must blame someone for our abundance of luggage, blame Marcus. He told me to take my fine gowns to impress the ladies of English society with our stunning American fashions."

"I hope he isn't as free trading business advice with the English as he is sharing American fashions."

Christa chuckled. "You know he isn't or you wouldn't be entrusting him with the job of handling all your business affairs in your absence. He'll do a fine job, just as he always does. And he needs the extra work to help him forget Suko. I think he came to have very strong feelings for her. He's been more subdued, it seems, since she returned to Japan with Tohashi last year.

"Did you see Harvard's bon voyage note?" she continued. "It arrived this afternoon."

"Yes, Letty showed it to me. He's becoming a fine young man. He's intelligent, with good common sense, too."

"The hardships that have befallen the Haviland family forced him to mature beyond his fifteen years. To lose his mother so tragically and then his father shortly thereafter at sea were terrible burdens for a youngster to bear. His grandfather was a strong influence in helping him accept his parents' deaths, but now it's Harvard who must show the strength of will to save the family. I never dreamed Orin would lose his fortune. Of his entire empire, only Haviland Court itself remains.''

"War has a way of turning the tide of prosperity for many people,'' Trace explained. "Public opinion went against the loyalists long before the war ended last autumn.''

"I don't think Orin ever really recovered from Nevin's execution. To have one's only son hanged for desertion would be devastating to any man, but especially to a man as proud as Orin Haviland. That must explain why he's become a recluse.''

"You know I'll do what I can to help Harvard,'' Trace assured her.

Christa rose up on one elbow to look at him, her smile warm. "Yes, I know. Your generosity is legendary. Now, let me show you how generous *I* can be.'' She leaned down to kiss him deeply. "Have I told you lately how much I love you, my husband?'' she murmured, her eyes glistening in the lamplight as she echoed his earlier endearments.

"Not in the last few hours,'' Trace answered softly, meeting her gaze. "Tell me again.''

"Let me show you instead, my love . . .''

NANCY MOULTON

NANCY MOULTON has always been a confirmed romantic. Even when she was growing up in Toledo, Ohio, she spent many late nights watching swashbuckling heroes in old movies. However, romance didn't rule her life. After receiving a bachelor's degree in elementary education, she went on to become a teacher, wife, mother of two children—Heather and Ryan—and reader of historical romance novels. Then one snowy winter in Wooster, Ohio, overcome by the effects of cabin fever, Nancy gave in to the urge to write a romantic novel of her own. Four years later, she had a manuscript that finally satisfied her, which she then submitted to Avon Books. The rest, as they say, is history. Nancy still finds opportunities to indulge in her hobbies, which include watching movie classics, reading, doing needle crafts, painting, teaching children about dinosaurs, and collecting kaleidoscopes.

Each month enjoy the best...

THE AVON ROMANCE

in exceptional authors and unforgettable novels!

HOSTAGE HEART   Eileen Nauman
75420-7/$3.95US/$4.95 Can

RECKLESS SPLENDOR   Maria Greene
75441-x/$3.95US/$4.95 Can

HEART OF THE HUNTER   Linda P. Sandifer
75421-5/$3.95US/$4.95 Can

MIDSUMMER MOON   Laura Kinsale
75398-7/$3.95US/$4.95 Can

STARFIRE   Judith E. French
75241-7/$3.95US/$4.95 Can

BRIAR ROSE   Susan Wiggs
75430-4/$3.95US/$4.95 Can